# LULLABIES FOR SUFFERING

## TALES OF ADDICTION HORROR

# Wicked Run Press

For more information, contact: WickedRunPress@gmail.com

Edited by Mark Matthews
with assistance from Andi Rawson, Jason Parent, Glen Krisch
and Julie Hutchings (editor for Lizard)
Cover Art and Design by Dean Samed

**Wicked Run Press**

"The wicked run when no one is chasing them"
*Proverbs 28:1*

# PRAISE FOR LULLABIES FOR SUFFERING

"The stories in Lullabies for Suffering are the real deal, a plunge into agony and the ecstasy, the inescapable nightmare of addiction."
—ALMA KATSU, author of The Deep and The Hunger

"My emotions are exposed and raw, my stomach tangled, my shoulders sagged. This open-veined collection tore me up. Each story was captivating and sucked me in and led me on a dark and twisted ride."
—NICO BELL FICTION

"Beautifully Brutal."
—STEVE STRED, author of The Ritual

"These stories are brimming with sobering revelations and heinous aberrations."
—CHRISTA CARMEN, author of Something Borrowed, Something Blood-Soaked

"Beautiful, enlightening, revelatory. Everything that good fiction should be, in a manner that elevates both its chosen genre and the status of discourse on its core subjects."
—GINGER NUTS OF HORROR

"Brutal, raw, but still somehow elegant, Lullabies for Suffering plumbs the depths of addiction in its myriad forms. There are no filler stories in this anthology, just six punches to the chin."
—GLEN KRISCH, author of Little Whispers, Nothing Lasting, and Husks

"Lullabies for Suffering delivers time and again. Rarely do you come across a collection so well-versed in its life lessons and realistic horrors."
—AIDEN MERCHANT, author of Dead As Soon As Born

"Be forewarned—These dark tales are hypnotic, gritty, and full of torment."
—RICHARD THOMAS, author of Disintegration and Breaker, a Thriller award finalist

## ALSO FROM WICKED RUN PRESS

### GARDEN OF FIENDS: TALES OF ADDICTION HORROR
"What fertile ground for horror. Every story comes from a dark, personal place"
—*JOSH MALERMAN, New York Times Best Selling author of Bird Box*

### ON THE LIPS OF CHILDREN
"A sprint down a path of high adrenaline terror. A must read."
—*BRACKEN MACLEOD, Shirley Jackson Award nominated author of Stranded.*

### MILK-BLOOD
"An urban legend in the making. You will not be disappointed."
—Bookie-Monster.com

### ALL SMOKE RISES
"Intense, imaginative, and empathic. Matthews is a damn good writer, and make no mistake, he *will* hurt you."
—*JACK KETCHUM, Bram Stoker Award winning author of The Girl Next Door.*

# TABLE OF CONTENTS:

# LULLABIES FOR SUFFERING – AN INTRODUCTION

ADDICTION STARTS like a sweet lullaby sung by a trusted loved one. It washes away the pains of the day and wraps you in the warmness of the womb where nothing hurts and every dream is possible. Yet soon enough, this warm state of bliss becomes a cold shiver. The ecstasy and dreams become nightmares, and for the sick and suffering addict, we can't stop listening to the lullaby. We crave to hear the siren song as it rips us apart.

Such is the paradox of addiction, and dark truths such as these require a dark piece of fiction to do them justice. Welcome to *Lullabies for Suffering: Tales of Addiction Horror*. Just a few words before we start.

This collection is a follow up to *Garden of Fiends* but certainly not a sequel, for the scope is larger, and the volume bigger. *Garden of Fiends* injected horror into your veins, *Lullabies for Suffering* slices into your wrist while tenderly holding your hand. The goal is the same—an unflinching portrayal of addiction but with empathy for those affected.

As someone who has been in recovery from addiction for many years, and who now works in the field of substance abuse treatment, this project is very personal for me. If I am the only one who reads the kaleidoscope of voices that follow, it will all have been worth it. The talent on display in this collection is extraordinary and it was chosen with care. Some stories will strike you as horror with addiction as the theme, others simply as the insidious nature of drug use—damaged humans craving for highs and wholeness but finding something more tragic and horrific on the other side. All of the works are novella or novelette length, for once you step inside the world, you'll want to stay a bit.

Why addiction horror?

Horror has the capacity to speak to trauma in a unique fashion. It's a tone and technique as much as a genre, and what better way to capture the epidemic of addiction, and the barren emotional and spiritual states that come with it, than through a work of horror. Until you've had your mind and soul hijacked by addiction, it is difficult to comprehend, for in the throes of a craving, the desire to obtain and use substances equals the life force for survival itself. Imagine yourself drowning and being told not to swim to the surface for air. Obsessions should be so mild.

Lullaby aims to portray this affliction with honesty, empathy and understanding. As Joe Hill so aptly noted, *Horror isn't about extreme sadism; it's about extreme empathy*. As much as that term 'trigger warning' is overused, I feel it may be useful here, for some graphic depictions of drug use, as well as cutting, lie ahead, but always with an artful sense and bigger purpose.

Some words about the contributors:

### Kealan Patrick Burke

Kealan writes part Faulkner goth, part cosmic horror. After his brilliant story "Wicked Thirst" from *Garden of Fiends,* it was impossible not to ask for more. His story, "Sometimes They See Me," is a frenetic love story of two addicts bonding over art and constantly needing a fix for the cracks in their psyche. Powerful, rich, and imaginative, this story begs to be read twice.

### Caroline Kepnes

"Hypnotic and scary," said Stephen King of her work. Her novel *You* is one of the greatest second person point-of-view works you'll ever read, and the inspiration behind the must-binge series on Netflix. Kepnes writes in a unique tone of darkness, capturing our neuroses, sexual tensions, and internal dialogue with remarkable candor. Kepnes flexes these literary muscles in "Monsters," where the legacy and stigma of addiction spreads through generations. As she did in *You* and *Hidden Bodies*, Kepnes shows us monsters hide behind human faces.

### Mark Matthews

My own piece, *Lizard*, about a young girl growing up with two addicted parents, who then becomes the dreaded 'fentanyl final girl' after a mass overdose. She will do anything to make sure other children don't suffer as she did. Like my addiction horror novels, *Milk-Blood* and *All Smoke Rises*, it's a true story, even if it didn't happen. I hope you like this one.

### John FD Taff

*The King of Pain* is back and turning up the temperature to "The Melting Point of Meat" with a powerful story on the obsessive urge of cutting and craving for pleasure that comes with pain. His characters are vibrant but fragile, the cracks in their life where the light comes shining through. Melting Point is a savage, cosmic, visceral piece. A definite page-turner.

### Gabino Iglesias

An infectious writing style and contagious passion, Iglesias is a master of the mosaic. He weaves his sentences as part sledgehammer, part harpsichord, beautiful but savage. Try to pin him into one genre, and it will change with the next sentence. Iglesias is the author of the ground-breaking, award-nominated *Coyote Songs,* with more songs to sing. *Beyond the Reef* takes place in the 'barrio noir' of Puerto Rico where a new father fights both heroin addiction and Lovecraftian beasts who surround his island home.

### Mercedes M. Yardley

Mercedes is listed here last as the grand finale of a firework explosion. The Bram Stoker Award-winning author is criminally creative with a wit and whimsy that turns her prose to music. To read her works is to live deliciously and walk through a field of poisonous wildflowers. "Love is a Crematorium" is a bittersweet love story that only Mercedes could write and I think you're going to love. You'll understand how heroin, much like love, "is a crematorium that lights you up and burns you out at the same time."

There you have it. My hope is for this book to serve, as Franz Kafka said, "as the axe for the frozen sea within us." For there certainly is a frozen sea, and the result is a spiritual hunger for warmth and wholeness. Our fractured selves suffer and crave for healing—or if not healing, at least relief from suffering, if but for a little while. Reading, like addiction, can offer that relief. A sweet song of comfort. Thank you for taking the time to listen to these Lullabies for Suffering.

*-Mark Matthews*
*October, 2019*

# SOMETIMES THEY SEE ME

*By*

*Kealan Patrick Burke*

# SOMETIMES THEY SEE ME

*Kealan Patrick Burke*

## 1.

I MET CALVIN ON THE SINGING BRIDGE outside Rosewood Park on the night of December 24th. I'd gone there to kill myself, and though he never admitted it, so had he. It was there in his eyes, the same flat look of grim resignation I'm sure I carried in mine. Everyone goes there to die. It's become a cliché, but such things don't matter when the end of your life is concerned.

He'd been throwing scraps of paper down into the frozen water. The scene looked familiar to me, but it would take a while before I could recall where I had seen it before. In that moment, I was more intrigued by his posture and the aura radiating from his emaciated body.

"I can wait," were my first words to him, and his response bound us together until the end of the whole mess.

"For how long?"

The night was full of funny things, the first of them being that when I rounded the spider web of frozen trees and saw his dark figure hunched over the railing in the haze of cold moonlight, I felt a brief twinge of panic. Woman alone; strange man on a bridge. That I worried he might be a killer only tickled me later as we lay in bed together reminiscing on how fucked up it all was. If he'd turned out to be a homicidal maniac, it would have put a serious damper on my plan to kill myself. But that's the interesting thing about suicide. It's a personal thing, perhaps the *most* personal thing of all, the very last measure of control. Thus, having someone else do it doesn't count. Instinct will revolt if the executioner isn't you.

Rather than cast our bodies into the freezing current, we walked and talked, and retreated to his place among the unsteady tenement buildings in a part of town nobody thinks of as anything but a backdrop to the occasional nameless murder on the nightly news. There, on the second floor, by the cozy light of a host of guttering candles, we drank cheap vodka, laughed and wept and entered each other both spiritually and physically until sleep left us entwined in his stained and stinking sheets.

With his true nature written in sweat all over my skin, my dreams did not, for the first time in years, try to drown me in anxiety. I did not see the wallpaper, and I did not see the blood. I saw only magic.

I *knew* him.

And so our brief love story began.

## 2.

One of my late father's truisms, deposed while bribing me out of his life: You're only fine until you tell on yourself.

Calvin told on himself early on. He was an alcoholic and an addict, manic depressive, and possibly a narcissist. I don't know how long we meandered through those drunken days before I realized I knew more about him than he did me. That was because I asked questions, whereas he was content to let me be a mystery. Or maybe he didn't care. I guess the nature of your passenger doesn't alter the destination, and we were on the road now, familiars, headed somewhere together, even if the motion was an illusion. Our days saw us waking in his grimy, powerless apartment, fucking like we'd die if we didn't, barely bathing beneath the teardrop trickle of cold water in the calamitous bathroom, and eschewing breakfast in favor of whiskeys at a local dive bar, The Big Grand. It was a disproportionately austere name for a place where your feet stick to the floor and the regulars are only marginally more material than shadow.

From there, we walked the cobblestoned streets and ambled aimlessly through the nicer part of town, cackling when we found ourselves obstructing the urgency of the better-dressed and daring each other to antagonize the police whenever we caught them giving us the rooster eye. Bookstores and libraries provided succor, a spiritual peace that saw us return to something almost human, cowed by the awe of a hundred thousand voices clamoring to be heard above the din of reverent quiet. Only here could we be apart, like sinners to the confessionals that best suited our brand of sin, baring our souls without judgment before a godless jury.

Afterward, better educated, we reunited, rejuvenated by dead men's tales and hidden knowledge, and off out into the world we went again in search of more distraction from the ever-encroaching edge of the inevitable abyss.

Running beneath it all was an awareness of doom, of borrowed time, and of the secrets we were keeping from each other.

It would end, this little adventure, and probably not well.

## 3.

On the last of our jaunts into the city, three weeks since we first met, we stopped before the large plate-glass window of The Orchid Gallery. It was nestled between a secondhand bookstore and a Subway, within which, the employees stared out at us in an envy unique to the bored and underpaid. Displayed before us in the gallery window were a series of small paintings apparently floating in thin air against a backdrop of stark white. Each canvas depicted an explosion of colors in no discernible pattern, the kind of work Pollock was known for, only less agitated, and no less impenetrable. There was a softness to it that appealed to me, even though such art has always seemed to me at best nonsensical, at worst constrictive, even while it inspires paroxysms of desire among aficionados. How difficult is it to spackle a canvas in fury, and what is it we're supposed to see other than orgiastic chaos? But perhaps that's just me. I have an aversion to art I have never quite been able to reconcile beyond its tendency to constrain. How can such things move us when they require us to stand still? What is it they're supposed to say? I divine no more emotion from a slapdash mosaic of paint than I do a pile of coats on a floor.

"It's wondrous," Calvin said, and I watched my reflection second his appraisal with a treasonous nod.

We went inside. The gallery was one long narrow room with walls of white-painted brick and a lot less art than one would expect given the purpose of the place. Even the art that was there embraced too much negative space to the point that the sparse amounts of color seemed like an oversight.

One of the paintings caught Calvin's eye and held it. It was a small blue square in the center of an enormous rectangular canvas.

Within the square was a single red thumbprint. A simple placard beneath read: *"Identity" – by Doris Wiltshire.* Beneath that, the price. *$17,000.*

"Are they fucking serious?"

Calvin ignored me, still enthralled, and I couldn't help but wonder at the source of his fascination. I lingered dutifully until ants began to crawl their way out of my bones, and then I went outside for a cigarette.

Three cigarettes later, my patience expired. I needed a fix in my veins or a drink in my gut, preferably both, and Calvin was burning our time staring down a fucking thumbprint. It no longer mattered what it meant to him. Only the need mattered now, and he was its sole obstruction. When I looked through the window, I saw him turn to say something to me. Only then did it dawn on him that I wasn't there. His gaunt, pockmarked face screwed up in bafflement before our gazes met through the glass, mine hot enough to warp it. He nodded and hurried out to join me.

"The fuck was that about?" I asked him, my irritation evident in everything from my tone to the way I stomped my cigarette to death on the pavement, an act which gleaned a look of disapproval from a woman hustling her two oblivious children along before us. "And what the fuck are *you* looking at?" I feel bad about that. It wasn't her fault that she reminded me of my sister.

Calvin took my elbow and led us to the closest bar. He handed me a baggy and shoved me into the bathroom, where, after cooking up the dope with toilet water, he went down on me while I shot up, and we were fine again for a little while. I didn't climax, but that's nothing new.

## 4.

"I wanted to be an artist for the longest time, ever since my parents took me to Atlantic City and I saw those guys doing caricatures on the boardwalk. I was enthralled by them. Couldn't stop watching them. Couldn't move. Would have stayed there forever. These working joes getting to sit outside with the smells of the sea and the popcorn and hotdogs, painting likenesses of people all day long. Took me years to realize I wasn't very good and never would be, though I was featured for a while in The Vanderelli Room.

People seemed to like it and it excited me to be so positively appraised. I thought I might be going places, but I couldn't make the spark catch again. I felt trapped, so I moved, thought a new space might serve me better. Thought I might be able to make a living from it someday. The self-delusion of all budding creatives. We should be compensated fairly for our passions, shouldn't we? And if the world deems art should be free, then I propose that so too should living."

I didn't respond, because I knew there wouldn't be time before he started rambling again. Besides, he wouldn't have heard my answer even if I'd cared enough about the subject to offer one.

"But then I started to feel tired all the time. And down. Started to feel nervous over nothing. Couldn't get out of bed. Didn't want to. Couldn't paint. Felt like I was disappearing."

This at least was more interesting, a thread of commonality to which I could relate. I was quite adept at disappearing and the terror of unbecoming. It's why I still check my skin for the faded floral patterns of the wallpaper from my childhood home.

"It's frustrating, worse than the notion of death."

"What is?"

"The idea of never being good at life."

We ordered more drinks. I was floating above myself by then, tethered to my body by some biological arrangement to which I'd not been privy and trapped in the room by the distant engine drone of his words.

"A man bit me once," I said, simply because the words had been burdening my throat.

He'd been in the middle of his mournful pontificating but stopped to consider my words. "Bit you?"

"Former lover. Blind date. Hopeless alcoholic. Woke up at his place in the middle of the night and found him chewing on my arm." I roll up the right sleeve of my denim shirt to show him the oval ring of white em-dashes. "He woke with a craving for more alcohol and had none in the house, so he decided to siphon it from my veins."

"Jesus. What did you do?"

"I clawed out one of his eyes."

"Seriously?"

It felt like I was talking to him underwater, my words slow, emerging from my mouth like delicate brush strokes. "Left him there screaming. Don't even know if he survived it or just bled to death in the bed. I took the eye. Had it encased in Lucite. I keep it on my nightstand as a reminder to be cautious among men who don't know themselves."

"Whoa."

My grin feels like my face is made of butter and I'm gently scoring it with a knife. "I'm kidding."

"About the eye?"

"The biting part was real. I figure it was some fucked up fetish. The rest is the kind of thing you think of later when you're safe and it's too late to act on it."

I could tell he didn't believe any of it, but I didn't care. What was it all but words to fill a silence that didn't need filling? I wanted to fuck and sleep and get high and die, and none of that mattered either. If art requires you to be still, then life demands motion, given that there's far more of one than the other. We were cohorts in a heist, he and I, thrown together by our strange natures and mutual ambivalence for life, stealing whatever perfunctory moments of joy we could find amid the ruins of the world. There would be no consequences or penalties. We hadn't ended our lives, not yet, but inevitably we would, which freed us from the prison of obligation.

"I miss the rush," he said then, and even without knowing the flavor of highs to which he referred, I agreed. No rush is the same, and the first is always the best. Get clean and come back to it and it's like an angel is fucking your brain. There's no guilt, no shame. That comes later when you come down or when a well-meaning Samaritan decides to adopt your burden. You feel bad because they feel bad, not because you actually regret letting the angel fuck you.

"When I paint, I become someone else. Something else. I actually like what it makes me even if I don't have a name for it. But I can't do it anymore and it's left a void in me I only know how to fill with bad things."

"'Bad' is a relative term though' wouldn't you say?'"

By then, I was starting to return to myself, prematurely brought down by the counterweight of his melancholy, and it was getting old. We needed a change of venue, a change of high. My elbows and toes were starting to tickle from the dust of inertia. I looked around at the long rectangular room, built to mimic a train car if Union Pacific had a habit of filling their cars with neon beer signs, Christmas lights, old TVs showing Keno numbers and NASCAR, cheap tables, bar stools with ripped red leather for seats, and admitted only the dangerous and disadvantaged. There was an old glass rotisserie too close to the bathroom door, within which flaccid hot dogs turned like the vacant fingers of a wet rubber glove. An overweight woman with dirty blond hair wearing a T-shirt bearing the legend WHITE LIVES MATTER looked up from her game of pool and glared a challenge in my direction, cue held rifle-like by her side. As I had no intention of getting into it with anyone brave enough to stand so close to the forty-year-old franks, I returned my attention to Calvin.

"Towards the end, I started seeing things in the paintings. The stories behind them."

"I thought that was the point of art?"

He ignored me. "Instead of photographs, I saw the people who took the picture. Instead of paint, I saw the inspiration through the eyes of the artist. Often, it was wonderful to behold. I saw incredible things. I traveled through time, awoke in strange beds, walked unknown roads. I became other people in places alien to me. But it was not always so benevolent. Sometimes I saw terrible things. And toward the end, when it got really bad, sometimes *they* saw *me*."

"Who's *they*?"

He looked down at his empty drink and shook his head. "If I knew that, I suppose I'd know the true meaning of art, like seeing the face of God, but I don't."

It was getting late, and I was getting bored, so I punched him on the arm to jar him from his reverie. "Let's blow this joint."

"We should go home. I'm tired. Worn down to ash by the pretense of being human, of being sane, of *being*, period."

I rose, the chair legs barking like a startled dog. "Fuck that. We're young. The night's young. Let's wreck it."

He looked up at me then and there was such a naked fear in his eyes it gave me pause, penetrated the protective veil of my high and twisted my guts. It's a look better suited to my own reflection on the bad nights: the atavistic dread, the misery and desperation, the absolute fear that you've reached the end of the road, and all that's left is for someone to make it official.

I didn't allow the recognition of his fear to take root. If I did, I'd be forced to join him in his dull introspective meandering, and I was too restless. I needed to keep moving, keep going, keep the high alive, or risk having my nerves exposed to my own reality. If the face of Calvin's God was art, then the face of mine was Chaos, raw and bleeding, filling the sky in a universe of my own design. Looking upon it was to risk going mad, and I was always never less than halfway there. It demanded I look, but I couldn't. Not yet.

I braced my hands flat on the table on both sides of his empty glass. My hair hung in my face and I could smell the grease. "Look. You're having a moment. I get it. Your life didn't work out the way you thought it would. Welcome to the suck. We're both fucked, and that's fine. This rollercoaster doesn't go in reverse, so what say we ditch the self-pity and finish the ride? We're still here, you and me, primed for adventure, and if sometimes they see you, so what? I'm seeing you now and what I see is potential." I leaned over and kissed his whiskey lips. "What say we don't waste it?"

Now that the decision to leave had been made, the clamor from the bar beyond the radius of our table rushed back in, as if we'd been encased in a bubble all night.

"Hey," the barman bellowed at us, and in his meaty hands he strangled tapwater into the sink from a frayed, once-white dish rag as if it were our necks. "Order a drink or get the hell out. You two have been sitting there dry for, like, over an hour now."

"Have we, *like*, been sitting here, *like*, for over an hour? I just finished my drink, you fucking putz." I admit I was offended that somehow, in this squalid shit pit, *we* were the offensive ones, so I threw him a glare and kicked my chair back from the table. "We're leaving. Got reservations at a place that doesn't smell like your mother's ass."

The barman's long face turned the color of a pickled beet. "My mother's dead, you junkie bitch."

"Then it probably smells even worse."

Calvin's chuckle was the sound of a bathtub draining.

The toothless and ferociously bearded old man who had spent the greater part of the evening openly ogling my breasts from his corner of the bar called out, "Might not want to be drivin' drunk. Police're everywhere." His rubbery lips spread in a wide empty grin, exposing a tongue paler than a sundried dog turd. "I could give y'all a ride. 'Specially the lady." He cackled and I thrust a middle finger at him as the barman rounded the bar like a tornado.

Calvin shoved the door open and we staggered out on a wave of laughter into the chill night air.

5.

What followed is hazy: snapshots of pulsating lights and music, of altercations and raised voices, of broken glass and an irate Uber driver throwing us out somewhere short of our destination, of more raucous laughter, of fucking in the rain, of running from the police, and the taste of paint on my tongue. Eventually we found our way to a shitty motel, the neon light a beacon for sleaze like us. We had no pills, no coke, no heroin, but we had a bottle of cheap vodka and that would have to do until we had the presence of mind to formulate a proper score. There were tears, of course, from Calvin, who, in the absence of whirling lights and adrenaline, returned to his ennui.

"I don't know who I am. I don't know what I'm doing here."

"Does anyone?" My nose was burning and my veins felt hollow. I considered getting off the bed and just fucking him senseless if only to shut him up, but that required an effort of which I was incapable, and I wasn't sure he'd be up to it, so I busied myself with taping up the smoke alarm so I could have a cigarette. "Hey, how come you don't have any paintings at your place? Any of yours, I mean. I'd like to see some."

"I destroyed them all. Hardest thing I've ever done, but it needed to be done. It was a kind of cleansing. I hoped it would help."

"And did it?"

"A little. Not enough. Can I tell you something?"

"Anything, mi amore."

"I know why this is happening to me. I know why I can see things in the paintings that other people can't. I know why I can step through them into those worlds and see what the people who painted them saw. And I know why I'm being punished for it too."

I dropped down onto the bed and mumbled around my cigarette. "Good. Closure's good."

"It's because of my mother."

"Isn't it always? Mine used to slam me into the walls and force me to stare at the patterns on the wallpaper. If you're wondering why my nose looks like this, now you know."

"I'm sorry."

"Don't be. It was good for me. Opened my eyes to things."

"Like what?"

"Who we are beyond the artifice."

He swept his hair out of his eyes, which were gleaming. I've seen that look in the mirror many times before.

"Yes, yes, that's it exactly. I see things now because my mother used to make me stare at her paintings until I saw what she wanted me to see in them." He nodded at the picture on the far wall by the door. Housed in a cheap brown frame, it was a drab, acrylic picture of a farmhouse and barn. "She would have torn that one off the wall. Bad art disgusted her. She agonized over her work. Sometimes I think it's what killed her. It used to drive her mad that she couldn't properly nurture her work into being. Even when she sold them and they were received well, she said they were unfinished. She said the same of all her work. She hated it. And I feel that hate, still. It lives in me because I've never been able to shake the sense that she felt the same about me: an unfinished disappointment."

I was starting to get tired. It had been a long day, my system jolted by so many drugs while being softened by too much alcohol. My heart didn't know what to do with itself, so it was time to let it rest before it decided to quit.

"She made me stare at them for hours. I used to make up things I saw in them to keep her happy."

"That's nice. You were a good kid."

"I did it for so long and so often I started seeing the paintings move. It made me ill. I was sick for a long time. My mother got sick too. Cancer. She had my father set up an easel in her room, but not for her. It was for me. She wanted me to paint her, to preserve her suffering. She wanted me to be an artist. I didn't yet know how, so I couldn't paint her. I was terrified I would disappoint her. But I forced it, and what emerged was the kind of effort you'd expect from a twelve-year-old. After the last stroke was done, I turned the easel around to show it to her, but she was dead." He shrugged, picked at the dead white skin on his big toe. "I don't blame her. I loved her. She just wanted people to be able to see what she saw, so they could understand her, but she couldn't get the images right. Which means no matter how her work was celebrated, she died a stranger to the world. The same will happen to me."

"The same happens to everyone. Even if you're known in life, we're all strangers in death."

"It feels like my time's coming."

I don't like when the conversation turns this way, as it so often does among people like us. There's always a moment in which you decide you've had enough of being nothing, that it's time to put the eraser down before you vanish completely, that you're finally ready to make a fresh start. The problem with that resolution is that it's like deciding to build a house because you know where to find a hammer. The tool is nothing without the materials and the will. If you allow the vow to take hold, it becomes a bogeyman, terrifying in its implications, so to prepare for it, you make a ceremony over having one last bump, one last high, and that reminds you how ill-prepared you are for anything else. *Why in holy fuck would you ever want to face the world clean?* you think. Even if by some miracle you come out of it with your determination intact, where do you begin? Rehab? Here's the funny thing about rehab: it's full of people who smile and tell their stories and congratulate each other and applaud and give out coins and then walk back out into the world with no idea what to do with themselves. Maybe they have a nice 9-5 job, a supportive wife, some kids. None of that can expel the nagging feeling that something's missing from you, something's not right. It's as if some mad surgeon crept into your house and removed one of your lungs while you slept. You live in a state of perpetual dissatisfaction, of being a passenger on the wrong train looking longingly out the window at all the happy people traveling the right one. For no good reason, you randomly find it difficult to breathe. You have no friends who aren't junkies. You become an expert at spotting people who are carrying, and they're the angels beckoning a return to the fold. It's grief, it's mourning, and there's only one way to cure it. It's why they call it a fix.

So no, I didn't want to have this conversation now. Or ever. A day might come in which I turn a similar corner, decide to get my shit in order and try to make it through without chemical condolence, but that's not today, and it's not tomorrow, and it's none of your fucking business.

I threw back the covers and patted a hand on the bed next to me. "Come on, lover. Come to bed."

"I can't stop walking into those paintings," he said then. "But the last time…the night I met you on the bridge…that was the worst of all."

He rose unsteadily, and that was progress. His pupils were small periods on a page streaked with thin red lines. A bead of sweat hung suspended from his stubbled chin.

"Why's that?"

He pulled his shirt up over his head and the bones in his chest were like kindling beneath a dirty white sheet.

"Because I almost forgot how to get back out."

## 6.

Even under oath, I'll never admit to being an addict or an alcoholic, no more than I'd swear to have either habit under control. No denial for this girl, no, siree. Just evasion. I prefer to think myself caught somewhere in the middle, a woman without a country but with periodic access to GPS if I ever want it. Weeks go by in which, despite the all-consuming suicidal horror of detox, I don't take anything. Calvin called it Jilting the Dragon. It's good to jilt the dragon every once in a while, even if just to prove that I can, to engage in a brief reminder of what it's like to be back behind the wheel of my own life. But those are also the worst times, dark and frightening times, and I don't much care for them. The world thinks being clean is the respectable way to be, but it's also the hardest. Sobriety is a world of sharp edges and pain, and I will never understand why you wouldn't avoid it if you had the choice.

Andrea, my younger sister, wants nothing to do with me. No doubt she tells herself it's because I'm an addict. She acts embarrassed by me, though I've never given her any reason to feel this way. I've never done her wrong. The beating heart of the enmity between us then, has more to do with how she feels every time she thinks of me, not as an adult, but a child. My memories of her are bittersweet. For a time, we were close, but the schism began once my mother began to physically abuse me. To Andrea, my mother showed only love, and no sign of the abject hatred which one day materialized out of thin air. While I was getting my nose broken, or beaten with a wooden spoon, or being dragged by my hair along the hallway floor, Andrea was in the living room, pretending to watch TV, while watching our reflections on the screen. She has no reason to hate me, nor do I hate her, but I clearly remember feeling that our bond withered a little bit more every time I asked myself why she had escaped my mother's wrath, why I'd been chosen as the target of her fury. In my darkest moments, I felt an impulse to bestow upon my sister the same violence bestowed upon me, perhaps as a means of restoring some perverse balance, but I didn't have it in me. I think now she wants nothing to do with me because I'm a walking reminder that if not for me, the sacrificial lamb, her world would have been very different. There is, of course, no way of knowing if this is true. Any hope of divining such information would require us talking, and we don't do that. The deep cracks in our relationship are destined to remain unshored.

Perhaps because Andrea and the past had been on my mind, once Calvin and I finally turned in, I dreamt of my mother, and of that horrid wallpaper, and of blood pattering my shoes. Jazz music drifted down from upstairs where my father had sequestered himself in his study with a bottle of bourbon and his own cowardice. I began to turn my head in the feeble hope that if she saw the terror on my face it might wake her up, and my mother grabbed a fistful of my hair.

"Do you know what you are, you little cunt?" she shrieked at me. She was weaving on her feet so badly it was like we were engaged in a peculiar waltz. The medication did not make her this monster. The as-yet undiagnosed degenerative brain disorder did that. But really, to my nine-year-old self, the reasons mattered little. I just didn't want to be afraid and in pain.

I heard the tiniest little sob from the living room, almost lost beneath the Nickelodeon soundtrack of some cartoon. It didn't come again.

"You're a horrible, ugly, soulless leech," my mother shrieked at me, and shoved my face into the wall. The pattern filled my vision, became a world lit by disintegrating stars. I felt an explosion of pain and heard an awful dull crunch inside my skull as my nose broke.

All because I burned the eggs.

7.

When I woke, I could still smell them and for a moment, I thought of screaming, until the red neon flashed into the motel room and brought me back to myself. I was covered in sweat, my default state those days, the sodden blankets like plaster of Paris setting around my legs. In the process of freeing myself, I realized Calvin was not beside me.

"Hey," I said to the red-veined dark. "Where'd you go?"

When he didn't answer, I figured he was either in the bathroom, or had stepped outside for a cigarette. I slid out of bed, my head filled with sand, mouth with glue, and my stomach lurched as the night inside me looked for a way out. I hurried to the bathroom. It was dark. As I flicked on the dim light, I wondered if Calvin was outside, or maybe had gone to score. This last would have suited me fine because one of us needed to. In my experience, nothing halts the onset of the dreaded morning after better than a chemical extension. It's why alcoholics always keep a few beers in the fridge and vampires sleep in coffins. It's a protective measure against unwanted intrusion.

Eyes shut, I let the stream of urine loose. I was weaving on the seat, in danger of falling back asleep right there, but then a sound from the other side of the bathroom wall permeated the fog and I opened one eye, squinting against the fluorescent light. When I cocked my head slightly to better hear the sound, my gaze fell upon the sink, which was close enough for me to hit with my elbow in the confines of the squalid room.

The basin was spattered with blood.

And now, despite the still developing hangover and exhaustion, I was awake. I finished peeing, dabbed myself dry, and pulled up my panties. "Calvin?"

No answer.

Worried now, I splashed some cold water on my face, which washed away the Rorschach pattern of blood in the basin. The iciness of it shocked air into my lungs but brought with it the level of alertness required for an impromptu nocturnal investigation.

"Calvin? You up?"

I did not look at myself in the mirror. I try to avoid that as much as possible. Reflections are inveterate liars.

I left the light on and the door open so I could see the bed. It was still empty but for a cumulonimbus of wrinkled sheets, but now I could hear a swishing, scratching sound from the living room-cum-kitchen, or whatever the fuck you call those claustrophobic areas in motel rooms that aren't the bed.

The room was lit only by the intermittent hazy red light from the neon sign. Backlit by the light from the bathroom, I saw a distorted version of myself in the cheap television screen and thought of Andrea trying hard not to be aware of the horror. Beyond it, just beside the door to the room, Calvin was a hazy, agitated and indistinct shape.

"What are you doing?"

"Working."

"Are you okay? There was blood in the sink."

"It's not blood. It's paint. I needed red."

His hands were pale smudges in the gloom, moving like spiders over the painting of the rustic barn.

"It's late. Come back to bed."

"Do you know where this is?"

I folded my arms. Now that I knew he wasn't bleeding to death, I just wanted to go back to bed. "Where *what* is?"

"This barn. Do you know where the barn in this painting is?"

"No. How would I know that?"

"Have you never stepped into the painting to see for yourself?"

"Can't say that I have, no."

"I've painted a door in it for you if you'd like to see."

"I'm going back to bed."

"It's in a place called Rowan County in North Carolina. The man who owned the barn shot his wife and daughter six months after painting this picture."

"Calvin, come on. Come back to bed. Whatever you're doing, you can finish it in the morning. Let's get some sleep."

A great sadness fell over me at the thought of losing him. I'd known it was coming. I'd just hoped it would take longer.

The scratching and swishing continued. The cheap frame of the painting clattered against the wall. And then his voice, lower and slower than I'd ever heard it, the kind of voice a man gets when he's smoked too much and drunk too little, crept its way across the room.

"He swore in court he didn't do it, and he meant it too. He couldn't remember doing any of it. Couldn't remember staking their bodies up in the cornfield either, which was how he got caught. Guy next door came by to see how his neighbor had managed to make those scarecrows look so damn lifelike and yurked up his breakfast right then and there. Ran screaming back to his house and called the police. When they took John McAllister away, he said somebody with a grudge must have framed him. Get it? Somebody framed the artist."

The swishing scratching sound stopped.

*Thank God for small mercies.*

"They executed him. Framed and hanged like fine art."

"Why are you telling me this?"

He turned and his eyes were black holes. "You've been keeping things from me."

So here we were, our moment come. I'd wanted it to be so much different, but now I realize there's no way it ever could have been. From the very beginning, this was its natural end.

"I would have told you, if you'd asked, but you never did," I said.

I watched him limp toward me. One of his feet was broken and hanging at an odd angle, but he expressed no pain.

"You poor thing."

"What is this?" he asked me. "What have you done to me?"

It wasn't darkness that hid his eyes from me. He had either painted them black or they had been removed. Through his pale skin, his veins were black as winter trees and appeared to be moving, as if wrenched by the force of a subcutaneous storm. The shape of his body made no visual sense anymore. His bones, his joints, had come out of true and his skin rippled and bulged and twisted as if he were made of plastic. When he stepped into the light from the bathroom, I saw that his wrists were broken, too, which explained why he'd stopped defacing the barn. His hands hung like dead flowers from the withered stalks of his arms.

"Tell me," he said, sounding as if he was gargling blood. "Tell me what you've done."

"I will, love," I told him. "But first please understand that I have done nothing to you. I'm only here to make the end a little better."

**8.**

On the day my mother first slammed me into the wall, I detached from myself, went *through* the wall, and it was real. I was there, trapped in the narrow space between the walls. I could see the wooden framework, the wires, the cobwebs, the mice, and when I looked up, I could see through the floor to where my father sat weeping at his desk. I could see inside him and it was all gray, like a sky considering raian.

I am, or at least for a time I was, reasonable and sane enough to believe that what I experienced as a child, being able to see the mechanics behind the skin of things, was most likely delusional, a reaction to sudden trauma, or a psychological escape tactic. I told myself this for ten years before going to court-ordered rehab for alcohol after my first DUI. There, a sponsor named Stephen Carver became my guru. He encouraged me to allow myself to believe in the spiritual benefit of healing, to be open to other realms and possibilities. One of the possibilities I didn't predict was him trying to stick his hand down my pants on the one and only night I let him drive me home. I broke his nose, blackened his eye, cut off his dick and rammed it up his ass, all in my mind on the walk home after he threw me out of his car. But as I raged, ashamed at what he had almost done to me, shaking in fear of where that might have led, I saw him as if he had appeared right back in front of me. I saw *inside* him, from the liquor boiling in his stomach to the splintering of his bones, the perforation of organs, the collapsing of his skull, as his car collided with a snowplow. That didn't happen, of course.

Not that night.

It happened the winter of the next year.

So, *wow, you can see the future, huh? How come you're not a TV celebrity? How many books have you written off the back of this amazing superpower? When is the world tour?* The short answer is that it isn't a power at all. It's a lens, and one that only works when I'm high, just like I was the night I failed to miss all the creepy vibes Carver was giving me. It was the reason I'd called him in the first place. *I'm fucked up and I need help. I don't feel real and*

*I keep thinking my mother is coming for me.* And anything that only happens when you're high only makes sense to fellow addicts. Should I have donned a cape and told Stephen Carver he might die by snowplow sometime in the future? He'd have laughed and tried to finish what he started.

I let whatever this ability or hex is fade into insignificance as time went on, and if sometimes I knew little things about people they might not have wanted me to know: from their sexual proclivities and secrets to the fate awaiting them years hence, I put it down to the heightened perception any addict can claim because it's hard to disprove. If I told you you were going to die in a plane crash somewhere and then it happened in eight years' time, would you think to credit the source? Of course not. You'd be deader than hammered shit. Anyone else who might have heard such a pronouncement surely wouldn't remember the one night some homeless-looking heroin addict spouted wisdom from the stoop while you were walking by. When asked, I can't predict jack. When it could be most useful, it doesn't come. Why not parlay it into a means of the perfect score, you ask? Why didn't I rob a bank, buy myself a mansion, pull one over on a dealer and keep myself high for life? For the same reason I gave before. I couldn't summon it. It was random, and when it did manifest itself, it rarely gave me anything that could be useful in the moment. So, incredible as it may seem, I forgot about it.

Until the night I decided I had served my sentence on this earth and it was time to be done with it all. The night I met Calvin. But what I saw in him changed everything. It was true confirmation of other realms and the wonder of the unknown, and it instilled in me a reason to delay the end, for a little while at least.

Because Calvin wasn't even real. Not that version of him, anyway.

## 9.

"Picture your mother," I told him. "Really picture your clearest memory of her and tell me what you see."

"Why?"

"Just do it."

"It's the one I told you about. Her in bed, dying. Me trying to paint her."

"What was her name?"

"Eloise."

"Her last name?"

"I—"

"You don't remember it?"

"No."

"If I gave you a week, or a month, you still wouldn't recall it because you never knew it. What about your father?"

"What about him?"

"Do you remember him?"

"Vaguely."

"Can you picture his face?"

"No, why are you asking me all these questions?"

"The reason you say you can walk through paintings is because you came from one of them. I knew it when I saw you at the bridge, because I saw the bridge before, in a painting. It was called "End of Night" by Eloise Brunner. It depicts a haunted figure tossing scraps of paper into the river. I looked it up when we were at the library, and all the others she did. Among them is the self-portrait she painted when she had terminal cancer. She painted a figure at the foot of the bed of the son she'd lost in Afghanistan. His name was Calvin. He's depicted as the artist in the painting. It's called "The Release." I don't understand the how or the why of it no more than I understand it of my own ability, but I see you, Calvin. Just like she did. I see you, only you're just a figure from her painting. You're not the son she lost. You're fragments, a fractured, malformed thing, crammed full of confused emotions and the yearning of a dying mother."

He was silent but for the drip-drip-dripping of paint from his hands.

"You are all the sketches that didn't work. Your mother painted this version of you into life. Until then, you didn't exist, and when she died, she left you behind, unable to function, an unfinished thing driven half-mad by the need to be complete. Getting high is too loose a fix for such a rigid problem, Calvin. You can't chemically force yourself into reality, so you use it to forget that you're *not* real."

He might have shaken his head, or perhaps it was neon's dance with the dark.

"Do you know why we're together, what attracted you to me on that bridge the night we went there to die? It wasn't just our common goal, it was that *you* saw in *me* what I am. I'm like you. I've seen the inner workings of things invisible to most. Unlike you, I can't step inside art, but I can see inside you, Calvin, and there are so many colors desperate to get out. You tried to paint them out, but that's not your destiny. That's not why you want to die. You want to open yourself up and let the paint run free, because *you* are the art, and you will forever suffer until you let yourself become it."

He didn't argue because I wasn't telling him anything he didn't already, on some level, know to be true. I watched him weep and the tears were thin rivers of sky-blue paint.

I wanted to touch him, to comfort him a little, but it was not yet time.

"Do you trust me?"

"I don't know."

"Can you?"

He nodded.

"I love you, Calvin. I love everything that you are and are not. I love your innocence and your grief. I love your confusion, your soul, and yes, I believe you have one. I love that you're lost and alone and unknown. I love that you're here and must leave. I love that I got to taste and feel and fuck and love you. I love that I got to see you and be seen by you."

"It was the only thing that was real," he said, and when he smiled, his mouth began to run until the lower half of his face looked like a puddle of petroleum.

"Your memories: the boardwalk, your parents, the bridge. She painted a life for you and all those paintings hang in homes and galleries around the world. Everything you remember is preserved and endless. You will live on through those, so this is not an ending, because art, and therefore you, cannot die, no matter what. I will see you again."

Gently, I put a hand to his cheek. It caved beneath my touch, and I closed my eyes as, with the softest of sighs, he collapsed in a waterfall of color to the floor.

I did not open them again until I had walked to the door. There,

I looked up at the painting of the barn.

It was much the same as before, only he had darkened the sky, and a figure, one must assume was himself, was standing in the door to the barn, one hand raised in greeting.

## 10.

I drank myself into a messy stupor, and once it passed and I could walk and the manager was hammering at the door, I showered and dressed and took a cab home. I don't like it here.

In the brief time I knew Calvin, I never invited him to my house. Part of that is good sense. Until I knew his true nature (as much as one ever can), I preferred to go on his journey with him and not fully invite him into mine. Another reason is that there are things the adventurous might uncover that I am not yet ready to explain. Things like the human eyeball in Lucite atop my nightstand, taken from the man who bit my arm and tasted oil, and the gilt-framed paintings in my living room.

My life is on that wall, and I don't know how to return to it.

My sister is there, reflected in the TV.

My father is crying in his office.

My mother is baring her teeth, clenching a fistful of hair.

Within these frames are the characters from my life.

All except the last one, which shows a bloodied patch of wallpaper and the shadow of a girl who is no longer there to cast it.

**About the Author**
Kealan Patrick Burke is the Bram Stoker Award-winning author of six novels, including the bestselling thriller KIN. His latest book is the horror collection WE LIVE INSIDE YOUR EYES. You can find him on the web at **www.kealanpatrickburke.com**, or on Twitter @kealanburke, where he thinks he's hilarious. An Irish expat who does not believe in ghosts, he nevertheless currently haunts a house in Ohio.

# MONSTERS

by

*Caroline Kepnes*

# MONSTERS

*Caroline Kepnes*

*YOU ARE A VIRGIN. You are eighteen years old and you've never done anything remotely criminal. Yes, you ate too many Devil Dogs, you played alone, and you got fat. But you lost five pounds before starting college. You've been there for your mother. You're there for her right now, in line with her at TJ Maxx. She likes to shop every time she comes home from rehab. You say you believe it when she says, "this time it sticks." You aren't lying to her. You aren't faking it. Every time feels like the time that it will stick and this time is no different. She pays for a bigger bathing suit—detox makes her thighs rub together—and she laughs with the woman at the register. The laughter is a good sign, a sign that it will stick. You pick at pink bubblegum that someone pressed under the counter. It sticks. Gum is sticky. There is no such thing as gum that doesn't stick.*

*Your mom swings her bag of new bathing suits in the air. "Come on!" she says. "Let's get outta here!"*

*Outside, it's summer, your first summer as a college student. You walk with your mother like you never left, like you're the same old kid. She picks up a penny and you never do things like that. You wish you were more like her, that she was more like you. Her sobriety never sticks and your virginity always sticks and she elbows you.*

*"Why so quiet?"*

*"Sorry."*

*"You want to get ice cream?"*

*You don't want ice cream but you want her to stay home so you say that you do. She drives the car. You ride shotgun, the virgin and the cokehead. You have never even smoked a cigarette and your mother has had so much sex. When she's clean the men are tidy and cold. They come from the Internet and they don't stay long. When she's using, the men are filthy and relaxed, like henchmen in a movie. There was that guy in the wife-beater who pissed on the deck. There was that married guy who wore suits and didn't take off his wedding ring when he sat on the sofa and hogged your TV.*

*"Soft or hard?" your mother wants to know.*

*She giggles like a kid at school. That's always her joke when you come to this place where they have ice cream that needs scooping and ice cream that comes from a machine.*

*"Hard," you say because no matter what you say she's gonna elbow you and embarrass you in front of the younger girl who's making your ice cream, blushing. There is no indoor seating area and you are jealous of the girl inside, roofed in. You bet her mother isn't a cokehead and then you turn red because what a mean thing to think you fucking virgin, you fucking loser.*

*Your mother's cone arrives first and your mind is full of dirty words, a car wash in reverse where the vehicles emerge covered in shit, in mud. Your mother licks her cone—vanilla—and if you weren't a virgin, you wouldn't notice the tip of her tongue. She wants to sit at a picnic table and she gets everything she wants when she's clean, when she can't have the one thing she actually wants: Coke. Blow. A bump.*

*Your cone isn't dripping and her cone is dripping and you sit across from each other like two people on a date except this isn't a date.*

*"Hey," she says. "Maybe we should get one of those Slip 'N Slides."*

*A couple of nasty boys who can't be older than twelve laugh at you, what a loser, he's here with his* mom. *You wish you were twelve. When you were twelve you didn't worry about being a virgin because twelve-year-olds can be virgins.*

*Your mother crumples up her napkin and hurls it at the boys and they leave.*

*You shouldn't disagree with her. Not when she just got home and the sky is hot and she has a brand new bathing suit and rehab is sticking. But those boys got to you, those kids who get to be the kid that you never were, free and mean. You bark at your mother because you didn't have the balls to bark at them. "I'm too old for a Slip 'N Slide."*

*"Don't be like that," she says. "Don't care so much about what other people think."*

*"I don't care."*

*"Yeah, you do and what a waste. What do you care if the neighbors see us having some fun? They'll probably wanna come*

*over."*

You used to stay with the Pyles who live up the street when your mom went away. You picture Mrs. Pyle in a one-suit, wet, in your back yard. *"No they won't."*

Your mother shrugs. You're right. No one in the neighborhood wants to come over. They've seen too many random cars in the driveway, sometimes black and whites with the red lights blasting shadows into the other homes. It's too quiet now. Your mother is bored of her ice cream, but she eats it anyway. You can't think of anything to say to her and you worked so hard to lose all that pudding on your belly this year. You don't want the ice cream but you eat the ice cream because you're a bad son. You don't believe it will stick. Not anymore. Not with her wanting to slide on a plastic tarp in the back yard. That's who she is, isn't it? She wants to slide, she doesn't want to stick. She pulls at her bra strap.

*"Well, we have to do something. The weather guy says it's only gonna get hotter tomorrow and we can't get the AC fixed. I have to pay the electric, the gas bill, too."*

Your house isn't yours, not really. Your grandmother gave it to your mom when she died, when you were in pull-ups. It still smells like a grandmother, like the house doesn't want to belong to you, to your mom who can't take good care of it. The words plop out of your mouth like upchuck. *"I'm sorry."*

Your mother stares at you. Her hair is wiry and her eyes are clear. They're so much scarier when she's clean, when she sees you, when she's not looking at you through a hazy veil of bloodshot eyes with her nose dripping and her skin sweaty. *"Sorry for what?"* she wants to know.

You can't think of anything smart to say and you don't want to say anything stupid and when she decides to go out later that night, it is your fault. All you had to do was say you wanted a Slip 'N Slide. When she comes home loud and not alone—he's filthy, he wears boots in summer—she is high and you know she's high by the sound of her giggles. She's a toilet that won't stop running and there's nothing you can do to slow the pace of her speech, to stop the chop, chop, chopping of her credit card. You hear him next, whoever he is, kicking off his boots and snorting your mother's stash. So you stay in your room. You don't play music to block out the sound of *them fucking. You deserve to listen to it. You are a criminal, the worst son on planet earth. You are a virgin and everything bad in this world, in this house, in your dirty mind, in your mother's bloodstream, it's all your fault because she was clean until you turned your back on her at that picnic table, until you refused to get on her side. When the filthy guy sticks his dick in her, when he grunts and you hear the headboard slam into the wall, you get hard and you put your hands on your body and those boys were right to laugh at you today. They're normal. You're the freak.*

### ARIEL

Ariel doesn't need a babysitter. She's twelve and some girls her age actually *are* babysitters. But her mom won't listen to reason.

"Don't compare yourself to other kids,' her mom said. "Trust me. It never works out."

Ariel tries another tactic. She tells her mom all about the babysitters, the girls who act so goody two shoes to her mother. They bob their heads up and down. They promise they won't have boys over or spend all their time on the phone.

"But then they do, Mom. All of them."

"Don't be a tattletale, Ariel. Just let me think."

Ariel knows when to leave it alone. It's been a weird few months. Her father isn't here anymore but this is a secret, something Ariel is not supposed to talk about, not with anyone. When they run into people at the grocery store, her mother says her dad is away on *business* and Ariel pictures him on top of a big pile of manila folders. It's a lie. He doesn't live here anymore. Her mother got an invitation to a wedding the other day. *Mr. and Mrs. Roger Pyle.* Her mother RSVP'd yes and Ariel peeled the card out of the envelope when she found it on the table by the front door. Her mother checked both boxes, like she's married, like her dad is going to come back for this wedding.

Her mother flips the pages of her little black notebook that she carries everywhere, even to the beach. Ariel's mother is beautiful, like a raven-haired queen in a cartoon and life is like a cartoon since her dad left. Ariel feels like she and her mother don't quite get to decide what happens every day, as if they are just characters in a show, as if a whole bunch of adults are in California, drawing their bodies with colored pens while another bunch of adults make up the stories.

Her mother pulls her long hair into a ballerina bun. "I could call Vince."

"Who?"

The question is a lie. Ariel knows Vince. He's the boy who lives up the street. His mother is a *loser* and Vince used to stay in the house with them sometimes when Ariel was little. She hasn't seen him in a long time and she forgot that he existed, but she knows exactly who he is.

"Ariel, he's a nice boy. He's home from college."

"But he's barely older than me."

"Six years is a big difference at your age, honey. He can drive. He's an adult."

"Can I just stay alone?"

Ariel's mother scoops the receiver off the phone that's attached to the wall. It's another moment that feels more like a scene in a cartoon, like her mother isn't deciding to call Vince, like the storytellers in California decided that she would, and so she does.

## Vince

*You're alone again.*

*It was fast this time. Your mother stole more bathing suits from TJ Maxx and instead of putting her in jail they sent her back to get 'treatment'. Other women get treatments too, but it's different. The girls in your dorm got spa treatments and one of the girls was always crying because her mother was in 'treatment'. You were sad when you learned it was treatment as in chemo, for cancer. There is no shame in that and you can't imagine what it would be like to have a mom who pays people to make her hair shiny or destroy unwanted killer cells. Wishing your mother had cancer is sick and you don't want that, you never would. You are still eighteen and you are still a virgin and after she left, you went to TJ Maxx and bought her a Slip 'N Slide. You felt mean and stupid standing in the aisle. Why didn't you do this sooner? You didn't set it up yet. You stare at the happy kids on the box, a white boy and a black boy on a healthy green lawn. Maybe you should throw it away. You are too old and too late, and it's like your mother always says, timing is everything.*

*She's right.*

*If you bought it when she wanted it, she would be here, slipping and sliding. All year your mother asked if you met any nice girls. All year you tried to find a girl to bring home to visit for the summer. If you had met a nice girl, if you had brought her home, she would have been there with you at the soft and hard ice cream place. She would have said that a Slip 'N Slide is a great idea because girls are polite to their boyfriends' mothers. If you'd succeeded, your mother wouldn't have slipped and slid back into rehab.*

*You pick up the box and put it in your closet and slam the door.*

*There are thousands of girls at the University of Wisconsin, but none of them would have you. They looked right through you and you could always feel them writing you off as doughy and odd. You wanted to grab them and tell them about the five pounds you lost, about the ten-pound weights you lifted, about how much you needed someone, how much your mom needed you to have someone. Maybe they knew that somehow. Maybe you're only supposed to want a girl for yourself, not for your mom. There was that one girl in your Child Psychology class with the small mouth and the long neck. She gave you a pen when you needed one and once ate lunch with you in the cafeteria. She told you about her parents, they were going on a cruise and you told her about your mother. She was back in rehab. The girl didn't sit by you after that and it was your fault. You said too much, too fast. It was okay for her to talk about a cruise but not okay for you to talk about your mom's roommate at Sunny Mountain Retreat. You picked the wrong girl. A good son would have picked the right girl, the kind who wants to hear the truth about dark things, but no. And that's why you're a virgin, you idiot.*

*The phone rings. You pick it up. "Hello?"*

*"Vince?"*

*It's a woman and you wonder if she's naked, how her tits would feel in your hands. "Yeah, um, hello?"*

*"Vince, honey, it's Mrs. Pyle up the street. How've you been? How you doing?"*

*"Oh hi." You gulp. "Good. Really good."*

*You know Mrs. Pyle. Barely. She says she's relieved that she caught you and maybe she wants you. Your pants bulge. Maybe she saw you when you walked to the store. Maybe this is how you lose your virginity and maybe fucking Mrs. Pyle will make you smarter and the next time your mom comes home, you'll be better. A man.*

*"Vince, honey," she says. And you are Honey—sweet, warm, and good. "This is coming out of left field, but I wonder if you're free to babysit tonight."*

*You say yes because you can't say no. Look what happened to your mom when you said no to her. The word of the day is yes and you're not a babysitter, but you can't say no to any woman who wants your help. You learned your lesson.*

*"Terrific!" she exclaims. "I really need to get out and we were in such a jam."*

*You take everything the wrong way. She doesn't want you. She wants to get away from you. "What time should I come over?"*

*"Seven," she says. "Oh and Vince, how's your mom? It's been ages since I bumped into her. Everything good?"*

*Your stomach turns over. Your insides are twisting up. You spent a lot of time in the Pyles' nice house when you were a kid. Every time your mother went away to rehab, you went to their home where the dishes were never piled up in the sink and their little girl was always toddling around with a plastic shovel while the AC hummed quietly, so quietly, always working, never broken. You weren't their son and that little girl wasn't your sister and when you liked sleeping in the spare bedroom, you felt guilty, like your mother would know. And when you got sullen and grumpy and played video games too much, you felt guilty, like you were ruining everything for the nice, perfect Pyles.*

*"She's great," you say. "She's on a trip with some work friends to some place up north. I can't remember the name."*

*Mrs. Pyle is so happy to hear that. You don't know why you lied. You want to protect your mother. You want the lie to be true. You wanted Mrs. Pyle to be calling because she wants your dick and this is your revenge, telling her how great things are in your house.*

*You put on fresh clothes. It feels good to have somewhere to go and that's another thing to feel bad about. You shouldn't be happy right now, not when your mother is in pain. You should get a fucking life. You did get a summer job, but they don't need you, not yet. Your deodorant smells good. Maybe Mrs. Pyle will smell you and want to stay home. You get your hopes up so easily but why shouldn't you? Maybe your mom is getting better. You're only eighteen. It's not like you're forty. Some of the biggest studs were virgins at eighteen you shouldn't get so down on yourself. Next year you'll be a sophomore and the girls will be a little busted up from the drinking and debauchery of freshman year. Next year they'll be ready for you—what a good guy, he's a babysitter so he must be great with kids—and they'll look at you a little more closely. Maybe that one with the short dark brown hair will let you borrow her Abnormal Psych notes when you miss class and maybe she'll ask you to have coffee with her and make fun of the pervy old teacher.*

*It could happen. You're a babysitter now, someone people trust with their children. You never babysat before. When your mother gets home, she'll be excited about your new second job. Maybe then her sobriety will stick.*

### ARIEL

Ariel doesn't jump up to say hi to Vince when he arrives. Her mother does, though, telling him he looks great—not true, he's squishy—and asking him about college—he's a *psych* major.

Vince stands like he thinks he's a man, a grown-up. Ariel's mom is writing things down, the phone number of the restaurant, the phone number for non-emergency police calls. She's saying all the things she always says to the babysitters, that she'll call, that he won't have to use these numbers.

"We're going out with some of Roger's colleagues," she says. She's lying again and it's always weird when her mother refers to her dad like that. As *Roger.*

"How is he?" Vince asks. "How's Mr. Pyle?"

"Terrific," her mother says. "He got a big promotion and he's on the road a lot, has to catch a late flight to Chicago."

When Vince picks up the piece of paper he seems even younger, like one of the boys at school. Does he know she's watching him? He doesn't look at her as much as she would like him to look at her. She wants him to look at her the way he's looking at her mother. Ariel is the star of this cartoon, not her stupid mother, lying, repeating all the stuff she already said, as if he's stupid, which he isn't. Vince goes to college. He's cuter than the boys at school, older and younger all at once. He keeps covering his mouth, as if he's about to crack up. She wants to tickle him and make him laugh, let him laugh. She doesn't remember much about all the time he spent here because she was young and her dad was still here. It feels so long ago, like those episodes are buried in canisters in the desert.

Her mother picks up the purse she calls a clutch and points at Ariel. "Be good." Ariel promises to be good. Her mother doesn't tell Vince to be good. She just kisses the top of Ariel's head and click-clacks out the door.

Vince asks her what she wants to do. She studies his puffy face. He looks like he cries a lot, like he's alone a lot, like he doesn't talk out loud enough. She decides right here, right now, that she is the boss of this new episode. She will decide what happens next. This is her house, not his, and he doesn't know anything about this kitchen, about her dad, about what he used to do when he came into her bedroom late at night. Vince doesn't know how the sink makes a funny noise if you don't turn it on hard enough. He is not like one of the girl babysitters either. He doesn't look at the clock like he wants time to pass so that he can invite a girl over to touch him. She can tell that he has no one who thinks about him. She misses her dad even though she shouldn't and Vince sticks his hands into his pockets.

"So, how's it going, Ariel? Did you have a good year at school?"

She asks the questions, not him. She tilts her chin. "How old are you?"

"Eighteen," he says. "How old are you?"

Nope. She asks the questions, not him. "Do you like college?"

He nods. "I just finished my first year. It's pretty great, yep."

"Do you have a girlfriend?"

That question is a fun one. It makes his skin turn red. "Yep," he says. "She's back home in Madison."

"What's her name?"

"Rhiannon," he says, and he turns even redder. Ariel is winning. Nobody in real life is named Rhiannon, except for that one girl at school and there's no way that Ariel would know *two* Rhiannons. He's lying. Already he stopped asking questions. He wants more questions because he wants to tell more stories about things that aren't true. This is fun, being in charge, and Ariel wishes that her dad could watch this cartoon. And then she feels fire inside because her mother told her not to think about her dad. Ever.

## VINCE

*A twelve-year-old girl sits next to you on this green velour couch. Twelve is young. It isn't even thirteen and she's sitting like she's older, but you can't blame a child for what she does. You are a sick motherfucker. You would never touch a child. You remember what you learned about in Child Psych—projection—and you wonder if that's what this is. If you're so hard up that you're fantasizing that you're with an older girl, age appropriate, one who's going through changes of her own and curious about boys, curious about you. Do you call the restaurant? Do you call the non-emergency police number? No. No. There is nothing to say. There is nothing wrong. It's all in your head, you idiot. You think because your mom is sick that all girls are sick. That's what this is. Projection.*

*You stare at the TV. Maybe you are cursed. Maybe your mother's sobriety can't stick because you are a bad curse for all women, all girls. You focus on the objective reality. You take inventory of the decor in the room, the blue shag carpet, a ticking clock and a flickering light bulb. The light bulb surprises you. Mr. Pyle is a Mr. Fix It and you don't remember a lot about your time in this house, but you do remember everything always functioning, never flickering.*

*"Be right back," she says. "I think I just got my period."*

*That's not normal. She's not old enough for that, is she? And what the hell do you know about girls, about periods? Only that it's not right for her to tell you about it.*

*You hear her flush the toilet and she returns and sits even closer. She pulls her hair up and runs her fingers through it. "Nope," she says. "Just being paranoid."*

*She's in charge of you and your eyes hurt from the flickering bulb overhead. You would get up and turn it off, but that would be wrong, turning off the lights when you're alone with a girl. You need that light right now, or else who knows? You might actually touch her. The thought makes you hate yourself because the thought is wrong. You wouldn't ever do that. But the world would expect that of you, wouldn't it? Fucked up virgin with a mother in and out of treatment comes onto a twelve year-old girl. Disgusting. Foul. Lock him up in prison and throw away the key.*

*"I'm tired," she says. "Pause the movie."*

*You pause* Freaky Friday *and sit there under the blinking bulb. It's a torture device, that light bulb. When she comes back, she's wearing a threadbare nightie. She turns off the light. She sits, but she doesn't face the TV. She faces you and she hikes up the nightie and she isn't wearing any panties. You should call them underwear. Not panties. If you tell her to put some on, that means you noticed that she took them off. If you don't tell her to put some on, then you are sitting alone with a girl wearing no panties. No underwear. You play the movie. You wonder what your mom is doing right now, if she's in a therapy circle with other adults like her or if she's telling her roommate that this time, things will be different, that timing is everything. Everything.*

## ARIEL

He's so weird. He's afraid of her. She's not scary. He doesn't tell her to put on panties and he probably doesn't even like *Freaky Friday* but he's watching intensely, like it's the type of story that's hard to follow. Ariel's mind swirls with wishes. She wishes he went to her school and she wishes he could sleep over and she wishes he could live in her house. He's safe the way most people are dangerous. If bad guys broke in, if her dad showed up to take her away, Vince would make him leave even though her dad is so much bigger, so much stronger.

She doesn't like it when her dad pops into her head. It isn't just because her mom told her not to think about him. It's *her* story now and she doesn't want her dad to be in the story at all anymore. She wants a fresh start, her and Vince. She pulls her legs to her chest and closes the window to her body with her nightgown. His whole body changes, like he's relieved. He is nice. Good.

She will let him be in charge now and she reaches for the snacks on the coffee table. "Can I eat a fruit roll-up?"

He still won't look at her. "You just ate one, Ariel. You don't want to get sick."

It's funny how he thinks that two fruit roll-ups will make you sick. Her mom would totally disagree. Her mom says children are resilient, nothing like adults, who can never bounce back from anything.

"I had a cherry one," she says. "Now I want a grape one cuz I can't get the taste out of my mouth. I hate when that happens, you know?"

He looks at her. He can't really be eighteen, not inside. He's like her. He's twelve. "Or," he says, all slow like. "You could go and brush your teeth."

She rolls her eyes like the girls at school who think her dad still lives here. "Whatever," she says. "I don't even care."

His voice changes, like he wants to be the adult again. "Does your mother let you eat two?"

Ariel doesn't want to talk about her mother. Her mother is the reason her dad was here in the first place, the reason Ariel exists. "My mom doesn't care what I eat. I mean, I'm twelve. I eat what I want."

"Okay," he says. "One more. But that's it."

She reaches for the box and takes two. She offers him the purple one, the one she doesn't want. "One for me and one for you."

He doesn't take it at first. She pictures them in the cartoon. His eyes are saucers and hers are smaller, but she is smaller, so it all makes sense, in context. Finally, he takes the fruit roll-up. He eats it like someone who was starving, scarfing it all down in one big bite. He was like that when he was a kid, too. Those were the good days, when she was too little to say all that much, when the carpets were all soft and sometimes Vince was over, and sometimes he wasn't, and all the time, her bedroom was just hers.

## VINCE

*You still don't know what to do. Something is wrong with her and you know it. It's like they say about porn. You know it when you see it. You eat another fruit roll-up, as if that will help, as if you don't know that gorging on Devil Dogs never helped your mother get clean, stay clean.*

*The light bulb doesn't just flicker. It sizzles. It's noisy. She exposed herself to you. You know it. You didn't look, but you saw. Your first vagina in real life and it was a child's. You should call your girlfriend Rhiannon to ask her for advice but she doesn't exist, does she? You should call the police, but it's too late for that now, just like it was too late for you to save your mother with a Slip 'N Slide. You fuck up everything and you choke on the plastic wrapper that you neglected to tear off the fruit roll-up.*

*She's laughing. "Omigod, are you eating the wrapper?"*

*You never grew up. You are a child. You still like to eat this crap and you eat too fast and the movie is growing on you and you reach for the box and she laughs. She's been watching you all this time, holding her nightgown over her knees. When she laughs, she looks more like her mother, and you can imagine her in six years, on campus, and it would be fun to eat lunch with her and your head is vile. Disgusting. She's a child and a minute ago you were concerned for her safety.*

*You fight a smile. You smile when you are nervous, which you are. "What's so funny?"*

*"Nothing," she says. "It's just neat to see you. It's weird how we're the same but we're not, you know? Like how we change but we don't."*

*She pulls the nightgown even tighter. It's not as see-through as you thought. The light bulb was playing tricks on you. Maybe it was all in your head. Maybe she never exposed herself. Maybe you were hallucinating because you want everyone to have problems like you. It's just a fucking light bulb and Mrs. Pyle did say that everything is great. You are the one who's fucked up. You. Not her.*

*"Hey," she says. "Is your mom really all better?"*

*You won't burden her. She's a child. "Yep," you say. "She's doing great."*

*"Phew," she says. "That's awesome. My mom always said that would never happen. She said it was sad but true that women who use drugs like her never get better."*

*You want to eat the cardboard box and all the plastic wrappers. Mrs. Pyle betrayed you. She betrayed your mom, your mom who always beat herself up about those perfect Pyles, how they always had their 'shit' together. And she would get down on herself for swearing in front of you, for using the word 'shit', as if you didn't hear swears at school all the time. Your mom tried so hard to be good like Mrs. Pyle. She sent them thank you notes and wasted money on fruit baskets and now to find out that all along, they didn't believe in her, not the way you did, do.*

*"Well," you say. "Moms say stuff. But mine's okay. I bet your mom's busy with your dad out of town so much."*

*That was mean and you crossed a line and you're not even sure why but you know you did. She drops her bare feet onto the table. Her legs are open and she pulls up the nightgown and scratches her leg. "It's okay," she says. But it isn't. "He's making a lot of money and we're going to Disney later this year."*

*"Cool," you say, and you've never been to Disney. She has more life experience than you, which is degrading because she is six years younger than you. But your mind is stuck on the nature of her experience. What is it exactly?*

*"Will your dad go, too?"*

*She moves her feet so that they press into the edge of the table. Her nightgown slips over her knees and bunches at her crotch. You said crotch. Not out loud but in your head and again you look at the phone. You should call the non-emergency police. Or child services. Someone.*

*"Yeah," she says. "If he wants to."*

*"Well, of course he wants to."*

*Her eyes are glossy. There's a new movie on the TV and she watches the two Lindsay Lohans scheme and plot. "He always gets what he wants," she says. "Always."*

*She picks up the remote control and slides her body into the corner of the sofa. She is done with you. She doesn't want to talk to you anymore and you failed to save her, to help her, to turn off the TV and say the right things and now the remote is in her lap and you would have to walk over to the TV and shut off the TV if you wanted to confront her. But you can't do that. You don't trust your dumb head because how could you? Look at your mom. Never sticking. Look at you, look at your legs—still pillowy in spite of how hard you tried living on celery and Diet Sprite. You're still soft, like ice cream, and this is the body you are stuck with and it sticks, unlike your mother's sobriety.*

*Eventually she falls asleep. You are afraid to make a noise, to wake her up. You pick up a blanket and lay it on her body. This is when the babysitter calls a girl to come over, to sneak outside and make out in the back yard. But you don't have a girlfriend. You go to Ariel's room. You turn on the light. You find her diary under her bed. It's mostly about boys at school and you go way back to read when you were around but you're not in there that much. You feel invisible. You turn the diary over and find a drawing on the interior of the hardback cover. It's a sketch of a girl, a body that's like a map. She has no eyes, no mouth, no nose. There are dozens of little dots on her anatomy, and all the little dots are in the place where her panties should be. Some are red and some are pink. You can tell when the red pen wore out when the pink pen was brand new, plump with ink, and you can tell when that one ran out, too.*

*You return the diary to its proper place. They are not the perfect Pyles. Your mother is a cokehead, but she never crept into your bed and touched you. You never drew pictures of your hurt body. You should have played along with the Slip 'N Slide. You lived in this house on and off for so long and you always thought Mr. Pyle was so great. You are a fucking idiot. A virgin. And for the first time in your life you realize that you are lucky to be a fucking idiot, a virgin. At least you aren't like Ariel.*

## MRS. PYLE

Yes, Mrs. Suzanne Pyle will have another drink.

She deserves it. She's working her tail off at home, at the office, trying to hold things together. She didn't rat out Monster because she needs Monster's money if they want to get the sink fixed, go to Disney. That doesn't make her a bad person. It makes her a practical person. She doesn't want to take Monster's money, but she *needs* Monster's money, and she's not an alcoholic either. She has a high tolerance. Her friends are judging her, glancing at her vodka martini, at each other. They're just like Monster. He threatened to go to the police about Suzanne's "drinking." Okay, so Suzanne drinks at lunch and was tipsy a few times she picked Ariel up from school. But nobody found out and nobody died and she's a damn good drunk driver, even if that's not the sort of thing that would ever hold up in court.

Monster is the bad one, not her. She's good, full of good ideas, like calling poor Vince from up the street to babysit. It was nice, the way he sounded on the phone. It was so obvious that he has a crush on her. Maybe he even thinks about her when he jerks off. It's a nice thing, thinking that this sweet boy who hasn't grown into his body enough to become a rotten man would load all of his lust on to her.

Gloria yawns. "So when is Roger back?"

"Oh, you know," she says. "Not anytime soon. This promotion is terrific, but he's on the road *constantly.*"

Suzanne knows that she's the kind of woman you believe. The cops would have believed her, too, but Ariel's been through enough. She doesn't need to play with an anatomically correct doll in front of a two-way mirror and Suzanne certainly isn't in a rush to tell her friends that she's getting *divorced.* (The cause: irreconcilable differences. Normal. Common.) Suzanne likes being thought of as married, as a part of *Mr. & Mrs. Pyle. Mrs.* Suzanne Pyle is someone who chooses the right man, the right blouse, the right babysitter. It isn't fair that she has to let go of that because of what Monster did. She hugs her friends. Bye. Bye. They look at each other, at her empty glass. *Fuck you, friends.*

She makes it home just fine, thank you. The cops didn't stop her. And if they had flashed their lights and pulled her over, she would have talked her way out of it. She pops a breath mint. She doesn't want Vince to smell the alcohol on her breath. The poor kid has enough to worry about, that cluster-fuck of a mother with her "addiction is a disease" nonsense. It's bullshit. That first line of coke is a choice, and Vince's mother is no different from Monster, who tried the same excuse with Suzanne when she caught him in Ariel's bedroom. *I'm not a monster. I'm just sick.*

Bullshit and Suzanne slams the car door. She fluffs her hair and freshens her lipstick. She sacrificed so much already. She turned down a promotion to stay home when Ariel was young. She loved it when Vince's mother would cave to her "addiction" and lose another dead-end job and go to rehab. What a high it was to sacrifice more of her precious time to care for someone else's child. She remembers young Vince gorging on her tuna casserole. No one ever taught him to eat with his mouth closed.

She opens the door. "I'm home!"

He's lost a little weight, but he's not there yet, probably still a virgin, the way he looks at her like he wants to pounce. She's still got it, she does. She asks him how everything went and she sounds sober. He shoves his hands in his pockets, no doubt willing the erection growing down there to quit. "Could I...Could we talk for a second?"

She cups his chin in her hand. "Of course, honey. You can always talk to me."

She directs him into the kitchen and her movements are deliberate. She doesn't have an itch on her waist but she scratches anyway, guiding his eyes to her ass. Still got that, too. "Can I get you something to drink? Water? Beer?"

"I'm okay," he says. He sits at the table. Awkward. Awkward because his mother never took care of him and he's completely overwhelmed by Suzanne's caring ways. Suzanne's having a beer because Suzanne deserves a beer. She pops the can. Pffss. "Honey," she says. "I get the feeling your mom's not doing so great."

He clenches his teeth. The rage he must feel, the guilt. "She's getting help."

Suzanne shakes her head. What a load of bullshit. *She's getting help.* Don't these people understand that it's not the world's job to help them? Monster was like that too, offering to see a *psychologist*, swearing that he would change, as if it wasn't too late, as if the damage could be reversed. He touched their fucking child. The end. Vince's mother chose cocaine over her fucking son. The end. These people have no will power and then they want pity. She takes a long sip of her Corona. They can fuck off. It's pretty simple that way. They're both monsters. The difference is that Vince's mother is the ideal monster, the one who lets Suzanne be the brave warrior, the one who never got her paws on her Goddamn daughter.

She throws Vince a bone and tells him that it's great to hear that his mother is getting help, as if "getting help" ever worked in the past. The poor kid just nods, with all the conviction of a sock in the washing machine. His childhood is shot. The only thing he can do now is get through college, get on his own two feet and find himself a girlfriend, a wife. But it's hard to imagine him ever shedding the baby fat, earning a consistent paycheck, paying a mortgage. Socks get lost in the dryer and no one ever knows who to blame, but Suzanne's sure of one thing—his mother should be dragged into an alley and shot, along with Monster.

"So," she says, in her brightest mom voice, the one that always lifts her spirits. "You're on your own at home, then? Must be kinda hard…"

He's too closed up to cry, to stand up for himself. "I'm taking care of the house," he says. "But she'll be home soon. It's okay."

"Right," she says, as if his unfit mother won't be spiraling down a mountain of cocaine before the end of the summer. She remembers those ridiculous fruit baskets, her chicken scratch on the thank you notes. Suzanne hates pears, and it was always mostly pears in those fruit baskets. Monster *loves* pears, and she remembers him slicing the cokehead's pears and feeding them to her fucking daughter. She opens another beer. Pigs. Monsters, both of them.

Vince's hands are shaking. He's holding them together but he's not doing a very good job of covering. "Vince," she says. "I meant what I said. You can talk to me. I know that this can't be easy. I'm here."

"I know," he says.

"And hey, if you want to stay with us, we have plenty of room."

"No...no, that's okay. I'm good at home."

"No, really, Vince," she begins, because the more she thinks about it, the more she wants him to move in. They are *the perfect Pyles*. This home is a safe haven and Vince needs to move in and make it all true again. It would feel so good to tell her friends. *My neighbor's kid moved in again...Another mouth to feed, but how can you say no?* She likes her house better with a man in it, and it would be nice to have someone in on the lie, even if he didn't know the whole story. Maybe Ariel would snap out of it, stop being so grumpy and realize that she's lucky to be alive, that we all are.

Suzanne doesn't let go of a good idea when she gets one. This is what she does at the agency. She pitches. She's selling Vince. He could stay in his old bedroom, the guest bedroom. "Naturally," she says. "We would never ask you to pay rent. If anything we'd pay you for helping out with Ariel."

"Maybe," he says, and his leg is thumping. He wants her. He's ashamed of his desire, ashamed of his mother. He thinks it would be cruel to move out of that house but he need*s* to move into *this* house. Suzanne is going to win this one. She doesn't say it to Vince—it's none of his business—but she worries about Monster coming back one night. That's what happens in all horror movies. Monsters return. And if Vince were around every day, well, he's certainly not physically intimidating, but at least Ariel wouldn't be alone and Suzanne wouldn't have to be self-conscious about getting babysitters for her twelve-year-old daughter when girls Ariel's age are out there babysitting. Right now, her friends believe her story, that they had a break-in while Roger was on a business trip, that Ariel is scared and doesn't like to be home alone. But kids are resilient and this charade can't go on forever. Suzanne saved Vince so many times and now it's his turn. She trusts him. She recognized innate kindness in him when he was a boy and it's still there now. He would never hurt a fly. She was attracted to the Monster for the opposite reason, because he seemed callous enough to compete, to earn, and you reap what you sew. But then you buy more land and you plant more seeds. That's what Vince is, a new seed, a new field.

"Mrs. Pyle," he says. "I actually…I don't know how to say this."

She licks her lips. *Oh.* He's not as innocent as she thought. He really does want to fuck her and he's going for it, blushing. It would be nice to have sex again. She wouldn't have to go to the gym as much. She'd never let Ariel find out about it. They'd do it in his mother's house, assuming it's not a total pigsty.

She drops her voice. "Go ahead, honey. Whatever it is, it's okay."

"Well," he says. "I'm concerned about Ariel."

Suzanne's insides coil up like springs in a mattress. "Oh?"

"I'm probably being crazy," he says. "But a couple times tonight, I dunno, I took some psych courses this year, and I'm someone…Do you think anyone hurt her?"

No. Suzanne will not stand for this invasion of her privacy. Vince is not on her side and he will not passively reject her and accuse her of being a bad mother. Her daughter is fine and children are resilient and everyone fucking knows that. *Everyone.* Vince is a child. He knows nothing about kids, about life. He took a couple of courses and now he has the nerve to accost her in his own namby-pamby way, as if she didn't provide the only stability in the kid's fucking *life.* He's never been much of a talker. He never sent any thank you notes or fruit baskets. His mother did that. Not him. He never said how much he loved her tuna casserole and their big back yard with the good grass, unlike his crabgrass at home. Fuck him and his ingratitude. Fuck anyone who wants to focus on Monster instead of her. Ariel is *fine* and Suzanne is *fine* and she knows how to cry on cue. No waterworks, just a few teardrops because any mother is sad to think of her child not being well.

"Oh God," she blubbers. "I can't thank you enough. I know that's not easy."

The ingrate is all sweaty and puffed up, as if this is about him. "I'm sorry. I was so scared to bring this up, but I felt like I had to because she just seems...off."

"You did the right thing, Vince. It's like those signs at all the stadiums. 'See something, say something.'"

She sees that sign every day on the way to work and every day it kills her, as if you're supposed to see everything always.

"Is Mr. Pyle, is he really away on business? Did he...you don't have to tell me."

She will not snap. She will not remind this little shit that his mother is away on weakness and selfishness. She rubs her forehead. "It's good you brought this up now. This way, I can talk to Ariel when he's not here."

"I really hope I'm wrong."

"Oh Vince, I do too."

He stands, as if he gets to decide when to leave. "If you need me to talk to anyone...I don't know if that's how it works, I'm just saying, you've always been there for me...I know I owe you for all the nice things you did for me, I just wanna...I'm here to help you."

He finally said something true. He owes her. A lot. "Don't be ridiculous, Vince. You don't owe me anything. I'm in shock right now."

She brings him in for a hug. His stiff arms call attention to the lack of stiffness between his legs. Another insult. He thinks he gets to look down on *her*. She pats his back before she pulls away.

"Thank you, Vince. You're a good kid. I know it hasn't been an easy road for you and I know this took a lot of courage."

He stands tall, like he just figured out what to do with his shoulders. The arrogance is spreading through him like a virus, as if suspecting Ariel of being abused elevates him, as if he isn't the latchkey offspring of a *drug addict*.

"I think it's gonna get better, ya know?" he says. "For all of us."

She doesn't offer to pay him because she knows he won't take the money. He broke the deal, not her, and she opens the door because it's time for him to go the way of the Monster. "Absolutely, Vince, from your mouth to God's ears. Get home safe."

## VINCE

*You did it. You didn't get a woody when she hugged you. You saw something and you said something and this is the time your mother's sobriety really will stick. You open the door and run into your house and pull the Slip 'N Slide out of the closet. You didn't need a girlfriend. You needed to grow up. You needed to be a man, an adult with a responsibility in this world that didn't have anything to do with the apron strings, with your mother.*

*You open the sliding door and step into the back yard. You won't be a virgin for much longer because tonight you learned how to talk to women. You aren't fat. Your heart is racing and your body is a furnace. You pull the bright blue tarp out of the box and you toss the box in the dirt. Your mother is right. It doesn't matter what other people think. It doesn't matter that you're older than the kids on the box. What matters is that you do the right thing at the right time, before it's too late.*

*You breathe in the smell of the plastic. You spread the tarp on the lawn.*

*You hear the doorbell ring. You get a little hard in your pants, but that's okay, you're human. Of course you hope it's Mrs. Pyle. You pray she wants to thank you, to sit on your face and kiss you all over.*

*"Coming!"*

*You run inside through the back door to check your hair in the mirror. It's impossible, but you think you aged tonight, like you grew into your skin. Your bones are more pronounced. Your eyes are larger. You take a deep breath and you open the front door and it's a police officer you know, one you've met over the years because of your mother.*

## ARIEL

Ariel is eighteen years old.

She's the same age as Vince, well, the same age he was that summer. She thinks about that night all the time. She carries it around in her head while she's walking to class, while she's checking out books at the library. Her mother came downstairs. Ariel pretended she was sleeping. She was good at pretending by then. Her mother reeked of beer and she turned on the light. She hissed at the flickering light bulb and pulled up Ariel's nightgown and for a moment, Ariel thought it was happening again, that her mother was like her father.

She was but she wasn't.

Ariel can still hear the sound of her mother rummaging through her bedroom. She can still hear her cutting up the pages of her diary and sobbing on the phone to the police about what she came home to, how *stupid* she was to trust the unstable son of a *drug addict* with her precious daughter, who was naked underneath her nightgown on the sofa, in the dark. *No panties, Officer. None.*

Ariel found Vince online a few years ago. He lives here in LA too. He's just a person in the world, like her. He was never charged with anything. The police went to him the day after her mother called. They asked him questions, but it ended there. Suzanne didn't want to pursue a case. She didn't want little Ariel to be questioned. She didn't see how that would help. Instead, she started telling everyone in town about what Vince did. For the rest of that summer, Ariel listened to her mother talk on the phone about Monster, Vince, and how when the police went to see him, he was setting up a *Slip 'N Slide* in his back yard. How creepy. How perverse. Obviously, he'd been doing that to lure Ariel over to his house, to get her all wet. Why else would a kid his age use a *Slip N' Slide*? Vince was Monster now. He went back to college early. Ariel's mother said he was *lucky to be free, but Karma's a bitch. He will pay for this in other ways.* A few months after that, there was a For Sale sign in front of Vince's house. A few months after that, there were new people in the house.

Ariel still can't wrap her head around it, how comforting it was to hear her mother talk about Monster, even though Vince wasn't Monster. Her *father* was Monster. But you want your mother to love you, to protect you, and she supposes that anyone in her position would have reacted the same way. She was a child. She was helpless. She didn't have her diary anymore. She didn't defend him and she didn't tell the police that she took off her underwear, not Vince. The real Monster was gone and if she had ridden her bike to the police station and told them that her mother was a liar, what then? Her mother cried a lot. She told her friends it was *all her fault* and her friends always said she was wrong. *It was that monster's fault, not yours.* And that was true.

The GPS lady advises Ariel to turn left in 250 feet. She puts on her blinker.

She's a freshman at UCLA now. She chose LA because Vince chose LA. She's known where he lives since she arrived in August. All year, she thought about going to see him. She just kept not doing it. The same way she kept not asking her mother why she lied about Vince that summer. Not doing something becomes doing something, and it's hard to stop.

He lives at a small apartment complex on a side street in Hollywood. His mother died last year. It wasn't drugs. It was cancer. She parks in a loading zone. This might be a bad idea. She should have gone to see him sooner, when his mother was sick, alive. She should have gone to the funeral. But it was always something and she pulls her little satchel out of her clutch.

Just one bump. One quick snort. For courage.

She doesn't know what she's doing here but not coming was driving her crazy. This must be what it's like to be an addict—she's not like Vince's mom, she only does a few lines of cocaine every now and then—but she can't take it anymore, the burden of carrying around all this love inside of her, this guilt, ever since that summer. This is the only way for it to escape. Love and guilt can kill you if they stay inside.

She rings his buzzer. He probably won't want to see her. He might be looking out a window right now. But would he recognize her? She looks so different. So grown up. Someone leaves the building and she slips in through the door.

One more bump to shoot confidence down her spine. Nothing about this is easy and of course she has issues, monster parents, finals, and a double shift at the library tomorrow. You do what you have to do to survive and you don't survive unless you take action. She's not a kid anymore. She can't pretend that life is a cartoon, that you don't control your own actions.

She knocks on his door. Does he live alone? Does he have a girlfriend?

"Coming!" he cries and she wants to bolt. She wants another bump.

She ruined his life and he probably despises her, all those

rumors. All those terrible things her mother said about him to anyone who would listen, the lady at the bank, the neighbor across the street, the real police, the ones who don't carry loaded guns, the ones who whisper that it was only a matter of time before the kid turned out to be like his mother, *poisonous.* It's not too late to run. She could run. She should run. Sometimes she thinks about that *Slip 'N Slide,* how he didn't tell her to put on panties. She hears her mother in her head. She was young, traumatized. Maybe he *was* Monster. She needs another bump. God she is flying. She needs to get the fuck out of here before the door opens.

### VINCE

*In theory, you should be depressed. You're still a virgin. You did meet a girl junior year, but you couldn't get it up. She was kind about it. She said you should get help. She said she didn't want to try anymore. But you didn't want to try. You didn't get help. Better safe than sorry. Maybe you're just better off alone.*

*The buzzer goes off and you flinch. It's probably a mistake.*

*Your mother is gone now, and you ruined the last few years of her life. She could never get over what that "monster" Suzanne did to you. She told you over and over again that you were the world's best son, the best boy, the sweetest boy, the kindest boy.*

*You still remember the joy in her voice when she said, "You got me a Slip 'N Slide!"*

*The rage that followed was too much for her to cope with on top of the yearning for drugs and eventually, nobody believed in her, not even you, and she went to prison for knocking off a convenience store when she was high. That's where she died, behind bars. It wasn't the drugs and it wasn't even the cancer. She died of "complications."*

*You never asked to know what that means. You figured there's no point. She's dead. And death is simple. Life is what's complicated. You graduated but you didn't major in Psych. You have a job but you don't feel like the other people at work, the people who laugh easily. What the hell do you know about people? You never took another psych class after freshman year and everyone knows that kids who take psych classes go nuts. They decide they're crazy. They decide everyone's crazy. What makes you any different? You didn't read Suzanne Pyle right. She fooled you. For all you know, you were always stupid, imperceptive. You always thought your mother was going to get better. Every single time. No matter what. You could have passed a lie detector because it was the truth.*

*At night in the dark, you believe in yourself, in your eyes. You know what you saw, what you suspected, and you will never forget the pink and red dots in Ariel's diary. There is no doubt about what her father did. But in the morning light, your security from the dark hours when you're tucked in bed is gone. You go to work and you keep to yourself. You think maybe you were wrong about Ariel, about her father. Who says it was him? You don't know that. Ariel didn't tell you that. She didn't point him out in a line-up. You get in the car to drive home at the end of the day. You sit in traffic. You eat fruit roll-ups in the car and you leave the wrappers on the floor of the passenger seat. No one's ever been in your car but you. You think Suzanne was right about you. Maybe she sensed something was wrong with you, the way the doctors know a bad spot from a normal spot in an X-ray. You get home and mostly you stay home. You don't get out much and if you ever did get arrested, if you committed a crime, your neighbors would describe you as a textbook loner who keeps to himself.*

*The buzzer rings again and again you ignore it. No one's coming over. No one ever comes over. The mind fuck of death is that people who die don't die in your brain. She's been gone a year now, and you still think,* Is that you, Mom? *You wonder if that will ever stop, the desire to bring her back to life, pull her out of the grave and give her another chance. And then you think about that Slip 'N Slide. She never did get to slip or slide. You tore it off the lawn and threw it away after the cops showed up at your house.*

*Someone's knocking on the door now. But this isn't a horror movie. You're logical. It's not your mother and it can't be the police. You did not lay a hand on Ariel that night. You would never lay a hand on Ariel. The cops only visited you that one time and nobody pressed charges. But look at you. You live like a criminal who got away with something. It's probably just your neighbor wanting to know if your rent went up. But still you run around fixing things, hiding things. You close your computer. You throw Devil Dog wrappers into the trash. You do think it's the police. You think that they know you better than you know yourself, that they have access* to your mind, that they know how impotent you were that night at Ariel's house. You didn't call the non-emergency police. You were a monster in the worst way, the silent kind who talks to the wrong person—the mother—at the wrong time, at night, while her child sleeps in front of the TV, not in her bed, no panties. No underwear.

You don't look in the peephole before you open the door. If they've come to take you to prison, you won't put up a fight. You don't know how long you can go on like this anyway. You don't believe your eyes when you open the door and maybe you shouldn't believe them. You think you see Ariel all the time. You've never Googled her. That would make you a pervert, wouldn't it? And you think every girl is her and it never is but now is now and it's her. It is. She opens her mouth.

"Vince," she says. "Hi."

You don't say a word. She could be wired. She could be here to get your confession. She is beautiful, like you knew she would be. She isn't the girl in front of the TV in the threadbare nightgown and she is a woman. She has a purse, like an adult. She throws her arms around you and you are older too. You aren't the college kid whose mom just went back to rehab. You hold her in your arms. You feel her heart thumping in her chest, pressed against yours. You invite her to come in and she doesn't move. She looks around your apartment.

"Or we could go somewhere. I can drive."

She doesn't want to come into your apartment and you want to give her what she wants. You grab your house keys and your jacket. "Okay," you say. "Let's do that."

She is talking a lot and she is nervous, jumping from the big stuff (she's thought about you, she has) to the small stuff. Hollywood is uglier than she expected. You let her do all the talking. You let her push the door and you follow her into the haze. It isn't all sunny today and she parked illegally and she laughs about the absurdity of all the cars in this city and nowhere to put them.

"Makes me miss home, you know?"

She looks at you with eyes that don't scare you, eyes that tell you that none of this is real. You know those eyes, those cocaine eyes. They belong to your mother, to the countless others who slipped and slid around your house over the years when you were a kid. Yes, Ariel is on something. The amateur college psychologist in *you tells you that this is not a surprise. Her father abused her and her mother squashed it and she's not talking about any of that. She's just telling you about her boss, her finals coming up. She trusts you. She doesn't think you hurt her. She doesn't come right out and say it, but she won't break eye contact and she won't stop talking and she's here, on her own volition.*

*"Oof," she says. "I'm such a jerk."*

*"No you're not."*

*"No," she says, squinting. "I mean, I didn't even say I'm sorry about your mom. And I am sorry."*

*"That's okay," you say. "It's been a while."*

*Her phone rings in her purse and she grunts. "It's my mom. Do you mind if I take it?"*

*She steps away. She doesn't want to talk to her mother in front of you and you bet she won't tell her mother she's there. You go through the things you know about Ariel Pyle. Tiny things. You go back to the night your mom called to tell you that the Pyles got divorced. It was your sophomore year and your mom was mad as usual because she never did stop seething over those perfect Pyles. She was mad at you for not being angrier. She said you should want to stand up for yourself, defend your good name and you said you just wanted to move on.*

*"I'm only gonna ask you this once, Vince. Did you touch that girl?"*

*"No," you said.*

*"I knew that," she said. "I know that you can't believe I asked."*

*You were like a guy in a movie who gets shot and doesn't know it until someone else points to the blood. You didn't feel anything. You were on automatic. You did what you always do. You told her that she had to ask, that it wasn't her fault, that nothing is her fault. She started to cry. "I should have sent you to my cousin Gina's."*

*You said it again. "It's not your fault, Mom."*

*"Yes it is," she said. "Unlike Mrs. Pyle, or should I say Ms. Pyle, I take responsibility. I know I messed up your life, I know it every day. And that's the hardest part about this. If I'd been home, you wouldn't have ever been in that house. I put you there, me. And do you know what it's like to live with that?"*

*You were cold. Like blood was pouring out of your chest. You couldn't talk. You didn't tell her to stop crying. You didn't tell her it was your fault, too, that you were the one who started it by trusting Mrs. Pyle, by not calling the police. You would never want to win a fight with your mom because she could never win the fight of her life. It was your job to let her win, even if winning meant taking all the blame. Eventually, she blew her nose and she was calmer. "Don't you worry," she said, as if you were the one who was worried.*

*"Their perfect little family breaking down is the best revenge. Those monsters will get what's coming to them. It's only a matter of time."*

*You knew she was wrong. Mr. Pyle still had his big job and now it's obvious that Mrs. Pyle still gets to be close with Ariel. Ariel, who is leaning against her brand new car, telling her mom she loves her.*

*She ends the call and sighs. "Ugh, that's like the fifth time today."*

*Her pupils are tiny and you are back to being you, the good boy, the one who wants to help. You don't care that her mother lied about you and you know what Ariel wants. She wants a bump. She won't say it. She won't do that in front of you. She came here to fall in love with you because she wants to get back at her mother, but also because she likes you. She always liked you and you always liked her. You know the love won't stick. You know that it can't. Not when she's like this. Slippery. But this is what you do, what you've always done.*

*She sits on the curb and you sit next to her.*

*She breaks the silence. She says she's wanted to come see you every day for the past six years. Her words are like rain and you miss rain. She says she's always felt horrible about what happened. You wanted this, for her to come to you. She is the only person on the planet who can prove that you are pure of heart and she balks at you when you tell her what a relief it is to see her, to know that she doesn't think you hurt her.*

*"Jesus, Vince. Of course I know you didn't hurt me. I was there. You didn't do anything wrong. And I know what I did...."*

*You blush. You remember her on the sofa. You don't want to say the wrong thing so you don't say anything.*

*"It's like I thought if I acted strange, you would tell someone."*

*"I tried."*

*"I know," she says. "You tried to help me. And then my mother went and ruined your life and I clammed up. I didn't stand up for you."*

*You don't want this to be the story. You tell her that she was just a kid, that she did nothing wrong. She huffs. "Oh God," she says, as if she didn't hear you. "Don't do that. You should be mad. It's simple. You get this mom who's in and out of rehab and messes up your life and then my mom smells blood in the water and ruins your life."*

*"No," you say. "No one ruined my life. It's not that simple."*

*You mean it, you do. She heard you this time. She shifts. You shift. You are in this together now and this will be the gum that sticks to the counter, the bargaining that never ends. If you tell her that her mother is a monster, she will say it's complicated, that her mother was only defending you from the real monster, her father. If you defend your mother, if you remind Ariel that your mother wasn't cruel, just sick, she'll fight back because of her father. She'll say there's no difference. Sick, cruel. They're both selfish, your mother and her Monster. She wants things to be simple and you want them to be complicated and of course she wants them to be simple. What her father did is simple. Monstrous. And of course you want them to be complicated. The drug was the Monster. Not your mother. And deep down she knows that, but she wants you to be in the same boat, and you want to be in the boat with her. You will never strike a deal that makes you both happy. You could spend the rest of your life on this curb with her and she stands up. "Should we drive on Sunset or something?"*

*"Sure."*

*There is peace now. She needs to be the one behind the wheel and you needed her to choose you to ride shotgun. You are the virgin and the cokehead. What you need and what you want are two different things and having your needs met isn't as good as getting what you want, but getting what you want can ruin you. It's safer this way. You know how to slide into the passenger seat. You know how this ends. You see her rubbing her dripping nose and you look out the window. Maybe she has a cold. You've been alone for so long. It's better this way, on the road with her, with the sun breaking through the clouds. Driving gives her something to do with her hands. She's in control. You believe in her, you do. You start to believe that it's only a matter of time before she doesn't want to get high, doesn't need to get high. It happens all the time. People find the right person, the person who sets up the Slip 'N Slide right away. People heal each other and maybe Ariel's not like your mother, same way you're not like her father. Maybe, just maybe, this sticks.*

*"Hang on," she says, as she turns into the parking lot of a gas station. "I have to run in the bathroom. I'll be quick, I promise."*

**ABOUT THE AUTHOR**
Caroline Kepnes is the author of YOU, HIDDEN BODIES and PROVIDENCE. The hit Netflix series *You* is an adaptation of her debut novel. The upcoming second series is based on her sequel HIDDEN BODIES. Caroline was born and raised on Cape Cod, Massachusetts. When she was in high school, Sassy Magazine gave her short story an Honorable Mention in their Fabulous Fiction Contest. They also gave her a Smith Corona typewriter. After graduating from Brown University, Caroline continued writing short stories (on her computer, sorry typewriter) while embarking on a career in pop culture journalism first at Tiger Beat, then at Entertainment Weekly. She also worked as a TV writer on 7th Heaven and The Secret Life of the American Teenager. Caroline now lives in a quaint neighborhood in Los Angeles. She goes home to Cape Cod every chance she gets.

# LIZARD

by

*Mark Matthews*

# LIZARD

*Mark Matthews*

## CHAPTER ONE:
### Lizabeth and Becca

"YOU'RE AFRAID TO GO, aren't you?"

I grabbed the car keys off the wall hook as if this was proof she was wrong, but she wasn't. She read me faster with each passing month together.

"Something tells me I shouldn't go," I answered. "We need to talk about it. It doesn't feel right to leave after getting bad news."

Our petition to become adoptive parents had just been denied. After a home study, background check, hours of interviews, reference letters, and lots of painful waiting, we'd received the form letter in the mail. Becca was ripping it into pieces.

"You latched on to someone with a past," Becca said, sprinkling bits of the letter into the recycle bin. "I've done too much damage. I can't repair it. The world doesn't want me, I don't want it, and that's just how it is. Trying to shove myself into places I'm not supposed to fit just crushes me under the weight."

My fingers clenched into a fist and I held the car keys with one sticking out between my knuckles, the way I do when I'm scared, knowing that one carefully aimed punch in the face will turn an eye socket into a bloody keyhole. My fingers seemed to have a brain of their own, but there was no reason for them to be scared. This was no late night walk to my car or uneasy feeling of being followed by one of my parolees. This was Becca, but it was Becca's fears, her stubborn words, her volleying with charges followed by retreats into hidden intentions, that I directed my anger towards. I tried to relax, but my fingers wouldn't obey.

"I've seen you with kids, I've seen what it's like. It's magical. We can't just give up."

"It's not giving up, it's giving in. It's acceptance. If one agency thinks we're not fit to adopt—that *I'm* not fit to adopt—well then, they probably all will. The property in Canada can be a home, not just a vacation spot. Away from people and memories that trigger me everywhere. I know you want to be a mom, and I hate that I'm the reason you can't have a child in your home."

"There are other agencies…"

"And there are other couples. Couples who aren't same-sex, because people think kids need a dad, for sure not two moms if one has a criminal record and shot-up a shit load of heroin and then got clean and shacked up with her probation officer… We probably should have lied a little better about that part."

"There are other ways. A donor. A surrogate. Even the old-fashioned way."

"Ah, hell no. It's the ultimate sin to add a child to this world the way it is. No way, not in my body, not in yours, I don't want someone suffering with having a *life* because I'm selfish. If there's a child who needs me, we can talk—otherwise, I'm listening to the call of the wild. I'm not saying you have to go with me. Maybe you should cut me free, lose your anchor."

Her words speared me through the chest, impaled me into silence. Becca retreated to the couch and pulled her long-sleeve shirt down over her palms. I could feel her mind's eye swirling. I wouldn't leave until she said something else. I needed her to give me that.

"Go to your visit, Lizard, just don't fall in love with this one."

She gave me what I needed. The inside joke was our glue, and we were still stuck together.

The air outside surrounded me with a soft chill, enough to heighten my senses, but not clear my head. I'd forgotten something inside. I was missing something. What was it? Whispers in my head begged me to stay, said that it wasn't safe to leave Becca alone. The whispers were the soundtrack of my life, background noise from the scared, angry child inside me I'd learned to live with.

Maybe Becca was right, that I really was afraid to go. It was my first home visit with my new drug court caseload. I'd visited homes in the past working in probation for seven years—first misdemeanors, then youth diversion, then to felony probation. But after three rounds of interviews, I'd finally landed the position I wanted—a drug court caseload working primarily with mothers.

Not a career, but a calling. My own call of the wild.

As I drove away, I kept seeing Becca in the wilds of Canada on the property she'd inherited from her uncle that we'd visited so many times. It was a sanctuary without a trace of humans for miles, the only sound in the air dog whistles only her soul could hear.

*She'll be different once we have a child in our life.*

Becca's body was a sprinkler that shot out joy for kids to dash over and play, and it grew stronger with every year clean and sober.

Her charges were serious, but not terrible. She was on my caseload many years back for misdemeanor retail fraud to fund her heroin habit.

From the moment I met her, I could feel something in her heart. She was shedding her addiction, slithering out of her old casing like a snake, or better yet, a caterpillar in a cocoon waiting to grow wings and fly off to a glorious garden. Somehow the world hadn't destroyed her.

When our last probation meeting ended, she reached out to touch me, and for a moment, I thought she would touch my cheek. Instead, she placed her finger on my scar and traced it, back and forth, as if sensually strumming a secret chord.

"From the monkey bars," I answered, when she asked how I got the scar, but she saw through my lie.

Such a loss, a hidden hurt, when she discharged off probation, so I scheduled a ruse meeting and invited her for lunch, a "follow-up research study on successful probation experience." But the ruse didn't last long, we had a second date, and sooner than healthy, rented a U-Haul, and I started living with someone from my caseload, a recovering addict, seven years clean. Both of us lied when asked by friends how we met, only saying we had matching baggage. I'd be fired if work found out, and rightly so.

The tiniest things, like the way she poured sugar in my coffee, held the mysteries of the universe. *I love you forever, Becca, and that shine still glows.* We were wrapped around each other like the tattoo of intertwining green lizards etched onto my right shoulder.

*I won't fall in love with this one.* It would be impossible to love another, but also impossible not to love this new position. I was made for this, a fiery passion roared through each nerve ending while I was on the job.

I was on Amy Branagan's street, the lucky recipient of my surprise home visit. Rows and rows of small bungalows, near identical, with rooftops still wet from last night's rain. The squad car was already there, parked curbside. The officer rolled his window down as I approached.

"You want me to come inside with you?"

It was clean-shaven Officer Renfrew with the iron jaw.

"Nah, I'm good, but thanks. Just being here is enough, just in case you're needed."

I went to the front door, feeling invigorated, refreshed, rebooted, shaking off the insult that they had to send a cop as if I couldn't handle this better than any human alive.

If I had partnered with a man like Officer Renfrew, the adoption agency would have certainly deemed us fit for parenthood. You need to pass a screening to adopt, but anyone can have a child by birth, anyone can do the *ultimate sin* of bringing a child into this world the old-fashioned way. My own parents certainly never had to pass a screening, and all the hurt they had carved into my soul had brought me to Amy's front door.

## CHAPTER TWO:
### Lizard's Dad, Trey Baker, 19 Years Previous

#### All Narcotics in Time-Released Safe

Trey Baker read the sign as if it didn't matter to him, but it did. It mattered to every little sweat bead on his goose-bumped flesh. If his prescription wasn't behind the counter, he would blow-torch the door right off that time-released safe.

The pharmacist wore a white jacket, her skin was Middle-Eastern brown, and she was counting pills on a plastic tray. She seemed in a trance, so Trey shuffled his feet, hoping the noise would get her attention.

The pharmacist looked up from her pills. "One moment. Be well," she said through a grin.

*Be well?* He was trying to *get well*. He squeezed Lizard's hand. His own hand was moist with sweat, hers was tiny and frail, but a man who is holding his little girl's hand isn't someone who fiends drugs. He isn't someone who visits pain management doctors who, for a price, shoot out digital scripts to the pharmacy of your choice. He was just a hard-working roofer who was hurt on the job and needed some help to provide for his family.

The pharmacist walked to the counter. Trey braced himself for his worst fears. Last time he tried this at another pharmacy the response was, *Sorry, Mr. Baker, there's been an alert placed on this doctor, and we can't fulfill the request.* Bugs exploded inside each sweat bead, crawled around Trey's body, and then buried themselves into his flesh.

*Hold your shit together.*

He gave another squeeze to Lizard's hand. The pharmacist's eyes scanned down. He needed Lizard to smile, but instead, her face was contorted and her eyes twitching.

"He doesn't need this medicine," she said, her head tilted as if listening to a far-off radio station. "He's sick, and you're just giving him more poison. That's what *she* told me, at least."

*Not now with that crazy shit.* He clenched her hand tighter, trying to shut Lizard's mouth, but the words still hung in the air.

"And who told you that?" the pharmacist asked.

"She's got this voice that speaks to her," Trey interrupted before his daughter could say another word. "We're not sure why. Some say it's an autism thing, but I refuse to put her on the drugs they say I should. I hate taking anything myself unless I have to... I'm just here for a prescription for Trey Baker." He tried to sound confident but his voice cracked like thin ice under too much weight. *Don't let your hands shake.*

The pharmacist turned to the bins behind her and started sifting through the white bags. Digging, digging, digging. When she finally grabbed one and turned back to the counter, the creatures ripping his flesh apart stopped for a bit, as if sensing the end was near. Relief was coming. He accepted the bag of OxyContin with a smile. He paid with cash, gave her a nod, and received another blessing to "be well." He tried not to rush out the store—only dope fiends would rush out the store—and he was a dad, not a dope fiend.

To the car, so close. He opened the back door and guided Lizard inside. She hopped in dutifully, and he shut the door behind her then dashed to the front seat.

He ripped the white pharmacy bag open. The brown plastic

bottle, so sturdy in his hand, the twist of the white top, so sweet. He popped two pills into his mouth. *Ahhhh.* He loved the moment pill met tongue. His taste buds had a spot reserved solely for OxyContin. He grinded them between his teeth, releasing all their fairy dust sprinkles down his throat. Tiny pieces of little army men, that's how he imagined them, ready to march for him through his veins, and he was their general.

"She wants me to be buckled," Lizard said from the back seat. "She says it's not safe."

"Who says?" he asked, not waiting for a reply because he needed more of the marching white men. He pulled out two pills, placed them on a Metallica CD cover, and crushed them with an expired credit card under his palm. He shaped them into two powdery piles, glorious silver-white mountains ready to snort.

"She's screaming at me, Daddy. She doesn't need to scream. Why does she scream?"

"We're going to the park soon. Just chill."

Two snowy whites lay next to him. He bent down, held one nostril, and then snorted the Oxy deep into his nose. The army of white smacked into the base of his brain. *Ahhhh…* An electric current ran down his spine. He decided to save the last one for later, and tucked the *Master of Puppets* CD cover safely on the passenger seat.

*See, I can ration and make this bottle last like I promised.*

Life was beautiful. Glorious. He was ready to be a dad again.

"We're going to the park, Lizard, the one with the curvy slide and the turnabout thing that makes you dizzy."

Yes, the park. She needed it. The morning had a chill and he'd forgotten her jacket, but the sun would soon warm up the day, thaw the earth, and summon flowers from the cold ground. Lizard needed something normal, like a park, because there really was something wrong with her. He could hear her mumble from the back seat as if speaking her own language.

He stopped at a red light and cars zipped by in front of him, off to elsewhere, people with lives unencumbered by the weight of his war. He envied them. He pitied them. They would never know the beauty of a victory such as he'd just won, oblivious to his grandeur as they went off to other directions. He had different miles to travel, his daughter in the back seat and the chopped-up pile of

Oxy riding shotgun next to him. Oxy asked for his time, for his life, for his soul—just like everyone else who needed something from him. His roofing job needed him to show up early and work until sundown, his wife needed him to split the bottle of pills he worked so hard to get. His daughter needed someone who understood what the hell she was saying.

The general needed more from his fairy dust army to win this war.

The traffic light was still red. He leaned over the middle console, fast and fluid as a cobra strike. He placed the rolled-up dollar bill to his nostril and lined it up to the pile of Oxy…

*Thump.*

Lizard kicked the back of his chair, acting crazy again. No time to yell at her to stop, just stay steady. Dollar found its mark, vacuum snort, base of his brain coated in white.

*Ahhhhh…*

"Dad, she's still screaming, not whispering. She says I have to buckle."

His body was mush, his foot slipped off the brake, the car crept into the intersection.

T-bone strike.

The grill of a Ford Ranger rammed into the side panel of his Honda Civic. Glass shattered, suspended in air, then rained down like diamond confetti. His femur bone split open exposing the marrow, and the compound fracture sliced into his skin. In the back seat, nine-year-old Lizard had become a projectile. Her body whipped from one side of the car into the other and her tiny head smashed against the window. Her skull cracked, and she was deposited on the floor.

Silence followed. Lizard was unconscious, her father dazed, confused. His thoughts were shattered like the glass of the car. His bone had punctured through the thick of his thigh. His car sideways in the intersection.

Lizabeth in the back seat…

*Lizard.*

*Oh God. She's bleeding. Her eyes are closed.*

He tried to lean over into the back seat to tend to her but the sharp stab of a sword that was his femur bone stopped him. It jutted out of his pant leg, and blood soaked his jeans. He was going to bleed to death. He would die there. Both of them would.

*The pill bottle. Where is it?*

He had to find it. He fought off the pain with primal moans and clamored for it on the car floor, digging between Mountain Dew cans and fast food wrappers, ignoring the searing pain where the split bone had sliced through his leg. Tiny bits of glass were cutting his fingers as he searched, blood spots popping up everywhere. Outside the car, a crowd had gathered.

There. He finally saw it. The brown plastic bottle, white strip taped to the side, contents safely inside, and the bottle was secured in his hand.

*Ah good, everything is safe.*

They gave him morphine during the ambulance ride to the hospital. Hours of surgery followed, then a thick cast up to his crotch. Lizard had internal bleeding and the inflammation of her brain pushed against the confines of her skull. They stitched up her injury and wrapped her in bandages. *TBI: Traumatic brain injury* would be attached to her medical chart for life.

They gave Lizabeth Baker Tegretol for the seizures. The gave Trey Baker more drugs for the pain.

## CHAPTER THREE:
### Lizard's Mom, Kate Baker,
### Four Months After the Car Accident

Lizabeth Baker
Tegretol 100 mg
Take one tablet two times daily

"What about this? Will this take the edge off?"

Kate's husband, Trey, hobbled around the kitchen, holding Lizard's medicine bottle, sick and craving some dope. Kate was craving, too, with a bubbling gut and aching back, like termites were chewing at her spine with sharp, stinging fangs.

Every prescription bottle in the house, other than the Tegretol, was empty, and their regular go-to doctors had all been tapped out and couldn't help them any longer.

"Tegretol won't do shit for you. Even if it would—you want her to seize up again?"

Kate looked down at her daughter and remembered the seizures that started shortly after the car accident. Her muscles locked up, rigid and frozen, and her body shook with electric energy as if someone tossed a toaster into her bathtub. The vision haunted her nightmares, especially when she was dope-sick with demon sweat and devil thoughts, trying to sleep, but in her mind's eye, all she could see was her child in the throes of that seizure. The hospital had returned her daughter broken with a crack in her head that was impossible to patch together. From that crack, a darkness shone through. A spotlight onto their failures as parents.

*Maybe if you didn't almost kill her!* she wanted to yell back into Trey's face, but the argument would threaten to break things already fragile.

Every breath he took contained a groan, a cuss, a vow of revenge for an imaginary list of those who had wronged him years ago. Kate didn't throw these tantrums when she was dope-sick. She'd married a soft man. He knew how to hustle for his highs in the early days, but not anymore. Now, he was just another child to feed. One of her babies was nine years old, the other one thirty-two, and both of them were sick.

"We need to go to the ER," he said with conviction, itching at the top of his cast.

"Best you'll get is a Toradol shot. Maybe one dose."

"Google Tegretol. See if it will help."

"It won't fucking help. I told you."

Kate was cleaning the fridge and throwing out old leftovers. Nobody ever threw them out. It was always up to her.

"Lizard, you want a taco for breakfast? We got taco meat from last week. We'll put it in a pita. Come on, grab a paper plate."

"Fuck it. No Oxy, we need some *H*. Call your friend Bucky." Trey hopped on one leg. Each hop went *BOOM* on the floor like an exclamation point.

"Watch your language with Lizard in the room."

"She doesn't know what *call Bucky* means. I'll say it as much as I need to. *Call Bucky*. Call him now. You know all about it. Go get it. Go see your old boy and bring us some smack, because I know you need it just as much."

She'd seen Bucky shoot up heroin a hundred times while they lived together. Shooting some, selling some, using people until they were lifeless then discarding the carcass. It took years for Kate to realize Bucky was using her to stay afloat. When she finally broke free, she felt like an escaped hostage. When she met Trey, she felt rescued by a savior, certain it was going to be different. He was a roofer who worked hard and treated her well, but she'd fallen for the same man. Maybe a lesser man. Bucky was always holding heroin, and Trey knew it.

"Look, sweetie," he begged. "Please. I need it. Just until my leg heals. I've been in this cast for months. Once I get it off, I'll be fine."

His head was tilted in a sad, puppy-dog style. Seeing him like this made her own aching cells crave some dope just as badly. The disability money was gone, the prescription bottles were all empty, and the unwritten rule they lived by was to help each other fix up by any means necessary. They were each other's constant patients, dope-fiend voodoo dolls. The ultimate love was bringing back dirty money to get your partner high, and their love was about to get deeper.

Kate lay a hand on Lizard's soft hair. She pulled a few strands between her fingers and then traced a fingertip over the scar as if reading braille, trying to understand what was going on inside. The scar tissue was forming just above her ear. Three major bumps in descending order spread along a line from the middle of her head toward the front. Tiny ones surrounded it like a constellation.

"You're going to stay here, Lizard. You'll be okay."

"Please don't go," Lizard said. "He'll take my pills. That's what she says."

"Well, what *she* says doesn't matter. I say different. Come on. Go heat up your taco. I'll be right back. And take that fork off the plate before you zap it. Remember, no metal in the microwave. And take your Tegretol, you missed too many doses." Kate put the prescription bottle right on her paper plate and realized there were only a couple left.

The sunlight outside her front door felt like disinfectant and exactly what she needed. Just a short ride away to her old life. Bucky would be happy to see her, certainly wearing a smug look of, *I told you so, I knew you'd be back.*

Her car remembered the way to his house as if following a railroad track, and soon she was knocking at his front door. Bucky answered, and his eyes darted down both sides of the street.

"My Angel," he said, and gave her a full body hug with hips pressed and memories triggered. "You need to get high, don't you? I can always tell."

His house was full of ravaged souls, desperate humans who stayed as long as they could pay for more dope. She did not say no when he led her past them straight to his bedroom. The door closed, he undressed her, and then lay her on the sheet-less mattress. Her fingernails dug into his back muscles when he entered her, digging for an earlier time, a time before Lizard, before her body became so tired, and she found it. A momentary relief of her suffering, a release from her curse, thanking God loud enough for the house to hear when she climaxed.

The two packs of heroin were given freely, as she had hoped. Another time, she might have been offended, but the invisible thread that connected them had never been cut, only been tangled.

"You're carrying my water now, you know that. I'll see you soon, see you often."

Just having heroin in her pocket as she drove home seemed to wake up her blood cells from their cold hibernation. Winter was over, and she was eager for the turning of seasons. Kate hadn't shot up in years. It seemed she took on whatever addiction her man had at the time, some symbiotic relationship, taking the crumbs of highs that fell off their plates. In just a few minutes, she'd be smacking veins with Trey. He had no idea what was coming. He'd be morphed forever.

She burst through the front door of her house, certain there would be something inside to piss her off, something one of them did that she was unprepared to handle but needed to fix. Best to find out what it was and get it over with.

Trey was standing on one leg, looking even greasier than before, same sweat pants on with pant-leg cut off, same Detroit Tigers baseball cap on his head, face dotted with scruff. Lizard was lying on the couch. Eyes closed. Her cold taco was still sitting on the counter, untouched, with an empty brown prescription bottle next to it.

"What the fuck happened?"

"What the fuck took you so long? Damn it. She did one of those seizures. Started shaking and making noises the way she always does. I took care of it. She's fine. We made it through. Now please, do you have it?"

"What the fuck, Trey? We need to get her to a hospital," Kate took a seat on the edge of the couch and felt Lizard's forehead.

"She's fine. Can't even tell if it was a seizure, she just started babbling all crazy then her body got shaky. I put her in a soft spot just like last time and everything is fine now. Tell me you got it. Please, tell me you got it."

Kate ignored him. Her daughter's skin was clammy, her eyes just barely open, eyelids fluttering like a flower trying hard, but failing to bloom. Her lips were wet with foam from the seizure. Kate touched the liquid and put the foam to her own lips. It felt unnatural, tasted salty and acidic. It burned, even, as if what was inside needed to punish the mother for leaving her child alone.

There were cracks in her daughter, and more was seeping out.

*She would be okay. Right?*

Her heart was beating, she was breathing. It's always like this moments after a seizure.

"We need to take her to the emergency room," Kate said. "We need to go. Now. What the hell? Why didn't you text me?" Kate didn't need an answer. She knew why Trey didn't—because then she might turn around before she scored the heroin.

"I know. We do need to go to the hospital. Something's wrong with the girl. You know what she's like when she talks crazy, but we can't go there sick like this. One look at us and we'll go through that child protective service bullshit again. Be smart. Let's get right first. Can't we just fix up and then take her?"

Kate didn't need to answer, saying no wasn't an option. Delaying it was impossible. She'd get high and get by. She was Lady Madonna, three children at her feet, one stitched up in the skull, one broken and wrapped up in a cast, but the third child—the one screaming inside her soul, the one who needed to use dope to escape the suffering of existence, if but for a moment—was the king baby of them all and would be fed first.

She pulled Lizabeth into her arms, held her in a dead hug, then laid her back down on the couch. Lizard groaned, perhaps a *thank you*, perhaps an *I love you*, or perhaps talking to some imaginary being again in a language Kate just couldn't understand. She propped up her head, surrounded it with pillows, then went to the bedroom to boil up Trey's first shot of dope.

Trey's arm was so easy to inject. His virgin veins popped in vibrant blue, his flesh eager to be punctured. The blood she drew back was a rich shade of red. He flashed her one last look of gratitude before his eyes rolled in the back of his head and then closed. She boiled up another batch of dope, plunged the syringe into her own crusty vein until she was engulfed in warmth. She swore she wouldn't nod off to sleep the way Trey had, but soon her eyes were closed, and both of them drifted off to the same lullaby for suffering, and suffered no more.

She awoke to the hazy image of her daughter bedside, looking over them, standing there for who knows how long—hours, minutes, days, her whole life. Standing like a dead child with shoulders hung slack as if her bones had been dissolved, her spine and spirit sucked right out of her body.

"Come here," Kate said and pulled Lizard to bed with her. She held her close, smelled her hair, her skin, remembered her as an infant and how the scent of hope and freshness in each pore of flesh held such promise. But now her daughter was trembling, not from a seizure this time, but from fear.

"I'm so sorry, sweetie. I'm so, so sorry."


## CHAPTER FOUR:
### Lizabeth at Amy's Front Door

I knocked on Amy's front door with a tiny rap of my knuckle. I wanted a friendly entry. Nothing alarming. I heard footsteps moving in all directions, pattering quickly one way then the other. Cabinet drawers slammed. Finally, I heard steps coming to the door.

Amy's fingers cracked the window shades, eyes peeked through into mine, leering at me with suspicion. Facial recognition finally hit her.

"Agent Baker. You're here," she said as she opened the door.

"Random visit time. Amy, sorry to interrupt, but you knew it was coming. Just need to look around."

I stood my ground. Never go in unless invited. Amy needed to invite me inside and into her life. Drug court is voluntary. She could say no and opt out of the program at any time and instead serve her full sentence for writing bad checks. The alternative to five years in prison for her charges was drug court, a program specifically designed for those whose crimes were committed within the scope of their addiction.

"You bringing *the man* in with you?" Amy asked and nodded towards the police car parked curbside. The shadow of Officer Renfrew sitting behind the wheel was evident.

"He's on standby just in case he's needed."

Amy opened the door wide and waved me inside.

The rental house was new, and Amy hadn't yet stamped her brand upon its hide. A solitary, faded green chair sat where a couch might be. Cable wires snaked out of a TV into one wall, and a broom rested against the opposite wall. A pile of recently swept dirt lay neatly on the hardwood floor below. Across the main room, dish rags were stacked and folded on the kitchen counter, not yet packed away, as if Amy wasn't sure she wanted to commit.

Joshua, her six-year-old boy, sat at the dining room table. He wore a gray sweatshirt, Mackinaw Island written in orange letters across the front. He peered towards me, certainly one of many strangers to come into his life.

"Say hi to Agent Baker."

Joshua didn't *say hi* as his mom requested. Clearly not sure if he was supposed to. His eyes seemed broken, like shattered marbles that had been glued back together and stuck back in his sockets. He had that frozen look boys get, not trusting his instinct, hoping he was invisible, that the request to *say hi* would be forgotten and the two grown-ups could go on with their business that didn't concern him.

But what was best for Joshua—keeping his mom clean and sober—was my business.

"Can I take a look at that?" I asked, stepping towards the kitchen table and motioning to the picture he was drawing. He kept his head bowed in deference and slid the picture towards me.

"He's been drawing this same cartoon character he calls Piper-Pippen, over and over and over," Amy said, her hands stuffed deeply into her back pockets.

Piper-Pippen had a long, lanky body, and even longer, skinnier arms. His wiry hair stood up straight, waving wildly in the air. In each one, Piper was smiling—smiling so big and confident that the mouth and lips extended beyond the shape of his head. His eyes were little twists of metal, the barb on the barbed wire, and his arms the metallic strings. I didn't recognize this cartoon, but Joshua had clearly invited him deep inside his private world.

*Why cling to Piper-Pippen, why him?* This Piper-Pippen, who had certainly been there for him when his mom wasn't. Piper had been his friend, his dad, his God even, comforted Joshua while he lie in bed, maybe hungry, never sure what will come through the door after his mom scored her morning dose of heroin—her sickness like a humid mist, her cure like an ominous storm. Joshua knew truths nobody else would ever know, the secret camera into Amy's world. He'd seen the things she'd done to fill her golden arms that had now rusted.

*You are the one I am here for, Joshua. Artist, dreamer, admirer of Piper-Pippen, but I know you can't speak of things yet the way you might like to. Someday you will say so much. The scream you've been holding in will demand to be released, and on that day, others will hear and feel your power.*

"I just need to check out a few things, Amy."

We made the rounds. I had her open the fridge to make sure there was no beer inside, and had her open the cabinets, checking for contraband. I didn't expect her to be stupid enough to leave heroin lying around in full view, but where addicts get high, they always leave a trace—the plastic tips of syringes, the bits of cotton, the tiny baggies or tin foil.

I checked the bedside dresser, always a popular spot. I found one pill bottle on the ground next to the mattress.

"Melatonin bottle. Need it to sleep. Swear I haven't slept for real in months."

"I hear it helps," I said. I opened it up to make sure the pills inside were as advertised.

Back to the kitchen, where I looked in the sink for spoons with brown, burnt marks underneath. Nothing but two dirty dishes soaking.

"I hate getting ketchup off plates, so I let them soak. Josh dips everything in ketchup."

I searched the bathroom, easily the most dangerous room in any house, where the blades are kept to cut oneself, the pills to overdose on, where you can run and hide at any moment and do private things you would never confess. Not a trace of any contraband.

"The garbages—I need to look inside all of them."

A garbage is the mirror to the soul. She took me on a tour to the discards of her life. The white plastic bucket in the bathroom was full of tissues, the silver bin in Joshua's room scattered with colored pencil shavings. In the kitchen, I got a whiff of fried chicken from the discarded bones, but no human bodies buried inside.

The last place I checked was the basement. We descended the stairs together, side by side. The basement was just an unfinished, empty tomb—a washer and dryer against one cement wall, old furnace churning nearby. Even the spiders had no place to hide. Her house was clean, I was done here, but a few questions remained.

"When was your last Narcotics Anonymous meeting?" I asked.

"I went today. Joshua drew five Piper-Pippens while I was there."

"You going to counseling?"

"Therapist canceled on me yesterday. I showed up, and she wasn't even there."

"Your last drug test?"

"I got tested three days in a row this week. All my random urine drops are happening right in a row, like I've done something wrong. Like something is creeping up on me."

Amy stuffed her hands in her back pockets, curled her feet toward each other, and then did a subtle hop on her toes. She looked to the ground, then back at me.

"You can see I'm doing everything I'm supposed to do, and the judge has proof. I'm good. I'm clean. So why is a cop *on standby just in case he's needed?*"

She was still thinking of the police car.

"It's just a precaution. He won't be needed."

"But does someone think he *is* needed?"

"Amy, my purpose is to help you, not make you nervous. I'm sorry."

---

"I know. It's not just you. Anyone with a badge makes me nervous. They can do anything they want. Bring me in, violate my probation. It's just instinct. When I see a cop car I wonder what I'm doin' wrong—I wonder what they *think* I'm doin' wrong. My hands jump to my pockets to check where my bag of dope is. That's not gonna change. You seem like you really do care and give a shit, but you don't know what it's like to be an addict. It's a life you'll never understand."

All of us got quiet. Joshua's broken marble eyes looked up at me from the table. I wanted to respond to his mom with all the raging memories in my soul. My reply churned inside me, heating and boiling and ready to blow. Amy must have felt this burning and wanted it doused.

"It's okay, it's fine. I know I need this. I love my new life," she said. "Drug court is a second chance to be a better mom. I'm so grateful. I really am. Little things are starting to make me happy, like the taste of licorice or the sound Joshua makes when he sneezes twice, never once. People like me don't know how to be happy, but I'm learning, and the best part is, Joshua is growing to trust me. I have drug court to thank for all of that."

Her words swung like a pendulum inside a grandfather clock, one side then the other, to believing what she said, to wishing it were true.

"Just keep doing everything you've been doing, string some clean time together, and soon people like me will have no power over you. You'll find that when you aren't using, we can't hurt you. We don't hurt you."

That felt like a perfect conclusion, instilled a touch of fear, but mostly hope, and it was time for me to leave. This little family would grow. Amy would meet a partner who cherished her in the same way I cherished Rebecca, not despite her battle wounds, but because of them.

"How did you get that scar?" Joshua asked before I could get out the door.

"The monkey bars," I gave my patented lie.

He thought of my answer. He looked to his drawings and shuffled them. He wasn't satisfied. He had more questions.

"Will you be coming back here?"

"Well, that all depends. What does Piper-Pippen think?" I

asked this knowing that Piper would speak of hidden truths that Joshua wouldn't.

"Piper doesn't talk to other people, only to me," Joshua said.

"I understand that. And what does he tell you?"

"Well, Piper says you should come back soon. It's when you leave things happen," his eyes darted to his artwork on the kitchen table.

"What things happen with Piper?" I asked.

"Nothing with Piper. Not him. His arms are so skinny there's no room to poke a needle inside."

Something deflated in the air. Whatever was holding Amy up, spirit and spine and dignity, was hacked at with an ax, chunks flying, insides oozing, but Amy stood tall.

"Well, then, I won't come back for Piper, I'll come back just for you."

I gave him a wink on my way out the door.

## CHAPTER FIVE:
### Amy After the Visit

Agent Baker had winked at Joshua as if speaking some silent language only the two of them could hear. A secret code they alone could understand.

Amy shut the front door and waited for both the cop and Baker to leave her street.

*Don't watch them drive away. They can see you. They know what you do.*

She reached her hands into her back pockets and flicked at the packet of heroin with her fingertips, again and again. Each time her nails made contact she was comforted that the dope was still there. Each time a soothing warmth, like a blood transfusion, swept over her. The snake bite of the needle that was coming soon would wash away the cold shame for buying a pack of heroin in the NA meeting parking lot.

*God, just get rid of it*, she'd told herself on the drive home from the meeting while Joshua mumbled to himself in the back seat. Having heroin in her possession changed her chemistry. Every cell reacted as if a fire alarm had been pulled. Her body hadn't had dope in months. Her veins were rested and healed, but they had not forgotten.

Soon as she had heard the knock on her front door she knew it was Agent Baker. She feigned surprise, but knocks from people with power such as hers hit an octave easily detectable, a dog whistle warning, so she'd dashed about the house thinking of hiding the dope, but finally decided to keep it on her body. Safest bet. If the agent was smart enough to search her body, she knew how to reach inside her pocket and palm it, or worst case scenario, beg for forgiveness and understanding if the deception failed.

Agent Baker was an odd mix of cold and kind, but she'd never gotten high, Amy could tell. She'd never once felt the beautiful pierce of a needle, never knew the sick desperation. The only evidence she'd ever felt genuine hurt was the scar left above her ear from the monkey bars.

Amy had passed the random home inspection and Baker was gone, leaving Amy holding heroin in her pocket, her son drawing pictures. His habit seemed just as obsessive.

Joshua was waiting for her reaction about the surprise guest, anticipating her mood to crack, wondering if his mom was going to get upset. Amy refused to get angry. Joshua and her could survive everything. They'd survived worse than this. Nothing could separate the two. A cord still connected them, from her blood to his.

She took some Ritz crackers out of the pantry, carefully ripped open the sleeve, put peanut butter on each cracker, one by one, until a circle of crackers filled a paper plate. Next, a glass of milk, topped off with a kiss on Joshua's forehead before he started eating his favorite dish.

"You don't need to be scared of Agent Baker. She's a friend of ours."

"Is the agent coming back?" he asked, cracker dust coming from his lips.

"Doubt it. Probably not for a month, no surprises until then."

*And no drug testing for a week*, Amy guessed. After getting called in to pee in a cup for three days in a row, there would certainly be a gap before she was tested again. Her addiction knew this and spoke to her.

*The time has come. This is your window. You made it. You*

*did all they asked, you can get high today. You deserve it. Just this once. Then you can stop again.*

She had four months clean. She was finally doing something right. Strange as it felt, she had prayed to be at this very moment. Out of jail, in her own place, Joshua with his own bedroom. She couldn't fuck it up. She was living inside an answered prayer, and needed to remember the hurt that her sickness caused.

*You will always be sick. I can cure what ails you. You will never quit. You'll always come back to me. Always. Go ahead and pretend you're happy, but you can't fool me. I'm the only one who has what you need.*

Everyone was just waiting for her to relapse anyway. Think of how smugly satisfied they'd be. All those questions they ask her with a cynical tone and their subtle disappointment when she answered that, yes, she was doing what they asked, staying clean, following her drug court orders. Getting high again would restore order to their world-view. *Ah-ha! I knew it, she is just a junkie. Why did we ever think she could change?*

She pulled the pack of dope out of her back pocket and transferred it to her front. She gave a comforting tap-tap to her jeans.

"Does Agent Baker know where Dad is?" Joshua asked.

"No, she doesn't work in the jail, she works to make sure people don't go to jail. When you see Agent Baker it means your mom must be doing well. It means we've got nothing to worry about. We've got nothing but blue skies ahead."

She wished she could fill his head with futures so fantastic he'd be forced to draw pictures of carefree families having picnics on green grass, brilliant yellow sun overhead, checkered-red blanket, one magnificent tree for him to climb. Instead, he was brooding, his neck craned over his manic drawings, his black bangs dangling above his eyes. Occasionally, he pulled a Ritz to his mouth and licked off the peanut butter before crunching on the whole cracker. She felt her own tongue get dry watching him until he finally washed it down with milk.

*Remember the beauty when you are high. Remember what a happy mom you are. Your smiles. Your charm. Not this lifeless sack you've become. Your son needs you happy. He deserves it. You deserve it. You've worked so hard. Just one time. What are you waiting for? Let's go.*

Amy grabbed the broom resting on the wall and swept the pile to the corner, moving it yet again. She didn't have a dustpan to pick it up. The place was supposed to be clean when she moved in, but it was filthy, and there was so much work to do to make it her own. New furniture, a lamp or two, curtains. And more cleaning. And it was always so still and quiet. No creaks, no settling, no tick of some forgotten clock in the other room. Nothing. It was empty, lonely, like it had no past, and it was going to take a long time to carve her new life into its walls.

"Joshua, do me a favor? Draw me a Piper-Pippen, your best one yet. I'll frame it and put it up as the first picture in our new house. But take your time, okay? This is the big one. I'll be right back."

She walked with urgent steps to the bathroom. The fight was over. Resistance vacated her body and sweet relief filled its place. Why fight it? It was inevitable since the moment she let herself purchase the heroin after the NA meeting. She'd been fending off men giving tightly held hugs with octopus arms in the parking lot, most of them pleading with her to go for coffee. She rejected them all, except the offer from Chuck Hartzel, who offered a pack of something *so premium* she just had to try, and she paid him with crumbled-up singles.

She shut the bathroom door behind her but didn't lock it, just in case. *Remember what happened at Burger King.* She was finally safe and alone. Her heart thumped in her chest, drum beat booming. Leftover works, needle, spoon, and cotton were all tucked away where Agent Baker wasn't smart enough to look (panel behind the bathtub faucet).

Water, spoon, mix, flame, cotton.

And focus.

God, was she focused as she sat on the toilet seat and stared at the liquid getting sucked up into the syringe. A chorus sang inside her, the church of the holy praising this moment, rising to a crescendo each second closer to the shot in her arm.

Blue veins so lonely, so ready.

The prick of the needle punctured her, found a vein, blood was drawn. The chorus sang their loudest halleluiahs as she pushed in the plunger and an opiate orgasm ran up her spine. God did she love life, loved her son, so beautiful, all of it.

She heard footsteps approaching the bathroom. It must be Joshua, but he sounded faster than usual. There was more weight to each pitter-patter and the hardwood floor echoed. He was done with his new drawing, and she was ready to gloat over his artwork, to be the mom he deserved, not the depressed, sad sack of bones she'd become where everything was a chore and bitterness filled each thought.

*Wait, Josh, wait.*

*Don't see me like this.*

Too late. A squeak when the bathroom door opened.

Joshua was about to see her shooting up. Wouldn't be the first time, and it would require another long explanation on why he needed to be quiet about this, how his mom was okay and this is just what happens when people slowly quit drugs. They still had blue skies.

The needle was still hanging like an errant dart in her blue vein when she saw it wasn't Joshua at all standing in the doorway.

It was Agent Baker.

Their eyes locked. Amy was unable to breathe, unable to break her gaze. Hidden truths were revealed as if her skin had been shaved off. The beauty of the opiates surging through her veins retreated. The comfort was gone, her deeds exposed.

Agent Baker's face was frozen with shock, stuck in a silent scream. She inched closer in disbelief and leaned into Amy's face. Her skin seemed to be glowing red, her flesh twisted, made of flames burning with anger.

Amy wanted to plead, to pray, *you don't know how hard this is, how much I tried, but I can't do it, so please, just help me. I mean really help me. Not this bullshit cop and robber probation game you call help, but truly help me learn how to live without doing this thing I can't stop...*

But nothing came out of her voice box. Everything was getting sucked out of her body into the swirling eyes of this agent with a badge who had broken into her sacred place.

**"Do you know what I am going to do to you?"** Agent Baker asked in a voice that had sunk seven layers deep.

Baker stepped forward. Amy had no room to retreat. She was fully cornered, exposed, and sat helpless as Baker took hold of her trembling hand. With a fingertip, she traced Amy's vein, inching slowly from her wrist toward the sweet spot of the needle mark. She reached the syringe, grasped it inside her fist, then plucked it out.

*Pluck.*

**"Do you know what I am going to do to you?"** Baker repeated.

Amy shook her head, because she didn't know.

**"I am going to help you. You will never be sick again. Never."**

*Never sick again. Never sick again*—the phrase somehow made Amy's fear bleed out of her body, and she looked up at Baker like a starving baby waiting to be fed. Baker was an infinite mother, a sexless lover, knowing her in ways never before possible. The feel of Baker's fingertips had been surprisingly soft, warm, tender. It brought back memories of Joshua as an infant, his flesh pressed against hers when he was minutes old, fresh from her womb, moist with the miracle of life. The breastfeeding that followed was abandoned too early when dehydration hit.

But it was okay.

Joshua was going to be okay. Everything was going to be okay.

Baker held the needle with the tip sticking out between her fingers, and plunged the syringe towards Amy's eye. Her eyelid snapped shut, but the needle poked right through the tiny film of skin. *Pluck.* She could hear it penetrating into her moist eyeball, the pain piercing as if she'd been stabbed in the heart. Baker tugged it out, just a touch, and then pushed it in deeper, right through her eye socket, again and again, until she finally pulled the needle out entirely. The syringe dripped with moisture.

**"You've had your chance."** Baker attacked again.

Amy raised a hand but was too slow to defend her other eye when the syringe stabbed inside. A milky-white liquid mixed with crimson blood leaked out her eye, dripped down her cheek, then streamed into her mouth which had opened to scream. With each new stab, a new pitch out of her mouth, screaming Joshua's name to help her, pleading apologies, rattling the bathroom walls with howls, sure that the gods would hear her pain and save her, but instead the snake bites of the needle came in rapid fire to all parts of her body. Baker pulled the needle out each time and found new, fresh skin to puncture.

Amy collapsed to the ground a ripped-open ragdoll. Her veins had been sliced apart, her flesh speckled in bloody red holes, her arms held out in front of her as if in offering. Her face was stuck in silent peace, a permanent sleep, the fluid of her life running in tiny red streams and puddling on the white tile. She'd been blinded and unable to see the bathroom door swing open and her son standing in the doorway, looking at her one last time before she died.

## CHAPTER SIX:
### Agent Baker After the Visit

*Well, then, I won't come back for Piper, I'll come back just for you.*

I hoped Joshua really heard those final words. If not, I know he felt the power of the wink I gave before walking out the front door.

Becca was waiting for me at home, and I was eager to tell her how the visit went.

*Not a career, but a calling.*

I chose Amy first for a reason. Not out of suspicion that she was non-compliant, but out of hope. She was the reason drug court existed, the reason I decided to major in criminal justice and work in probation. Her pasty white skin had grown color the last four months. Long-sleeve black shirts gave way to sleeveless tops as the abscesses healed and scar tissue faded. Her timid green eyes became tinted with resolve. If she could continue to grow, shed her old skin, then maybe her soul could be repaired and her boy Joshua could be glued back together.

Amy had been in and out of jail for years, protesting in front of judges with tears and foxhole prayers to not lock her up, swearing on her child's grave that she would never use again, but instead, she got high with Joshua's dad and dragged her son along for the ride.

Amy had nearly lost custody of Joshua after she overdosed on the floor of a Burger King bathroom while Joshua was stuck in his booster chair, chicken nuggets, fries, and orange drink on the table in front of him. Joshua didn't even cry, just stared out the window at cars leaving the drive-thru and eyed the moms, wondering where his went. She nearly died on the floor of the locked bathroom that had to be busted open.

After she stole her mom's checkbook and wrote $3,000 worth of bad checks, the bank pressed charges. Josh's dad went to jail, but rather than join him, Amy received a sentence to drug court. First expectation was twenty-one days in a residential treatment center, then intensive outpatient counseling. Every two weeks, she stood before the judge to discuss her status. She had to visit probation each week and was called in for drug screens at random.

And she had to agree to surprise home visits.

*It went well,* I would tell Becca. *I'm aligning myself with her, best I can, but keeping a distance (you know I'm not good at keeping distance).*

*But the boy, Becca. You should have seen him—such a precious thing. I want us to have a child like him someday. No, I'm not getting pregnant, you're not getting pregnant. It might be a sin to bring a child into this world, but it's a worse sin to leave children who are already born to suffer.*

Being in Amy's house was like visiting my own childhood home. I was so familiar with the air inside a heroin household. I could detect things, sense things, sniff things out, and something still didn't smell exactly right. Amy still had a trace of that heroin film over her skin that addicts can't escape. She seemed stuck with that nervous twitch that happens in early recovery, always fragile, tip-toeing on the sharp edge of sobriety.

Whispers in my head, familiar chatter I could usually ignore but now growing in pitch, fed more suspicions.

In all our time together, including the day she faced years in prison if the judge didn't grant her drug court, I'd never seen her that nervous. Every week she moves among *people with badges* with a quiet, growing confidence, but not tonight. Tonight, she was fixated on the police officer out front *just in case he's needed.* Her body language was full of fluttering nerves, her arms continually crossing and uncrossing. She kept poking her fingers into her back pockets while I looked through the nooks and crannies of her new home.

*When I see someone with a badge, I pat my pockets to see if I have some dope.*

*Piper says you should come back soon. It's when you leave things happen.*

I needed to go back.

My arms turned the wheel before another synapse fired in my brain. I took a right turn into a dollar store parking lot, a quick circle, and I was on my way back. I would think of the excuse for my return when I got there, but barging back into Amy's life was my job. It was needed. I didn't want anything to sabotage my hopes. I wanted Joshua's prayers answered. I was the answer.

I parked in the driveway. Officer Renfrew was long gone. I bounced up the front porch, knocked. Waited. Knocked. Waited. No way could they have gone right to sleep or left. They were in there.

I didn't wait for an invite. I opened the door.

Quiet.

And stillness. Enough that I could hear the sound of dust settling. Crouched behind the green chair, Joshua sat with his knees pulled into his chest. I hadn't noticed how skinny he was, wiry legs, wiry arms, like Piper, too skinny to put a needle into, and at that moment, too terrified to get up from his safe spot against the wall.

"Joshua, what happened? Where's your mom?"

Joshua pointed, his arm straight as a street sign, his motion commanding. I obeyed. I walked straight to the bathroom, the most dangerous room in any house.

I wasn't going to knock. Wasn't going to ask to be invited in. I opened the door, praying all I'd see would be Amy's look of surprise as she brushed her teeth, and I'd leave with humble apologies. Amy's anger would be righteous, and her belief that those with badges abuse their power confirmed.

The door swung open, and the image exploded like a fireball. Amy looked up at me.

The syringe dangling from her vein, the look on her face, the scent of despair, the sound of her gasp—it all hit me like a flash of lightning, blinding my eyes and searing into my skull. My flesh sprung icy goosebumps, tiny hairs stood on end. Bile burned in my gut and rose into my mouth. Amy had abandoned her child same as if she'd left him wrapped up in a dumpster, and the anger was a shotgun blast into my brain stem. The explosion shot power through me, made me get up into her face.

I took her hand in mine and traced the flesh of her arm. I thought of ways I might rip the skin off her bones, forcing the snake to shed its skin.

***"Do you know what I am going to do to you?"***

The voice didn't feel like mine, didn't sound like mine. The words themselves tasted foul. Something else was coming out of my mouth.

I inched my finger up her arm towards the needle. Her skin trembled at my touch. I plucked the syringe out of her vein. My hand acted on instinct and closed around the needle, making a fist, with the sharp metal point sticking out of my knuckles like a claw.

The sword stabbed with sweet efficiency into her eye—the first of many.

The rage that followed was a bloody nightmare, forgotten in content but not in tone. It was a nuclear explosion of anger and rage, and after it ran out of fuel, I was left staring at the bathroom mirror at the strange sight I'd become.

Ugly and twisted, a face as disfigured as the emotions and hurt that hid beneath. The beast still talked to me in my dreams, whispered to me from the dark places, spoke through the crevices at the bottom of my skull, but it hadn't shown itself since I was a child. It was back and awake. The killer again had shown her face.

Joshua was at the doorway, staring at the bloody carcass that used to be his mom but now lay on the floor in a pool of heroin-tainted blood. When he finally turned to look at me, the Lizard, the chameleon, I wondered if he saw my true face—the face I first saw so many years ago.

## CHAPTER SEVEN:
### Lizard, 18 years previous,
### One Year After the Car Accident

Mom and Dad were fighting about what to do with me, and their voices were like bouncy balls banging off the walls. I was in bed with a blanket wrapped around my head like a bonnet, but I could still hear their voices through the door.

*"Lizard's dead asleep. Come on. Let's go."*

*"We're not leaving her alone."*

*"Then just let me go score."*

*"You always take too long."*

*"I'm not leaving you alone again with Bucky."*

I wanted them to leave and let me sleep, but they didn't, so I got out of bed and went into the kitchen. I started pouring a bowl of Reese's Puffs, pretending I hadn't heard them arguing.

"Stop that, Lizard," Mom said. "We're going out for donuts. We have to stop by a friend's house, and then donuts. You okay with that?"

It didn't matter if I was okay with it, but I did want a donut.

We drove through empty streets, the clock on the car with *5:52* glowing in red. Misty rain seemed stuck in the air, and I watched drops stream down the window until we finally parked on the sad street. It was early morning, still dark outside, and I wished I was at home. Stars glistened and burned in the black sky. The houses on this street seemed faded and grey, some empty and abandoned with bricks falling off and roofs burnt up.

My dad stood at the door and knocked so hard it sounded like his knuckles were made of metal. I clung to my mom's legs.

No answer, but I could hear music coming from inside.

My dad leaned forward with a huff and banged louder. I finally heard deadbolts and locks being undone, and a man appeared at the open door.

"God damn if it ain't Trey and Kate, here for breakfast," he said. He wasn't wearing a shirt, and his pants hung down so I could see his underwear. A gun was tucked inside his waistband. I wondered if this was the person they called their friend. I was hiding behind Mom's leg. His eyes looked down at me in surprise.

"And the whole family is here. Fucking special."

"Not my idea," said my mom, wrapping an arm around me.

I could feel my dad's nerves rattle as he spoke. "I know it's early, but we're sick. You got new shit last night, I know that. I got money."

"Not ready yet, still cutting, weighing and packing, but if you want to wait, come right into our lobby."

My dad shuffled his feet.

"How long?" my mom asked. "We just wanna score and go home."

"Take as long as it takes, or you come back, or you wait, but this shit gonna blow you out."

We went inside. Mom held my hand.

The house was small, like ours, just one TV room and a kitchen next to it, and it was stinky, like an old laundry pile. There were at least ten people inside, some of them smoking cigarettes and it made everything look hazy. I could feel eyes buzz around me like flies, and I could see sadness sweating from their skin. Two were younger than the rest and sat in front of the TV playing Xbox football, saying the *F* word back and forth. Everyone else was just waiting, watching, smoking.

I recognized their look. They were sick. Sick like my mom and dad.

"Fucking Bakers. Why'd you let him inside?" someone shouted from the kitchen. "Weighing this up, and then you can have some, but sit your ass down first."

His voice was so loud that everyone looked. He was the commander inside this place, I could tell. He was staring right into me, like he knew me, recognized me from someplace I wasn't supposed to be. I clawed up my mom like she was a tree and I needed to climb to safety to survive—like Simba from the stampede in *The Lion King*.

"Wait one fucking minute, Baker. You brought your kid to my house?" he said, staring me down.

"We just want to score and go. It's fine, she's fine. Aren't you fine, Lizard?" my dad said, and I knew he wanted me to say yes.

"Fine? Fine? What the hell is wrong with you? Hell, this kid probably isn't even your child. Might be mine the way Kate using that velvet purse of hers. Bringing a kid to a place like this... Shit, nobody worth being a parent would do that, don't deserve to be a parent… You hear that, kid? Your parents don't deserve you."

My dad grumbled angrily, like a thunderstorm far off nobody but me knew was coming. And with thunder comes lightning. Only the medicine would quiet his storm, and even though a car smashed into us leaving a drugstore once, I wished we could go there for his medicine like we used to, instead of a house like this.

The first time I saw my dad using the needle he looked at me with his mouth hanging open and said, "No need to go to Walgreens anymore," as if I should be happy for him. After that, nearly every morning, Mom and Dad found somewhere in the house to use the needle. Sometimes, I sensed them doing it in the other room behind closed doors because the house got a certain kind of quiet. Other times, I looked through the crack in the partly-open bathroom door and could see a slice of them angled in the mirror. Their faces were twisted, their eyes scary. I started seeing the syringes in the garbage and bruises on their arms. THEIR smiles happened less often, and even when the smiles showed up, they couldn't be trusted.

In my private moments, alone in my room, I prayed to God it would stop. God didn't answer, but the Whisper did. Her voice came from my dark closet, telling me to stay in bed because, *"You don't want to know."* The day the car smashed into me, she whispered, *"Your daddy's sick, and he's just getting poison."* In the car ride home, the whispers changed to screams, yelling at me to get buckled (but I never got buckled). The day Mom left me alone with the taco that I never ate, the Whisper warned me Dad was going to take my medicine.

Sitting in this smoky, stinking house, the voice murmured that I wasn't supposed to be here, that I needed to get out. The eyes of these people were all over me as they scratched and twitched.

My mom was sitting on the ground, and I sat on her lap. She played with the back of my hair, her fingers moving like a comb down each strand. "What kind of donut do you want?" she asked in my ear so close I could feel her hot breath.

"Glazed. With sprinkles."

"Good choice. You always make the best choices," she said, and kissed the side of my neck. Her lips were warm, moist, nice.

"How old is she?" a woman asked. She had a tiny yellow tattoo on the side of her neck, and I tried to see what it was but couldn't. I wanted a tattoo someday.

"Ten. Just had a birthday," my mom answered.

"How did you get that scar, sweetie?" the woman asked me.

I put a finger on my scar, wishing nobody could see. When I first got the stitches, I tugged at them so much I was afraid my head would leak out. The doctor said it probably made the scar even worse.

"Monkey bars," my mom answered.

"Well, she's precious. Mine's eight. I'm seeing him this weekend."

The mom was the same as most of the men, her skin greasy, her movements shaky. I watched her suck on a cigarette and then blow smoke into the air that curled up into twirling circles, hypnotizing me for a minute before it disappeared.

"Time to cook. Ante in," said the commander, stepping from the kitchen.

People jumped up. The Xbox kids left their controllers on the ground. Cigarettes were tapped out in beer cans. They all scurried to stand in line, holding cash in their hands, in front of the man called Bucky. He was like the ice cream man and they were kids waiting at his truck. I felt my stomach empty, like it was eating itself. I wished I'd taken a few bites of those Reese's Puffs—instead, smoke and dirty laundry stink swirled inside my belly.

"Let's bring this home. We can be back in twenty minutes," my mom said to my dad.

"Oh, hell no, babe. I'm too sick to drive. We can fix up fast here, then home. It's not like she's never seen," my dad said, talking about me as if I wasn't sitting right there on Mom's lap.

"Lizard. I don't want you to look, come on. Go sit at the table. Play with my cell."

Mom led me to the opposite edge of the kitchen table, turned the chair towards the wall, and asked me to sit down. She took out her phone, tapped on the Candy Crush app, and handed it to me. She left me there, staring at the wall near the basement stairs.

I pretended to play Candy Crush like she wanted me to, but all my attention was on listening to everything behind me. I heard skin being slapped; *smack, smack.* I heard the flick of lighters. I listened to their mumbles. I could feel their concentration. I imagined I could hear air let out each time the needles poked through their skin. *Pfffff.*

I had to see. I turned my head to look for just a bit, and in a flash saw Bucky aiming a needle into his arm, just below his muscle. Another person had their shoe off and poked between their toes. One was looking into the wall mirror and poking into their neck. If they saw me watching I'd be in trouble, so I turned back.

I held out my own arm before me. The blue veins ran like highways from my elbow to my wrist. I smacked my veins with my palm the way I'd seen my parents do and imagined the red bits of blood inside the blue vein scattering about.

When would Mom and Dad be finished? I wanted to leave. To have a donut and be home instead of alone and staring at the wall. Not far from where I sat, I could see the top of the stairs leading to the basement. Black and white checkered linoleum stairs went down to somewhere even darker than here. I put Mom's cell phone on my lap, placed my hands together, locked my fingers, and held them to my chest to pray.

*God, please get me home.*

I could feel Bucky behind me at the kitchen table, his heart thumping in his chest. The beating made this house seem alive. My parents were farther away, and if Bucky wanted to hurt me, Mom and Dad couldn't help. I imagined him dragging me down to the basement to a place I would never be found.

*Please, God. Get me home. Make this stop. Let me know you're there, God, give me a sign.*

I squeezed my fingers together, feeling each knuckle, and then I heard the answer.

**I'm here.**

The whisper came from the basement, from down in the dark. I squinted, expecting to see a pair of glowing eyes looking up at me. I wanted to see the face of the girl who whispered to me, but there was only blackness.

*You're here?* I asked softly.

**I'm always here. I've been here from the start.**

*Where did you come from?*

**I was with you in your mother's womb. The drugs went to my body instead of yours. I protected you, surrounded you, I kept you alive. I will always keep you alive. You need me.**

*I need you for what?*

**To protect you.**

*I don't understand.*

**You need me now, because now it's the ending.**

THUMP.

Something crashed to the floor. The noise made my skull vibrate.

I looked down at my feet and saw Bucky. He'd dropped off his chair to the ground and fallen even closer to me. His arms were sprawled out and his eyes were looking directly up, partly open. His pupils were rolling back into his head. His mouth was open and drool gathered at his lips. The needle still stuck inside his arm. He was like a wizard stabbed by his very own wand.

The commander had fallen.

This wasn't right. Someone needed to help. But who? Not me, someone else.

I grabbed Mom's cell. I reopened the app. Just play Candy Crush like she asked and everything will be okay.

The cussing got louder behind me. Every word spoken sounded like alarms ringing. Things were wrong and getting worse.

"Don't shoot this shit."

"Andy's nodding."

"Transou ain't right."

"Damn it."

I needed to look. I finally turned.

Everything was different from before.

One of the young boys was on the ground, not far from where the black Xbox controller lay. His body was twitching on the dirty carpet. The woman with the yellow neck tattoo was still sitting on the couch, but her head kept drooping, chin falling towards her chest, then pulling up, then falling down, as if her head weighed too much and she couldn't hold it up. It finally went down for the last time, and her whole body fell with it. She toppled onto the floor, and I could clearly see the yellow tattoo on her neck. It was Tweety Bird.

A man next to her turned to look, his mouth opened to speak, but before he could say a word, he dropped to the floor alongside her.

More kept dropping, too many to track, like a bunch of puppets whose strings had been cut, their bodies lay slack on the floor, everything tangled. Nobody spoke another word. The only noise was gurgling and raspy lungs trying to breathe. The heartbeat of the house was fading and the breathing getting slower. The man named Bucky was trapped like a bug on his backside and wasn't even trying to get back upright.

*Mom and Dad.*

I got up from my chair to get to them. The room looked like a grenade had gone off. I had to step through the bodies on the floor. I walked over Bucky, pretzeled on the ground. I walked over the mother who was supposed to visit her son this weekend, and I imagined her missing the meeting and him wondering why.

I got dizzy, and I fought with every muscle to stop my brain from bursting out my scar. A seizure was coming, but Tegretol wouldn't help, and I wanted to go home.

Mom and Dad were slouched against the wall, leaning into each other and resting like two weary travelers. Dad's needle was on the ground, but Mom's needle still poked out of her arm. The tiny slits of her eyelids were open, and the pupils inside rolled around but didn't look back.

"Mom!" I cried, giving her a shake. "Mom!" I said in a higher pitch, hoping it would wake her up.

Foam came out of her mouth. Tiny bubbles of spit gathered on her lips and then drooled down her chin.

"Mom!" I kept shrieking, and with a finger tried to open her eyelid, but it snapped back closed. Her skin felt cold and was changing colors with each second. A lighter shade of alien blue.

"Dad, you have to help!"

I shook his shoulders. His body was loose, his head flopping around like a bobblehead doll, like it might fall off his neck and roll on the ground. His eyelids cracked for a moment. I could see one sliver of his eyeball inside before it completely closed. His body fell over onto the floor.

My thoughts screamed with prayers and cries. Someone had to wake up and help me, but nobody did. If I could only have a seizure, just black out and be like them, then we'd all wake up at the new place together. Instead, I was forced to feel and see everything while my heart inside was bleeding tears. It wasn't fair. I wanted to crawl onto Mom's lap, dig my way into her, and feel her arm on my shoulder the way things were just moments ago.

I turned to look over the room of bodies, wishing someone would help, sitting with my parents behind me. This was the same way we sat in our last Christmas picture we took at Sears. I loved that picture. I used it as a bookmark. I felt so special wearing my fancy clothes with my parents behind me, smiling so big with love in their eyes. Now their eyes were closed, their mouths hung slack, their lips were blue, and drip-drops of a strange liquid bubbled down their chins.

I needed to get the phone and call for help.

*ARE YOU SURE YOU WANT TO DO THAT?*

The whisper startled me because it was louder, more powerful. The words boomed inside my chest cavity.

*Yes. I am sure. I need to call 911 for help. Something terrible happened.*

**I know what happened. They all injected a deadly dose of fentanyl. All of them. And if you call 911, people will come and save them with Naloxone, and we don't want that.**

*Why not?*

The voice didn't answer. I was crying and scared and I wanted to huddle in the corner. I hated being alone.

*WHY NOT?* I asked the voice again, so loud it had to answer.

**You have suffered more than a child should. There is more to come if this doesn't stop. I will help you. I'm going to give you what you want.**

The voice seemed to be coming from every mouth in the room. Tiny bits of foam erupted on the lips of faces as it spoke. First one mouth moved, then another, like a concert of dying people.

**Tell me what you want,** the voice repeated. This time coming from the lips of the gamer-boy. He was going to look so sad at his funeral.

*Show me who you are. What do you look like?*

**TELL ME WHAT YOU WANT.**

*I want Mom and Dad never to do this. Ever again.*

**Okay. I will make that happen. Tonight is the last night.**

My head scanned the room, daring the voice to show her face, but instead I just heard more words.

**I CAN MAKE IT STOP. FOREVER. NEVER SICK.**

*No, you can't. It's up to me to save them.*

I looked at my parents on the ground. Their bodies seemed empty, and I could feel their souls seeping out of them, ready to go to Heaven or Hell. I squeezed the cell phone. I knew what to do. So many times I had thought about calling 911 from my house when I saw my parents' eyes close, their bodies in such unnatural shapes while I tucked them in. I never called, but I worried until my stomach felt sick. Every time, their eyes eventually opened, but not this time. This time I needed to call for help. All these people needed me to save them.

I dialed 911 on Mom's cell phone. The operator picked up on the first ring.

"What's your emergency?"

"I'm in a house where people are using drugs. I know it's drugs. They're all dying and I need help.

Yes, I'm safe.

No, I don't know where I am.

No, nobody else here can talk to you.

I don't know how many people, a lot of them and nobody is awake.

I'm Lizabeth Baker. I'm ten years old. I'm on a street. I don't know where."

***NOW YOU'VE DONE IT.***

The 911 woman kept talking, telling me to stay on the phone and stay safe, and I begged her to be faster. Mom and Dad's skin was changing colors. I reached down and grabbed Mom's hand in mine and tried to warm it, but instead it just made mine colder.

***YOU DON'T KNOW WHAT YOU ARE DOING. THEY HAD THEIR CHANCE. THEY CAN'T LOVE US. THEY WON'T LOVE YOU. I KNOW THIS WILL NOT MAKE SENSE TO YOU NOW, BUT SOMEDAY IT WILL.***

The voice screamed at me from every single body on the ground, shaking the roof like a jet flew overhead.

***YOU WILL SEE WHAT I LOOK LIKE. PREPARE YOURSELF.***

I tried to tell the 911 operator my parent's names, Trey and Katlyn Baker, but I couldn't speak.

My stomach spasmed. Bile filled my mouth. It tasted like acid and was burning my tongue, my gums, my lips—even my teeth seemed to sizzle. My body froze. Arms and leg muscles stiffened. This was the big seizure that all those little seizures were leading up to, but this time my brain was fully awake and I could feel everything.

The bubbling liquid filled my mouth, gathered on my lips and dripped as if from a leaky faucet. The bile tasted revolting, foul, same as the whole room smelled, like dying bodies, smoke, and vomit.

I dropped the phone and fell to the floor, gagging, gurgling. I couldn't get any air, and if I didn't breathe soon, I was going to die.

My brain couldn't pray, my hands couldn't move. My head was spinning like water draining down a sink, swirling and swirling, taking me down with it. The acid finally boiled hot enough to come spraying out from my lips and shoot onto the ground.

I could breathe again, but I couldn't stop vomiting. My own breath made me nauseous.

A puddle gathered below me, looking like a melted snowman, getting bigger the more I threw up. I heaved, took a breath, heaved some more. My whole gut was emptying, coming from some deep cavern, until finally my insides were piled onto the floor.

Then the puddle before me started to rise up.

A tiny whirlpool, whipping in circles, turning from liquid to solid—and a person was emerging inside it all. First little legs, then a body, then arms. It stood up from the ground and straightened until I was eye to eye with a girl in front of me, just as tall.

She had one ear pierced, just like me—Mom had pierced my ears at home, but my left ear had closed, and I left it that way. She was skinny, just like me—I was so skinny I couldn't find real Levi jeans that fit me and could only wear Wrangler. Her eyes were the same hazel, with a green middle and brown outsides.

But it wasn't exactly me, because her entire head was bald. She had no hair, no eyebrows, just one big scar over her whole face. Every bit of her skin was scarred as if burnt, and her flesh was stuck in the shape of the flames, twisted and discolored.

It had to hurt to have skin like that.

I wanted to scream. I wanted to hug her and not let go. I wanted this mirror of myself standing there to shatter and disappear. Then I'd wake up back in bed and start over with a bowl of Reese's Puffs.

The voice spoke to me, face to face, eye to eye, for the first time after all these years.

***THEY HAD THEIR CHANCE.***

She grabbed the cell phone off the floor. The blue light illuminated her damaged face. She poked the red button and hung up on 911.

**We need to do this fast before they get here.**

The scar girl started with my dad. She positioned herself behind his shoulders and grabbed him from behind. She was too small to move his weight, way too small. I knew because I'd tried to drag him before—but I was wrong. She moved him on the first try.

She was stronger than I was.

She dragged him across the floor. His face flopped around, but his eyes stayed closed, his body slack. She grunted from the effort—she was getting tired. Her scar tissue face was turning red. She moved like she knew exactly what she was doing, like this had been planned for a long time. Dad's body was at the top of the basement stairs, and with one final grunt, she pushed him down.

The crashing noises descended. Like a rock bouncing down a pit, I heard his bones smashing down the stairs, then finally stop at the bottom.

**We need to do this fast,** she said again, and moved like an insect across the floor over to my mom. She grabbed Mom by the shoulders and started to tug.

"No!" I screamed, and I reached for Mom's foot, took hold of it.

**We need to do this now. They had their chance.**

The girl was too strong. She yanked Mom's body free from my grip, and in an instant, the angry girl had scooted her body across the floor to the basement steps. The needle was still stuck in Mom's arm and went sledding down the stairs with her. It felt like my own bones were breaking when I heard her body crash down the stairs, and reminded me of the day my head smashed against the car window.

I dashed to the steps to look. The stairwell was steep. The kitchen light shined on the top few stairs but not the bottom. The black-and-white checkered stairwell went to Hell, I was sure of it, and I decided to walk down.

The basement was dark. The air felt dusky, mucky, like a swamp. My parents were just dark shadows on the ground, but I could tell their arms and shoulder blades were out of place, certainly busted and broken, and their heads smashed apart more than mine ever was.

***By the time they check the basement, it will be too late.
They'll die like they are supposed to.***

I couldn't see the scar girl anymore. I could only hear her
voice.

***Nobody will ever hurt you with heroin again. I'm with you
always.***

The darkness of the basement engulfed me like a hot bath,
and I wanted to lay down next to my parents and die with them, all
three of us in one final Christmas picture. The basement was going
to be my tomb if I stayed any longer. Then I heard the sirens.

I felt summoned to walk up the stairs. The voice stayed
behind as I rose up and saw lights flashing outside the front window.
Ambulance workers busted through the door. First, a young man in a
blue uniform, then another man behind him.

They scurried about, checking each person, calling for more
help. They had their own, different needles to revive these dying
people, and started poking the bodies. Some of the people were
revived, coughed up more foam, and then they were taken out to the
ambulance. New help kept arriving. A policeman took me outside.
The sun was burning bright. Morning was over.

*Check the basement*, I wanted to scream, *check the basement*,
but each time I tried, my mouth seized up and the whispers told me,
***No, don't. Don't. They are dead, let them die***.

She wouldn't let me scream, and that scream has been stuck
inside me all my life, eating at my organs, tainting the scent of my
breath.

I spent the rest of my childhood years in three different foster
homes, and I never told anyone about the scar girl. Even after all the
therapists they had me talk to. Even after being interviewed by a
journalist who did an expose on the Fentanyl Final Girl, the one who
survived in the house of horrors, where eight people died, only four
survived. One had to be forced into a coma and put on ice in the ER
but woke up delusional, seeing scarred-faced demons. Another
survived but overdosed the day he was discharged. (This time,
nobody could save him.) One of the boys playing Xbox survived, the
other did not.

The fourth to survive was Bucky, who lived to sell another
day.

The journalist helped me find the boy who never got the visit from his mother, the one with the Tweety Bird on her neck. I swear he could hear the whispers that nobody else could. Not my whispers, but his own.

I never want anyone else to be that boy.

## CHAPTER EIGHT:
### Lizabeth in the Bathroom with Joshua

Joshua stood upon restless legs, more nervous than I, after taking in the blood-stained bathroom and realizing his mom had been murdered. His eyes stayed glued to the ground as if awaiting punishment, as if he were responsible for the mess. His fingers fidgeted, silently snapping, his head bowed in deference to my next move. The moment swirled outside of reality, like we were spinning a different direction than the rest of the earth.

I might have cried. I might have screamed. I might have checked Amy's pulse to confirm she was really dead, but I didn't need to. Whatever presence inside me that was responsible wouldn't have stopped had she not been killed.

My brain fast forwarded to how I wanted to spend my last moments before the coming storm. Arrest, handcuffs, press coverage, standing before the judge with a policeman behind me when the judge read my sentence. I'd be incarcerated alongside those who I'd been responsible for sending to prison.

My life was over. I killed myself, and I sliced inside this poor boy's heart when I'd murdered Amy.

I needed to get to Becca and explain to her what happened in my own words. Becca—the one person who knew me, the only woman who mattered. She was Mother Universe, proof of redemption, of understanding. She would accept my darkest sides. I needed a moment in her arms, swaddled in safety, one last time before I completely shattered.

"Joshua. I am going to call for help. The police will come. An ambulance. You sit in the green chair and when they get here, tell them I did this. I'll be at my house waiting. I need to go home and tell someone who I love what happened. To confess what I did. To be with her before they take me to jail."

How can I leave him here? This house was stained and the walls were moaning in pain. Joshua heard it all, felt it all, but he didn't move, as if in catatonic shock.

"Joshua, you should leave this room. You shouldn't see this anymore."

I tried to escort him out of the bloody bathroom, but he put an arm up to stop me. His strongest move yet.

"Will they put you in jail?" he asked.

"Yes, but I deserve it," I answered. My hands were red as if I'd been finger-painting with his mother's blood.

"No, you don't. I knew this was going to happen. Piper-Pippen warned me my mom was sick and killing herself. He told me he would find someone to help, and I think that person is you."

"Joshua, please, people will come for you."

"Take me with you. Don't leave me here."

"Police will know what to do better than I do, they'll be here soon, they can take you. Please, go in the other room," I pleaded, I cried, the phone unsteady in my hand and ready to slip from my fingers. I dialed 911 with trembling fingers the way I had so long ago.

And then I heard her.

*You're making a mistake.*
*Take the boy with you.*

When the operator answered I didn't say a word, despite multiple requests to declare "the nature of my emergency." I held the phone away from my ear, as if keeping it from my body would stop my confession.

*Do I really want to confess?*
*No, she deserved to die, she had her chance long ago.*
*What to do?*
*Leave the body, take the boy.*

I stared in silence at Amy's body on the ground, hoping that the dead might talk to me one more time, that words might come from her mouth, forgiving me, telling me that she understood why I killed her, thanking me for finally putting her to rest, and begging me to take care of her child.

How could I explain myself to the operator on the phone, who seemed just a voyeur to this tragedy? She couldn't understand. The judge, the jury—they would never understand. Neither would the journalist who'd certainly want to interview the Fentanyl Final Girl who'd become a killer.

*How can I explain myself?*

**You can't.**

Joshua bent down beside his mom. He reached his hand towards her face. Her cheeks were dotted with syringe holes, and blood streamed down like mascara-lined tears. With one finger, he touched her flesh.

"I heard fingerprints stay on things forever."

All my crisis training, all my trauma training, meant nothing, for this little guy was suddenly in charge, while I felt lost.

The 911 operator kept asking, "What is the nature of your emergency?" The world needed my answer.

"Somebody died. Please send an ambulance to 15356 Ellen Drive. Check the bathroom."

I hung up.

"Get your stuff."

Joshua gathered things as if he'd been ready for this evacuation plan for years. Taking his drawings was his first priority.

One last look at Amy. I needed the image of her murder burnt into my brain. Her body seemed punctured by a thousand thorns, her eyes mutilated, her jaw slack. I had failed her even before tonight. We had failed her. We never really helped her. Police and punishment and threats did nothing to stop the addiction, we needed to find a way to dig inside her hijacked brain, but never could. Maybe love for your child, for your partner, for your own life, mattered not when the lizard brain of addiction took over.

I shut the front door of the house. I left the dead behind, and I took the child away into the night.

## CHAPTER NINE:
### Lizabeth Drives Home

My grip on the steering wheel was sticky from blood. It was my birthing blood, my red badge of courage.

I was a mom, driving my child to safety. Joshua was buckled up securely in the front seat and gazed straight out the window to what lay ahead.

I've always had poor boundaries in my work. I'd once left Christmas gifts on the porch of a single dad who had lost his job. I'd delivered groceries to another man who'd been living off of Kraft Mac and Cheese as his only meal. I once befriended a woman under a fake Facebook profile and sent her messages of support.

I'd fallen in love with yet another.

And now I was bringing a probationer's child home, and I planned to smuggle him across the border to Canada. First, I needed to tell Becca what happened and convince her to go. I wanted more than my bloody hands as exhibit A, but the face of this young boy, suddenly an orphan, as exhibit B.

I rehearsed my opening statement.

Something came over me. Something came out of me. Amy was going to die of an overdose, I know it (That's not true. That's your monkey bar lie and she'll see through it.)

Let's leave for Canada. All three of us. Tonight. You were right. I didn't fall in love with this one, I killed this one, and now her son has nobody. We have a duty to care for this child. He wants to go with us. Foster care will tear him apart.

I'm not fit to adopt anymore either. I have a criminal past, worse than Becca's, and I needed to run to our safe room before I got crushed under the weight.

They would have questions at the border. I could show my badge to the border agent and explain that his mother just got incarcerated, and I was transporting him back to his family. Yes, we need two people—he's a minor—you don't stay alone with minors. Then we'd descend through the white-tiled tunnel to Windsor, driving through leaky walls where the Detroit River drips all around, then ascending into Canada, emerging out a birth canal into a new life.

I pictured Joshua and I on the cabin porch, the forest overgrown around us, the only sound of humans the occasional plane overhead, not an interruption, just a reminder of how isolated we were. We'd sip iced tea, waiting for Becca to get back from her hike. She likes to hike alone where there's no trail, no matter how much the thicket tries to stop her.

The fresh air will penetrate every cell. The wild will accept us.

We could get fake names, new birth certificates. Becca's

uncle knew people in Canada, he had friends in strategic places. I got a guy for that, was always his answer. Well, we would need things done, but I had to get Becca's buy-in first.

I pulled into an empty driveway—no sign of Becca at home. Where is she?

Joshua stayed in the foyer as I dashed about the house, expecting to see Becca, but each room was empty, mocking me, laughing. She left without you. Couldn't you see it coming? She told you as much. The rejection by the adoption agency was too much. I knew it. I could sense it, but I left her alone in the house anyway.

I was a single parent suddenly, on the run with nobody to help me. I needed to move fast. How long until people with badges showed up? I was like Amy now and would always be afraid of people with badges. Joshua saw the terror in my eyes. I was just another person who let him down, who didn't know how to live.

I can't do this alone. Not without Becca.

My dark fears were washed away when shining headlights appeared in the driveway. Joshua and I squinted out the front window and watched Becca get out of her car. I watched her walk to the house as if witnessing Jesus walk on water, coming to save me. As soon as she stepped through the front door, I started to explain.

My rehearsal was useless.

Everything changed as I spoke. Voices in my head clanged in confusion. She coached me through my narrative with her eyes best she could, knowing that I was out of balance and needed an anchor. Becca had been in situations like this before, when the unexpected moments of life surprise you sharp as a papercut. She could hear the blank spaces and pauses between my words. Her skin changed like a chameleon to her environment. She was a lizard, just like me.

"You called 911 from her house. They'll be here soon."

"I was on a private line."

"They can unmask that."

"How long does that take?"

"Doesn't matter, you said a cop was there. They know about your visit."

Becca eyed Joshua standing there in silence, trying to decide if the boy was really up for this. He smiled back at her in a way I'd not yet seen—a reassuring curl of his lips, a brightness to his eyes, a sadness of needs unfulfilled. It was a weapon of warmth for times like these. He was a survivor with an arsenal of tools buried in his heart, I'd certainly not yet seen them all.

If Becca had told me I was crazy, that I needed to get a lawyer and turn myself in, that the foster system would be okay for this child, I would have obeyed her command. Instead, she commanded otherwise.

"Clean up. Take a shower. You're bloody," she said. "We'll need to hit ATMs. We need to pack. I'll get the suitcases from the basement. Joshua, we're taking you with us."

## CHAPTER TEN:
### Becca in the Basement. One Last time

The luggage had been gathered, ready to fill, and Becca sat alone in the basement trying to let the truth take root.

Lizard killed someone.

Killed someone.

Everything had changed. An officer of the court, a probation officer, her partner, the woman who worked with the dirge of the city and had always come home clean, now had her hands stained with blood.

Becca had listened to Lizard tripping over her tongue, trying to rationalize the act of murder. Lizard made excuses, she placed blame, all to make her actions easier to digest. Becca knew the taste of excuses, she'd tasted them in her own words for years, crimes committed that nobody would ever know. Money stolen from those who thought they misplaced it, thousands of dollars of retail fraud, but she'd never caused physical harm the way her partner had. Lizabeth had just torn a body apart.

Lizard was still the person she wanted to be with, to run away with, maybe more so now than ever. There's a beast in everyone—sometimes it's an addict, sometimes it's a killer.

Becca sat in the basement, not far from a dirty pile of laundry that would never get clean and the exercise bike that gathered dust. The dust seemed thicker now, chunkier, and the weight of above was ready to crash down. She was alone in the depths, below it all, holding on to a lost love.

In one hand, she held a pack of heroin, in the other hand,

works to get high. Before their flight to safety in Canada, she was going to shoot up some dope. One last time. It was perfect.

Lizard let her beast out, and now it's my turn.

She'd been rejected so many times before, the adoption denial was the final excuse to let the dam break free.

You never forget how to get high. You never stop loving it. Soon as Lizard had left for her home visit, Becca got in her car and drove the familiar route to buy heroin. She then rushed home to use it, her stomach bubbling in anticipation, expecting to find an empty house, but instead found Lizard with bloody hands and an orphan child.

The face Lizard showed her when she walked in the door was a mix of panic and desperation, spinning in a blender. You finally look like me, Becca had thought. You finally need my help like never before. But first, a snakebite into my veins and the golden rush of heroin.

How many times had she dreamt of this moment? This magic elixir that gave her love like nothing else could. Becca had felt defective from the moment she was born, and heroin was the only fix, the only cure, the one thing that took away her affliction. Somehow she'd learn to love the defects, to live with them instead of cure them. For seven years she'd been stuck in a cage—trapped in a cage of not using— but she'd learned to live inside that cage. There was freedom in that cage. There was love from Lizard inside that cage. Now she was busting out.

She waited until she heard the pipes rattle from Lizard's shower before going through the routine of cooking up. Her vein was easy to hit and seemed to pulsate with pleasure in response to the needle point. She drew some blood, mixed the red cells with the brown nectar of the gods, then plunged the needle in. The syringe was a second heart that pumped life, and a beautiful opioid orgasm followed. Her spirit was awakening after being asleep for so long, bathing in the heavens that had descended into this basement.

One last time, oh God, I can feel your welcoming hand, the warmth of a mother's womb. A lifetime of wonder.

Then she heard the footsteps. A devil was descending, and each hoof clanked upon the metal strips on the basement stairs. The devil was coming back to Hell to remind Becca what happens when she gets high.

The monster was upon Becca in an instant, stood tall over her, knife raised over its head. Foam gathered on her mouth and dripped from her lips. Becca shrunk in the chair.

The monster was Lizard. Or almost Lizard. She had a face full of scars and her hair was scalded off her body as if she'd just walked through a fire. Her breath was foul. Her eyes determined. The tiny slit of a scar just above her ear, the first part of Lizard's body that Becca had ever touched, had grown like wild weeds over her entire face. Becca always thought the scar was just poorly-sewn stitches on a teddy bear that would one day rip open and the stuffing inside would come spilling out.

Today was that day.

Lizard's eyes bulged out of her face and burned with rage from the ultimate hurt. The killer had found a new victim.

Becca felt a howl build in her lungs, ready to release, but nobody would hear. She felt an apology in her heart, but nobody would care. She was stuck waiting for one last slice into her body— one last time.

## CHAPTER ELEVEN:
### Lizabeth in the shower

"Clean up. Take a shower. You're bloody," she had said. "We'll need to hit ATMs. We need to pack. I'll get the suitcases from the basement. Joshua, we're taking you with us."

Becca was on board. Her voice revealed her trepidation, but she had accepted me, despite my confession, and was with me—with us—for the run to Canada.

I stood in the shower washing off the blood and baptizing myself for our new life together as parents. I wanted the water scalding hot, to beat down on my flesh and hurt upon contact, for my sins would not be washed away by anything mild. If there were steel wool to clean off the blood, I'd have used it. The red water swirled at my feet. Amy and her heroin-infused blood went in circles, down the pipes, draining into the city.

A city I had to escape.

Soon as Amy's smack-filled blood had been cleansed from my flesh, my own blood started to boil. Something was wrong. I sensed it, smelled it. My gut swirled, my breath turned foul, and my head pulsated. I could feel the tiny capillaries in my brain cells expand from the surge.

Another seizure was coming.

An intense vomit.

The angry girl was triggered. She grew from a seed inside my womb to a raging little beast ready to unleash her wrath.

It pulled me out of the shower. My skin was so hot the water sizzled and dried as if on a grill. I put my clothes on over flesh turned to scar tissue. Tornado sirens were shouting in my head, turning to words.

***CHECK THE BASEMENT. SHE BETRAYED YOU. CHECK THE BASEMENT.***

My legs weren't my own. They moved me to the kitchen, and I watched my hands pull the largest knife out of the butcher block. Joshua was sitting at our kitchen table, doing his artwork. A dozen Piper-Pippens were spread about the table with their arms stretching, reaching outside of the pages and into reality, just skinny metallic tentacles, sharp as my knife. Their faces were smiling as if they'd just heard some dark secret, and their eyes swirled in tiny barbed wire twists, hypnotizing, Joshua's eyes transfixed just the same. The flock of Piper-Pippens and their creator bore witness as I left them to walk the stairs to the depths below.

There I found her, the person I used to know as Becca, heroin works lying by her side. My fingers clenched the plastic handle of the knife. My head screamed for me to use it.

***SHE BETRAYED YOU.***

*No. She just had a slip.*

***SHE'S NOT FIT TO BE A PARENT. CUT HER UP.***

*It's my fault. I burdened her with too much weight.*

***CUT FREE FROM YOUR ANCHOR AND LEAVE WITH THE BOY. HURRY. THE POLICE WILL BE HERE SOON.***

Becca's pupils had retreated into tiny dots. She knelt before me like a helpless sacrifice victim, trembling in fear before a brutal god. I could smell the heroin in her veins, reeking out her pores. The same scent from my childhood home that stuck to the walls, that hung thick in the air while I ate cold SpaghettiOs, praying my parents would wake up while I went to bed alone. The whispers from my closet I used to listen to for comfort had now turned to screams of rage and were in full control.

**SHE BETRAYED YOU. TAKE CARE OF HER.**

*How could she?*

**KILL HER.**

I couldn't refuse the commands any longer, and the butcher knife slashed down upon Becca's head. She screamed. The blade cut into the side of her scalp. A perfect incision just above the ear. We had matching wounds.

Her blood dripped from the cut. I cocked the knife back for another strike. She held her hands up in defense, and I struck again, right into her palm. A stigmata wound with more blood—a deeper, richer red, as if I was chopping into the sticky sap of a tree. Primordial ooze seeped from her screams, from her tears. Chemicals exploding. I felt Becca's spirit like never before, like I hit a secret spot of her soul that was leaking into my own.

**FINISH HER. WE HAVE TO LEAVE.**

Becca was crying like a bloody newborn. A fresh coat of red paint covered the side of her head and her palms. Her plasma hung in the humid basement air, soaked into me, coated my lungs, my veins, letting me know for an instant what it was like to be her, living with the beast of addiction, then being slaughtered by the one who was supposed to love you.

She's been sliced up like this her whole life.

**FINISH HER.**

*I can't do it.*

**THEN LEAVE HER TO BLEED TO DEATH. THEY WON'T CHECK THE BASEMENT.**

*Don't check the basement.*

My mom and dad died in a tomb just like this. I felt their presence inside Becca's blood, coming into my soul through osmosis, the consciousness of all addicts penetrating my skin, all of them victims as much as villains, seeking love, comfort, understanding same as I did as a child, but being hurt instead. Seduced by a sweet lullaby full of promises but finding only suffering.

**KILL HER. SHE BETRAYED YOU. LIED TO YOU. SHE'S NOT FIT TO COME ALONG.**

I'M NOT KILLING HER! I shouted back. I summoned a collage of memories with Becca; nights in bed, twirled up in white sheets, eating mint chocolate chip ice cream. Watching her pick up her five-year sobriety chip, a glorious golden moment. Kissing the flesh of her neck, her blood beating just inches from my lips, nourishing us both with love and tenderness that I couldn't live without. How could I even consider this?

My skin stopped burning. I felt the scar tissue retreating. The angry girl returned to her place in the pit of my soul, nestled in some spiritual womb, a seed I would not feed any longer.

I had fought back the Whisperer. I had beaten her back to retreat.

I fell to my knees. I dropped the knife. My empty hands cooled with relief. I embraced Becca for all that she was, fearful at first she'd reject me, but she succumbed to my touch. I hugged her. We swayed to music that only we could hear. She apologized in my ear, I apologized back. We shared fluids and blood-soaked lives and became one.

I was holding what I needed. She understood what came over me, that it wasn't really who I was, just something hidden deep in my cellar. It was time to retreat to our safe room, the garden of our new Eden at the secluded cabin in Canada. Her cut would heal; we'd have our scars. We'd parent Joshua as if he was the first boy ever born.

But we were not alone in the basement.

The presence of cold metal snaked up my skin. A spider-like shadow dashed across the floor. My eyes caught sight of a tentacle growing like a barbed wire weed beside me.

It was an arm. First one, and then two. Skinny arms. Too skinny to poke a needle into and attached to a child with metal twists for eyes. Each strand of his wiry hair seemed to hiss, ready to strike.

**"SHE CAN'T COME WITH US."**

The voice came from some dark place in Joshua's heart, the murky depths where screams deferred got locked inside, waiting for their release. Joshua had transformed into Piper-Pippen. The cold metal, cartoon monster, who was his comforting light in the darkest of times, now controlled his creator's heart, and the beast refused to let Joshua be hurt by heroin any longer. Only one mom was fit, the other rejected.

**"NEVER AGAIN,"** he said, and the basement shook.

He wrapped his razor-sharp, barbed wire arms around

Becca's neck and squeezed. She gasped for air. Blood dotted her neck. Her fingers tugged at the metal noose cutting through flesh, threatening to sever her head right off.

I screamed loud enough to wake both God and Devil, begging Joshua to understand, that Becca can fight this war and win, don't kill her for losing one battle.

His metal twists of eyes had grown too cold. All he could understand was the rage and hurt he'd held in so long. The trapped scream in his heart was finally exploding. He squeezed tighter, his arms a barbed wire python cutting off the oxygen to her brain. Becca's face changed color. She had no air to breathe, no air to scream. Her eyes screamed for me to help her in the language of the dying. Save me Lizard, save me from him.

I begged, I pleaded. I yanked at his arms until my fingers grew bloody again, but the ball of rage that was Piper-Pippen wouldn't give. He only squeezed harder, and smiled his maniacal, cartoon grin.

I grabbed the butcher knife from the ground. It was all that was left. It was either let Becca be killed or put the knife into Piper-Pippen's heart. I had to do something. I had to decide if I should kill again. One of them needed to die. I couldn't take them both.

**ABOUT THE AUTHOR**
Mark Matthews is a graduate of the University of Michigan and a licensed professional counselor who has worked in behavioral health for over 20 years. He is the author of On the Lips of Children, Body of Christ, All Smoke Rises, Milk-Blood and the editor of Garden of Fiends: Tales of Addiction Horror. He lives near Detroit with his wife and two daughters. Reach him at WickedRunPress@gmail.com

# THE MELTING POINT OF MEAT

by

*JOHN F.D. TAFF*

# THE MELTING POINT OF MEAT

*JOHN F.D. TAFF*

THE KNIFE, IT'S A ZIPPER, RIGHT? It lets me open up and share the things that are inside me. Things that I'm too embarrassed or repressed to share.

Yeah, that's what I believed at first.

It lets me feel things that I am too numbed to feel.

Stupid now, huh?

Too many nights spent with teenage girlfriends, alone in my upstairs bedroom. While my parents snored away obliviously downstairs, we listened to My Chemical Romance or Death Cab for Cutie, talked about who was lame at school and who was lamer, huffed model glue or cans of air we lifted from Staples. You know, the kind that you use to blow crud from your computer keyboard. Blew our minds better than boys or music…or, fuck, even each other.

With a pocket knife that used to belong to my grandfather, we cut ourselves. Tentative, whisper-thin streaks down our arms, not vicious or deep like the boys we knew who also did this, who would then stand around and watch the blood patter around their feet. No, just enough to break the skin, to draw a red hairline. Just enough for the long-sleeve T-shirts we favored to cover. We winced as we did it, but we giggled just as much.

It was something to do, right? Something to share. Something that made us feel liked we understood each other when we really didn't even understand ourselves.

I mean, how could we?

But it also opened *something* within me.

When I did it, for a few seconds after, in the hazy adrenaline high of the pain, I would close my eyes—*but I could still see.*

Patterns, like some abstract thing close up, the details of it sharp and clear as if my eyes were open and pressed too close to clearly make it out. Like waking up hungover, sprawled across someone's cheap-ass Ikea throw rug, my eyes fluttering open onto its weave of coarse fibers twisted together with cat fur and curls of pubic hair.

I couldn't tell what it was, but each time I cut, each time I rode the blissful waves of pain, I saw it. Saw a little more clearly.

And like the endorphins that coursed through me each time, I wanted more.

To *see* more.

#

When was the first time I realized that pain brought pleasure?

In other words, when was the first hit I took, the first buzz I felt?

No, it wasn't in college or even high school. It was far earlier than that, in grade school. Can't remember exactly how old I was, probably six or seven, but I was out riding in our little cul-de-sac. It was a beautiful summer morning, all sun shining and birds chirping. Dogs barking in the distance. The static of cicadas providing background white noise.

That was back when parents would let their children, even little ones like I was, play outdoors out of sight. I think my mom was in the backyard hanging clothes on the line. Or more than likely on the phone with one of her cronies, seated at the kitchen table, twirling the cord and smoking Pall Malls one after the other, crushing them out in the chipped *Lake of the Ozarks* ashtray, bitching about my dad or having to deal with me during the summer break.

So there I was, racing all by myself. Don't remember having any friends with me that day. Round and round the center island of our little pocket street, on a bike or tricycle maybe. I can't precisely remember. Probably a Big Wheel, you know, the pink Barbie version my parents bought for me instead of the regular model with the red body, yellow fork and black wheel. Pink wheels? Yeah, whatever.

So I was out riding and took the curve too sharp and too fast, ended up wiping out spectacularly. Spilled ass over teakettle into the street, sliding across the concrete on my belly as if I'd just successfully stolen a base.

My little top protected my belly, but my short pants (probably a matching Garanimals outfit, knowing my mom) didn't offer much protection for my bare legs.

I lay there for a minute, dazed. When I rolled over, I saw the Big Wheel canted up onto the curb like a shipwreck, one of the rear wheels still turning slowly. Then I looked at my legs.

From shin to slightly above my knees, they were scraped by the rough concrete, the skin rucked up like pills on a favorite sweater, exposing raw flesh underneath, blood already beading there.

I remember staring at it for a long time, trying to make sense of it. Not what had happened, I knew that. I wrecked, wiped out. No, I mean the *why* of what I saw there, my scraped legs stretched before me.

I could already feel the pain, the hot stinging of all that abraded skin.

But I also felt, over it or under it, *pleasure*, the tingling of something warm and enjoyable... enjoyable, yeah. Something that felt distinctly *good*, like my mother brushing my hair out or lazing in the sun by the side of a pool. It was comforting, and I lay back staring at the blood on my legs and had that feeling, that epiphany you don't get very often in life of putting two things together and getting the larger picture.

Right there, sprawled in the middle of the street, I acted on that. I wanted more, with the same ache I felt when my mother snapped the television off mid-cartoon. And it was all good until I heard something that I eventually realized was my mother screaming.

She found me there, lying belly down on the street, in that sort of upward dog yoga pose (not that anyone had heard of that back then), dragging my body across the rough concrete, sanding the skin away, leaving a pale line of blood in my wake.

As she tells the story, my eyes were closed, my face almost transported into rapture.

She thought (still thinks) it was something sexual, unseemly precocious in nature. Me humping the concrete and leaving what looked like a smear of menstrual blood. And in front of the neighbors and all.

It was nothing of the sort, though it was entirely about pleasure.

And that indistinct, wholly malleable line between pleasure and pain.

But mostly about my *need* for both.

#

There were no sororities for me in college, no ma'am, even though my mother was a legacy at one of the biggest on campus. I crushed my mom in a whole lot of ways, I'm sure, but I never saw her more defeated than when I told her there was no way I'd be rushing her sorority. There'd be no dressing in whatever passed as the latest "in" fashion, no batting my eyes at the frat guys trying to ply me with beer to get into my panties, no sitting around having tea parties with flowery cups and linen doilies.

Whatever.

I obviously had no idea what went on in sororities and still don't and don't care.

My mom was disappointed, though, and I carried that in a backpack of other disappointments I lugged with me all the time, everywhere.

No, no sororities. I went into the dorms, where I settled in with a roommate from Missouri who introduced me to her profound sleep apnea. I, in turn, introduced her to my own brand of casual bisexuality. Within a month or so, we had our own little band of *gurrls*, kind of like our own sorority. We hung out, listened to Nine Inch Nails and Azar Swan. We dyed our hair ombres of dark turquoise and violet and garish pink, painted our nails black, wore ripped fishnet stockings and skirts that barely covered our asses.

And we cut ourselves.

As with all the other stuff, I showed them how. None of them had ever done it before. None of them had ever eaten pussy, either, but I showed them that, too.

By then, though, I had stopped believing that the knife was a zipper. I had changed the focus of why I did what I did.

My belief then was that we are balloons, and that our skin is a thin layer of material, like latex, holding all the swollen things within—the rush of blood, the twist of sinews, the slick conviviality of organs. A flick of the blade against the thin barrier that held this in, and it could be exposed for all to see. Nothing quite like sitting around in your dorm room naked with a few of your best buds, high AF, sliding a thin boning knife down your inner thigh, its miniscule, icily sharp tip leaving a furrow in your skin, like a boat skimming across a red sea.

Where before there had been little pain in my knife's meanderings, now it was more definite. I scored my flesh more deeply in college than in high school, deep enough for the little tip to disappear beneath my tight, white flesh, blood beading from the pores behind it.

The first time I had been brave enough to do this, Little Miss Missouri gasped, turned her head and yakked in the trash can her parents had given her, the one that sat beside her bed, the word *Princess* bedazzled across its pink steel side. The smell of her cheap wine vomit momentarily blotted out the sugar cookie scent of her Yankee candle, whose flame was the only light in the room.

As she freaked, I climbed into her bed, my skin sliding against hers. She thought I was trying to comfort her, and maybe I was. But as one hand went to her face to caress her cheeks and brush the tears away, to shush her trembling so that no one would batter at our door wondering what was wrong, the other slid the knife slowly, gently along the side of her breast.

She might have gasped as I did this, thinking it was just me, just my finger toying with the side of her firm, corn-fed tit. That I might trip a finger across her hardened nipple, before I...before...

I lowered my face to that bloody tit, sucked powerfully, then darted my lips to hers.

I saw her powerful confusion as she tasted herself on my tongue. She wept as she came, and we lay there bleeding, together.

Hello, my name is Livy, and I am addicted to pain.

#

The first hundred or so times I cut, felt the pain coursing through me, I didn't pay much attention to what my eyes showed me.

It was freaky, sure. But I was more caught up in the moment, in the trill of my nerve endings firing, transporting me to a place where there were no worries, no stresses, no concerns.

But eventually I realized that I am neither using the knife as a zipper nor that we're just blood-filled balloons. No, I came to know that I was actually trying to *see* more clearly. That the pain was trying to show me something large and profound. An unknown further from my rational perception than even Bro Culture and organized religion.

And I was quickly becoming hooked not just on the pain, but whatever it was that the pain was trying to show me.

#

I slid easily through the digestive tract of college, was shat out with little aplomb into a life I barely understood. Full-time job? Expectations? Responsibilities? I'd like to say I saw all this coming, that I knew it loomed like the tiptop of the head of some huge *kaiju*, tearing up the landscape just over the horizon.

But I didn't.

I spent four years drifting through coffee houses, doing the occasional paper or homework necessary to keep my solid C average, going to parties and concerts, seducing a whole procession of unlikely girls—from my sophomore Comparative Religions prof to a few of the cheerleaders of one of our school's basically worthless sports teams. I think it was football...or maybe basketball.

Whatever.

And then, suddenly, there I was in real life. And it sucked. Hard.

But pain, oh, pain was always there for me when I needed it.

And I *needed* it.

But unexpectedly, the cutting wasn't enough. Cutting seemed so juvenile, so tentative, so demure, even when I learned to cut deep, through the skin into the bright, red quivering muscle of my arms and thighs.

Not enough to help me cope with the sheer blunt force of reality.

Pain is a gateway, I was understanding.

And I was simply unable to get through the opening cutting afforded me.

It offered me a peephole.

I needed a window.

#

The sun slid through the slatted blinds like rays of dust. Early morning, rosy gold, easy light filled the bedroom, and Livy lay on her back, arm thrown over the pillow next to hers, staring at the pockmarked ceiling.

At her side, a thick, brown woman lay curled atop the bed, her skin dusky in the golden light. An eruption of dark curly hair sprayed over her pillow. Livy watched her round stomach, uncovered, rise and fall with each shallow, sleep-filled breath, her breasts drooping to either side of her chest.

Livy smiled, licked her lips, tasted the girl—Rayne? Rana? She couldn't remember. Reaching out, she touched the girl's hair, played with a few strands of it, letting it slip through her fingers, then grasping another few strands.

She rolled over to more closely study the girl's massive tit closest to her, deep olive skin finely pored, with enormous areola. As one hand toyed with her hair, her other gently prodded the girl's nipple, watched it tighten, harden.

The girl stirred at that, and Livy leaned in close, exhaled her warm breath over that erect nipple, watched the brown flesh gather, furrow.

"That's a nice way to wake up," she muttered, stretching and moaning under Livy's touch.

Livy moved closer, snuggling into the warm cleft of the girl's body. As she did, she untangled from the twist of the bedsheets.

There, at the end of the bed, was a large, irregular blood stain.

The girl—Raina, Livy finally remembered, relieved—craned her neck up to take a look.

"Yeah, about that..." she said.

"Don't worry," Livy murmured, burying her face in Raina's side. "We were both pretty drunk."

"It made a mess," Raina protested.

"I'll clean up later."

"Doesn't it hurt?"

"Of course it does. That's why I asked you to do it."

With waves of that pain drumming through her foot—seemingly intensified by talking about it—Livy wrapped herself around Raina and let the pain carry her away.

#

Later, in the bathroom as Raina snored, Livy sat on the edge of her bathtub, foot raised, propped on the edge of the sink. She examined the damage. The entire nail of the big toe of her right foot was torn away. Blood crusted the toe, slithered down her foot, and dried in a Rorschach blot at the base of her ankle.

She reached for a small kit case on the corner of the sink, unzipped it. Methodically, she pulled out a bottle of peroxide, a tube of Neosporin. Leaning back, she turned on the hot water in the tub, grabbed a washcloth, waited for the water to get hot.

Washing her foot thoroughly, gingerly daubing at the angry red of the exposed nail base, she cleaned the blood away. She wrung the washcloth in the flow of water from the bath, turning it momentarily pink.

She cleaned the nail bed delicately with peroxide, applied a blob of the ointment, then wrapped her toe in gauze, sealing it with a piece of white tape.

Livy could still feel it throb beneath the bandages, sending delicious pulses of buzzing warmth up her legs. She considered taking a few ibuprofen to take the edge off, but quickly dismissed it.

*Why harsh the buzz?*

She zipped the kit shut, set it back onto the counter.

Now, to get rid of the girl.

#

Raina dawdled at getting dressed, and Livy tried to suppress her growing annoyance. She sat at the small kitchen table outside the bedroom, sipping at a cup of black coffee, drumming her fingers on the table's surface.

"Never done anything like that…with anyone," Raina's voice floated in from the bedroom. Livy heard movement there, the rustling of the bed linens, clothes.

She rolled her eyes at Raina's statement. How many times in her life had she heard that?

"You mean the toe thing or the rest of it?" she asked, letting her tone slip partially into snide.

"The toe thing, of course," Raina huffed, sounding as if she were pulling on her jeans. "You'd be surprised, though. I've met a bunch of people that have that same...whaddaya call it? Fetish?"

Livy sneered at that word. How she hated it. Her fetish, was it? *Fetish* seemed such a suburban word to describe what she saw as normal as breathing or eating. Taking a piss wasn't a fetish, was it?

*Well*, she supposed, sipping at the coffee, *it could be.*

"Really?" was all she could allow in response.

"Yeah," Raina said, coming out of the bedroom, shrugging back into her retro Black Flag T-shirt. "One of the professors on campus is doing a study on pain. I've met a few people who are involved, people who're into that shit."

That thought piqued Livy's curiosity. A study on pain.

"What exactly are they studying?"

Raina shrugged and reached over to play with a strand of Livy's hair that had fallen across her face.

Livy was finished with pleasantries and intimacies, but she let Raina toy with her hair, at least until she answered.

"Not sure, but it's pretty hush-hush. They're paying people to participate in the studies, some nice coin from what I understand. I hear they're studying how much pain a person can endure, what it does to 'em. But..."

Livy tilted her head away from Raina's hands.

"But?"

Raina sighed, pulled her hand back. "I've met three of these people at parties. Never saw 'em again."

#

*Addicted.*

It's not a lovely word, is it?

I never liked it. I never liked thinking that I was beholden, to a person or a thing. I never liked the sound of needing something more than I could control. Of not being able to quit, of failed promises to stop. I was either cutting or thinking about the next slice, the next slam of a door against my fingers. Acting on it during the day, dreaming of it at night.

*Addicted.* I hate it.

Plus the word has *dick* in it.

Okay, that was a joke, but an honest one.

When did I realize that I was addicted to pain?

Right after high school and before college is when that particular curtain parted.

I was in love in high school. Who wasn't?

Her name was Jennie, and she was brilliant, beautiful, daring. And I loved her, loved her with the true, absolute, overly dramatic, gushing heart of an eighteen-year-old.

That summer we spent after graduating high school was idyllic. Making out in darkened, beer-smelling basements as music blared all around and boys hooted at the voyeuristic thrill of us kissing.

We made out in cars with the windows open, warm summer air flooding over us, pulling our long hair into streamers, carrying our laughter away.

We made out at friends' pools and darkened movie theaters where the air smelled of fake butter and dried, sticky soda and she tasted of strawberry lip balm.

And finally—literally—we made out at a swimming hole, just a few of our close friends at a pond on one of their parents' properties. Under a blazing July sun, unadulterated by clouds or propriety, we stripped off and dove into water that was muddy and smelled faintly of fish. We played and splashed, dove and swam blindly under the water, grabbing for each other's legs and asses.

We drank Boone's Farm Strawberry Hill and Everclear with grape Kool-Aid. We sunned ourselves on huge beach towels, applied lotion and zinc oxide, sprayed our hair with Sun-In.

And we talked, gabbled, really. About each other, about the coolest guys and prettiest girls. About the colleges we were all going to in just a few weeks.

One by one, as the day waned, the girls left, and it was just me and Jennie. She lay beside me on her towel, toyed with braiding and unbraiding my hair.

We were going to school soon, different schools.

And that was the end of it.

She told me as she braided my hair that we needed to grow, see other people. That this was an opportunity for us both to embrace.

Oh well, right? I mean, boo-fucking-hoo. How many relationships are ruined in that huge, gaping chasm between high school and college? It seemed so naïve, so innocent, so fucking small-town America.

I couldn't do much more than laugh. I thought it was light and effervescent on the cooling air. I'm sure, to Jennie, I sounded like a maddened hyena.

She left me there, stretched nude under the early evening sun pushing through the trees that skirted the edge of the pond. Its light was colored golden-green, coruscating over the brown sheet of the water.

I felt the wind toy at my hair, and it reminded me of her.

I sat, pulled my knees up and rested my head there, thought of crying.

My hand, blindly, found a rock near the edge of my towel, the size of a good orange. The fingers curled around it exposed the promise ring she'd given me just a few months prior. A stupid thing, a girlie thing. A thin band of silver and some tiny flake of a blue stone she told me was sapphire, but was probably glass.

We'd laughed over it, but I wore it every day since.

No more.

I tore at it, trying to get it off, trying to remove the reminder of her I carried with me. It refused to slide over my knuckle. I twisted and turned it furiously, sputtering in anger.

Then, the rock.

I flipped it to my other hand, splayed the ring hand's fingers on the ground, brought the rock up until it eclipsed the sun.

Down, hard onto the ring. But mostly the finger.

A surge of pain roared up my arm, and before I could stop myself, I brought the rock smashing back down again and again.

Each time, that pain burst over me, washed things away. My threat of tears, yes, but also all thoughts of that other pain caused by Jennie. Her departure. Her absence.

I felt disconnected from my emotional wound but fully embraced by this physical one. It seemed nurturing and kind, even sexual in a way.

With each blow of the rock, the pain seemed to soften into pulses of warmth that throbbed up my arm, lapped against my consciousness like the waves of some deep, uncharted ocean.

I saw the vision even then, though it took me years to recognize it. It opened onto me as if a slit had been cut in my closed eyelids, and the darkness came rushing in. But it wasn't the darkness of the night sky and the glittering grains of its stars. No, it was some deeper darkness, something bigger than that, bigger than empty space, at once ancient and otherly.

And from that, swimming across my vision like a glimpse of some unimaginably huge leviathan, an indistinct pattern there in the darkness behind my closed eyes; something vague, as if glimpsed through chiffon. Something I couldn't quite make out.

All I knew then was the pain. I orgasmed from it and passed out.

When I came to, it was night, full-on summer night, stars scattered over a hazy sky and crickets crazily *skree-skreed*. I pulled myself up, my hand throbbing. I put on my clothes, gathered my stuff in my good hand, and made my way to my car.

Under the dome light, I could see my hand was a mangled mess. The promise ring was gone, as was much of the skin of the back of my hand. The ring finger was crooked as hell, bent and smashed, as were the two fingers on either side.

Oh, shit, yes, it was all broken. The next day at the emergency room, I was told I'd shattered quite a few of the bones in that hand. I told my mother that I was so upset I punched a rock. Close enough to what had actually happened. She bought it so easily. I knew she just wasn't comfortable pressing for the actual truth. It wasn't the first time she'd ignored the scars tattooed across my flesh, the telltale marks I did my best to hide, and she did her best to overlook.

And for the next few weeks, alone in my room most of the time, I toyed with the broken fingers jutting from the plaster cast signed by no one. I pulled at them, pushed them, anything to elicit the delicious waves of pain.

It wasn't just easier to deal with this pain than the Jennie-induced pain.

It was preferable.

And I clearly needed it.

\#

Livy was able to extract the professor's name, a doctor really, from Raina as she frog-armed her out the door that morning.

Alan Atryx, Ph.D., Senior Director of the Laboratory of Cognitive Physics for the big state university that dominated the little Midwestern town. He taught classes, mostly upper-level independent labs and arcane genetics courses. He was a faculty member of the applied physics program, though Livy had no idea what any of that meant, and was stymied as to what connection existed between pain addiction and applied physics.

She sought him out in the school's online page for the department's faculty, but didn't learn much. Tenured, been at the university for 15 years. Plain looking, with a receding hairline, a Van Dyke beard and hipster-looking wireframe glasses. He looked as if he wore short-sleeved white button-up shirts complete with a pocket of pens. A nerd. A geek. A dweeb.

Not a professor who studied pain or the people who pursued it.

Livy wondered if Raina had been wrong, if she'd misheard or misunderstood what people had relayed to her.

#

The music pulsed and blared. Some unidentifiable Euro Techno dance stuff. The DJ, promoted on the club's fliers out front, was hidden behind his rack of instruments and turntables, effaced by the blasts of multi-colored strobe lights and his own bulky hoodie and ball cap. He bobbed and weaved, alternately throwing switches and huddling over his laptop.

Livy was covered in sweat from dancing to the frenetic music, her Radio Buzzkills tank top sticking to her collarbone, a line of perspiration clinging to her spine. Her hair swung about her face, matted with moisture. Salty lines tracked from her forehead down her cheeks.

The girl who'd gravitated close to Livy smiled as she caught her eyes through the thick curtain of her hair. A little mousey, Livy thought, but she liked a mousey girl. Perhaps they'd go back to her place, play a little, shed some blood.

As much as Livy enjoyed the dancing, the hectic thrum of the music, the enclosed heat of the club, she needed a fix. She needed to feel that electric slice of pain coruscating from whatever body part she injured directly into her brain. She needed that surge of dopamine, needed to bathe her nervous system in it.

But more than that, she needed to *see* again, to catch a glimpse of the elusive thing that her open, pain-free eyes couldn't discern.

She needed…*needed to see more*.

Maybe this girl would go home with her and use one of the many crowbars Livy kept on hand—knife or hammer or paddle—to help her pry that door open, get a better look. Lately, she'd found herself more often than not home alone, curled into a ball on the floor, body wracked with pain. Fingers and limbs sticky with blood, smeared over the tiles, drying on the edge of the bathtub. Tears down her cheeks, urine-soaked panties clinging to her when she'd hurt herself so badly her bladder would void.

She kinda missed having a person there with her, to be there as she rode the waves of pain and pleasure, to be with her as she came down, to hold her, comfort her maybe.

Then, of course, to leave.

Livy sidled up to the bar, took an empty seat among the other crushed people, sitting and standing, trying to get the bartender's attention. Livy waited her turn patiently, still breathing heavily, still sweating profusely.

As she turned to scan the room, someone appeared before her, startling her with both suddenness and proximity.

"I wondered where you went," the girl shouted near Livy's ear. "I thought I'd scared you off. Or bored you."

Livy found herself smiling. The girl was evidently not as mousey as Livy had believed.

"Neither. Can I get you a drink?" Livy said, half turning to see if bartender was any less busy. She wasn't.

"Sure. I'll have a 7 and 7," the girl said. "And I bet you'll have…wait a minute, let me guess."

The woman stared intently at Livy through her wireframe glasses.

"Something unexpected. Not beer. A gin and tonic, maybe."

Livy found her smile widening.

"How'd you guess that?"

"Just a good cold reader of people, that's all. If you're buying me a drink, can I sit here?" She gestured at a seat that Livy hadn't seen had opened.

"Sure, of course!"

Livy swiveled around and gestured to the seat just as the bartender came and took their order.

"If I'm buying you a drink, can I at least get your name?" she asked.

"Daphne," the girl said.

"That's funny, you really look more like a Velma," Livy said.

Daphne shrugged, tilted her head, and instantly Livy knew that she wasn't the first or even the fiftieth person to ever draw that comparison.

"Well, at least a sexy Velma," she said, trying to salvage the situation.

Daphne smiled, and Livy was certain that smile was sincere.

The bartender returned, Livy paid, and the two clanked glasses before sipping their respective drinks.

"You come..." Livy asked.

"You a townie or a uni?" Daphne asked at the same time.

The two laughed, each took another sip.

"Your question first," Livy said. "I was a uni, now I'm a townie. You know, couldn't get away and all."

"Okay," Daphne laughed. "I guess you were gonna ask me if I come here often?

Livy nodded.

"Not really. I work a lot of odd hours, don't often have the time to get out and do this," Daphne said.

"Yeah, I come here...well, a lot, I guess. Never seen you before. Glad I did."

"Me too."

The DJ took a break, and the two spent the next fifteen talking about themselves in the kind of rushed generalities reserved for two people circling a pick-up before the music began again.

As Livy felt she was close to closing the deal, Daphne did something unexpected. She reached out and touched the hairline scars that crisscrossed Livy's arm.

At first, she said nothing, just let her fingers brush softly across the raised bits of dead, pink flesh, playing them like a tonearm across the grooves of a vinyl record. Livy felt goosebumps race across her skin, and she exhaled loudly.

Daphne leaned in, even though the DJ was still on hiatus.

"Do you cut yourself for pain or pleasure?" Daphne asked, so close that Livy breathed in her warm breath, redolent of cheap whiskey and lemon-lime soda.

"Both, but not anymore," Livy said before she realized the words were spilling past her lips.

Daphne raised an eyebrow, but said nothing, didn't stop tickling Livy's arm.

"Not cutting, anyways. You can only cut so deep before things get too serious. Nah, I've moved on to other stuff."

"Such as?"

Now it was Livy's turn to raise an eyebrow. "Let's just say more pain. And if you want to know more than that, there's a place I can take you to talk about it."

"And where is that?" Daphne said, clearly knowing exactly where Livy hinted.

And in about twenty minutes, they found themselves there.

#

The next morning, Livy opened her eyes onto light streaming through the blinds of her bedroom, carving paths in the dust that spun lazily in the air.

She breathed in and smelled something that was not familiar. Turning her head, she saw an unexpected lump under the covers, then remembered that she'd brought someone home with her.

*Darnelle? Dolores?*

Livy leaned up on one elbow, stared across the bed. She saw the girl's spray of auburn hair across the pillow, her glasses folded neatly on the nightstand.

*Daphne.*

Her movement stirred the other girl, and she rolled over, blinked.

"Good morning," she said, breathing in deeply, breathing out slowly.

"Yeah, so, if you're the kind to linger in bed, grab breakfast together at some local café…" Livy began.

"What time is it?"

"I dunno, about seven, I guess."

"Shit. I gotta get going. Work and such," Daphne said,

throwing the covers off and bending to the floor to find her clothes.

"Well, I had a great time," Livy said, watching her backside as she found her jeans, slipped into them, pulled her bra and shirt on.

"Yeah, me, too," Daphne said, pulling on her boots. "But I gotta say, your scary talk of pain never really materialized."

Livy rolled her eyes. "Yeah, well, about that. I think I just wanted the company."

"Sure thing," Daphne said.

Livy bristled at how breezily the other girl accepted that. As if she didn't believe her claims of pain-induced pleasure. "Well, I mean, I normally do get into stuff that scares a lot of other girls away."

"I'm sure you do…really," Daphne said, lacing her boots.

"Look, I've broken fingers, cut down to the muscle, hammered my toe fucking flat. How's that?" Livy felt a little flare of anger now, as if her credentials were being challenged.

"Okay," Daphne said, turning to face her on the bed. "It's just that, in my profession, I see a lot of people addicted to pain and pleasure. *A lot.* It's no big deal."

"Your profession?"

"I work on campus. I'm a lab assistant for a scientist who's studying pain."

Livy blinked.

"Dr. Alan Atryx?"

Daphne's brow furrowed.

"How'd you…?"

"How'd you like to grab a quick breakfast at a local café?" Livy asked, fumbling for her own clothes.

#

Livy watched Daphne slide the meticulously cream-cheesed half of her French toast bagel into her mouth, then chew methodically, rolling her eyes and bobbing her head before she swallowed and answered the question.

"I can't really tell you too much about it," she said, licking a smear of cream cheese from the heel of her hand, nearly derailing Livy's train of thought. "It'll screw up your responses."

Livy frowned. "But it's definitely a study on pain, addiction to pain?"

Daphne cocked her head. "Sort of."

"Well," Livy said, reaching across the table and staying Daphne's hand from sliding in another bite of her bagel. "Can you get me in? Can I be part of the study?"

"You want to be a lab assistant? Or...do you want to be part of the study? I mean, a subject."

"Yes!" Livy said, so loud and excited that other coffee drinkers, at least the ones without their ear buds in, turned and stared. "Yes, a lab subject. I'm a natural."

Daphne considered this, her hand still clutched by Livy, the half-eaten bagel poised in mid-air.

"Okay, if you let me eat my breakfast, I can see what I can do about that. But I need to finish so I can get over there. And I should warn you that Dr. Atryx is particular. Very, very particular."

"That's okay," Livy said. "I doubt he's met anyone exactly like me."

"You'd be surprised," Livy said, looking doubtful as she shoved the bagel in.

#

When does it become too much?

Have you ever thought of that? I doubt it. Few addicts, myself included, do. Why would you?

But think about it with me for a minute. When does the need for something, the raw, aching desire for something, become an addiction?

What's the razor line between the two? When do you finally reach the point where you need a substance to fill that huge, gaping hole in your life? And nothing else can?

When does the desire for two doughnuts become the obsession, the need to eat two or three or a dozen every day?

That sounds silly, I know.

So when does the happy, playful *let's try a hit of meth* turn into the overwhelming need to tweak until you're scratching at the lesions under your hair, staring at your suddenly loose grey teeth in the bathroom mirror, shaking, shivering, desperately needing that next one, that last one, that only one?

It's as subtle and shifting as that indefinable line between pleasure and pain.

What a question.

If an addict knew that, knew the invisible line, where it was, what lay beyond it, do you think they'd ever cross over? Do you think they'd willingly trade simple need for addiction?

If you are an addict, you know the answer to that question.

Yes. Resoundingly yes.

#

And that was how Livy found herself, three days later, in a cold, antiseptic room deep in the basement of the extraordinarily secure Cognitive Physics building, strapped to a table, stripped down to bra and panties and hospital gown, wired from head to toe.

She looked across the room to the large window that opened slightly above, overlooking where she lay. It was just plain glass, the technicians behind not embarrassed or discomfited by what they were doing, at least not enough to demand one-way glass. Three of them milled about back there, white lab coats, hair pulled up, all wearing glasses.

Livy waved at Daphne, who waved timidly back evidently cautious about showing too much deference to Livy.

The two techs in the room, one of whom was obviously the medical lead, strapped a blood pressure cuff around her upper left arm, making sure the finger sheath measuring her pulse was taped snugly. He reached above her head to click some apparatus on a table behind her, then leaned in close.

"Okay, we're ready. Are you?"

"Yep. Ready and rarin' to go," she answered, to which he frowned a little.

"Now, you understand we're going to hurt you, right? Things are going to be…well, *unpleasant.*"

"Counting on it, doc."

His frown deepened.

"The panic button is strapped to your left arm," he said, indicating the almost comically large red button on an elastic strap there. "Punch it, and you're done. We'll end the test as quickly as is possible."

"Got it."

"The first few tests will be purely chemical. We have some pretty nasty pharmaceuticals that can cause all sorts of internal pain without leaving any permanent debilities. The other three tests will be more...physical."

"I read all the literature and signed all the waivers, doc. I'm good to go. Really."

He looked at Livy, curious yet doubtful.

"All right, then," he said, rising and turning away. "Let's begin."

He made a motion toward the folks behind the glass. Livy raised her head and looked back toward Daphne again, smiled broadly for her.

Daphne nodded briskly, turned her attention to a bank of computer monitors.

Livy heard a chime from the intercom in the room, and the last tech came close, lifted the first of four syringes from a neat row of them arrayed on a small stainless steel table to her right.

Livy felt the needle slip in, a little tickle of pleasure, nothing more.

It took a few seconds, but Livy squirmed on the table. She felt a curious itch build in her skin, as if it crawled with formication. The sensation was unexpected. She was prepared, aching really, for some initial bomb of pain that would overwhelm her, but she saw this for what it was. Testing, cautiously measuring her ability to absorb pain.

But it grew until it felt like every square inch of her skin was crawling with ants. And not just swarming, stinging, piercing her, filling her with their venom.

Twisting atop the table, she vaguely noticed her arms and legs were strapped down, inhibiting her movements. As awful as it was, it was still fairly mild on the pain scale, ultimately only tickling at her pleasure center.

After the letdown of knowing that this wasn't going to give her the experience she sought, she relaxed on the table and lay there passive, staring at the ceiling.

She could hear the quiet ping of some instrument, the muffled voices of the techs in the next room. She sighed, hoping it wasn't all going to be such a letdown. Anxiously waited for the next syringe.

She heard the click and whoosh of a door opening, the sneaker-clad footfalls of the tech re-entering the room. A hand lifted the second syringe, and Livy barely felt its tip slide into her, blurred by the dying sensation of creepy-crawlies. The tech wasn't even out of the room when the substance injected into Livy's bloodstream exploded like a fireball.

Almost literally, Livy thought, remembering how shots of that cinnamon-laced liquor felt as they landed in her stomach. That initial blast and *wow!* of detonation, then that delicious wave of heat spreading from it.

Whatever this stuff was, it seemed to burst out not from her stomach, but from all of her, as if the explosive was in every artery, vein and capillary. It lit her blood afire and burned there, lingering like that liquor did on her breath, her lips. But this stuff…oh, this stuff was liquid pain, intense and unremitting.

She twisted a bit at its whole-body embrace, felt it ignite the neural pathways within her that only moved in one direction, like the slam of a body against a pinball machine can only lead to *Tilt!*

Pleasure sifted down from all this, a soothing sprinkle of snow against a sunburn. Her twisting atop the table turned to writhing, stretching her legs against it, curling her toes. A moan escaped her lips, became a burst of gathered breath that gasped from her like an exhalation of her very soul.

She closed her mouth to tether its end inside her, felt the feeling disperse, ebb, ebb, slip away finally.

She shivered on the table, as much from the shadow of that pleasure as from the cold.

Another chime, then, and the door opened behind her.

She breathed heavily, not quite panting but desperate to get that feeling back, desperate to cling to that life raft of pleasure adrift on the expanse of the bleak sea of her life.

The tech leaned in.

"This one takes a moment. It's two drugs. The first counteracts the injection you just had. The second…well, you'll definitely feel it when it kicks in. I'll be nearby with the counteragent for it. If you want to tap out, end the experiment, slap the button there on your left arm. I'll give you the shot immediately."

"Please, please just do it," Livy moaned through clenched teeth. "Please, I need it. I need you to do it. Give it to me."

Vaguely embarrassed by the junkie tone of her voice, the wheedling, almost sexual need there, Livy swallowed hard, focused straight on the tech's face.

"Please."

The tech acquiesced, plucking the third syringe from the table, bringing it to her arm, plunging the chemicals into her.

She had time to watch the tech step back, place the empty syringe onto the table, then take up the fourth one, the last one.

Livy saw that her hand was shaking, the tip of the needle wavering, sparkling in the creamy light of the fluorescents.

And then it all went blank.

What fluttered through her mind, like short glimpses revealed in the burst of a strobe, were those images seen on grade school videos about nuclear war. The blistery, ascending, expanding burst of a hydrogen bomb. The strange, midnight shots of the pressure wave rippling out, bursting over houses, utterly shredding them, carrying the now disparate parts off into the radioactive night.

Livy felt the way it might have felt to be inside those images. Whatever the substance was they'd injected her with detonated in her body like the death of a star, first imploding, collapsing into her center, then violently exploding, throwing everything that was her, all of her, out, out, out.

Livy shrieked, and her body arched up on the table, head jittering on its surface, her heels drumming against the bottom. And in between, frozen like an electric arc, Livy's body strained against the restraints that held her to the table.

She knew she'd bitten her tongue, could taste the blood trickling down her throat. But the pain was lost in that cataclysmic, annihilative supernova of agony. It eclipsed anything Livy had ever felt in her life, wiping her mind clear of the first syringe's pathetic effects and even the more robust effort of the second syringe.

The pleasure from this was also more than she'd ever experienced, nearly more than she could take in. Almost as if she was a keyhole that was capable of accepting only the first few cuts of the key.

But those few cuts released all of the tumblers inside her.

Her body arched like that for an entire minute. Livy was

vaguely aware that the tech had stepped forward, the syringe in hand, waiting for some sign that Livy wanted to end this.

Livy didn't want to end this, though. Never wanted to end this. *Ever.*

But she was aware that the pressure wave of the detonation had swept through her, the vanguard of that pain had passed.

But as that faded, the curtains of her closed eyes raised, and she could see.

Something unimaginably huge and unbelievably sinuous twisted across her vision, completely filling it. She could sense the movement almost more than see it, so close was her focus on whatever the thing was.

It seemed segmented or composed of sections, moving together as smoothly as water. Iridescent midnight purple where colors shifted across its surface like oil on water.

And then it was gone, and she was left staring at the blank insides of her eyelids, her muscles taut and exhausted.

Slowly, she lowered herself to the table. Her back ached, her calves burned.

But more than that, she felt the usual after effects of one of her highs. Slightly anxious now, exposed atop the table, cold. Her mouth was completely dry, and she felt panic setting in. At the edges of her frayed senses, an overwhelming lethargy was creeping in. She knew that she needed, more than anything else now (except, let's be honest, another hit of whatever that drug was they'd injected into her last) was to crawl into bed, pull the sheets up over her head, and crash.

That, at least right now, was not going to happen.

Her eyes fluttered open onto the unforgiving fluorescents. She blinked and licked her lips with a tongue that felt like a lizard's.

Someone approached. A shadow fell over her. She assumed it was the tech, maybe with some other syringe meant to slip inside her and make her feel better. She prepared to wave her off.

"That's all," came a reedy, male voice. "I'm afraid we can't use you in my study."

Livy lifted her head.

It was the man she'd seen in the staff listing on the department's internet page. Dr. Alan Atryx. He looked down at her, a bit fussily she thought, then looked over to the window where a few of the techs still clustered.

"Wait," Livy said, but he ignored her and walked back toward the door.

As he reached for the knob, she said the only thing she could think of.

"But I saw it. I really *saw* it this time."

Dr. Atryx turned, and, surprisingly, smiled at her.

#

Pain addiction?

Like what the fuck, right?

You can't be addicted to pain. Addiction is for things like meth or coke or oxycodone. Booze or pills or pot. But not pain.

How the fuck can you be addicted to pain?

Something my mother used to say to me, after I was stupid enough to tell her.

You don't see addicts crouching in dark alleys bashing their heads against the bricks, do you?

You don't see someone willing to trade a blow job for just one hit.

You don't see junkies lounging on filthy mattresses in derelict buildings breaking each other's fingers.

But come on, if Robert Palmer was right, and you might as well face it you're addicted to love, then why would pain be so far off the mark?

I've never stolen money or cruised dangerous streets in bad parts of town to get a fix of what I need, but I have traded sex for it plenty of times, so what? I've wheedled and begged for it, foregone relationships because of, forgotten to eat or drink or go out of the house for long periods. Felt the deep ache of withdrawals, the cravings, the thrill of the fix, and the desperation to do more.

Point is, I've done everything a good addict would do to score a hit of what I need. What I'm addicted to.

Besides, pay attention.

I've already told you.

I'm addicted to *two* things.

And I already knew at this point that one of them was gaining the upper hand on the other.

#

One of the drab, generic lab techs (not Daphne) led Livy to a drab, generic room, where her clothing hung limply on wire hangers inside a flimsy Ikea pressboard wardrobe. She dressed quickly, sitting on the lone plastic chair scooted across the room, up against the featureless beige wall.

When she was dressed, she opened the door to find the same lab tech still standing outside, waiting.

"Come with me," she said, turning down the long beige hallway, walls unadorned, floors of the kind of hard speckled linoleum favored by institutions. "Dr. Atryx wants to speak with you."

Livy followed, wondering if this woman was the one who administered the syringes to her. Who had stood by watching while she writhed in pain on the cold medical table.

*My kind of girl,* Livy thought to herself. *Maybe I'll see her sometime out at the club. Or under my sheets.*

She walked behind her through a bewildering series of turns and cross backs, to a nondescript set of elevators. The tech pushed the button, smiled thinly at Livy.

Livy considered saying something to her, but what crossed her mind were only stupid things like *Come here often?* or *So, when do you get off?* She decided instead to remain as quiet as the tech.

The elevator doors finally opened. Inside, the car looked as if it had arrived straight from the 1950's. It was painted a scuffed light green. The buttons were simple black ones, unlit. The entire car was draped in heavy, quilted fabric, the kind movers use in freight elevators to prevent furniture from banging around.

Once inside, the tech inserted a key card into an unidentified slot under the numbered buttons, and the car lurched into motion. Livy had no idea what floor they were on. The buttons went from 4 to B, and they were clearly going down. But either the car moved in almost ancient slowness or they descended well past B.

Just when Livy began to feel that there was something truly amiss, the car heaved to a stop, and the doors banged open. She followed the tech down another series of hallways, these dotted along their length with windowless metal doors, most bearing placards with a series of numbers that seemed not part of any pattern nor meaning Livy could discern.

At one of these doors, just like any of the others, the tech stopped, waited for Livy to stand beside her. Then, she opened the door onto a simple office. A potted, obviously plastic fern stood in the corner. Two chairs faced a plain wooden desk. Nothing was on the desk, not a pen, not a photo, not a piece of paper.

And behind it sat Dr. Alan Atryx, looking as if he had been sitting there waiting quietly this entire time.

"Thank you, Marcie," he said, and she backed from the room, closed the door. "Please have a seat. Livy, is it? Splendid."

Livy turned, saw what looked like relief wash over the tech's face as she closed the door behind her.

"So, you performed adequately on the first set of tests. But what you said there at the end, well, I'm not going to lie to you. That stopped me cold."

Livy turned back from the closed door to face Dr. Atryx. His demeanor was now wholly different than it had been in the exam room. There he seemed brusque and annoyed. Now, he came across more like a game show host, casual, almost jovial.

"Well, I'm still not quite sure what this is all about," Livy said, looking around the small office to find something, anything that signified that the man actually worked here, that this wasn't just some room he happened to wander into and sit behind an empty desk. But there was nothing. Cubicles at the DMV had more flair than this space.

"Let me just stop you right there," he said, raising a small, manicured hand. "You're here for what you think is a pain study, am I right?"

Livy blinked. "Well, yeah, I thought so."

"It's not *really* a pain study. At least not *precisely*."

Livy waited because it sounded to her as if he was now going to launch into an explanation of exactly what it was. But he didn't. He simply stopped talking, staring at her across the desk.

"Then...what is...it?" she stammered.

"Well, that's it, isn't it? If it's not a pain study, what was all that up there?" he asked, circling a single finger up toward the plain acoustic tiles of the ceiling. "I mean, why would we just put you through all that? Yowtch!"

With that, he practically leapt from his chair, pushed it back behind him and jumped to his feet. Had Livy been a more excitable person, she might have yelped in fear. As it was, she did flinch.

"So I suppose we owe you some kind of explanation, don't we?"

He came around to her side of the desk, stood fairly close to her in this small room. She could smell him now, a combination of seemingly disparate odors—chalk dust, breath mints, some kind of cheap aftershave and something else. Something that underlay them all, just a hint of it, a whiff with every breath Livy drew in. Something that, weirdly enough, made Livy think of that unknown thing she saw through the door pain opened inside her. Something slick and sinuous and almost greasy.

That foundational smell was sort of musky, sort of sweet, sort of spoiled, and she closed her mouth against it, held her breath.

"Well, I guess so…"

"Not that you didn't get anything from it, though, right?"

At this, he winked lasciviously at her, and she might not have been more surprised if he'd have licked his lips.

"Let's go. I have something to explain to you, but I think we need a little cheerier setting."

Livy hesitated. She was becoming surer and surer that whatever this strange little man wanted to show her might involve her eventual appearance before a Title IX Board of Inquiry.

"It's certainly nothing like that," Atryx said, holding the door open for her.

Confused, Livy stood and followed him back into the hallway.

#

"Are you familiar with any studies of consciousness? Of, say, sleep and its whys and wherefores?" He looked across the table at Livy, who stared at him blankly.

After following the strange little scientist through the rabbit's warren of blank hallways somewhere underneath the building, he'd led her to the foyer at its first-floor entrance. Afternoon sunlight beamed through its airy atrium and played off the abstract aluminum sculpture that sat in the pool of a fountain gurgling away at the center of the space.

They were seated in two cushiony lounge chairs nestled behind the fountain from the main entrance. A few people milled about here and there. A coffee kiosk near the main bank of elevators bustled with what Livy assumed were researchers getting their afternoon fixes.

These were not the elevators she and Dr. Atryx had just ridden up on. That was farther back, behind an unmarked security door.

Everything that had occurred so far today—from the actual medical tests to this on-the-go discussion with Atryx—was all so surreal that Livy had simply detached her questioning mind from what was going on. Not able to make much sense of it, she just took it all in.

"Sleep?" she asked. "I'm not sure I understand."

"No, of course you don't," he said, managing to sound condescending and not condescending all at once. "Let me explain a few things that may sound digressive, but will ultimately tie back to where we are now. Will you indulge me?"

Livy didn't reply for a second, so thoroughly had she detached herself, but Atryx's lingering look carried such a weight of expectation that it eventually hammered through her stupor.

"Oh...I...sorry," she stammered. "Of course."

Dr. Atryx uttered a little, fussy sigh, then proceeded.

"Sleep offers somewhat of a mystery to researchers. Prior to going to bed, your brain is very active, very alert. Brain waves are cycling up and down at thirty or forty times per second. Like Buddy Rich on steroids."

He paused a beat, waited for a reaction from Livy. But she had no idea who Buddy Rich was, and Atryx moved on.

"So, frenetic, erratic brain waves prior to bed. Got it? Asynchronous, no predictable rhythm. How does all that result in sleep? Well..." he explained, then paused to consider his next words.

"Picture a music concert, some sort of alternative rock from the looks of you. The audience is packed, restive. The stage is set with a single microphone. Everyone in the audience is talking about different things to different people, all at the same time. This represents your brain prior to sleep. Each audience member represents a different brain cell, each occupied with a different yet important activity. Everything is chaotic.

"But then sleep comes. This chaos becomes synchronized. All that chatter in the audience calms down, and everyone seems to be suddenly singing the same quiet, slow song. It's as if something or someone has taken the stage with a commanding presence, commanding enough to get every single member of the audience to sing along at its volume and cadence."

He paused to see if Livy was still paying attention. Apparently satisfied that she was, he continued.

"In the brain, the singer, if you will, is something in the middle of your frontal lobe that emits these slow waves of non-rapid eye movement sleep. That single organ or cluster of cells is what opens your brain to sleep. It organizes the millions, the billions of chaotic cells that compose your mind and focuses them on that one thing. Opening the doorway into sleep.

"I'm after the same type of thing, but on a wholly different, cosmological level. I'm attempting to organize the chaos of humanity in much the same way, to bring a disparate group of consciousnesses together for a single purpose that we'd otherwise never have."

Livy shook her head, trying to organize Dr. Atryx's flood of words into something that made sense.

"What does this all have to do with pain? With me?"

Dr. Atryx smiled. "If we're to keep with our charming analogy, pain is the song we need to get the audience to sing. And you, Livy, you, I think, are the singer. And I desperately need someone to lead my chorus. That is, if we're going to open that door and see…really see…what's behind it.

"Think about your answer, my dear. Be certain. Do you want to fully see what you've only caught glimpses of your entire life? Are you ready?"

"Yes," Livy answered without considering the implications of everything he'd said. "Absolutely fucking yes."

#

Livy went home propelled on a wave of perplexity and anticipation the likes she'd never experienced before. Perplexity because she still had no clear idea what Atryx had been trying to say. Anticipation because she still somehow felt that he held the key to the one thing she wanted above all else.

That perfect hit, that ultimate high she'd been seeking, the orgasmic blast of hurt that had become her life's one overriding need, that one sublime toke of pain that would push her right to the edge—of herself, of her consciousness, of death. She wasn't sure which, not even sure she needed to be sure.

That one hundred-percent, uncut, unadulterated line of pain so pure it would unlock that doorway inside herself, to finally, *wholly* see what was on the other side.

She wondered, as she sat curled in her bathroom, smashing at the third toe on her left foot over and over with the hammer she kept under the bathroom vanity for just such occasions, she wondered if her doorway was the same Dr. Atryx was attempting to open.

*Bang! Bang! Bang!*

And if so, what would they find on the other side?

#

A few nights later, Livy lay in bed absently flipping through her dog-eared copy of *Hidden Bodies,* not really watching an episode of *Dateline.*

"I want to possess all the dark yellow copies ever made and keep them in the basement so that only Amy and I can touch them." She loved that line, loved its inherent addiction.

Something about Joe's obsessions—with books, with killing—stuck in Livy's head, like a plug of hair in the shower drain, refusing to be washed away. His addictions (and, frankly, those of most of the other characters) spoke to her so truthfully, she'd read the book at least a dozen times.

Her cell rang. Not expecting anyone, she peered down on its illuminated screen to see a picture of Velma from *Scooby-Doo.* She'd humorously added this to her contact should Daphne prove to be a more-than-once hook-up.

Smiling despite her best efforts, she answered the phone.

"Well, hello there, kitty," she purred. "Long time no hear."

There was an awkward pause.

"Umm, yeah," Daphne said. "Look, if you really want to be a

test subject in this study, meet us here at the lab building, out front, at 10 p.m. There's a little field trip involved."

"A field trip?" Livy asked, momentarily nonplussed. "OK, errr, do I have to bring anything. A permission slip from my mommy?"

The attempt at humor was lost on Daphne as she had hung up.

#

When does it slip over, eh?

When does an addiction cross into something that flirts with death?

All addictions ultimately do. You understand that, right?

I don't care if you're addicted to sour cream or crystal meth. Everything that becomes an addiction leads to death. Full stop. Literally.

I'm well aware that every addict's family—*my family*—has already rehearsed the late night phone call where some unknown voice tells them their loved one is dead. But I'm also well aware that addicts only fear death because it means we'll no longer be able to get our high again.

What that death looks like takes its form from the particular addiction. Whether it's slumped in the grungy bathroom of some doom metal club, a twist of hose tied around your arm, a needle stuck in a vein. Or on a gurney in an operating room, surgeons valiantly trying to bypass your fat-clogged heart. Its shape may be endless, but in the end it's all death.

Did I answer the question?

When does an addiction become death?

From the very first nip of a needle, the very first spoonful of sour cream.

Death is there, waiting, tapping its fingers restlessly but confidently.

From that moment on, you can't do anything but ride the rails. Oh and by the way? Those fuckers are greased.

Yeah, I know what you're saying. You're saying the obvious. The thing that everyone says, sitting on their La-Z-Boys, feet up in their living rooms, Fox News blaring on the television, staring at the wife's Precious Moments figurine collection. You're saying just *get off*. Stop feeding the beast.

*Just stop being addicted.*

I got news for you, Nancy Reagan, it's not as easy as all that.

Imagine, then, how hard it would be to get out from under *two* addictions.

#

And that was how Livy wound up in a black Tahoe, the kind favored by modern-day television G-men, blindfolded and chatting with Dr. Atryx as they made their way to an undisclosed location.

She sat between the good doctor and someone else, someone who seemed more solidly built than Daphne (whom she hadn't seen at the meeting location anyway) and smelled decidedly male.

*Axe body spray,* Livy sniffed. *Ugh. Is there anyone on the planet other than a teenage virgin who think this shit smells good?*

She kept that to herself. She'd stayed mostly quiet since they slapped the blindfold on her, forcibly helped her into the car.

"Am I finally going to see the Batcave?" she joked. "I've been waiting my whole life for this." No one laughed or responded, so she retired the comedy act for the evening.

Besides, Atryx did most of the talking. At some point during the 30-minute ride, she realized that he was one of those men who liked to hear himself talk. A lot.

"So, after digressing last week with you in our little chat about sleep, we're now going to explore Native American culture a bit. Again, though this will seem pointless, believe me, it's pointed. And it tees up what I'll be showing you tonight."

She felt him fidget next to her, as if barely restraining his delight in what it was he was about to tell her.

"But first, you stopped me by saying something last week while you were still strapped to the gurney. Do you remember what that was?"

Liz turned to him. She was somewhat surprised that he was just bringing this up now.

"Sure. *I saw it,* is what I said."

Through the blindfold, Livy could swear that she felt him smile at that.

"You did, indeed. In fact, you also said, 'I *really* saw it this time.' Emphasis on the word really."

"Yeah."

"That's important, because *seeing* is the whole thing here. The big enchilada. Pain is the key, you see. You just might be the singer to get the choir in tune, as it were, but we must never forget that pain is the key."

Livy didn't interrupt, so Atryx pressed on.

"Focused pain is the key to open the door. But until this point, I couldn't find anyone who could withstand the sheer amount of pain necessary to turn the tumblers. Then I understood. I wasn't looking for a single person to internalize all that pain. I mean, it's too much. It would—and did—kill the average person fairly quickly, before we got so much as a peek.

"What I needed was a choir of pain, a whole host of people. And a choir director to unify and harmonize the entire thing. As I said, that might be you. I hope it is. But remember…pain. It's all about pain."

He took a deep breath, and Livy could feel him positively vibrate next to her.

"Even with a choir and a director, the music has to be correct. Just the right pitch, the proper intensity. What could we do to produce the absolute apex of human pain and suffering without killing the singers prematurely?"

Livy now shifted in her seat. As keen as he was to share his secret, she was eager too. To get this soliloquizing out of the way so that they could get onto whatever the fuck they were getting on to.

"I'm going to go out on a limb here and guess that you're as much a student of Native American studies as you were sleep or cognitive physics."

"I'd say that's a safe bet," Livy said.

"Fine. Back in the heyday of this country, the Lakota had a charming ritual known as the Sun Dance. Variations of it were shared across various plains tribes, but it was generally a ritualized way for young men to offer sacrifice for the wellbeing of the family or community. Most of the rituals centered on a trial of physical endurance. Some of them, the ones we're most concerned with, took it further.

"These involved scarification, blood-letting, or other methods—in addition to good, old-fashioned hallucinogenics—in order to produce enough pain to invoke a trance state. Some of those methods generated sustained levels of pain most people in Euro-indigenous cultures can't even begin to contemplate. Where we're going tonight, I'll share with you exactly what I mean."

The car, as if to punctuate Atryx's words, began bouncing on its springs, crazily rocking the passengers inside. Livy suspected that they had left whatever main road they'd been on and were now on some backroad far from campus.

Evidently, the basement of the Cognitive Physics building wasn't even enough to shield what he was doing out here.

For that, he needed the kind of buffer zone that only wilderness could offer.

#

The car crunched to a stop, and Livy heard doors open. Hands took her left shoulder gently, guided her out. When she stood by the side of the car, those same hands removed her blindfold.

It was probably around 11 p.m. They were somewhere far enough from the campus that the dull haze of the city lights was muted. The stars shone overhead crisp and clear, and the crazy cicadas filled the air with their perpetual buzzing.

Livy blinked a few times, not really from bright lights, more from the tightness of the blindfold being removed from her head. But there were lights there in the darkness, large security fixtures perched on the top of a huge warehouse-like building whose corrugated steel walls reached at least two stories into the night.

Turning, she looked past the top of the car she'd just climbed from. A narrow gravel road, like a grey string in all that black, twisted the way she'd assume they'd come. All around was a dark, midnight green ocean of cornstalks, rustling in the gentle breeze. The light from the building fell onto the first row or so of the field, illuminating it like a Bierstadt painting.

The building itself was entirely reminiscent of the long, bland hallways she'd walked with Atryx. No windows and only one plain, unmarked door. No signs, no bright colors, no logos or indication of any kind as to who owned this building or what transpired inside.

That, as Livy was about to learn, was entirely by design.

#

The single door opened onto an antechamber small enough to surprise Livy. Only Atryx and Livy went inside, the driver stayed inside the car, and the man who'd sat next to her remained just outside the door.

Inside, a concrete pad and a flight of metal stairs that climbed just one level. The interior of the stairwell was lit by few fixtures and, in another detail that seemed surreal, an illuminated Exit sign above the door they'd just come through.

"No elevators here. After you," said Atryx, ever the gentleman.

He followed her, and Livy felt that same aura of barely repressed excitement bleeding off him. He was evidently anxious to show off something housed in this farmer's field warehouse, but with all his talk, she had no idea what it could be.

Their footfalls clacked on the metal steps, reverberating in the narrow chamber. At the top, another plain door, this one with a card reader attached, though Atryx never bothered with a card. Maybe with his seniority he didn't need to. As he approached, the mechanism simply clacked, and the lock turned green.

Through the door was another of the repetitious, long hallways, this one sheathed in the same corrugated steel the building was constructed. Several doors broke the monotony, but Atryx walked to the very end, probably a football field's length. There another door, which clacked welcomingly as they neared.

He drew it open onto a good-size room, larger than the operating theater where they'd run the tests on Livy. It was crowded with computer gear and monitors and other electronic paraphernalia. The room itself was dark, the ambient light coming from all the technology. Two techs seated at consoles turned in annoyance as the door closed, immediately stiffened.

"At ease, lady and gentleman," Atryx said, ushering Livy in. The two returned to what they were doing, studiously avoiding any attention to the visitors.

Livy took two steps in, her brow furrowing.

The wall opposite was almost entirely glass, a great window that showed the darkened interior of the structure, which stretched into the darkness. The steel ribs of its walls and ceiling visible, what Jonah might have been witness to after his ingestion.

But that wasn't what stopped Livy.

She wasn't entirely sure of what she was seeing, so she stepped farther into the room, went right to the glass.

At first, it looked almost religious. Row after row, aisle after aisle of what appeared to be crucifixes hanging suspended a foot or two off the floor. These, like the structure of the building itself, stretched as far as she could see.

As Livy stared, something clicked into focus.

These weren't crucifixes, these were *people*.

Dozens and dozens—*hundreds!*—of people, suspended above the warehouse floor, arms splayed out, arranged in neat little rows like an army of crucified Christs.

"What. The. Fuck," Livy muttered.

"Pardon the religious overtones," Atryx said, with his remarkable capacity to seemingly guess what she was thinking. "It's purely unintentional, I promise."

"I don't…"

"Behold, the choir, almost—but not quite—invisible," he said.

Livy felt her mouth go dry, unable to make sense of what she saw. Nothing in her experience, nothing in reality prepared her for such a sight.

"Would you like to go down and see your flock?"

#

When does the addictive substance transcend the addict's ability to process it?

I'm not talking about death here, we already covered that.

I mean when does the thing you crave become too much for the puny vessel that is your body to process?

I'm talking about a high so profound that your body can't even cope with it. Something so outside of human perception that it pretty much just overloads your ability to experience it?

Some people I know have tried psilocybins, mushrooms to

you noobs. Hippy addicts, sure, but that's not a high that can be carefully titrated. Difficult to know exactly how much is in each one. Some of them have said that they've had at least one trip where the psilocybin content of the particular 'shroom was so off the charts that it knocked them onto their asses, almost literally just left them drooling onto their hemp carpets.

No happy trips over rainbows, no distorted landscapes, no intense realizations.

Instead something so immense, so profound that their little human brains couldn't even hallucinate big enough to comprehend.

What happens then?

What happens when the trip doesn't kill you, it consumes you?

What happens when the trip eradicates the *you* of you?

We're all just meat, really, in the end.

What exactly *is* the melting point of meat anyway?

This thing that Atryx was doing. It was pushing ahead exponentially. He might just find whatever that was.

And for the first time, I found myself capable of pushing that limit…*my* limit.

That snake of my addiction stirred somewhere deep within, coiled, made itself felt.

Made damn sure I knew it was hungry and needed to be fed.

#

There was an elevator in this part of the building. Evidently if you could make it into the *sanctum sanctorum* of this place, you could access the elevator, too. Dr. Atryx took Livy down, just one floor. This elevator featured digital controls, its ride far smoother than the secret elevator back at the campus.

When the door parted on the ground floor, Livy saw that the aisles were designated with little illuminated markers at their feet, reminding her of the indicators on airport runways. Each featured a combination of letter and numbers that meant nothing to Livy.

Atryx led them down what she supposed was the main drag, speaking all the way, as was his wont.

"Remember what I told you about the Lakota? The Sun Dance?"

She hadn't really been paying close attention, but she nodded.

He smirked a little, as if knowing she didn't.

"Some tribes, to induce that all-important trance state, pierced the flesh of their braves, inserted wooden dowels to which leather thongs were attached. These warriors were hung by these from the ceiling of a sweat lodge, sometimes after ingesting sacred medicines. They dangled there, high and in excruciating pain, until they had visions. Sometimes they hung there until the dowels ripped their way through the flesh, and they fell to the ground."

Livy looked up in the dim blue light and saw there were men and women, each mostly nude, sheer briefs protecting at least some of their modesty. Closest to her was a man suspended about eighteen inches off the ground. A series of tubes snaked around his head, a breathing apparatus affixed over his mouth.

His arms were stretched cross fashion, kept flexed by the steel rod that entered his skin just under one shoulder blade, re-emerging under the adjoining. Thin cables attached to the rod, vanishing into the unseen expanse of the ceiling. Blood leaked from most of his wounds, trickled down his buttocks and legs, plipped to the ground.

"What I got from the stories of the Lakota was the idea for a form of pain that seemed intense enough to do what we needed, yet not so much as to kill the patient," Atryx said.

Livy stared at the hanged man. She silently prayed that, as her gaze drifted up, his eyes would be closed. If they were open, if they bulged from their sockets with suffering and terror, she thought she might just bolt and run.

But they were closed. She could barely make out the young man's respiration, rising and falling. His mouth, though, distorted by the clear plastic respirator mask, was twisted, contorted in unutterable agony.

"They're drugged, of course. Barely. Just enough to keep them comatose, not enough to dull the pain. Can you imagine the racket if they were all awake and screaming? With these steel walls?"

Livy found it difficult to breathe. She flinched, nearly putting out a hand to steady herself against the man's thigh.

"Here's where we come full circle to the first analogy I

made, the one involving sleep research and consciousness. We found that we could induce the level of pain we required, but we couldn't coordinate it, couldn't focus it. Then I realized that what we were missing was that conductor I mentioned. Just as the brain itself requires those cells in the frontal lobe to lull the rest of the brain to sleep, so, too, did our study. But more than that."

Livy turned to him. "You needed someone who *saw*. Someone who already had begun to see whatever it is you so desperately want to see."

"Precisely."

"Well, I want to see it too. Desperately."

"That's my girl," Atryx smiled.

#

They didn't just hang her up right then and there. No, there were preparations to be made. They drove her back to her apartment in the same black Tahoe, blindfolded, seated between the security guy and Atryx.

Livy found that she was trembling now, in dread or anticipation or both, just as Atryx had on the drive before.

The car deposited her at the door of her building. It was after midnight, quiet on her tree-lined, residential road. The streetlights cast everything in an orange glow. A cat screamed in anger somewhere close, and the muted sounds of music pulsed from some apartment on one of the upper floors, only the bass making it down to the street.

The security man helped Livy out, removed the blindfold. Once she stood on the curb, Atryx's window whirred down.

"A messenger will deliver a packet of papers for you to sign and return. He'll wait as you read through it and make your mark," Atryx said. "Don't eat or drink anything all day tomorrow. Between the pain and the drugs, you'll definitely be queasy. Don't want to vomit all over yourself, do you?

"We'll pick you up here at midnight tomorrow. And, though I shouldn't have to say this, don't tell anyone."

The window whirred back up, and the last thing Livy saw was the doctor's smile, like some psychotic Cheshire cat. The car sped away, disappeared into the evening, the light from the dusk-todawns sliding over it greasily.

Livy went upstairs, collapsed in bed without removing her clothes or even bothering to turn off the bedside lamp. She fished out her phone, toyed with calling Daphne, to tell her what had happened, thank her. She stared at the cartoon image of Velma, then swiped the phone off, set it onto her nightstand.

She supposed that Daphne already knew.

Besides, that snake she'd felt earlier, the very embodiment of her addiction that had begun to uncoil within her, was now hissing and rattling, making its presence very known.

*Tomorrow,* she thought as she closed her eyes and tried to sleep. *Tomorrow you'll likely get more than you know what to do with.*

*And me?*
*Well, I'll see, won't I?*
*I'll finally, definitely see.*

#

Though it was warm outside, even after midnight, it was cold in the warehouse. Livy hadn't noticed it before, probably because she was fully clothed then. Now here she stood, tits out, a thin brief covering her ass and privates. She couldn't see her breath in the air, but it seemed to her that she should.

She trembled, too, but she knew that wasn't because of the cold.

That had to do with watching the technician with the thick steel bar, the other with the tray of scalpels and forceps. The gleam on all that metal made Livy's flesh crawl deliciously with goosebumps.

Dr. Atryx stood to the side, far enough back that he wasn't overwhelming, but still a presence, with his wire rim glasses, tailored suit, and all-purpose grin.

The techs helped her onto a gurney that had been wheeled in place. She climbed onto it, eyes fluttering at this additional layer of coldness as she laid back on her stomach, let her arms fall loosely over the sides.

She kept her eyes closed as they slid down the waistband of her skimpy briefs, gave her a shot in the ass. She hadn't been expecting this and flinched as the needle dimpled the skin.

"That's just the narcotic," Atryx said. "Our version of Lakota medicine."

Livy felt nothing from the injection other than the deep sting in her cheek.

"We're going to make the first incision through the skin and fascia. We need to access the space between your *trapezius* and *latissimus dorsi*," said the tech with the scalpel. "Needless to say, this will hurt."

He sounded like he was the same tech who'd been there for her original tests, who'd also warned her of the impending pain.

He didn't understand that, to Livy, it wasn't a warning, it was a promise.

She felt the scalpel touch her skin, slide through, cut, cut deeper.

An icy tendril of pain fanned out in a skein across her back, and still the scalpel sliced, deeper than Livy had ever attempted. She felt someone press a pad against her back, to catch the blood, she guessed, but that pressure was swept away by the stinging heat of the incision.

Her feet jerked involuntarily, and she felt the old familiar warmth suffuse her body, the flood of dopamine over her brain. As the tech made the second incision, Livy cried out and tried to bury her face in the metal of the table.

She felt like she'd been butterflied. The feeling of her shoulders being cut open, fanned out like angel's wings was unsettling, but the storm of pleasure that washed over her effaced all that.

Livy scarcely felt the steel bar as it was threaded through the slits the tech had made, the tug of the cables being attached.

The techs lifted her from the table, set her feet onto the ground.

Atryx stepped near, put his mouth to her ear, whispered. "Time to sing, little angel. Time to open that door and see what's behind."

Distantly, she heard a whirring.

The cables attached to the bar lost their slack, the bar itself tightening against her back, forcing her arms out. The techs guided them gently, until they extended straight from her body.

And then the cables went taut, and Livy lifted from the ground.

As she rose, the injection's medicine asserted itself.

But as Atryx had warned (or was it promised?) it didn't mask the exquisite pain.

As she ascended, as her toes grazed the ground, a supernova detonated in her skull, expanding, eradicating everything before it.

She heard, as if removed from herself, a scream tear from her lips. Her stomach lurched, flopped like a landed fish.

And she experienced movement, a definite sensation of rushing toward something, not upward as she might have guessed, but moving forward, propelled not by her dangling feet but by some emotive force that hurtled her out, out, out.

Before all went dark, she was punched through something gelatinous, a thick, frangible membrane that separated where she was—*who* she was—from something, somewhere else.

Livy *saw*.

#

She floated in blackness that had depth, that had texture, that had presence. She felt her arms stretched to her sides, her toes pointing down, as if those directions had any meaning.

Her eyes were closed, yet the sensation of seeing something, some essential fabric of the boundless space that surrounded her, transcended her sense of sight, her entire reliance on physical senses at all.

Pain excoriated her. The muscles supporting her weight tore against the steel rod that penetrated them, the raw slashes through her flesh burned like lava. Agony screamed through her, rang her entire body like a bell, thrummed in every limb like a plucked guitar string.

More than that, though, she had a sense of all of those other hanged people behind her in the warehouse, as if their pain coursed through her, too. Tuned and focused in a way that she still felt impossible.

It built, the pain coursing through her like the ultimate of highs, piling up like a great wave against her shore, a tsunami of pain and pleasure that were indistinguishable now, merged into one overwhelming sense.

But the coil of her addiction asserted itself, rose within her, demanded more.

She needed *more* feeling, *more* pain, *more* than even this universe could seemingly give her. She thought that whatever lay beyond the door she'd just opened could offer that.

At what price, though? Satisfying addiction always came with a price—blood, tears, life. It was always something. Now, she understood the price wasn't just for her. *Everyone, everything everywhere* would be the price of satisfying the suddenly cosmic addiction that rose within her.

And she would pay that price, *any* price, *every* price.

She reached her decision. It was no decision, really.

As if accepting that bargain, something flared within her, a pulse of pure sensation igniting what was left of her, throwing it out into the endless void, spreading every atom of her until they were all distant, disassociated specks with no further bonds, to each other, to her, or to the untold dozens of people back in a warehouse she now could only dimly remember.

Movement off at a distance. Something gathered in the darkness, apart from the vast cloud of atoms that used to be...*Livy?* Something so vast, so primeval that it transcended space and time.

It existed before and after, in this dimension and every other, possessing a cosmic, alien intelligence so awesome it was almost a physical presence itself, separate and apart from the growing bulk of the thing.

As the atoms of who she once was brushed against it, motes of dust in god's eye, she felt its attention shift towards her, a seismic hunch of shoulders that rocked the foundation of the cosmos where she floated.

If she had thought the pain she felt—the attraction that still held the atoms of what were once her essence in some sort of weak electrical bond—had reached its apex, she was wrong. At the shift of that malign presence's attention every disassociated particle cried out, screamed into the void, vibrated in distress so profound it seemed to generate its own gravity.

But it was nothing compared to that presence, the deep, deep malevolence roiling about it, coagulated from the very darkness it coiled in. For her? For what she was doing?

*No,* she realized.

For existence. Hers. Its.

All of it.

It existed out of time and space, hatred as foundational as the cornerstone of a great building.

It reviled her, truly, ultimately, but it wasn't anything personal.

Just as it transcended reality, so, too, its hatred transcended all.

It twisted before her, revealing more of itself, millions, *trillions* of cilia across its entire hideous surface, spreading across the cosmos, crawling through the death clouds of stars, palping distant planets.

*Everywhere.*

It was infinite, a cancerous presence that suffused the very fabric of dimensions.

As its attention flicked from her, indifferent now, the bits and pieces of her imploded. She was hurtled together, slammed back with enough power to cause her body—she realized she was back in the warehouse now—to sway on its supports like linen on a clothesline.

The feeling, *every* feeling, fell upon her, as unfamiliar as the day she was yanked from the womb. Crushed into her, all of it now bringing only pain. Every sense seemed attuned to it, no light for her eyes, no sound for her ears, no odors or textures. Pain was the all-encompassing sense now, and all her organs were tuned to that frequency only.

Dimly, she felt the steel rod finally rip its way through the muscles, strained beyond their capacity to hold her weight. She dropped to the floor, fell to her knees. She felt every speck of grit, every grain of dirt bite into her knees, the soles of her feet.

She held her hands before her, slick with blood, dark red in the gloom of the warehouse. She looked down at her body, at her feet. They, too, gleamed with blood.

In a daze, she stumbled forward, turned. Behind her, she saw most of the others had fallen, too, milled about in confusion, disrupting the neat rows and aisles they'd been organized in.

Closer now, she saw they were covered in blood as well, their bodies glistening in the null light.

She flexed her fingers. Every movement stung with pain, every curl of muscle and shift of weight.

*Skin.*

Her skin was gone, stripped away, exposing muscles and sinews, the white sketch of bone.

Around her, they all screamed, the screams ringing out, filling the warehouse, as they realized what had happened. Shrieking, they staggered into one another, each beseeching each, some falling to their knees like stricken penitents. Blood slicked the ground, spilled from the split of their shoulders by the steel bars that had suspended them.

Livy realized that she was screaming too. Her throat felt raw. Droplets ran down her face, and she wasn't sure if it was blood or tears.

That wasn't all. Everything around them was undergoing a radical transformation. The air thickened, dense and warm like a dog's breath. As Livy watched, the walls of the warehouse slumped, evaporated like water on a griddle, exposing the raw weal of the night sky above. The girders and beams vaporized.

Livy turned back, looked up where the control room was. She was sure, even from this distance, that she saw it melt away, saw the lab-coated figures of the techs effervesce. Even Dr. Atryx melted like a candle, slumping into nothing as the control room itself lost cohesion. Fittingly, the last thing Livy saw of Atryx was his smile, distorted into a Daliesque sagging grin, the corners of his lips curling to his ears, his bottom lip drooping past the dissolving bank of consoles.

The warehouse dissipated completely, the steel rods, the cables, even the blood on the ground. It spread like ripples on the surface of a pond. The vast sea of corn surrounding where the structure stood cleared like a fog, the road, the trees on the horizon, the glow of the distant university town.

All gone, erased like a sand mandala by the wind, wiped clean.

Still, the chorus behind her screamed, their wails ascending into a clear sky that also peeled back, tatters and wisps of it giving way to smudges of that familiar absolute black.

One by one the stars winked out, vanished.

The barren earth beneath her feet was all that was left, the only thing that seemed separate from the encompassing darkness. Save for her brethren, the chorus of pain that fanned out behind her, still screaming their song into the emptiness above them, trying to fill the space between the dead stars.

As her humanity drifted away, carried off by the pull of that song, she thought briefly of her mother, so disapproving of everything about her. Of beautiful, lost Jennie, what might have been. Of Daphne, what might have been. The cartoon image of Velma floated into Livy's mind, frayed at the edges like a worn carpet, then no more.

Livy (if she was even that person anymore) lifted her bloody, skinless head to the infinite blackness surrounding her.

What she saw awed her.

The thing, that great presence in the void, twisted over them, lovely in its awesome serpentine shape. Iridescent ebony scales covered it, each a chiaroscuro of beautiful, heretofore imperceptible shades of black.

It unfurled across the entire upturned bowl of the sky, emptied now of stars and galaxies, of comets and moons, of planets. Collapsed, yearning for something to fill it.

Because of her decision, because of her bargain, her insatiable craving, the thing did just that, expanding as it uncoiled, infinite segments of it slithering into the farthest reaches of space.

Standing there, she screamed her pain into that dark cosmos, her choir behind forming a perfect dreadful harmony. That thing inside her, a smaller version of the one filling reality, shifted too. Moved with purpose, grew within her, pulsed out along her wail, unwound into the ebony emptiness.

She lifted her gaze, saw her addiction unwind from her, slither and slide up into the twisting *S* of that *other*. What had seemed so immense inside her she now saw was tiny, insignificant.

As her consciousness, her awareness of self, of being Livy, faded, she saw the squiggles of those behind her ascend, join the infinite bulk of the other, remoras latching onto something that dwarfed them on a scale that was too immense to be quantified.

The sole remaining blip that was her, that was Livy, faded, shredded away as the warehouse had, as Dr. Atryx had, as the fields and trees, her mother, even Jennie and Daphne had.

Only her addiction remained, joined to the addiction of her

choir, joined to the great addiction that was all that existed now, twisting through every nook of reality. It had gained access through the door she'd opened, her life…all life…traded away for a fleeting pleasure, a happy trip, the ultimate high.

For she got what she'd wanted. She faded on that cold comfort.

But she *saw*, oh Livy surely *saw* before she faded into the universal addiction she'd traded it all for.

She saw it all.

**ABOUT THE AUTHOR**
John F.D. Taff is a multiple Bram Stoker Award nominated author with more than 100 short stories and seven novels in print. *The End in All Beginnings* was called "the best novella collection I've read in years" by Jack Ketchum, and it was a finalist for a Stoker Award. His fiction has appeared most recently in *Shadows Over Main Street* 2 and *The Seven Deadliest*, and his latest short story collection *Little Black Spots*. A story in that, "A Winter's Tale," was also nominated for a Stoker. His epic novel *The Fearing* was released serially in 2019 by Grey Matter Press. Robert McCammon called it "Epic and powerful." His work will appear soon in the collection *Midnight Land,* as well as in a new novel, *He Left*. He lives in the wilds of Illinois with one wife, two cats and three pugs. Follow him on Twitter @johnfdtaff or learn more at his blog johnfdtaff.com.

# BEYOND THE REEF

by

GABINO IGLESIAS

# BEYOND THE REEF

## GABINO IGLESIAS

BEING A PARENT AND BEING A JUNKIE are almost the same thing.

Both pull at you with an undeniable strength that makes you feel like you're at the mercy of something infinitely more powerful than you could ever imagine. Both things affect your health in myriad ways because they destroy your sleep patterns and come between you and eating and exercising. Both things make you tired, happy, sad, desperate, angry, and frustrated. Both things become so ingrained in your life that you can't fathom existing in their absence. Both things demand all your money and suck up all your time with the power of a thousand black holes. Both climb to the top of your list of priorities with incredible speed and an unapologetic forcefulness that shatters your sense of control and fragments your sense of self. Both can fill you with joy one minute and then replace that joy with absolute dread the next. Both become the core of what and who you are. Being a parent and a junkie are two things that can make you feel the true power of a warm embrace and then fucking kill you, shatter your soul, or make you do incredibly dangerous things without a second thought.

I know these things very well because I'm both. I know because I'm writing this in a shitty motel room in Condado, Puerto Rico, and I hope that whoever finds me turns this in to my wife and, more importantly, to my daughter Angelica. My daughter is my life, and I hope reading this will help her understand that her dad was a good man. Yeah, a flawed man, but a good man nonetheless. I also hope whoever reads this believes every single word I'm about to write, and then spreads the words so that no one else ends up in the same position I'm currently in.

As I write this, there's a darkness coming, bubbling in my very bones, haunting me from the streets. I don't have much time to write. I know it. The thing I fear most is just outside that door...

First, let me say I never meant to become a fucking junkie. Hell, I don't think a single addict out there started out looking to become a junkie or knowing where that first taste of dope would lead. Becoming an addict doesn't happen in a day. Just like falling in love or getting old, becoming a junkie is something that happens to you over time, like a glacier creating a canyon, and it's something you never notice until it's too late. Yeah, drugs are so damn glorious they shut down the part of your brain that dishes out common sense. If you, like me, didn't have much of it to begin with, you're royally fucked.

The way in for me was stress. Financial stress. Professional stress. Every damn kind of stress you can think of was eating me up. Stress is an acid that corrupts your insides and destroys your mood. Stress is like high blood pressure; a silent killer that rusts you from the inside out until you're nothing more than a husk of whatever it is you were before stress devoured you.

I'm a first-generation college student. I paid for my college degree doing odd jobs and taking whatever money I could get in loans. My parents and teachers had convinced me education was the way out of the barrio, and I believed them. Little did I know they had no idea what they were talking about. Everyone has a pocketful of solutions for you, but if you look at them with a critical eye, you'll soon realize they are in trouble themselves. In my case, I listened to those who talked about education like it was the rope ladder that would allow folks like me to climb out of every hole. What they didn't tell me is that the best thing you can do when you're done climbing up that rope is to make a noose, insert your head, and use it to hang your overeducated-ass from the nearest tree.

In my case, all I had at the end of four years was a useless degree in anthropology, a ton of debt, and some awful decisions. If you take anything from this, my dear Angelica, make it this: every person you meet is two or three bad decisions away from being a junkie, homeless, dealing with a horrible disease, or getting a bullet to the back of the head. The kicker? All humans are born flawed, naturally defective. All you can aim for is making the right decisions most of the time so that things balance out positively and you keep your life, and your sanity, together. I love you with all my heart and hope you read this someday and decide not to judge me.

Protecting you from the horrors I have unleashed is the reason I'm in this shitty room that smells like cigarette smoke, wet carpet, and broken dreams.

After four hard years and graduating college, I couldn't even afford an apartment. I had no job. I had no money to feed myself and I had no other option than to move back home. That meant fighting with my father daily. If I wasn't out there knocking on doors or working construction, in his eyes, I wasn't even trying. It didn't matter to him that I spent hours every day looking for opportunities on my phone, sending out resumes, going on interviews. None of that mattered because he was struggling himself and I was just another mouth to feed.

You know what? I understand him now. I really do. Being a father is so strange, so difficult and scary, that I've learned to forgive parents who fuck up. You kids don't come into this world with an instruction booklet. Instead, we have to rely on our heightened senses, a few instincts, community support, and a bunch of baggage and nonsense that older generations shove down our throats.

I'm rambling and I don't have time to ramble, so apologies when that happens. My head hurts, I keep stopping to pace the room and look out the window. I'm not sure how much time I have before the outside world comes crashing in. You need to know how it started.

I was broke after college, living at home, and was ready to do whatever I had to do, and then something happened.

Six weeks after graduation, when I was ready to give up and go wash dishes, my friend Tony offered me a job selling stolen jewelry at the beach. I was an anthropologist, I studied cultures, I would do great at sales, right? I spent each day on the beach hustling customers while breathing in ocean air so rich with salt I swear it mutates all of us. Most days were spent looking at women in bikinis and old dudes walking their dogs, but when it was overcast and the beach empty, I'd remember horror movies I watched and thought about strange creatures coming out of the ocean at night. I didn't make much money on those days, but the pay was enough to hand my father a few bags of groceries and get him off my back. Then one day a guy put a gun to my face and took every ounce of gold and every diamond I had and left me with stained underwear and a profound aversion to criminal endeavors.

I didn't give up. I don't give up. Ever.

After the jewelry thing, I managed to land a job. I was hired by an insurance company to look through old files and figure out who had fucked up and when. According to the woman who hired me, someone with my education would be able to "think outside the box" and identify problems. I hated the job from the start, but it paid well and I needed the money. I moved into a 244-square foot studio near San Juan with my first check. I was able to afford food with the second. Soon, I could afford weed, which made me forget work in the afternoons. It took me back to my high school days and getting high on the beach. It made me feel carefree as a crashing wave. Then a guy at work named Juan who was always happy introduced me to Oxycontin.

We had a team-building day. They shoved us into three old school buses with busted ACs and drove us to a hotel. During a panel on empathy, I asked Juan why he was smiling since what we were listening to was the most boring shit ever. He looked around, put his hand in his front shirt pocket, and gave me a white, round pill. I swallowed it dry. Half an hour later the stuff they were telling us about made me smile just as wide. I was hooked. If weed was good, Oxycontin was great. On Oxy, not giving a shit became much easier. The world was softer, my stress seemed to have relaxed. Nothing mattered. I felt…strong and free.

The bad thing was that I soon needed more. I needed something stronger to make the world softer. That's when heroin came in like a heroine.

Like most things in life, it happened by accident. A great childhood friend caught me popping an Oxy during a small party at his house and he introduced me to heroin. He took me up to his room and pulled out a little box where he had all his stuff. I watched him fix up, like he was a damn chemist and phlebotomist, cooking the junk, and then drawing some blood from his vein, the darkness spiraling into the syringe like thick, slow-moving smoke, and then pushing in the plunger. It was mesmerizing, A beautiful ritual. My turn was next.

"You'll never forget me, my man," he said. "You'll never forget the first person who helped you shoot up. This shit will change your life." He was right. When I think of the darkness born of that moment, I remember his face and his eyes buried under that deep brow. I only needed help shooting up once. I learned quickly how to do it on my own. I went to college, remember, I'm educated.

I'd like to say heroin was like laying down in a field of

flowers while the sun's rays caress my face, but that's not it. I'd like to say it's like scratching a deep itch, but that's not it either. I'd like to say it's like summer vacations or Saturday mornings, but they all fall short.

Have you ever felt the hand of God inside you, as if he reached his palm into your chest, caressed your heart, and nothing but his good grace and beauty pumped through your veins? Well, that, my dearest Angelica, is what heroin feels like.

After discovering heroin, everything else blurred together. Heroin made me float through life on a cloud of comfort. On good days, going to work high meant reading through files while the radio played smooth jazz. On bad days, it was a few hours of suffering through sweat and cramps and cravings and looking at the clock every two minutes while thinking about getting a fix.

People often talk about drug addicts in derogatory ways and fail to realize that there are many addicts out there who, like me, learn to be functional and work right alongside the rest of the living like some secret breed. Junkies cut your hair and mow your lawn. Junkies go to school with you and cheer from the sidelines during your kid's little league game. Junkies teach your kids at school and serve you at your favorite restaurant. If you live in an expensive neighborhood, chances are your neighbor is popping pills and swallowing them with wine. Yeah, addiction is everywhere. The world is rough, so we become addicted to social media. We become hooked on booze or porn. We get addicted to money and sex and lying. We become addicted to a million things that help us escape reality. I became addicted to heroin because it was an airplane to paradise. It was poison, but it felt like medicine, a magic elixir that unveiled the splendors and beauty of life.

Somehow, I pulled it off. Yes, I did. In fact, my entire life became better while I was using heroin. I didn't get to enjoy every second of it and some of what happened is a hazy memory, but the end result is the same: I met an incredible woman named Crystal and we started dating. We liked each other. We loved horror movies and stand-up comedy. We fell in love and got married. We moved into a bigger house in Carolina. Low income housing, but relatively clean. We had a beautiful baby daughter and we named her Angelica because she was an angel and that is a perfect name for a little angel with eyelashes so damn long they belong in a cartoon.

Yes, that's you. I still think you are an angel.

Anyway, I was there for all of those events, but I was also absent. Life as a junkie is what happens between fixes. You can be doing something, but you're never fully there. If you're high, it's like you're hovering above the moment at all times. If you're not high, you're there but a part of you is thinking about getting a fix. Being an addict is living in the interstitial space between fixes, in the desperate moments between getting what you crave and worrying about how obvious it is to others that you need it. The day you were born? I got high in the parking lot. Holding you sent electricity down my arms and filled my chest with something akin to warm cotton candy. I know that was love, but it was love on heroin, and as I held you, I was worried about getting high again. And that's the worst thing about heroin: it gives and it takes away. It makes things simultaneously brighter and darker. It beautifies while corrupting. It amplifies things as it infects them. It makes your life more bearable as it kills you.

Fast-forward five years. I was still at the insurance company, still unhappy, and still stressed. I still had loans to pay and now I also had a mortgage, a car, a phone, car insurance, all the expenses that come with having a baby...you get the idea. I also had my junk habit. That's not easy on the wallet.

I was broke and things were only getting worse. Just like love or friendship, heroin's ability to take your reality and make fucking balloon animals out of it erodes over time, so you do more and it costs more. And that cycle never ends.

My second foray into crime was a couple of months after you were born. The day you were born was the happiest day of my life, but it also scared the shit out of me. It's easy to save enough money to keep your junk habit when you can squirrel money away here and there and don't have any major expenses. That changes when you have to buy diapers and formula almost daily, your spouse is at home recuperating and emptying the fucking fridge every night, and you have a small tower of medical bills on the table that look like a stack of white pancakes. In order to give myself some breathing room, I decided to try out something I'd read about in an article a few months earlier.

On a Tuesday night I left the house at around 11:20 pm. I had to get diapers again. This time, however, I was going to take a little detour.

Instead of going to the usual Walgreens, I drove sixteen more blocks and parked in the side parking lot of a small credit union. Believe it or not, it's a place most folks don't visit at night. Rumor has it a young boy riding his bike was run over by a lady leaving the bank and students who live in the apartment complexes nearby claim they often see the kid, whose arms are missing, wandering the parking lot. Los Desmembrados, they called it, wandering spirits killed in car accidents who are missing their limbs. Our version of La Llorona, which haunts lonely roads. Just one of many legends that come from this island, like the angry spirits of Tainos murdered by Spaniards in the rivers of Yabucoa, or the strange creatures that inhabit the murky waters of the inlet of Guanica. The list goes on and on. If you haven't seen these types of strange things on these streets, you haven't lived here long enough. Maybe they do see a ghost, but when addicts need money, these things don't matter.

The parking lot is pretty big, surrounded by trees and the ATM was at the back of the building, so I felt somewhat comfortable. I pulled out my phone and pretended to text for a while until a car pulled up. A man with a black trucker hat and a black shirt stretched tight around a prodigious gut stepped out. He would have been hard to handle. I kept playing with my phone. Midnight was quickly approaching and I was thinking about heading back home when a second car pulled into the parking lot. This time the driver was a woman. She looked like she was in a rush. She wore a blue pencil skirt, a white shirt and her heels cracked against the asphalt. She made it to the ATM and went through the motions. My brain started showing me images of a nice bundle of cash and converting it to heroin. The woman was in a hurry and wasn't paying attention. I was thankful for that but thanking God at that time struck me as fucking blasphemy. I was going to hell already, but there was no need to make things worse.

I knew about ATM cameras and I wasn't going to risk it. I pulled a hat down tight over my eyes and stepped out of the car, casually strolling toward the woman's car. She noticed me, but it was too late.

"Don't make a scene or I'll shoot you."

My voice was surprisingly calm. I was in control. Desperation changes people, and never into something better. I was no different. I was a calm junkie pretending to be okay. Her eyes betrayed nothing, but her body went as rigid as a board. I touched the side of my body slowly, hoping she would think I had a gun.

"Say hi to me like you know me and then put the money in the front seat of your car. I swear I'm not gonna hurt you."

She wasn't convinced. Her eyes darted around the parking lot. I needed to bring her back to me and slash any dumb ideas that could be popping into her head.

"Hey, look at me. Walk this way. Put the money in the car. Now."

She didn't move. I thought about the ATM camera. I thought about someone else coming into the parking lot. I thought about rotting in jail like a fucking idiot while my wife and baby daughter sat at home, alone and in need of food or diapers or a hug.

I bolted.

On my way home I prayed. I prayed that she hadn't seen and memorized my license plate. I prayed that no red and blue lights would blossom in my rearview mirror. I prayed that money would just fall out of the sky so I wouldn't be tempted to do anything that stupid and dangerous ever again. I prayed for a better job or some new opportunity. Then I listened to the silence as I drove and thought about how the only constant thing when it comes to God is his unresponsiveness.

My hands were shaking when I pulled into the garage. I walked into the house and was about to throw my keys on the table when I remembered the diapers and formula. The drive back to Walgreens was the longest I'd ever done.

Sadly, I knew I wasn't finished. My brain kept thinking about ways to make easy money. I thought about stealing and kidnapping. I planned out holding up a convenience store. I thought about getting a mask and trying the ATM thing again. I thought about hanging out in the parking lot outside the mall and sticking up the last stragglers making their way out of the movie theater. I thought about going through the purses women left unattended at work. All of it struck me as too risky for the small reward I'd get. Nothing was worth not seeing you again. Nothing.

Then the perfect opportunity presented itself.

To help keep myself functional during work hours, I relied on clonazepam. I popped them throughout the day. They took the edge off everything and submerged the world in a fuzzy warmth that made being at work without a fix bearable. The only downside was more trips to meet my dealer.

We met at the parking lot of an old panaderia every Thursday at 5:45pm. When I got there, he was sitting in his car, screaming into his phone. When he saw me, he yelled once more and hung up. He rolled down his window.

"How are you, Adam?" he asked.

"I'm doing okay, Marco," I replied. "All good with you?"

"Yeah, I'm good."

"You sure? You seemed agitated on the phone."

Asking your dealer questions like this is never a good idea, but junkies aren't the smartest people.

"Yeah...this shit you're using to stay mellow when you're feeling sick? This shit is mostly for bougie white folks in Condado and students who are too afraid to take something stronger. It's big business. I have a dude who helps me make deliveries. You know, just the pills. Anyway, the problem is he looks like a fucking thug. He should be playing a bad guy in the movies instead of trying to be one in real life. He's always getting pulled over because of the window tints on his car and they don't let him into buildings that require an access code because people get scared. He just had to skip another delivery. He was having a cigarette next to his car when some crazy motherfucker popped out of the house with a .45 screaming about neighborhood safety and keeping the place clean. He just called to say that he's waiting for me now."

"Waiting for you here?"

Marco looked at me and frowned.

"Why the fuck are you asking all these questions, man? You want your horse or not?"

"Yes, I do. And I'm asking because I can help you," I said.

"Help me? How da fuck can you help me?"

"Look at me," I said, stepping back and doing a turn. "I'm clean. No facial hair. No tattoos. I dress like I could fucking do your taxes. My car is a piece of shit with regular windows. I don't stand out."

Everything I said to Marco was something I had already thought about. A lot. Keeping up appearances is crucial when you have fucked up arms and thighs and feet and spend an inordinate amount of time looking for a vein and then plunging a needle full of wavering mirages into your flesh. Once you start using regularly, veins disappear, harden, track marks show up easily. I wear long sleeved shirts for work and sweat my way through.

"Yeah, so?"

"So I can make any drop you need. The way I look means no one will pay as much attention to me as they do to your current delivery man. He looks like a criminal. I look like a fucking pizza delivery guy."

I won't recount the rest of that conversation. I'm short on time to write, this hotel room is shrinking, the evil I've uncovered is closing in, and there is so much to say. The point is this, and you already probably saw it coming, Angelica: I started doing deliveries for Marco. I would do them right after work, during lunch, or whenever I had to go get formula at the grocery store or diapers in the afternoon. It was easy. I got paid in junk. There was more money in the house. Mom got flowers. You got toys. Bills got paid. I was happy. Things were good for a couple months.

Then things went bad and got really fucking dark.

I met Marco at the usual parking lot on a Thursday like any other. He handed me a few packages and then asked me if I was willing to do him another favor. He said he'd keep me high for a month. I should have asked what it was all about. I should have realized that when a drug dealer asks you for a favor your response should always be no. I should have walked away from the whole thing and continued to save my pennies and pay for my junk like any regular God-fearing addict. But I did none of that. The idea of free heroin was too powerful. It was a bright light inside my brain that blocked out all rational thought. Free horse was the only thing I could think of. I immediately said yes.

The gig was relatively easy. All I had to do was accompany one of Marco's men to a transaction, bring a shotgun along, and try to look like a bad motherfucker and someone who would pull the trigger at the least provocation. I was neither. He knew it and I knew it. However, I was a desperate junkie, and that means I was willing. That was something we both knew. I wasn't what he wanted, but I could offer what he needed. That, Angelica, is life in a nutshell: people looking for something they want and mostly having to settle for some knockoff, lesser version.

The night it went down, I told your mom I was going to meet my boss at a café to go over some special files he wanted me to study in detail. I sweetened the lie by telling her he was going to pay me a little bonus for that work. It would be easy to fake because I would be saving money all month instead of buying junk. I thought it was a brilliant idea. After so much darkness, the clouds had parted and a little ray of sunshine was shining down on my head. It felt good.

You know how dangerous things always seem to happen in slow motion in movies? That's not how they go down in real life. In real life shit goes south quickly.

I met Marco's man at the same spot I always met his boss. He was waiting in a black Chrysler 300 with windows so dark they looked like black mirrors. The car sat on thick tires wrapped around matte black rims. When he saw me approaching, he lowered the window and told me to get inside. The smell of weed wafted out as soon as I opened the door. I climbed inside and shut the door carefully. The man was wearing a beanie and black jacket. It was hot as hell outside. He looked as out of place as a guy in a bathing suit walking around Anchorage in January.

The man turned to me and said his name was Ronny and then explained what I was supposed to do.

"Play it cool. Your job is to just look like you don't take shit from people, you copy me?"

I was wearing my oldest jeans, a pair of black sneakers, and an old black T-shirt. That was my version of a badass.

"I'm gonna give you a shotgun as soon as we get there," said Ronny. "You know how to use it?"

"Not really."

"Fuck."

He looked at me and I could tell he was thinking about whether I'd be useful or not. Apparently, I was the only option, so he continued.

"It's easy. You have four cartridges in there. Before you walk in, make sure the safety is off. If you can see a little red dot at the top, that means it's off. You can't shoot the thing with the safety on, so remember that. Got it?"

"Got it."

"Okay, good. You seen fuckers pump a shotgun in movies,

right?"

"Yeah."

"Cool. You're gonna do that. Pull back hard and then pull forward. You'll hear a clacking sound each time. Clack-clack. That means there's a live round where it needs to be. If you have to fire, aim in the general direction of whatever or whoever you wanna fuck up and pull the trigger. It's pretty hard to miss with a damn shotgun. After shooting you can pump again and again if you need to. Three more times. I didn't bring any more ammo. If you have to shoot that thing four times for some reason and still need more…well, you're fucked."

His words weren't meant to comfort me, and they didn't.

What happened next happened incredibly fast. Adrenaline was rushing through my veins and accelerating everything around me.

We left the parking lot and Ronny drove all the way into Old San Juan and then down into La Perla. I hope you've never been there, but I'm sure you've seen it. La Perla is a ghetto sitting below the walls of Old San Juan. It pushes against the water and is the most important trafficking spot in the Caribbean. Poverty is rampant, but it's also home to some very rich drug lords. The place is trapped between the water and the huge walls the Spaniards built to protect the city. There's only one way in and out. This had made it easy to control. Cops don't go there anymore. It's a dangerous, violent place where a lot of people die every year.

Please, do not ever visit this place. Ever. Stay away and keep your mother away. Make sure no one you care about goes there, especially near the water.

After entering La Perla, Ronny drove until the road ended where there is little lighting but lots of privacy. There was a white SUV already waiting. We both exited the car and walked around to the trunk. Ronny pulled out a blue backpack and a shotgun. He handed me the gun and pointed at the top of it. I pushed the safety off.

"If you so much as fucking aim that thing anywhere near me, I will kill you. We clear?"

I nodded.

We made our way to the tiny corner of land jutting into the water. As with every chunk of beach in La Perla, it was rocky and the sand was dark brown. The ocean breaking over the reef about a hundred feet away drowned every other sound around us. The combination of rocks, darkness, and waves made the place feel forbidden, like nature had built its own barbed wire barrier. We had just gotten there and I was ready to get the hell out already.

As we approached, I saw two men waiting for us close to the water. The way they were dressed threw me off. Both were wearing long coats, dark pants, huge boots, and large hats pulled down over their faces. If Ronny was out of place because his jacket made no sense in the Caribbean heat, the folks I was looking at belonged to an entirely different universe where common sense plays no role.

Ronny walked up to the men and stopped about five feet in front of them. I stayed a few feet behind him to his right. I wanted to see everything but stay separate. I figured taking part in the transaction that was about to go down would be worse than just being a witness.

"Gentlemen, I have your package."

Ronny smiled. The two figures said nothing. Not being able to see their faces made me extremely uncomfortable. Even before getting into a fight people will look into their opponent's eyes. You already know they say eyes are the windows of the soul. Whether that's accurate or not is debatable, but I like to look at people in the face.

"The last package...Ronny...not good."

The one who spoke was standing in front of Ronny. His voice sounded horrible. Imagine a fat man with emphysema choking on pancake syrup and you have an idea of what he sounded like.

"What do you mean not good? You know we always bring you the best shit, man. Always."

"Not good...Ronny!"

The voice had a wet quality to it that I'd never heard coming from a human throat before and it sent shivers down my spine. Then he said a word I couldn't make out. Something that sounded like "sick" or "thick."

"Listen, man, this is premium shit, okay? You know Marco likes you and your...people. He wouldn't fuck you over. We've been doing business for a long time. You know he wouldn't do that."

The man in front of Ronny lifted his hand and pointed at him. The hand was grey and only had four fingers, and I could swear it was webbed. I was so scared I forgot the gun until Ronny stepped back and looked at me. He wanted me to act. I lifted the shotgun.

"Settle the fuck down, man!" Ronny yelled at them with my shotgun to back him up. His voice was a few octaves higher than it had been before. Realizing he was nervous made me even more afraid. I looked back at the man's hand. It was dark and I was sure the lack of light was playing tricks with my eyes. His hand couldn't be that color, and yet it was.

The man started speaking a language I'd never heard before. It sounded like Russian or Turkish but being spoken by someone with a slashed throat.

"Stop!" said Ronny. "I have no fucking idea what you're saying. You want the junk or not?"

"No! Poison!"

The scream came from the second man. He stepped forward, brought his hand up, and removed his hat. The only way I can describe his face is like that of an aborted abomination concocted in a lab, like they were trying to mix an ape and a fish with a touch of toad thrown in. His skin was a dull grey, his lips were humongous. There were only a couple of slanted holes where his nose should have been, and his eyes, which were bigger than any eyes I'd ever seen on a human face, were unnaturally round and covered in a milky membrane. He had no hair, no ears, no eyebrows.

"You made us sick," said the...*thing* with the huge eyes and lips. He turned toward the water. In the distance, right where the deep blue of the sky met the reef, three other figures were standing. They had slim bodies, huge heads, and unnaturally long necks and limbs. My eyes darted back to the two creatures in front of us. Subterranean. Amphibious... whatever it was, these were not humans like you and I, Angelica, and my fingers clenched on the shotgun as if I was holding you tight, for at that moment, I didn't think I would ever see you again. I only had four shots.

My breathing was speeding up and my heart was pounding in my chest like a tiny caged gorilla.

The one who had removed his hat held a grey finger up to his face and took a step forward. Light from the street fell on to his face.

"You...made sick!"

The initial shock of seeing his batrachian features subsided and I looked at where he was pointing. There was a lesion under his left eye. It looked like those horrendous lesions caused by krokodil, that semi-synthetic drug that folks use because it has similar effects to heroin and morphine but that makes your flesh rot. I'd seen a few junkies with deep lesions, so I stayed away from krok. The jagged hole in this thing's face was horrendous. Something thick and black was dripping from it. In the center, yellowish flesh speckled with black surrounded a hole where I could see bone. I heard Ronny gasp.

"Are you saying our horse did that to you? That's not possible. You know we always deliver the goods. You've never had any trouble with our stuff, man. There's a lot of pollution in this water and mayb—"

The creature who was still wearing a hat lunged at Ronny. Ronny tried to jump back. The creature landed on him. The backpack went flying. They fell to the sand in a flurry of black leather and greyish limbs. The hat flew off, the mask was gone, his face was revealed. He looked just as monstrous as the others.

I looked up just in time to see the second fucker moving my way. I pumped the shotgun. Clack-clack. I pointed at the thing's chest and squeezed the trigger.

The blast broke the night in half, its echo ricocheting against the gigantic wall and filling La Perla with the sound of a cannon. The shotgun threatened to rip my arms off. The creature shrieked and stumbled back, flailing his arms as if he was trying to catch something that wasn't there. His long coat flew open. I saw the thing's white, scaly belly underneath and it made me pump the shotgun again. We all fear otherness on some level, some primal response to things we don't know, and my own lizard brain was taking over.

The thing landed on the sand in a sitting position. I let out a scream that entered my ears and sliced my soul with a blade of ice. I was seeing and hearing a fucking monster. A real monster. Before I could squeeze the trigger a second time, a muffled gunshot came from the floor next to me. I looked down. Ronny was doing his best to push the creature off of him.

In front of me, almost inaudible to my ears because they were ringing from the shotgun blast, I heard something like a wet cough. The creature I'd shot had its mouth open, coughing and gagging. Rows upon rows of tiny black teeth reflected the scant light that reached its face, and an inky liquid sputtered out of its monstrous mouth. Its outstretched hand reached toward me, the grey triangle of flesh between the webbed fingers clearly visible. I pulled the trigger. The blast opened a dark hole near the top of its white chest and pushed him onto his back. It twitched once and stopped moving.

I felt something on my shoulders and turned, ready to fire again, but stopped. Ronny was standing there, covered in the dark blood of this strange species. He was still holding his gun. His chest was pumping up and down like he'd just run up a dozen flights of stairs.

"Let's get the fuck outta here!"

Ronny picked up the backpack and started running back to the car. I stood there, looking at the two creatures on the sand. Something strange happens to your brain when the impossible becomes real. It shuts down. It cracks a little under the weight of a new truth that had previously been inconceivable. Depending on their significance, new truths can freeze you. The two creatures in front of me were real. I'd seen and heard them. They were bleeding black blood on the sand, their strange bodies unmoving so my eyes could take in their reality. Still, even with the evidence in front of me, a part of my brain was screaming *No! This isn't real!*

I heard Ronny shout behind me. I pulled my eyes away from the bodies on the sand, turned around, and ran the same way we'd come. As I reached the end of the sand, I turned around. I wanted to make sure those things weren't following me. What I saw then froze my blood in my veins. A lot of people talk about abject horror, but few of us ever get to really experience it. That night, I experienced it.

The two bodies on the sand weren't moving, but closer to the shore, another ominous body was emerging from the water. Each second it got closer and I got a better look. It was naked, the body was humanoid, but it was clearly not a human. It was hunched over and its arms reached almost all the way down to the sand. Its legs were skinny and it walked like it hurt to do so. His mouth reminded me of watching videos of fishermen hauling giant groupers out of the water. The whiteness crawled up its neck and dark slits opened.

The creature was horrific. I was mesmerized. An amphibian thing was walking out of the ocean on two legs. I was in the middle of a horror movie and I couldn't move. I heard the engine of Ronny's car roar to life and the spell was broken. I turned and ran as if the thing on the shore could break into a run at any time and tear me to pieces with that huge, horrendous mouth.

I jumped into the car and we burned rubber out of La Perla. Nobody spoke until we were almost at the parking lot behind the panaderia.

"What the fuck was that all about, Ronny?"

"Listen, man, it wasn't supposed to go down like that. I don't even know what to tell you. Usually we just hand them the backpack full of dope and get the money or they tell us where the money is. I...I don't fucking know what that was all about. Call Marco and talk to him."

I knew asking more questions would get me nowhere, so I didn't ask any. Five minutes later we pulled into the parking lot and I opened the door. I wanted to go home. I wanted to see you, to breathe in your wonderful smell and listen to the small sounds coming from you. I already told you that being a parent and being a junkie are very much alike, and cravings are a huge part of it. The presence of your children, seeing them happy and knowing they are safe at that moment, is as relaxing as the best drug in the world, and just as addicting. I needed that. My body was halfway out of the car when Ronny talked to me and made me jump.

"The shotgun stays, man," he said.

I hadn't even realized I'd been clutching it that whole time. I checked the top, clicked the safety on, and gently placed the butt of the gun on the floor. Ronny didn't seem in the mood for another single word, so I closed the door. He peeled out of the parking lot, his lights quickly merging into the avenue in front of the panaderia and then vanishing in the distance at a high speed.

I got in my car, turned it on, cranked the AC, and sat there like an idiot, turning the night's events in my head over and over. There was an argument in my head:

*That was impossible.*

*You saw it.*

*That didn't happen.*

*You killed a creature on that beach.*

*Strange fish-human hybrids don't exist.*

*One of those things almost killed Ronny and the other had the same plans for you.*

When the argument stopped, the questions began. What were those things? The question was one I could not ignore. I needed answers. And I needed a fix.

I drove home in silence. I walked into the house, checked on you and your mother, and then went to the bathroom and took care of myself. The dope wasn't working as it should. I felt clammy and the junk was buzzing but failing to explode inside me, like a bad electronic song with a superb buildup that fails to deliver on its promise. I felt itchy and dirty, simultaneously tired and wound up.

Eventually, I crawled into my bed. Darkness overcame me in waves. Sometimes it resembled sleep and sometimes it was just fear. Then I fell asleep and the fear got worse.

I had a nightmare. I woke up in the middle of the night to strange sounds. I sat in bed, trying to identify what the sounds were. They came from down the hallway near your room. Something like a dog slobbering on a bone. I jumped out of bed and ran to your door. The sounds were louder. I panicked even though I had no idea what was going on. Every parent has a sixth sense, especially in the middle of the night, and mine was telling me something was terribly wrong. I started praying.

I barged into your room and threw the light on. Two figures stood over your crib. They looked exactly like the things I'd seen walking out of the water. Both had blood running down their atrocious faces, their huge lips barely touching as they ate. One lifted its fishy head and looked at me with its humongous eyes covered in that white film. Then it opened its mouth and shrieked. The sound pierced my ears and I had to close my eyes and grab my head because it felt like it was about to explode. The shrieking stopped. I looked at the monster again. It stood in the same place, its glistening lips still open. Bits of flesh were visible inside its mouth clinging to the rows of tiny, pointed teeth. There was a touch of white inside as well, crunching like carrots.

They were eating you, both your flesh and your bone.

Seeing the two creatures hovering over your crib, lips parted and coated in blood like huge fresh wounds, ripped a scream from my throat. I ran to them, ignoring the danger. I wanted to see you. I needed to believe you were okay, even if I knew you weren't. Three quick steps into the room was all it took. My perspective changed. I could finally see inside the crib. Your pink pajamas were shredded and soaking in a pool of blood. I knew that mess was you, or what was left of you. I screamed so loud it became silence, unable to move, rage and fear tensing every muscle in my body. The creatures came to me. They reached out for my face, their long fingers drenched in your blood.

Thank God I woke up.

I never managed to go back to sleep that night. Instead, I stayed in your room and listened to your breathing until your mom walked in to feed you.

The next day at lunch, I rang Marco. He seemed distracted and said he'd rather not talk on the phone. Given his line of work, I understood. We agreed to meet at our usual spot, except this time we would go inside and get some coffee. I called to tell your mom I was going to work an extra hour or two on the new project. If being a junkie has one benefit it's the ability to lie even to those you love most without even thinking about it.

Once Marco and I were sitting down, twin cups of coffee steaming in front of us, Marco looked at me.

"I didn't know shit was gonna go down like that, Adam," he said, genuine concern or regret from that realm in his voice. "I wouldn't have asked you to go if I'd known."

"Thanks for saying that, Marco, but it doesn't really matter to me right now. What matters is knowing what the hell I saw on that little beach. Those things weren't human, but they talked to us. They were fucking angry. They attacked us. When we—"

Marco brought his hand up. The gesture did its job: I stopped talking.

"Not here," he said. "Finish your coffee. We'll talk outside. I just needed the caffeine."

I blew on my coffee obsessively and downed it in three or four sips. I kept looking around, convinced people knew Marco was a drug dealer.

A couple of minutes later we were sitting in Marco's car.

"So what the hell were those things, man? I need to know. I need some fucking answers."

Marco was looking out his window. The world around us kept going. People were getting coffee, walking their dogs, driving to and from a variety of places. They were all oblivious to the horrors that inhabit our reality. Just like me until the previous night, they all ignored the monsters with which we share our space. The idea made me want to exit the car and start screaming about it in the middle of the street. I didn't even care if I sounded like a crazy person because by then I had started doubting my sanity. Some overpowering sense of self-preservation kept me glued to the seat, eagerly waiting for Marco to answer me, to shine some light on what I'd experienced.

"The shit I'm about to tell you has to stay in this car. We clear?"

"Yeah, Marco, I just need to know what those things were. And if I'm in danger," I said.

"Ronny texted me that shit had gone south but I only know so much. He left the backpack in a secure spot and vanished. He never replied to my texts. I haven't been able to get a hold of him since his last text telling me the deal ended badly. I have no idea all that went down. Can you fill in the details?"

"Sure, man," I said. "We showed up. There were two dudes at the beach. Except they weren't dudes. They were…creatures. Fucking fish walking on two legs and talking. Ugly as hell. Ronny had a backpack with him. He tried to give it to them, but they started complaining. They told Ronny the last batch had made them sick. Then they attacked us."

"And yet here you are. How so?"

"You know I had a shotgun. I put two large holes in one of them and Ronny took care of the other one, the one that attacked first. We left the bodies on the beach."

Marco took a deep breath, looked at me, and shook his head like a man who is forced to face something he really hoped he wouldn't have to. I knew the look well. I saw it in the mirror every day.

"You already saw them, so there's no reason to lie to you," he said.

He sounded like he was talking to himself, not me.

"Listen, Adam, you're gonna have a hard time believing what I'm going to tell you, but it's the truth. I'm only gonna tell you because it might be good for you to be on the lookout."

"On the lookout for what?"

"Just…fucking listen to me. My uncle was a big shot in the Old San Juan. He ran La Perla for many years. Twenty years ago. He came up the ranks like everyone else. He started as a foot soldier and eventually inherited a solid set of dealers and connections in Mexico,

Cuba, Miami, and Colombia. He took a decent business and made it explode. He turned those few solid contacts into a fucking empire. He was the first one to bring more than one delivery a day. He learned that the Coast Guard wasn't a fan of hanging around the dangerous, choppy water near the reef, so he used smaller boats to get the stuff to the shore. If the small boats got stuck he'd send folks out in jet skis to get the shit and bring it in. He also liked to send a message to his enemies. If you fucked with him, he would kill you and then have his men take your body out to the reef and tie it there so the fish and crabs would feast on you. Then the bodies started..."

Marco stopped talking. His eyes were still glued to something on the other side of the window. He hadn't made eye contact with me. He was obviously nervous, and that wasn't helping my own nerves much. He inhaled audibly.

"The bodies started disappearing. My uncle told the men to use better rope because he wanted his enemies to see the bodies when the tide was low. That was the whole point of going through the extra work of tying them to the reef. He also wanted cops to know that La Perla wasn't a place they wanted to fuck with. The men listened and did as they were told, but that didn't work. My uncle grew frustrated. He told his men to use chains instead of rope. The chains failed to work. At first he thought it was sharks. Maybe they were getting to the bodies during high tide. A large shark was probably strong enough to fuck up some chains, so he started using more. The bodies kept vanishing. Then he got the idea that maybe people were doing it. Enemies saying they didn't give a shit. Whatever. He made some of his men stay out there at night.

"Well, they never saw a god damned soul out there, but the bodies still disappeared. It was obviously something under the water. He had to know, so he went out there himself with some men, a fisherman's light, a dead body, and waited around. What he saw was...well, he caught the things in the act of taking the fucking body away. Everyone on the two boats saw the same thing. There was something out there, something not entirely human or animal, feeding on the bodies my uncle's men were leaving.

"Now, that part of the story is somewhat clear. You know, it's easy to understand. The men who went with him were witnesses. Whatever. The point is that what comes next is what's really hard to explain, and maybe even harder to swallow."

Marco looked at me for the first time. Something like anguish had taken over his features. He looked the way all men with heavy secrets look: broken and tired. I felt a connection with him for the second time that day. I knew all about feeling haunted by your secrets. I knew all about skeletons in the closet that never feel like they're buried deep enough. I knew about secrets that would keep you up at night with the possibility of shattering your entire life if they were ever exposed. Marco kept talking.

"My uncle started going out there whenever they had another body. He was obsessed with those things. He wanted to see them, to figure out what the fuck he was dealing with. Rumor has it he somehow established communication with those things. According to my mom, one of them climbed onto the boat and...started talking. The story goes that their species had lived off the coast of Massachusetts for generations. Then something happened, not sure what, but it had to be big, and they had to look for a new place to live. They ended up here in Puerto Rico, off the coast of Old San Juan. They'd been there for years. The water is always rough by the reef and there's almost no boat activity out there because of it, so they were comfortable for a long time. My uncle kept going. He was obsessed. He developed a relationship with those things. My mom says he started using them for jobs on land. Whatever. The point is those things kept feeding on the corpses, but then something weird happened.

"My uncle was killing too many junkies. You know, motherfuckers who didn't pay their debts and assholes who started dipping into stuff they were supposed to be selling. My uncle was dumping bodies full of heroin and those things got hooked on it. Got themselves their own habit worse than you. Apparently they have the ability to...I don't even know how to describe it. Like I said, they are in the water, living on the reef, but they are also out of the water. Some of them are normal enough to stay out of the ocean for hours. The point is this: they started showing up at my uncle's house. They had figured everything out. They were infinitely smarter than my uncle had guessed. He got scared. Those things had information. They knew how many boats were coming in. They could destroy the whole drug trade if they wanted to. They didn't threaten my uncle, but they asked him for whatever was in those bodies, so he started selling them heroin.

"The relationship stayed that way for years. Before he died, he talked to me about the whole thing. At first I thought he had lost his fucking mind. You know how when folks get old and their brains start slipping. But that wasn't the case. He had some of his men take me out there. He wanted those things to get to know me before he died. I was the new boss, so I was going to be dealing with them. I went out there and one of them climbed on the boat. I was scared shitless. I'd never seen anything like it. Then that fucking thing started talking. It sounded weird as hell with those huge, unmoving lips, but I understood it. Their main concern was to keep things as they were. They'd become addicts, all of them, the whole damn colony were junkies. They needed me to keep the supply flowing. I promised them nothing would change. You know how you look at someone's face when you're talking and the way they look back at you or the way they smile gives you a hint of whatever is going on in their heads? That shit was lacking in this conversation. Those huge eyes never blinked. The lips didn't move much or smile. It was...what's the term? Expressionless. Whatever. It freaked me out. I wanted to keep them happy and keep them away from me. When I took over and the business got too hot for me to take care of everything, I took Ronny with me one night and did the same thing with him. He's the one who's been dealing with them since. This was about two or three years ago. Sometimes I still see them outside my house or swimming close to our boats when a big delivery comes in. It's weird. It's like they want to keep those fucking fishy white eyes on everything. Always watching. Whatever."

Marco stopped talking again. I was glad he did. The information I'd received was too much. It was incredible, but it fit well with what I'd seen and heard the previous night. I could believe it, but I didn't want to. The thought of strange humanoid things living out on the reef and feeding on corpses while also walking on land and interacting with us was too much for me. It was like someone had lifted a veil and shown me that my version of reality was weak and easy to shatter. I wanted to go home. I wanted to go straight to you, Angelica, kiss the top of your head, get a fix of dope, and forget everything. Sadly, Marco had more to say.

"I've had to deal with those things since I took over. You know, with Ronny's help. We hand them the junk and then someone brings us money the next day. The whole thing freaks me out. Did you get a good look at them?"

"It was dark out there, but I think I did," I said.

"They're horrible. They…they shouldn't be. They seem smarter than us. I still have no idea how they get shit done on land, but they do. They come out. They even kill people. I know because I've seen it happen to people who cross them, to folks who go out there to see if the rumors are true. One time a Cuban took a shot at one of them from his boat. It was a new guy. I guess he didn't know any better. The boat disappeared on its way back. Those guys never made it back to Miami. Another time, a guy went out there with Ronny and started asking questions. It was too much for him to process. He put his hands on one and pushed it around before Ronny dropped the backpack, apologized, and yanked him outta there. A few days later the kid came to see me. He said strange men in huge coats were following him around, showing up everywhere, hanging outside his place at all hours of the night and vanishing every time he opened the door to go confront them. Then I stopped hearing from him, no answer from his phone, until Ronny found him. He was in the tub. We never found his head."

Marco stopped talking again. He looked deflated and scared. I could tell he was done. His posture changed. He slumped on his seat, his body a weak, bent period at the end of his long explanation. I had to say something because I still had a huge question hovering around in my head.

"I believe you, man, but there's something I don't understand. They were blaming Ronny for being sick. One of them had a nasty wound on its face. They were saying the last batch was bad. What the hell was that all about? Did you try to mess with them? After what you told me, it doesn't seem likely," I said.

"I think I know what that was all about. We sold them some bad junk, but I assure you that was an accident."

Marco looked at me. There was something else in his eyes now. I'm a junkie, so I recognized it pretty quickly: guilt.

"What do you mean by bad junk?"

"We tend to cut our stuff with safe shit. Talcum powder. Sugar. Detergent from the dollar store. Powdered milk. Baking soda. Whatever. Junkies are only good business if they're still alive, you feel me? A dead customer is a lost dollar, so we try to keep our shit relatively clean. This time around we brought in two new guys,

Dominicans, who needed a gig. We were moving a lot of product and were short on hands. We gave the Dominicans a few keys and asked them to cut it. Apparently they used rat poison. I think the damn rat poison is what made them sick. I'm not a scientist. Shit, I don't even know exactly what those things are, but they'd never complained before, so my guess is that the rat poison fucked them up. They reacted to it or something, something about their species was hit even harder than a regular human's body. Different DNA."

"And this means what for us? Why did they attack Ronny and me at the beach?"

"I have no fucking idea, man," said Marco. "I hope they all die from it, but I doubt that'll happen. If half of what old timers say is true, those fuckers are resilient. They don't overdose, that's for damn sure. Others have tried to get rid of them before with no luck, rumors are, even the U.S. Government. I'm sure they've paid the consequences. I don't know what the fuck we're gonna do. For now, just watch your back. You know, until this thing cools off. I'm gonna tell Ronny to drop off a free delivery for them. Premium and uncut. With a note, you know. A gift. Sort of an apology so they know we meant no harm. It was a fucking accident."

Watch your back. That's what he said. My paranoia ramped up to eleven. Then Marco said he had some business to take care, so I got out of his car and he left.

Once again I sat in my car and thought about everything. My veins were aching for a fix, muscles cramping, my brain was begging me to give it the magic chemicals that made it slow down a bit, but I needed to think, to process, to try to understand. More than anything, I needed to come up with a plan to keep you, your mother, and myself safe.

There was no denying that what Marco had told me was true. At least some version of it. I had seen the damn things with my own eyes. That said, I had questions. Lots of questions. Do you know what people who went to college do when they have questions, my dear Angelica? They do a bit of research. I was an anthropologist and had never heard of anything even remotely similar to those things living on the reef, but that didn't mean no one had ever heard of them. I had to cure my ignorance, and the easiest way to cure ignorance is with heavy doses of information. I was finally going to put my damn degree to work. I was going to use the rope ladder to climb out of this dark hole I was in.

Now, I'd like to tell you that I went home, got a fix, and rested until the next day. Only two of those happened. I went home and got a fix, but didn't get any sleep. I was afraid of nightmares, which I knew would come, so I stayed awake and watched you sleep as my body and brain dipped in and out of the beautiful heroin nirvana. I breathed in the air you exhaled. I watched your eyes twitch and imagined your dreams. I became one with every ounce of your flesh.

It was my thirst that broke that spell. I went to the kitchen to get a glass of water. Our kitchen sits opposite two large windows that look out at the street and the houses on the other side. I had looked out those windows a million times and seen people walking and cars going by. I was also high and being high makes your brain operate like a phone call from another country on a landline made by someone wearing a wet towel around their face. That's why it took me a moment to realize what I was looking at. Outside our windows, right across the street from us, was a figure. It was standing behind a neighbor's dilapidated truck, bathed only by the light of the moon and the bit of yellowish haze from a nearby lamppost. It looked gangly and was covered from head to toe with a long coat and hat. It was a look I unfortunately knew very well. The vision made fear's cold, strong fingers seize the back of my neck and squeeze.

I knew what the figure outside our window was and I knew it was looking for me. My life was in danger. I can't explain exactly how I knew but I was sure it was true. That figure was one of those things and it was looking straight at our house. I had put a shotgun blast into one of their brothers, and this smarter species wanted revenge.

My options were limited. I didn't have a gun, and going out there with a large knife struck me as stupid. The idea of leaving the house and trying to talk to the creature crossed my mind, but willingly leaving the safety of the house unarmed seemed like the worst idea in the world. Especially since it would mean leaving you and your mother alone.

When faced with awful choices, human nature often takes the path of least resistance and immediately falls into a state of inaction. Instead of going out there or even approaching the window to get a better look, I stood were I was and kept my eye on the creature outside.

Time passed. The thing didn't move. Neither did I. Time is a strange thing when your blood is full of junk. It stretches like cheap bubblegum and then collapses on itself. A half hour can seem like an eternity spent in an alternate dimension and a few hours can go by in what seems like a five-minute power nap. I tell you this so you can understand I'm not lying when I say I have no idea how long I stood there, watching the figure on the other side of the street. Eventually I needed a bathroom break. My body started moving toward the bathroom before I realized I was doing it. When I came back to the kitchen and looked out the windows again, the creature was gone.

I went back to bed after that. I wanted your mother to feel me next to her because I didn't want her to worry. I think I managed to do the opposite. I fell asleep and the nightmare was there waiting as I feared. It was short, but brutal.

A creature was dragging me into deep water by my leg. I was screaming. My hands were bloody from trying to hold on to the reef. The beach was deserted. The thing had its nails buried in my flesh. It pulled me toward the other side of the reef. Soon my shirt was gone and the sharp rocks were digging into my flesh. Saltwater entered my wounds and made me scream louder. Then the last rock slipped away from my bloody hands and I was quickly pulled underwater. The creature held on to me, dragging me deeper and deeper. Light fractured and blue darkness began to surround me. Rays of light danced above me like empty promises. My chest ached and then my body inhaled against my will. Ocean water invaded my lungs and stung my nostrils and the back of my throat. As the darkness threatened to swallow me forever, I looked down at the creature below me. I saw its greyish body moving through the water effortlessly, the awkwardness I'd seen on land replaced by an animal agility that spoke volumes about its strength and speed. Finally, just as black clouds were entering my vision, I saw the peaks of buildings. There was a city beyond the reef, a secret city no one knew about where I would spend all eternity.

I woke up screaming, sweat running down my face. Your mother woke up. I never went back to sleep. Instead, I paced the house like a maniac until the sun was out. Every time I went to the kitchen, I pretended not to look out the windows, but I did. The thing was still there. A Profundo. A deep one. That's the name that popped into my head. It worked as well as anything else.

The next morning I skipped work and went to the library at the University of Puerto Rico in Rio Piedras. That library had been my home during my last year as a student. I knew where every classic anthropology tome sat on those endless rows of dusty shelves. This time, however, I didn't know exactly where to start, so I talked to the old lady at the counter who, according to silly student lore, never left the damn place. I asked her for books dealing with coastal folklore, human-fish hybrids, strange sailor narratives, and books on legends from the ocean from across the globe. Then, just as she was rattling one last name off her computer screen, I remember what Marco had said and asked her for anything they had on the history of Massachusetts.

I spent the next five hours the same way I'd spent countless days as a student: reading.

Humans have always had a strange relationship with the ocean. It gives and it takes away. It leads to discovery and destruction, to new opportunities and to war. The ocean carries diseases from their points of origin into new territories. It contains strange creatures and sunken ships. The ocean feeds us and we serve as food for some of its denizens. Humans have understood this forever, and our tales reflect that in a plethora of cultures.

As I was expecting, the ocean is also full of monsters. Giant whales. The kraken. Enormous sharks. Strange serpents. Evil mermaids. Various beasts and blobs that live in the remote darkness near the ocean floor or that hide in the pitch-black trenches no human has ever seen. The list goes on and on. Then there are also beasts that belong to certain cultures, that have only been seen in certain spots and most say belong to the realm of dreams. There are strange turtles that kill, monstrous jellyfish, dangerous octopi, and fish big enough to swallow boats. None of them were what I was looking for.

I was about to quit when I found something that made me keep reading: the Qalupalik. I made a copy of what I read so you could see it and know that your old man isn't crazy. The chunk below is of poor quality because the machine was running out of toner, but I thought it was important. Anyway, here's what the book I was reading, *Underwater Demons: A Bestiary of the World's Oceanic Monsters,* by Marcus Matthew, said about the Qalupalik:

*In Inuit culture, the Qalupalik is a human-like creature that lives in the sea. The humanoid fish is said to possess long hair, green or grey skin, and elongated fingers that end in long, sharp fingernails. According to Inuit mythology, the Qalupaliks like to inhabit reefs near human settlements. The creatures wear an amautik, which is a handmade pouch Inuit parents use to carry small children while working or during the day. The purpose of the amautik is as simple as it sinister: the Qalupaliks use it to take away children who disobey their parents. According to legend, the Qalupaliks eat the children. However, there are many rumors and even a few poems that talk about the Qalupaliks coming ashore to trade with the locals.*

*While it is generally understood and accepted by the academic community that the narrative is one used to prevent children from wandering off alone and playing by themselves near the water, certain members of the academic community point to the fact that the Inuit have a long history of disappearances and a high rate of child mortality, especially in coastal settlements. While this is far from enough evidence to support the existence of some humanoid water creature that devours children, Inuit songs, stories, poems, and mythology give the Qalupalik a privileged position and the creature is seen as something to be avoided at all costs, even by adults with no children.*

That was something. Humanoid creatures that lived near reefs and took children away from time to time. It wasn't an exact match, especially because the Qalupaliks were rumored to have hair on their heads but, as I said, it was enough to keep me going with my research. Half an hour later, I found this:

*Just like a few other cultures across the world, the Scottish also have a humanoid resident of the deep that is known to interact with humans on water and, occasionally, on land. In Scottish mythology, Selkies, or Selkie fowk, which roughly translates to "seal folk" or "seal people," are mythological beings capable of therianthropy, which is the mythological ability to metamorphose into animals. In the case of Selkies, they change from seal to human form by shedding their skin and then from human to something akin to a skinny seal with arms whenever they enter the water again. They are said to inhabit reefs near human settlements and to use their abilities to walk on land to interact with humans.*

I had enough to pique my interest and to let me know I was on the right path, so I kept reading. The book gave me versions of humanoid creatures inhabiting reefs near places where people lived all across the planet. These creatures were possibly the Qalupaliks or Selkies, but the drug-laden bodies they were feeding on had mutated them into something new. These things I called Profundos.

Knowing that other cultures had some version of it made it all better and worse at the same time. The worst thing about it was that the descriptions were eerily similar: green or grey skin, long fingers, batrachian features, and the ability to move around on land.

Without meaning to, I finished Matthews' book. I took a break after and went to get a sandwich from the university's cafeteria after telling the librarian to hold my books for me.

I ate, but I can't remember what was between those two pieces of bread. The information in my head was too much to process. I kept having the same revelation when I stopped focusing on one thing and looked at the bigger picture: humans have been sharing their lives with residents of the reefs seemingly forever. We have tried to get rid of them before, but we've never managed to.

It was almost time to go home, but I wanted more. I wanted one last look at some books that could add a tiny piece to the crazy puzzle I was putting together.

The first book I scanned after lunch yielded nothing except rehashed entries about some of the creatures in Matthews' book. The second contained a bomb.

Karla Ocasio, a professor at the University of Texas at Austin, had turned her dissertation of a small town in Massachusetts into a book: *Drowning the Truth: How the Government Destroyed a Town and its Residents.*

I'm running out of time—there is so much to say, but with each sentence, it feels like I'm being watched closer—so I'll just leave you with the gist of the book:

Innsmouth was a coastal town in Massachusetts founded in 1643. The town was known for shipbuilding before the American Revolution. Unfortunately, like many other towns, Innsmouth did not survive the shift to other types of businesses and a new way of living destroyed the town. Young people left in search of new opportunities and the residents that stayed behind became reclusive. According to the book, a series of disappearances led authorities to the town. All official records of what was seen in Innsmouth are sealed, but three weeks after launching an investigation, the government took over and used explosives to detonate the reefs that sat a few hundred feet in front of the town. But the story doesn't end there. After they destroyed the reef, many of the folks who were living in the town were taken away by Federal agents. They never came back. However, there are no arrest records or proof that anyone from Innsmouth was incarcerated or forced to move elsewhere. They simply disappeared. The fact that they bombed the shit out of the reef and felt the need to throw people in government vehicles and make them vanish is more than enough to convince me that something terrible was going on, something they didn't want the public to know about. I knew what those *somethings* looked like. The things I'd seen were descendants of those that had survived the bombing in Massachusetts. Or maybe they were the same. I had no idea how long those things lived.

Knowledge is weird, Angelica. One thing you will learn in life is that knowledge always comes to you fragmented, so it always feels incomplete, always leads to more questions. How well you get to understand something often depends on your ability to take pieces of information and build a puzzle to get a clearer picture of what you're dealing with. That is one skill academia tries to give you. It was the one element of being in college that I enjoyed. Seeing things come together is almost magical. It makes you feel like you can see the real world right underneath the false one. Unfortunately, not everything you see is good. This was one of those instances. I took pieces of folklore from around the world and observed a few patterns. They made me uncomfortable. If what they suggested was true, then anyone living near a reef anywhere around the world could potentially be dangerously close to creatures that have been around as long as we have. Hell, perhaps they even preceded us. The point is that the history of Innsmouth felt like the missing piece of the puzzle. There was something out there, just beyond the reef. It was something that had been around for a very long time. It also apparently possessed enough power to scare the government of the United States of America so bad that they decided to use bombs to deal with the situation.

The second thing you should know about knowledge is that it's often not comforting. Knowing things is scary. Understanding how the world works is something incredibly depressing. Seeing the inner working of society will make you see institutionalized racism everywhere. It will show you how misogyny is alive and well. It will show you how all of us who aren't rich are cogs in a system that's incredibly oppressive. It will show you that system has been designed to prevent us from moving up on the social ladder. You will learn that privilege is basically the idea that something isn't a damn problem because it doesn't affect you personally. Anyway, I digress. I need you to have answers, I want to finish everything I have to say. I'm starting to panic and want to put in here all the life lessons I might not get to teach you. Let me get back to my damn story before something happens and you never hear the end.

As you can imagine, my first reaction was thinking I need to get the hell off the island. Our beautiful country is 100 miles long by 35 miles wide. San Juan, where you were born, is like a finger sticking out into the ocean. We are all surrounded by water. If there is something in that water, we can't escape it. Oceans. Rivers. Even lakes. From what I'd learned from the rest of Matthew's book, there were also instances of humanoid creatures inhabiting bodies of water inland. In other words, I was fucked unless I moved to the moon. I had no money to go anywhere. Yeah, I know, I'm coming back to money again, but that's how it goes for poor people. Lack of money is at the core of most of our problems. I had no money to run away. I would never leave you and your mom alone and there was no way I could explain my situation to your mother. Every time I considered it, the image of that creature hanging out outside our house came back to me. The only thing I knew for sure was that I needed to get a gun.

My first thought was to call Marco. If anyone could get me a gun in a hurry it was him. He picked up on the second ring.

"Yeah?"

"Marco, it's me, Adam."

"Did you hear about Ronny?"

"No, I don't know anything about Ronny."

"Ah…so why are you calling then?"

"I'm calling you because I need a fucking gun, but now I want to know why you asked me about Ronny, man."

"I'm…I'm sorry I got you into this, Adam," he said. "I had no idea it would turn out the way it did."

"It's too late to be sorry. What I need now is a big fucking gun, not an apology. What happened to Ronny?"

"Ronny's dead."

Two words and my world shook a bit, the edges blurring under the weight of Marco's revelation.

"Dead?"

My question was stupid. Marco hadn't stuttered. Still, some part of my brain wanted confirmation, as if Marco would suddenly crack up and tell me he was bullshitting. Instead, I got details. Details I wish I hadn't gotten.

"He wouldn't pick up his phone so I sent someone to check on him. Someone had broken into his home. My man found him next to the bed. His body had been opened. Whoever did it took most of his organs. The guy I sent ran out, scared shitless, then he realized how fucking crazy he would sound if he came to me with that story, so he went back inside and used his phone to make a video."

That's all I needed to know. That's more than I wanted to know. I could picture Ronny looking out his window and seeing a figure in a long coat in the opposite side of the road, looking at his house in the middle of the night. Once again, fear's cold fingers grabbed the back of my neck and tried to squeeze me to death.

"I saw the video, Adam," Marco said, making me jump when he unexpectedly broke the silence. "There were these…things inside him. They looked like large black tadpoles with teeth. They were wriggling around, eating him from the inside, eating whatever was left of him. When my guy went to leave the place he saw a purple chunk of guts on the floor. This guy isn't a fucking doctor or anything but he thinks it was a liver. He said it looked like the liver his mother used to cook. Guy's a tough son of a bitch, but he said what he saw, and the memory of the liver's smell as it cooked, finally got to him. He vomited. Then he cried."

"So these things that came for Ronny. They attacked him at the beach, we killed them, and now they somehow still got him. They got him on land. What the fuck are we going to do now?"

"I don't know what you're going to do, but I'm getting the fuck outta here for a while. I have enough good people here. I can run this shit from my phone for a week or two. I hope this thing blows over. I'm done dealing with those fish people or whatever the fuck they are."

"I hear you, man, but I don't have that option. I'm broke. I have a family to protect. I have to stay here. I need dope for a week and I need a gun. The least you can do for me is hook me up, man. I was there with Ronny. They saw me. They saw my face. I...I've seen one of them hanging out in front of my house."

Marco's silence was pregnant with guilt, but I was sure he was also debating whether he should help me or if he should hang up the phone and never answer my calls again.

"Sure, I'll give you some smack and I'll give you a gun, but you need to know that a gun won't do a damn thing. You think Ronny didn't have a fucking gun?"

I hadn't thought about that. My brain was jumping between the horrific images Marco was putting into my head and the all-consuming need for a fix. I knew heroin would make some of the fear go away. Then I asked myself the most fucked up question of all—what if they could smell the heroin inside me? What if the poison coming out in my sweat smelled like lunch to them? What if eating me wasn't just the Profundos getting their revenge, but getting their fix?

"I hear you, Marco, but I need some kind of protection. I need a gun."

"My plane leaves at five thirty. Meet me at our spot in an hour."

Then he hung up.

I ran home to get a fix after the phone call. The hit almost knocked me out, but something stopped me from nodding out. It was your mother's voice yelling at me from the second floor. She said we needed diapers and formula and wanted to know what the hell I was up to. She sounded more worried than angry. I ran out of the house, jumped in my car, and drove away. Explaining was not an option at that point.

Fifty minutes later I showed up at our usual spot and Marco's car was already there. He had the windows up, but I could see a dark silhouette behind the wheel. He seemed to be taking a nap. I walked up to the car and touched my knuckles to the glass. He didn't react.

Any smart person would have seen Marco's lack of a reaction and left the place, gotten back in their car, and hauled ass out of that parking lot. But I was not smart at that time because I was high, so I did none of those. Instead, I reached for the handle and opened the door.

Marco's face was frozen in horror. He was slumped on the driver's seat. A huge cavity opened up just below his sternum and went all the way down to his genitals, which were missing. I'm not a physician, but I could tell his lungs and stomach had been removed. Same with his intestines. The cavity was making a sound. I couldn't help but lean in closer. Sitting in his lap, more or less where his testicles should have been, there was a puddle of black goo. Inside the black mush, round things were swimming that looked like tadpoles with very large heads and fully formed teeth. They had no eyes. They wriggled around as if trying to rip tiny chunks of flesh from the massive wound they swam inside of.

I slammed the door and looked around. It was still light out. They had done all of that in the light of day while people could see. *If you haven't seen these types of strange things on these streets, you haven't lived here long enough.* Then I remembered the gun, so I opened the door again. There was a gun in the passenger's seat. I leaned over Marco's body, which was more of an empty husk, and grabbed it. I shut the door again, walked to my car, got in, and sped all the way home.

I thought being home was going to comfort me somewhat. I really thought that seeing you and your mom was going to ground me, that it was going to take the fear down a few notches and center me. It didn't. Protecting both of you was still my main goal, but now I had no idea how I was going to do that. Two men were dead, and they were both more dangerous than I was. My nightmares came back, yet my eyes were wide open. Visions of those things feasting on your flesh invaded my brain and made me feel lightheaded with anxiety. I pulled the gun and thought about what my next step should be. You tossed about in your crib as the sun painted the sky purple. I couldn't stick around and I knew it.

You know those times when you know exactly what's going to happen but you go through the motions anyway? I had one of those moments. I went to the kitchen and looked out the window. The figure I knew would be standing on the opposite sidewalk was there as expected. I ran upstairs and kissed your soft, small head. I knew what I needed to do.

An hour later I was pulling into the parking lot of a cheap motel in Condado, El Tropical. It was very close to Old San Juan and La Perla. I checked in with the bag I usually take to work, went to my room, and sat on the bed with the gun I'd taken from Marco's car in my hands. It felt heavy and solid. I knew it could spit death whenever I wanted it to, but even that brought me no comfort. Then I remembered that my laptop was in the bag along with the copies I'd made at the library. That's when I started writing this.

I write this to tell you that I love you and that no matter what goes down you and your mother were—are—the best things in my life. I write to tell you I'm sorry that I wasn't strong enough to stop using junk when you came into this world. I swear I tried my best given the circumstances, but not everyone has the power to do things like that. Hopefully, you'll never have to find out if you have what it takes.

I write this hoping it will show you that I'm not a bad man, just did some bad things. Some dumb things. We all make mistakes. Mine just happened to be bigger, more expensive, and infinitely more dangerous than the mistakes of most others.

I also write this to give you a few lessons, to show you a few things about life that I learned the hard way and that I wish someone had told me about. I write this to tell you that life is unfair and painful, but that it's also beautiful and full of happy moments that make all the bullshit worth it. Holding you in my arms is something I wouldn't change for the universe. Kissing the top of your soft head felt like a tiny miracle every time, and I would go through everything I've gone through a million more times if it meant kissing your head even just one more night, if it meant holding you against me for one more minute.

I guess I also write this to tell you about those things from beyond the reef. Spread the word. Tell whoever you think can help. Bomb the fuck out of them. I'm not convinced that will get rid of them and they won't just find somewhere else to go, but at least they won't be here, they won't be near you.

I have stopped writing this a few times to check out the window, and last time I did, there was a figure standing at the end of the parking lot. He was looking at me, wearing the hat and long coat and…well, you already know. I can't say I was surprised. In fact, I was expecting them to show up.

You see, when Marco and I were talking in his car the terror and the ache in my veins were blinding me to a few things. His fear was contagious. Marco talked about them as if they are indestructible, like they are ghosts with sharp teeth that can come for you and there's nothing you can do, but he's wrong. I killed one of them. I blasted it twice with a shotgun. Black blood poured out of its body onto the sand of that cursed beach and it died the way all living things die. You can fear a lion or a snake, but they are animals and you can kill both of them. When they die, so does your fear. I have a gun and I will kill as many of those things as I need to convince them to leave me alone. If they leave me alone, they'll leave you and your mom alone. If they don't get the message, I will put bullets in their damn heads until there are none left.

Now I'm going to print this out in the little office they have in the lobby and put it in my bag. I'll also email it to myself and to your mom. The message will get out somehow even if something happens to me, but nothing will. Those things die like all living things die. They've been invading my nightmares but now I will be their worst nightmare. Watch this junkie become a hero, Angelica, watch your dad finally be strong enough, because I'm making my last stand. I did my last bit of dope, and once it's gone, it's gone for good. When I get back in this room I'm going to sit on that bed and wait for the thing outside to try and get inside. I have a little surprise for it. These fuckers will learn to stay out there beyond the reef or I'm going to turn them all into sushi.

See you soon, baby girl. I love you.

## ABOUT THE AUTHOR

Gabino Iglesias is a writer, editor, journalist, and book reviewer living in Austin, Texas. He is the author of COYOTE SONGS, ZERO SAINTS (both from Broken River Books), and GUTMOUTH (Eraserhead Press). He is the book reviews editor at PANK Magazine, the TV/film editor at Entropy Magazine, and a columnist for LitReactor and CLASH Media. His nonfiction has appeared in places like The New York Times, the Los Angeles Review of Books, the LA Times, El Nuevo Día, and other venues. The stuff that's made up has been published in places like Red Fez, Flash Fiction Offensive, Drunk Monkeys, Bizarro Central, Paragraph Line, Divergent Magazine, Cease, Cows, and many horror, crime, surrealist, and bizarro anthologies. When not writing or reading, he has worked as a dog whisperer, witty communications professor, and ballerina assassin. His reviews are published in places like NPR, Vol. 1 Brooklyn, Criminal Element, The Rumpus, Heavy Feather Review, Atticus Review, Entropy, HorrorTalk, Necessary Fiction, Crimespree, and other print and online venues. He teaches at SNHU's MFA program. You can find him on Twitter at @Gabino_Iglesias.

# LOVE IS A CREMATORIUM

by

Mercedes M. Yardley

# LOVE IS A CREMATORIUM

Mercedes M. Yardley

IT WAS SATURDAY MORNING and Kelly was mowing the lawn. The grass smelled good and his shirt was stuck to his scrawny body in a sweaty, happy way. He was tired. Good-work tired.

A beat-up green car pulled up and parked in the middle of the dirt road to his house. Joy got out, her blonde hair more disheveled than usual. She wore a HEART band tee and was holding her arm in a disturbingly careful way. Her mascara ran down her face, and her eye was red and puffy. It was going to be a glorious shiner.

She moved toward him and even her walk wasn't quite right.

"Joy," he said, and turned off the mower. He jogged over and she threw herself into his arms.

"I'm sweaty," he said, because it was the automatic thing to say. He meant to say, "Whatever happened, we can handle it." He meant to say, "I'll kill your father this time, I really will." He meant to say, "You're safe here. I'll never let something like this happen if you stay with me." But "I'm sweaty" is what came out of his mouth.

"I can't do it anymore, Kel. I can't." She pulled back and her brown eyes were angry and wild, so un-Joylike, and Kelly nearly took a step back, she looked so fierce.

"I'll kill him if he touches me again, I swear I will." She bared her teeth, and suddenly she was all fireballs and fury and deep, poisoned seas. "I'll chop off his hands. Then I'll chop off his head. I'll stab him in his creepy staring eyes, so help me!"

Kelly pulled her close again, holding her while she sobbed and raged and wailed. He felt her soul grind to dust in his arms. Felt her lose the strength that anger and terror gave her.

"I love you," he whispered into her hair after she had become quiet. His shirt was doused with sweat and tears and probably tasted like a salt lick. He wanted to run his tongue down it to be sure, but instead merely dipped his head and sucked on his shirt collar.

"You're the only one who does, Kel. The only one in the whole world."

She raised her face to look at him, and he studied her

cheekbones, her bruised eye, the way her lip had been busted open. *Again.* He looked at her injured arm, looked away, took a deep breath and reached for it, but she cradled it closer.

"Remember going roller skating as kids?" he asked.

Joy blinked.

"What?"

"You were always Hell on wheels. Busted your face up something awful. I'd see you like this all of the time."

She tried to smile, and Kel felt curiously close to crying.

"A portent of things to come, huh?" she asked.

"Maybe."

"If I remember right, you were always trying to put me together then, too."

Kelly smiled. It was a goofy smile, full of teeth and something dark he was trying to hold back.

"It's my job. Always was. Always will be."

He kept his tone light, but Something Serious ran underneath it, and it was this Something Serious that Joy latched on to.

She took his hand in hers and studied the length of his fingers, the squareness. These were hands that had never hit a woman, never hurt a child. Quite the opposite. These were hands who had washed away dirt and picked out baseball bat slivers from her young fingers. Hands that staunched blood and applied bandages. These were healer's hands.

Joy held Kelly's hand up to her cheek, over her eye. He ran his fingers gently down the bruises and imagined blood vessels knitting themselves back together, swelling, receding. He wished the pain to disappear, but when his fingers left her face, she winced and her tight lips told him she was still hurting.

"I always expect you to have magic in you, Kel," she said, and he grinned that goofy grin again, but he felt that his eyes had gone primal and a little bit dangerous.

"What's goin' on, Joy? You have something real big on your mind."

She dropped his hands and stepped back as if she needed to give him some distance, some formality. It was almost like a business proposition. He somehow felt undressed, like he should be standing there in a church suit with a leather briefcase, his shoes polished nicely.

She squeezed her eyes shut.

"I'm leaving. I have to leave. He was going to kill me this time, I know it."

"Joy—"

"I *know* it," she said, and opened her eyes. He saw everything then, and soon he was nodding his head.

"Okay. Okay. So what are you going to do?"

She looked over her shoulder at the car.

"I have a bag. I have a little bit of money. And I have his car. I thought I'd just drive until I couldn't drive any more, then sell it. After that, I'll walk. I'll…I dunno. I'll sleep in ditches. Find a city, get a job. I don't know," she said again when he looked at her, "but I can't stay anymore, Kel."

"Did he break your arm?"

She shook her head.

"I don't think so. It's just awful sore. But I can't go back."

"You could stay with me and my parents."

She stood on her tiptoes and kissed his cheek.

"Sweet Kelly. You know I can't."

"They just don't know you like I know you. If you stayed, they'd get that chance. I could talk 'em around, you know I could."

Give them enough time and they could see past the donated hand-me-downs and the dilapidated trailer, Kelly was sure of it. Joy was so much more than Buck's daughter, and his parents would realize it. But seeing the way Joy babied that arm, he knew time wasn't theirs to spend. Her dad was mean at the best of times, but the fear in her eyes was stark. Kelly's stomach felt like he had eaten something sharp, something pointy with spines. The edge of a newly hewn axe, or the point of one of Buck's knives.

"He'd come looking for me, and I don't want you to get hurt. You or your family."

"He doesn't scare me," Kelly said automatically, but they both knew it wasn't true.

"It's okay, baby," she said, and kissed him. She tasted of blood and Orange Crush Chapstick.

They'd only kissed a few times, out where nobody could see. The kisses were deep and they were funny and sometimes they laughed and a time or two Joy had cried. But the kiss this time was saying something deeper. It was a Last Kiss. That's what Kelly was afraid of.

"Got any money?" she asked him. Her lips were still so close to his that he felt them move. She didn't want to pull away, to have that distance between them. He didn't either. He blinked and felt his lashes flutter against her cheek.

"Some."

"Come with me," she said, and burrowed her face into his neck. She pushed her body as close to his as she could get it, and his arms went around her automatically.

*This is how it's supposed to be,* he thought, and the grasses and dust around him nodded yes, yes, this is exactly how it is supposed to be.

"Joy, I—"

"Please don't tell me no. I don't know if I can do this without you. I need you to be with me."

His heart hurt. In the best of ways. In the worst. Her hair smelled like sweat and lavender and something else that tugged at the very base of him. He put his hand to her scalp and pulled it away. His fingers were red and sticky.

"What did he do to you?"

He almost didn't recognize his voice. It was a dark thing, roiling and full of teeth. It hurt as it came out of his mouth, and he had to bite it back.

Joy's fingers fluttered to the wound in the back of her head, hovered, and then moved away. She tried to step back but Kelly held her closer, rested his chin on her head, careful not to hurt her. Her body was fragile, made of spun sugar and spider webs. There was only so much pain the human body and mind were meant to take, and then everything exploded into showers of shadows and powder.

"When are you going?" he asked. His voice was gentle this time. It was just right.

"Right now."

"Let me throw together a bag."

She pulled back and looked at him. Her eyes were huge and full of hope and pain and wariness and disbelief. Kelly remembered the first time they had held a rabbit from the fields. It was tiny and furry and dying, an accident from a lawn mower, if he remembered right. Her eyes had looked that same way. There was magic in the world, but also death and horror. He knew he was making the right decision, then. Knew it was what needed to be done. He couldn't send this broken little bunny out into the world to die alone. He needed to be there with her to soothe the wounds, to keep the monsters away. He needed her to do the same thing for him.

"I'll never leave you, bunny," he told her.

She blinked rapidly in the sun, her smile crooked and a little unsure.

"What's with the new name all of a sudden?"

He shrugged, kissed her forehead.

"It fits you."

He packed a duffel in only a few minutes. What does a teenage boy really need, after all? He took his wallet, thought about it, and took the envelope of grocery money from the kitchen cupboard.

*Mom and Dad.*

His handwriting was fast, hard, gangly, like the rest of him. He wrote quickly, a born lefty, dragging his hand through the ink before it had a chance to dry.

*Joy needs me. I promise to call.*

He pondered over it, whether to say it or not, but then he thought of his mother reading the letter.

*Love you,* he scrawled, and stuck the note to the fridge with a magnet.

Joy was sitting cross-legged on the hood of the car. Her eyes were closed, and whether she was sleeping or praying, Kelly couldn't say. Seemed that both did the same amount of good, far as he could tell.

"Ready?" he asked her.

She opened her eyes and stared at him for a long time. He wondered what she saw. A boy in a sweaty shirt holding a duffel bag and a couple cans of Squirt. This was who she was going to depend on. He looked down at himself and frowned.

"Guess I should've taken a shower. I didn't even put the mower away. Sorry, Joy. I just thought, what if your dad is comin'? I was just thinking of being quick, not really of anything else. Maybe—"

Joy slid off the hood. She stood on tiptoe, bumped noses with Kelly almost playfully, and then she kissed him again.

*Not a Last Kiss,* he thought hazily. *A First Kiss. The First of their adventures together. This is the beginning of everything.*

"I love you, Kelly Stands," Joy said. "From the bottom of my heart, I do."

His stomach did flipflops and leaps and he found it strangely hard to talk.

"I love you, too."

He did. And she did. The way she blushed and wrapped the fingers of her good hand into his shirt sleeve told him all he needed to know and more.

He tossed his duffel bag into the backseat of the car.

"Mind driving, Kel? My head hurts something fierce."

He opened the door to the passenger seat and helped her in.

"Here," he said, and pulled a bottle of aspirin out of his pocket. "Got something for your head."

"Thank you, baby."

She swallowed it dry while Kelly walked around, hopped in the driver's seat, and started the car.

"You're sure about this?" he asked her.

"Absolutely."

"Then let's go."

She leaned her head against the window. She slipped her hand into his.

A few hours and they were outside the state line of Alabama.

#

They drove until the car ran out of gas. It was a good five hours of driving. They filled it up two more times before they decided that was far enough.

"It's time to ditch it," Joy said. Her eyes were red and her face was white from exhaustion, but she still looked happier than Kelly had ever seen her.

"All right."

Kelly had wondered how they'd sell the car, but it was easy. Joy took a deep breath and wandered up to a pair of long legs sticking up from under a truck in a driveway. She bent down, and the legs slid out and turned into a young man, who unfolded himself and stood up.

Kelly watched Joy put her hands in her pockets, tilting her

face up to see the stranger. She squinted in the sun and something in Kelly wanted to stand between them, to look the other man in the face and see what exactly his intentions were. Something else wanted to duck quietly into the background. Kelly felt himself actually bunch up in the passenger seat of the car, getting smaller and smaller before he forced himself to stop, to stretch out.

Joy pointed at the car and the man followed her gaze. Kelly waved awkwardly, put his hand down. Joy stood on tiptoe as if she was whispering in his ear, and Kelly didn't like the way his stomach tightened when the man bent close to listen.

The man straightened. Nodded. Reached in his back pocket for his wallet. He handed folded money to Joy, and then laughed when she hugged him with her good arm. He put his hand on top of her head like it had always gone there, like he had been teasing her about being short all of her life. They looked like old friends.

*She could have just as easily been born here,* Kelly thought. *He could have been me.*

The thought of this man, this stranger, being her parallel-world Kelly made him get out of the car. He ambled over a bit too casually.

"Hey," he said, and didn't like the sound of his voice, the note of question and concern and danger and warning wrapped up inside of it. Uncertainty and chainsaws. High fives and electric fences.

The man nodded back, his grin wide and easy, and Kelly almost hated him more. All was right with his world. This was a man who knew where he was going to sleep that night, who didn't have to worry about Joy's fitful cries as she dreamed, who didn't have the responsibility of being the last one awake, watching to keep them safe.

"Joshua here will take it," Joy said simply, and that was that. It was over for her. Car discarded. Item checked off her list. Joshua swooped in to save the day.

"You'll want to paint it or…whatever, pretty soon," she told Joshua, and he nodded again.

"Gotcha," he said, and Kelly looked down at his feet. They were large and his sneakers were still stained from mowing the grass. How long would these shoes last? Suddenly the weight of what they were doing hit him, crushed his chest in a way that nearly made him gasp.

Joshua studied him, seeming to really see him for the first time.

Joy slid her hand into Kelly's, almost timidly, and his fingers curled automatically around hers. She was shaking, and he noticed that her bright smile was tight around the corners, her eyes a little bit too wide.

"Right. Thanks, Joshua," he said, and then he was walking down the long dirt driveway with Joy at his side, their legs swishing through the grasses.

"We're going to be okay, bunny," he said, and as soon as he heard the words, he knew he believed them. He squeezed her hand and she squeezed back. He made a face and soon she was laughing up at him, her nose scrunched in the way that told him she was truly happy, not worried about passing her English test or hiding her shiner or wondering whether or not bones would break this time.

"I sort of dig you," he said, and laughed when she mock hit him in the chest.

"You're lucky that I sort of dig you right back," she said, and then she stopped and leaned against him.

"Thank you," she said. Her voice was thick and heavy with her sincerity. "Thank you, Kelly."

He hugged her, tucking her body protectively against his, and it felt right. This was how it was always supposed to be. He knew it, had known it since they were children, when she would flee through the trees to his house in the middle of the night, afraid of her mother and her father, of the screams and new holes in the wall. She didn't want to stay in his room, but asked him to come stay beside her out in the trees.

"Remember when I'd pull my blanket out through my window?" he asked her. "And we'd go back by the woodshed to sleep? We were safe there."

"How could I forget, Kelly? It was the only time I slept. You said you'd keep watch, that you'd be the last one awake, watching so my father wouldn't find us."

She was speaking into his shirt, burying her face into him like a newborn kitten.

"I loved you then, did you know that? Always, always. If my daddy found us, he would have killed us. But you still came."

"You were always there for me, too," he said. "You know it worked both ways. You were there whenever I needed you, and that was an awful lot."

She pulled away and looked at him. He saw himself reflected in her irises, realized that she saw him and through him and made him even more *him* than he actually was. She saw someone strong and safe and dependable, an eight-year-old boy who turned into an awkward almost-man, but he was enough for her. He was everything, and his heart felt strangely light and happily strangled at the same time.

"I'll always come for you," he said simply, and the flurry of kisses on his face made him smile, made him laugh with the purity of *being,* and then they were walking hand-in-hand by the side of the road again, and even when night came and they were forced to sleep outside, without Kelly's blanket, it wasn't frightening. It was childhood, just like old times, and the scent of her hair and the cut grass was what heaven would smell like, he was sure of it.

#

Joy had nightmares during the night, but each time she would twist and cry out, Kelly would whisper, "I'm here," and "you're safe," and "I love you."

The *I Love Yous* didn't come as natural as he would have thought. They were still unsure and sounded a bit grandiose, but they were real and sincere, and it pleased him that each time he whispered this, she quieted and turned toward him.

That's what love was, he thought. Being the warm blanket for somebody else. Being the rain that brought their parched roots back to life. It was being their tether so they didn't float off into space. It was growth and pain and responsibility. Love was a crematorium that lit you up and burned you out at the same time.

Joy woke up with sticks in her hair.

"I'm hungry. Are you?"

"Starved," he answered.

They walked until they came to a filthy old gas station. "Dilapidated" came to Kelly's mind, possibly for the first time in his life. They used the restrooms and washed up, then bought prepackaged sandwiches and drinks. They counted their folding money with an intensity that made the attendant behind the counter take notice.

"Where you headed?" the attendant asked.

"Nowhere in particular," Joy said. "What's around here?"

"Not a thing."

Joy was biting her lip a bit too hard. The attendant watched this, too.

"Where do you live?" Joy asked, and both Kelly and the attendant were taken back by this.

"About two miles up the road."

"Where's the nearest city?"

"Probably Macon." He pointed.

"Goin' there anytime soon?"

Her voice was breathless. Hopeful. This is what hope sounded like. It sounded like a young girl asking a stranger for a ride to the city.

"Nah." The attendant's gaze narrowed. "Whatcha looking for in Macon?"

"Work. You're sure you're not going that way?"

"Nope."

Joy shrugged.

"Too bad. Later."

The bell dinged as she pushed her way out the door. Kelly was right behind her.

"What was that? That guy gives me the creeps. He'd rob us blind and leave our bodies in a field somewhere before he'd help us. What did you do that for?"

Joy kept walking, fast.

"Because he scares me, Kel. I knew he wouldn't help us. But now if he's looking for us, or wants to tell my daddy where we went, if there's a reward, he'll be looking in Macon. And that's exactly where we won't be."

"Where will we be?"

"I don't know and I don't care. But not anywhere close to here. We'll go somewhere wonderful. Somewhere just for us. Any place you've always wanted to see?"

There were people who dreamed of Egypt and Turkey and Thailand and other exotic places. Kelly had never done that. He assumed he'd be working right in town, or pretty close to it, all of his life. Just like his daddy and his daddy's daddy. There wasn't any shame in it.

"I don't know," he said. "Never thought of it. You?"

"Anywhere," Joy said, and that was it.

Anywhere. He was pretty sure they'd make it.

She smiled up at him, blonde hair blowing in her eyes.

"Keep your expectations simple and you almost always get what you want," she said, and squeezed his hand. "Then everything else that happens, well. It's just a gift."

He wanted to tell her that she was his gift, but it was too hokey to say. Maybe if he thought it hard enough, she'd hear it.

"I never thought I'd get you," she said simply. The honesty cut through his teenage bone and sinew. He flushed, and she laughed when she saw it.

"You're my wish," she said, and jumped up to ruffle his hair. "I'll always take care of you. Always."

#

As they walked, the heat, the humidity, the car exhaust, and the long Southern grasses crowded in on Kelly's lungs, making them smaller and fuller and unable to work. The air was all dust and dirt and pollen and his lungs sucked it in, shrieking for oxygen, but each breath had less air than the last. He collapsed on the ground, gasping, pulling in dirt and bits of weeds into his body, into his throat, and he felt them lodging there, making a home, taking root.

"I have you, baby. I have you," Joy said, but words alone couldn't make him well, and they both knew it.

Joy left him lying there, sprawled on the ground with his duffel bag as a pillow, and she ran to the road.

"Help!" she screamed, waving her arms, and a pretty young thing radiating hope and desperation in the Southern sunlight would make anybody stop. A car slowed down immediately, and she leaned in the passenger window.

"I think my friend's having a terrible asthma attack. Could you help us? Please?"

The driver seemed doubtful, but Joy's eyes sparkled with tears, *real* tears, honest-to-goodness tears, and the driver realized he had a chance to be a hero. The time for heroics seemed long past, left someplace back in the war, but here was a woman who needed help to save a person she cared for, and this driver was just the one to help them.

He hopped out, grabbed a backpack from his trunk, and followed the girl through the weeds until she stopped at the side of a tall, lanky boy, just this side of manhood. He'd curled up into the fetal position and was breathing in dirt with every gasping breath.

"This won't do," the driver said, and he pulled the boy up, cradling him.

"You need to sit up," he told Kelly. "And you need to take deep breaths. Deep ones, son. Darlin', open that bag and hand me the inhaler, would you? My stepson uses one. We keep one in every vehicle."

Joy's hands shook, but she unzipped the bag and did what he asked.

Kelly was gasping, taking in half a breath, less than that. Joy watched his face, reaching out to briefly touch his blue lips.

"This boy needs a hospital," the driver said. He started to pull Kelly to his feet. Joy helped him.

"We can't go to one," she said. Kelly was draped over her, and she kissed his cheek over and over as she and the driver pulled him to the car. "We don't have any money. And they'll take him away from me, that's what they'll do. They'll bring him back home. We can't go back."

The man looked at both Kelly and Joy, and then sighed.

"Okay. Fine. Let's do what we can."

Joy hopped in the back seat and pulled Kelly in beside her. The driver leaned in and checked Kelly's eyes.

"Good, you're back with us. Keep breathing, boy. In and out. Good air filling your lungs. Hold on to that pretty girl next to you and I'll get you someplace safe."

Kelly rested his head on Joy's shoulder and closed his eyes. He felt her hands run across his face. He remembered those hands holding cotton candy at the state fair last summer, beautiful and graceful even though two of her fingers had been broken and bandaged.

"Are you okay, baby?" she asked him. Her voice was as sweet as honey. "Are you okay?"

"Okay," he managed, but any more words were too hard to

say. He breathed in and out, in and out, for what seemed like a very long time.

The car stopped.

"Just a second," the man said, and stepped out.

Kelly struggled to open his eyes but they were too heavy. "Is he...?"

"He brought us to a motel. I don't think he'll tell anybody."

They didn't say another word until the driver opened the back door.

"Come on, kids," he said. "I'll help you."

"I can walk, sir," Kelly say politely, but unfolding himself from the backseat took more energy than he expected.

"I know you can," the man said, "but let an old man feel useful."

They made their way up the metal steps and the man opened the door with a keycard. The room was small and dingy, but clean enough. It had a bed, and that was all that mattered to Kelly.

"I'll just lie down for a second," he said, and was asleep immediately.

The driver filled a plastic cup up with water and handed it to Joy. She pulled Kelly's shoes off his feet and then took it.

"What are you going to do now?" the driver asked.

Joy drained the cup in two gulps. The driver refilled it and handed it back.

"Guess we'll rest up for a day and then head out again. Thank you so much, sir."

The driver sighed.

"I don't like it. You know I don't. Asthma is scary at best, fatal at worst."

Joy paled, but the man continued.

"But I can see how stubborn you are about not going back to wherever you came from, and from the looks of you, you actually might be better off. So stay. And take this. He should keep it on him. Just in case."

He dropped the inhaler onto the cheap motel table. Then he slid a couple of soft, worn bills there, as well.

Joy's lip trembled.

"We won't be able to pay you back."

The man smiled.

"You don't have to. I get the sense you've had a bad time of it. Not everyone is out to get you. Get yourself into the city and away from all of this dust. You seem like good kids."

He nodded his head, stepped out of the room, and quietly pulled the door shut behind him.

Joy looked at the money on the table. She looked at Kelly asleep on the bed. She kicked off her own shoes and curled up next to him. She watched him breathe for a very long time, in and out, clean breath after clean breath, careful not to fall asleep until she was certain he was safe.

#

Kelly woke up with sunshine in his eyes and an ache deep in his lungs. He groaned and stretched out. His stocking feet were hanging off the short bed. He could see his big toe sticking out of his right sock.

"Baby?" Joy was right there, her eyes wide. Her hands were baby birds, fluttering here and plucking there. She tested his arms and chest and neck and collarbone as if she was afraid he had shattered apart during the night.

The way his body and head felt, perhaps he had.

"Hey," he said, and that was all he got out. A simple "hey" and then he was breathing in her hair as she flung herself at him. He was choking again, going under once more, but this time it was a glorious thing.

"I'm okay," he assured her, and he very nearly thought of sitting, oh yes he did, but it felt so good to lie there, rest his weary body, and simply take a second to bask in the experience that was a happy, relieved Joy.

"Never again, never again," she told him. "We're not walking in those weeds any more. Look, the man from yesterday gave us some money and we're not too far from a bus station. That's what we should do, Kel. Buy two tickets and go as far as the money will let us. But maybe breakfast first. Are you hungry?"

Was he hungry? His stomach had more teeth than a barracuda. He could eat everything ever cooked in the world. Yesterday, he swore that if he walked past one more cow chewing its cud, he'd leap over the fence and bite the animal right on its haunches, he was so hungry.

"I could eat," he said politely.

Joy looked at him. She looked at his face and his body that housed his traitorous lungs. She looked at his one pale toe poking out of his stupid sock. She looked hard and then she covered her face and laughed. She laughed so much that tears slid out from under her fingers. She laughed and then she was sobbing, and then she was laughing again.

Kelly didn't know what to say. He laid his hand on her knee and waited until her breathing had righted itself.

"I'm sorry," she said, wiping her eyes. The bruise was starting to heal up some. That made Kelly happy. "I don't know why that was so funny. I just.... I need you, Kel. You're my North Star and the thing that always sets me to rights. You're something special. What would I do without you?"

He struggled to sit up.

"Feed me and you'll never have to know, bunny. But if I don't eat soon, I'll waste away to clear nothing, and that will be the end of me. Then you'll be alone."

"Don't say it."

He grinned.

"Alone and forgotten."

"Don't you say that!"

He tickled her, and her pale hair in the sunshine was the prettiest thing he'd ever seen.

"Alone forever and ever and ever, unless you feed me right now!"

She laughed and this time he laughed with her. They tickled and fought and kissed, and then they kissed some more, this time with more intensity. Joy pulled the curtains, and the sun prowled around outside, wondering why it wasn't allowed in. Years from now, when he'd think back on his last truly happy moment, this was the one that would come to mind.

#

The money was carefully tallied and bus tickets were purchased. After walking through the weeds, the bus felt like a grand thing, a chariot of the finest paint and steel. Kelly sat in the window seat with a freshly showered Joy asleep on his shoulder. This was how it was always supposed to be.

The woman in front of Kelly turned around in her seat.

"Where ya from?" she asked.

Kel's mind stopped, a rabbit frozen at the sight of danger. This danger was wearing a kerchief and had sparkling eyes, but danger all the same."

"Um. Utah."

She raised one eyebrow. "You're going the wrong way for Utah."

Kelly shrugged. "I want to see everywhere."

"And your girlfriend. She from Utah, too?"

Kelly felt his face change. It went dark, pulled itself into an expression he didn't know his face muscles could make. He briefly imagined that he looked at the woman through slitted pupils like a cat, or a venomous snake. He tightened his arm around his sleeping Joy.

"You have something against Utah?" he asked, and the woman turned herself around.

Kelly leaned his head against the window. His limbs still felt heavy from yesterday, the brush with fragility, the way that his body took in new flora and fauna and rejected it. At home he mowed the lawn and ran outside without issue, but this was somewhere different. All of this was…different.

Kelly wondered about his mother, who would be beyond hysterical by now. He bet she lit up the phone tree at home, calling all of the neighbors. He wondered if Joy's dad was one of them.

He shuddered, and Joy made a small sound in her sleep.

"It's okay, it's okay," he whispered into her hair. "It's me. I'm awake. I'm watching over you."

They rolled closer into the city and Kelly tried to keep his soul from crumbling in despair.

"We can do this," he whispered to Joy. "We can."

The city was gray sky over gray cement over gray pavement. Rain shimmered down and pasted the wet garbage to the street.

"Joy," Kelly said, and nudged her. "We're here."

They grabbed their bags. They grabbed each other's hands.

"We made it," Joy breathed, and Kelly bit back his desolation.

She turned to him. Her eyes shone with tears that had nothing to do with broken bones or terrified humiliation. "He'll never touch me again," she said, and Kelly could hear Joy's heart sing. It was a cheerful melody in C Major.

"Never," he agreed. "We won't let him. He'll never find you."

He had always read about happy tears, but he hadn't ever heard them until now. They sounded sweet. They sounded like horror. Kelly and Joy strode away from the bus station like two people who had purpose, but this was a lie.

They never had such little purpose in their lives. After the bus tickets, they had only enough money to grab a fast food hamburger two times.

Twice.

At home, Kelly would be downing burgers and spaghetti and milkshakes and whatever his mom would place in front of him. She understood lank teenage boys with hollow legs and grumbling stomachs. But here, food was harder to come by. After five days and two hamburgers, things felt dire.

"I'm hungry, Kelly," Joy said. She wrinkled her nose in frustration. "I thought it would be easier than this."

"It will get better," he said, and he hoped with all of his might that this was true. It had to be the case, didn't it? Like that old saying; *When you are going through Hell, keep going.*

"I know it will," she said, and her hand wrapped in Kelly's was still what mattered most. It was safe and cool and unbroken. He thought of her fragile little bird bones and held on a little tighter.

"How long do you think you'll stay?" she asked him. She was looking at the ground, far too carefully, and he knew she didn't want to see what was in his eyes. "I mean, before it becomes too much and you'll go back?"

He thought. He thought slowly and carefully. They had barely slept in days, but had walked around the city holding hands and pointing at buildings. He'd never seen anything so tall and imposing in his life.

"We're going to live up there," Joy had said, gesturing at the tallest apartment building she could find. Its windows shone like stars. "We'll wake up every morning and look down on this city and all of the people and know that we own it, Kel. It's going to be something real special."

It was a different place when you were up high. They'd rode in elevators and climbed stairs and being at the tippy top of the world changed the bleakness of the city. It opened beneath them like a cavity, a void. It showed the gentlemanly hollows beneath its concrete cheeks.

But down here from the street, they were face-to-face with the trash and refuse that this tall utopia excreted. Sewage rats, that's all they were. Kelly bared his teeth briefly.

"That depends, Joy. When are you going to be ready to go back home?"

She was shaking her head adamantly before the words were fully out of his mouth.

"Never," she said. She pulled her hand from his and crossed her arms across her chest protectively. "I'll stay here for a hundred years before I ever set foot back in that town again."

Kelly shrugged. "Then you just answered your own question. I'll stay here for a hundred years. Wherever you are, that's where I'll be, too. You'd just better get used to it."

She searched his eyes then, looking for the anger or deceit that she was half afraid would be there. Kelly gazed back, his face as wholesome and open as fresh ears of corn at the supper table, or a new bottle of milk.

"How did I get to be so lucky?" Joy asked, and Kelly laughed. His stomach growled at the same time.

"Guess it depends on your definition of luck, bunny," he said, and Joy's bright smile told him that she was the luckiest girl in the entire world, that she wouldn't change a thing as long as it meant they were together. They could have a room in the penthouse or a little cottage by the sea or sit side-by-side, chained in the gulag and it wouldn't matter as long as she had her Kelly.

That night was the first night it happened.

Kelly squirreled food out of a public dumpster. He used his long orangutan arms to reach in and pulled out a fast food bag full of trash. In amid the plastic forks and dirty napkins was a container containing a half-eaten salad and most of a chocolate chip cookie.

"Dinner is served," he said, and although he and Joy winced as they first touched the old food, the spiked mace in his stomach insisted he eat it.

"Put the pride away, you fool, and feed me," his stomach demanded, and Kelly, being a very good Southern youth, did as he was told. A quarter of a salad and a bite of cookie wasn't enough to satiate him, but it was enough to convince his ravenous body that he was, at least, trying.

Within two weeks, all pride was completely gone. They became more furtive. Their movements became darting. They went after garbage cans and dumpsters, pulling out half-eaten meals in Styrofoam and dining on rewrapped cheeseburgers with gusto. They scavenged deftly like the street mice they had become.

"Chinese, lover?" Joy would ask, and they'd eat quickly, using their hands and wiping them on the cold concrete later.

Their bodies stank and Joy's blonde hair turned into straw after washing it in gas station bathrooms with hand soap. Nobody wanted to hire two high school dropouts who wore the same clothes day after day.

"Please, sir," Joy begged. It was her third job interview that morning, and the look on the man's horsey face said everything. "I'm smart and I learn really quickly. I type well. I just need a job. I'll do anything."

He eyed her too closely. "Anything?"

She stood up, her hands fisted at her side.

"Not anything." Her voice was quiet with rage and she stomped out the door. Kelly met her outside, saw the way her mouth bitterly twisted, and wisely said nothing.

More weeks passed. She was shrinking away. The skin was pulling too tight over her face and her ribs were showing even more than normal. But Kelly, skinny to begin with, looked like a corpse. One evening Joy looked at him and studied the way the gray light of the city washed the color from his face.

"I love you," she said, and he broke out into his goofy grin.

"I love you, too," he answered, and his glowing face bobbling over his scrawny body broke something in Joy. She kissed him, long and deep like she was stealing his taste away. He was a treasure to save for later. Something to think of during the bad times.

"I'll be right back," she said, and touched her forehead to his. "Save my spot, okay?"

"Sure," he said, and watched her walk down the alley, disappearing in the warm steam from the manhole covers. Save her spot, she said, as if people were scrambling to steal their particular section of gritty horror town. But Kelly was dependable, and Kelly was truthful, and if Joy asked him to save her spot, then he would guard it with his life.

She returned nearly an hour later with a bag of fast food in her hand.

"Here," she said, and sat down. "This is all for you. I already ate."

His stomach roared and ached as he opened the bag. The smell was teenage heaven.

"Fresh?" he asked hopefully. It was more than he dared.

Joy smiled, but something was lost there. "Fresh. Eat up, Kelly."

He wanted to enjoy it. He wanted to take his time and savor it, but the burgers called his name too loudly. They were decimated, the burgers swallowed and the fries pushed into his mouth six at a time. When he finished, he licked his fingers, each one, starting at the thumb and working his way down.

"That was good, Joy. Thanks," he said, and leaned his head against the wall. "Where did you get the money for it?"

She shrugged. "I had something to sell."

"What?" he asked, but she didn't answer. She slid close to him and pulled his arm around her.

"I'm not feeling so well, Kel. Mind if I take a quick nap?"

"I'll stay awake," he promised, and kissed her bird-nest hair. She settled into a fitful sleep, squirming in a way that reminded Kelly of frightened kittens, and he whispered over and over that she was all right, that he was here, that she shouldn't have to sell herself to feed him, that she could deny it all she wanted but he wasn't an idiot. And he loved her anyway, always, no matter what, he murmured, and that's when she finally quieted.

He held her all night long and hated this horrible bone-gnaw city.

#

It began little by little, bit by bit, like leaving a cobalt blue bottle hanging on a tree in hot summer nights, and watching the rain fill it up. Joy's spirit began leaking out of her eyes and her mouth while she slept, and something else began to take its place. What was left of her began to be distilled, perfect and pure, precious little drops of Joy. He could let each taste of true Joy rest on his tongue for hours, to be delighted over, and it was a glorious thing when he could get it.

It became harder and harder to obtain.

Joy traded her time and her body for things. Food mostly, at first. Sometimes for something that seemed precious at the time.

"Hey, pretty girl," a man said to her one night. She was standing with other kids in an alleyway. They pretended to talk about movies they liked and boys they had dated, but it was an open ruse. They were really standing there in order to be seen, to show how their skinny legs would wrap around a person's waist if they could pay. Their thin, bony fingers became deft at undoing zippers, buttons, and clasps. They picked at food in the trash heaps and shoved them into chapped lips like tiny racoons. Kelly stayed in the area, too, but far enough away that he didn't intimidate the customers with his tall frame. He crinkled himself into the smallest ball of bones and rags that he could, trying to look as harmless as a newborn puppy without milk teeth.

"Hey back," Joy said, and Kelly turned his face away so he wouldn't have to see the way she arched against the man, the tiny buds of her breasts attempting brazenly to be those of a fully-grown woman.

"I don't have much money on me," the man began, and Joy immediately turned away.

"Then I don't have much time."

"But I have something shiny and I have some beers back in my car."

Joy pretended to study her manicure. Her nails were bitten so far that they showed blood, the tender skin around her finger shredded and torn.

"I don't work for beer," she said.

"That's just a bonus," the man said, and held something up. It was a necklace, a cheap chain and some kind of pendant that glittered and reflected the sad streetlights. "How about this? Something pretty for the pretty lady."

Kelly would think back to this moment often. It would come to him in dreams, completely unbidden. He'd be running down a grassy hill with a herd of wild horses, their hooves pounding around him. He'd have his arms out like an airplane, feeling the wind and freedom and the exhilaration of being in wide, open spaces with these beating hearts of feral muscle, and then he would stop. He'd pull up short, trapped in this piss-scented alley, and the horses would thunder on without him. He'd stand, and see his Joy staring at this cheap trinket like it was the most beautiful thing on God's green earth. He'd try to reach out to her in this dream, to raise his hand or shout her name, but the most he could do was watch helplessly as she reached out to touch the pendant, pull her hand back tenderly, and turn to walk away with the man.

She didn't come back that night. Not at all. Kelly waited, his hands shoved deep into the pockets of his hoodie, his head against the rough brick wall. He stood straight and stretched, not caring if he looked like a long shadow unboxing itself from its dybbuk prison. He paced back and forth, his feet scraping against the broken bottles and used syringes that littered the area.

"Knock it off," a short girl with ratty black hair said. "Your creeping is going to scare guys away, and I'm sick as hell and need something to fix with."

"I'm waiting for Joy," Kelly said, and glowered at her.

The girl was unmoved. She looked at him with eyes that seemed cloudy. She had to have been born like this, hopeless and bored. She couldn't have ever been a tiny little girl with a favorite stuffed animal who loved riding on her father's shoulders. That couldn't be true.

"I don't care who you're waiting for. Do it somewhere else."

She turned away, her small back blocking him as firmly as any bolted, metal door. He wanted to throttle her, to pick her up by her slim throat and shake, shake, shake her while her legs bicycled in the air. He wanted to see her face purple and her mouth open, see her tongue starting to protrude as she tried to scream, as she tried to breathe, as she—

Kelly reared back, gasping. He realized that his hands were reaching for her. He tucked them up under his armpits and hurried away.

It started to rain, a cold, cheerless rain. It wouldn't make the flowers bloom. It wouldn't clean the streets or wash heavy makeup away, leaving rounded cheeks fresh and cool. It just plastered wet hair to faces and made the night feel even crueler. It made every hope and dream sodden. It did, however, run down Kelly's face and drop from his nose and chin better than any tears ever could.

He walked all through the night.

During the day, he caught a few hours of sleep next to the vent by an old laundry. It smelled like mold and dryer sheets. He thought of his mother and curled up around himself. After feeling good and sorry for himself, he painfully got to his feet and looked for Joy.

He looked all day.

And then all night.

The next day he ate a crushed up taco shell and drank as much water from a public water fountain as he could hold. He thought his stomach would burst. He sloshed away. No Joy.

No Joy that night. Or the next day.

The sun made noises like it was time to retire.

"Whoops, time for bed," the sun said, and the city widened its sleepy eyes in horror. "Time for me to rest and for the things of the night to come alive and take hold. It is the hour for things to hiss and creep and take the tender hearts of the young in their teeth. Fare thee well."

Shadows swept long and deep, turning the daytime parks and playthings into that which was dark and sinister. Kelly himself felt his arms stretch and elongate, felt fangs protrude and his walk turn into something prowling like a wild animal. He was no longer the good-natured, corn-fed boy who bagged groceries and helped little old ladies out to their car. He was here. He was Joyless. Anger built a fire in his chest and fed it with logs of resentment and shards of glass.

He scuttled with the other wild things away from the edges of the light, preferring to teeter outside where the darkness was deep and horrific and hungry.

He bypassed his usual route and walked around the back of a boarded-up store. He smelled filth and something sharp that reminded him briefly of gasoline. If he had a match, he'd burn the entire city to the ground with all of them inside. There was so much trash and refuse around that the area would catch immediately. He'd make a wall of fire so high that astronauts would be able to see the fire from space. A burning, roaring inferno on a hill should never be hid under a bushel, so the Bible said. He'd burn the evil out.

He nearly stepped on a bag of soggy rags covered in fallen leaves. He adjusted his footing and then stopped, suddenly. He saw something move.

"Ugh, a rat," he thought, and his first thought was disgust. His second thought was whether or not he could catch it. Could he grab it in his shaking hands and bash its head against the concrete ground before it had time to bite him? How much meat would a rat have on it? How would Joy feel if she came strolling by and saw her Kelly with actual meat cooking over a fire? Would that be enough for her to forgive him for not protecting her?

He blinked rapidly and wiped his nose on his sleeve. He crouched down, looking for something to hit the rat with, if that's what, indeed, it was.

It wasn't. The leaves moved again, and he saw fingers poke out. Just a flash of dark skin. He fell back onto his butt, scrabbling away in surprise. Then his mind cleared. This was a hand. A moving hand.

Somebody was buried under the trash and leaves.

He sprang forward, grabbed the hand, and pulled. What he thought was a pile of garbage was instead a man who looked a few years older than him. His face was slack and his eyes refused to open. Kelly pulled the leaves from the man's face and tried to get him to speak.

"Hey. Hey! Are you okay? Sir?"

The man wouldn't sit up, and Kelly couldn't make him. He kept falling limply back to the ground, moaning. He slurred something out, but Kelly couldn't understand him.

It was there, on his knees behind the garbage bins, that he heard the most beautiful sound of his life.

"Kel?"

His name, whisper-soft, and suddenly his ears pricked like those of a dog.

"Joy? Joy, where are you?"

He crawled on hands and knees, completely ignoring the man who was again unconscious beside him. Back in the farthest corner, tucked away from the streetlights and police sirens, was Joy.

"Oh, bunny!" Kel exclaimed, and clasped her to his body. Her head lolled, her eyes rolling back until he could see the whites.

"Bunny, bunny, you're alive. You're alive. I'm here. I found you. It's me, your Kelly. I have you. Everything is okay. You're safe."

He was lying. He knew he was lying, but he didn't care. He would promise her everything if she would just stay with him, and he did. He promised her heaven and hell and a home with a hundred milk cows and flashy cars and everything she ever wanted. She'd bathe in champagne and dress in new clothes, a different gown for every single day.

"You'd wear it once and then throw it away," he said, and his voice sounded different to him. It was high like a child's. "Or we could donate them to people who live on the street. We'll box them up, and wrap them like birthday presents, and we'll bring them to this very city with all the food we could carry, and we'll give them out. Right here. It will be like Christmas every single day. People will be walking back here wearing nothing but fine things. And it will never rain. Can you imagine what that will be like, Joy?"

She didn't answer. Kelly could feel that her body was warm and she was still breathing. Her T-shirt was torn and bunched up, exposing her filthy bra. The rest of her clothes were missing. She was completely naked from the waist down, and Kelly's mouth trembled at that. He wrapped his arms around her, pulling her onto his lap, and cradled her. He covered as much of her body as he could.

She had needle marks in her arms, fresh and raw, and they nearly made him sob. They were ugly against her white, white skin.

His traitorous brain filled in the blanks and showed him how Joy had spent her last seven days. Human monsters poked sharp needles through her soft flesh, into her fresh veins, injecting evil into her blood, telling her lies and filling her with poison love and a sinister high. If he had protected Joy, she would not have needed to feel that high. He would have given her that high.

"No, Joy," he said, and buried his face in her hair. Something foul had been rubbed into it, but he didn't care. "We escaped your father. We're here together. Come back to me. Don't go away again and leave me alone. You're all I have."

He tried to pick her up, but he wasn't strong enough. She was deadweight against his twiggy arms, now starved of all their muscle. He wrapped his arms around her, pulling her onto his lap, and cradled her. He covered as much of her body as he could with his hands, giving her as much privacy and body warmth as possible.

"I'll sing to you. Would you like that? How about a little Whitesnake?"

He sang every old song he knew. He went through all of the classics, all of the old rock that he and Joy had listened to through the years. After he sang those, he did some country and even some R&B, although he didn't know much. After that, he made up words to tunes he vaguely knew. Hymns and old tunes that his grandfather used to play on the phonograph when he was just a kid. The sun was just peeking over the city to assess the night's damage when Joy finally stirred.

"Kel...ly?" she asked, and peered at him through slitted lids.

"I'm here," he said quickly. He tried to smile but his mouth wouldn't work. It opened and attempted valiantly to turn up at the corners, but he knew it was just a big, blank maw of darkness. He could swallow Joy and the stars and the world and the universe with the huge void inside of him. He closed his mouth and swallowed instead.

"Joy. I'm glad you're awake. I've been watching over you."

"Shin—y," she said, and her hand moved toward her breast. It was clumsy and heavy. Kelly grasped her fingers. She pulled away weakly, and gestured to her chest.

Around her neck and under her shirt was the necklace. The pendant was a star made out of something that looked like glass. It shimmered dimly in the light of the rising sun. It was beautiful and horrible and Kelly wished he could worship it and break it between his back teeth. He'd grind it up and spit the bloody shards onto the sticky sidewalk, hallelujah, all praise be to its name.

"Yes, it's here," he said, and wrapped Joy's nearly lifeless fingers around it. That despicable, coveted thing. "It's beautiful. I hope you keep it always."

She turned her head toward Kelly's chest and fell asleep. It seemed much more natural this time, a healing sleep instead of near death. Her chest rose and fell and her heart stretched and beat. Blood rushed back and forth, to and fro, hurriedly spreading disease and who-knows-what to every part of her body.

"What did I miss?" the sun asked, shining over the city. "Today is a brand new day, full of beauty and promise."

Kelly traced his fingers down the needle marks on Joy's

arms, terrified of the holes in her skin, that an infection had been injected inside her, and the infection was about to spread and replace her soul.

He let his tears fall.

#

They had been gone for several months. Kelly had hoped things would get better, but that was his usual, optimistic nature. Sweet boy. Poor boy. Boys like him had their souls ripped away and their hearts cubed and put through the meat grinder. That was just the way of it.

Joy had turned into a bundle of sticks. Her eyes peered out from dark circles, and her lips were perpetually cracked. Half of the people she solicited roughly turned her away.

"You don't know what you're missing!" Joy screamed back at them. She was usually so drunk she barely managed to stand. This particular time was no different. "Think some other girl is going to give you such a good blow?"

"Joy," Kel said, putting his hand on her shoulder. She jerked away from him.

"What, you gonna preach at me now, you goodie-two-shoes? Tell me how I'm not taking care of my holy temple?" She gestured at her body with both hands, and her eyes were burning in the hollows of her sockets. Kelly knew she was spoiling for a fight, but he wasn't going to be the one to give it to her.

"I got a couple hours of work today. I have some food."

He handed her a small package wrapped in tinfoil. She grabbed it greedily.

"Ah, thanks, Kelly. You're so sweet. Always thinking of me."

"Always," he said. "Come sit and eat with me."

He took her hand and led her to a spot near the wall. She sat down unsteadily.

"I want to see you happy, Joy," Kelly said. He kept his voice quiet and even, the same way he used to when talking with a scared cat or wounded pup.

"I'm happy," she said, her mouth full. "Food makes me happy. Hey, you didn't bring me anything else, something else I'm hungry for, did you?"

He shook his head.

"Just that."

She finished and wiped her face carefully with her fingers. For a second he saw the Old Joy, the True Joy. She used to fastidiously wipe the blood from her face so nobody would know what happened at home. He knew. The entire school knew. Everyone in town knew, but that didn't help her much, did it? It was all a façade. Joy pretended that everything was perfectly normal and so did the town. Whatever kept the status quo, right?

He had never hated his home town as much as he did at that very moment.

"What?" she asked, looking at him. "Why are you staring at me?"

Kelly smiled, and it was real.

"Just admiring your beautiful face," he said truthfully.

She laughed.

"Stop it. I know what I look like."

"Like sunshine," he told her. He ruffled her hair with his hand. "Like Joy."

"Like Hell itself came here walkin', and I know it, baby. You think I don't, but I do." She leaned back and looked at where the stars would be without the city's light pollution. "I used to be pretty."

Kelly slid closer to her and put his arm around her.

"Don't say that, bunny. You're still pretty."

Her laughter sounded more angry than mirthful. The sharpness of it startled both of them. Kelly felt like it was a sharpened shiv that found its way beneath his skin and into the tender part beneath his ribs. She continued twisting it.

"I see myself, Kelly. I know what I look like, how I act. Sometimes I'm so horrible to you, and it's like I'm inside of myself, watching. I know I'm hurting you. I want someone to hurt the way I do, but nobody cares except for you. So I hurt you, and that hurts the rest of the world. But it isn't right." She took his hand in hers and looked at him intensely. "I do love you, Kelly Stands. Sometimes I almost forget it, but it's true."

He cupped her dirty face in his thin hands.

"I love you right back," he said simply. "You're my Joy."

"That's correct, sir," she said, and leaned in to kiss him.

His lips touched hers and he remembered their sweet, awkward kisses behind the woodshed, or in the barn, or once in the supply closet at school. She was in there looking for board erasers. He had been sent in for paper towels.

"Oh, sorry," he had said, and shuffled his too-big feet in his too-small shoes. "I didn't know you were in here."

She had whirled around, her eyes wide, her blond hair spinning around her like a halo or firefly glow. He had never seen anything so startled or wild or pure. She slid past him to the door and her hip bumped his. His hand came to the small of her back to steady her, and he wasn't sure how it happened after that, but suddenly his mouth was on hers and her arms were wrapped around him so tightly that he thought she was going to squeeze his heart until it popped like a balloon. Even if it did, it would erupt with sweet Joy-colored confetti.

He kissed her now, leaning his body into hers the slightest bit. She responded, pushing her breasts against him and sliding her tongue into his mouth aggressively.

He pulled back just a little, but she mashed her lips against his and moaned. It sounded like theatrics, not like his Joy. He felt her fumble against the button of his jeans. The fingers of her other hand slid searchingly into his back pocket.

He ripped himself away, breathing hard.

"What are you looking for, Joy?" He growled like a beast. Naïve Kelly had disappeared along with the memory of that day in the supply closet, of the sweetest kiss he had ever experienced. He felt his face furrow as he grimaced.

Joy pressed herself into him again. "I'm not looking for a thing, baby," she said, her mouth against his neck. She moved to his earlobe and bit gently. Kelly hissed in his breath and Joy took that moment to surge into the corners and hollows of his body. She was a liquid and he was a container that needed to be filled.

He was drowning. He was drowning in Joy. Her hot mouth and clutching fingers made him want to sprint down the alley away from her and also hold her so tightly that she melted into his skin. They could share one body, become one person. She could run through his veins like the heroin she wept for in the middle of the night and they could both get high together.

This thought splashed over him like filthy water from the gutter. His senses cleared. The heady vapor of Joy and her scorching kisses lifted enough that he realized her hand was in his pocket again.

She was going for his wallet.

"Joy," he groaned painfully. "Stop."

She mistook his disappointment for passion.

"Never, baby," she said, and deepened the kiss. Kelly slowly slid his hand down her arm.

"Yes, baby," she whispered, and moved against him.

He circled his fingers around her wrist, and then grabbed it roughly. Joy squeaked and the wallet fell from her hand.

"What is this, huh?" he asked her. His voice was hoarse from want and pain. "You're stealing from me? From *me*, Joy?"

"Baby," she began, but Kelly pushed her away and shot to his feet.

"Joy," he rasped, and there were a thousand emotions as he said her name. His eyes threatened to spill tears. He was going to be just another teenager crying on the sidewalk, another little boy bawling because of some girl. "Do you think I'd honestly keep anything from you?"

She peered up at him from the ground. Her mouth moved like she was trying to say the words "I'm sorry" or whisper his name. Perhaps she was simply telling him to go to hell. He dashed his sleeve against his traitorous eyes. They threatened to expose him for the absolute child that he really was inside.

"I've given you everything I have," he said, and winced when his voice broke on the last word. "I don't have anything left. I walked away from everything I had for you."

"Kelly," she said, and sorrow and something shinier flashed across the surface of her eyes for just a second. Then the moment was gone, and her gaze drifted to the wallet on the ground.

Kelly's stomach went cold. He could imagine what they looked like to someone standing far away. They didn't look like lovers at all. They looked like two destitute people who just couldn't find it in themselves to care anymore.

Kelly's chin trembled slightly.

"Do you remember," he asked slowly, "the day of my asthma attack?"

She didn't move, but her body language told him she was listening.

"You saved me that day, Joy. You ran out into the road and got help. If it hadn't been for you, I would have died."

Her voice was low.

"If it hadn't been for me, you wouldn't have been out there. You would have been at home where you belonged." She climbed unsteadily to her feet. Kelly almost reached out a hand to help her, but what was the use? How could you hold a ghost? You can't. You have to let her whoosh right through you on her way out the door.

"You would have been home," she continued, and her voice was rising, "with your *mother* who loves you, and your *father* who thinks you hung the moon." She hit him with each emphasized word. He took the blows stalwartly. Her frail hands were too weak to do any damage to his body, but each time her tiny fists struck out, his heart shattered in half. The pieces of it became smaller and smaller until he thought his blood would cease flowing through his body without anything there to pump it.

"You'd be home going to *school* and dating other *girls* and finally being happy, Kel. You'd be happier without me, I know it. Now don't deny it," she said as he tried to interrupt, "because I know what you want to say. But you would honestly be better." Her hands fell to her side. They stood bathed in the sick glow of a neon sign.

"I have to see you every day, knowing that you're here because of me. Starving, because of me. Because I'm too selfish to make you go home. I can't deal with it. I can't look at you because it hurts too much."

He tried to say something. He was a beaten dog and she was holding a stick made of words. He cringed and shuddered at what she was going to say next, but he couldn't leave. He just couldn't. That wasn't what a loyal dog did.

"I'm a cancer, Kelly," she said, and her voice was crystal clear. The slurring was gone. She was clear and wholly present for the first time in months. It terrified him. The sheer force that was Joy was almost more than he could bear.

"Joy," he said. At her name, her eyes flicked to his. They held each other's gaze for a very long time.

"A cancer," she repeated. "Sure, it will hurt at first when you cut me out. You'll have to heal. But then everything will be better."

She put her hand on his chest, curling her fingers into his shirt like she used to. Back when Battered Joy and Terrified Joy and Desperately in Love Joy were the same person, and he had been Her Kelly.

He put his hand on top of hers.

"I don't want to cut you out. I want you with me, always. Even like this."

But the moment was gone. It had flown by as the best things always fly by, and she was gone. The heartbreak and craving were back, her body trembling in want of the next fix, her brain eaten alive by the insects swarming inside of it. The insects would keep swarming, desperate and hungry until they were fed the one thing they wanted. Needed.

Her eyes fell back to the wallet still lying on the ground.

Kelly teetered as though the world had dropped out from underneath him. That's what it felt like. There was stability and his steadfast love for this beautiful, broken, bizarre girl, and then suddenly there was…nothing.

"I don't have any money in there, Joy. I used it all on food."

Her tongue darted across her lips. Too fast, like a lizard's. Kelly was afraid that if she met his eyes again, he'd discover she had yellow, slitted reptile eyes.

"On food, Joy," he emphasized. He could see the cogs turning in her head as she studied him and the wallet, gauging how long it would take for her to swoop it up and pelt down the alleyway.

"Take a look inside if you don't believe me," he said. His voice sounded like an echo of itself. He sounded utterly defeated.

She cocked her head and looked at him. The craftiness on her face destroyed anything that resembled the old Joy. This wasn't the woman he loved. This was just some desperate stranger looking for an easy mark.

He slowly turned out his pockets, one by one. She watched carefully.

"Look," he said, turning around so she could see him from all angles. "No money. No other food. No score, nothing to trade or sell. I've given you everything I have. All of it."

Her lips twitched as if in disappointment. Her skin was clammy, sweaty, her flesh in constant motion from a million muscle cramps inside. She slowly slid down to the ground by his wallet.

He held his hand out to her, and held his breath. His hands were cracked and dry, the fingernails bitten. They weren't the hands of a boy who could save her. They weren't the hands of a boy who knew how to be saved.

She picked up the wallet. She opened it. She looked at the picture shoved inside. It was the two of them, two years ago, smiling into a camera that some random friend had held. Kelly was grinning his easy, ridiculous smile and his arm clumsily draped around Joy. Her eyes were screwed up against the sun, her head thrown back in laughter.

She looked for a long time. She traced her finger over their faces and clothes as if she had never seen them before, as if these were new beloved people who had amazing adventures and lives that she wanted to commit to memory. She'd sit at their feet and ask how they met and what their favorite flowers were. The boy looked like somebody she could marry and have babies with and trust to raise their children with love. The girl looked like someone she wanted to share her secrets with. They could sit in her bedroom at night, braiding each other's hair and gossiping about the things that happened at school.

"Do you remember?" Kelly asked. He hardly dared to breathe, lest this skittish animal bolted and broke away. "We used to be so happy. We can be happy again."

Joy finished opening the rest of the wallet and ran her fingers through the billfold and tiny pockets. She came up empty. She looked disappointed before regarding Kelly with a fake smile and blank eyes.

"Hey, baby, maybe you could go out and score me something good. I need to get away from all of this for a while."

She slapped the wallet into his outstretched hand and walked away, disappearing into the cold darkness of the alley.

#

This time Joy had kept her distance for nearly a week, and each morning Kelly woke up alone instead of with Joy—Morning Joy—who was the most desperate, the most foreign and infected and sick and irritated. It was like a thousand mosquitoes were nipping her skin and she would do anything, sell anything, or take anything to make them stop. Kelly stood in front of a store that sold glass sculptures and he studied them through the window. Maybe if Joy was with him, she'd look into the glass and be cured from the inside out. The glimmer of glass made the stars shine beauty into his veins, and there was no room for anything else.

"Pretty, aren't they?"

A voice to his left, down by his elbow. He turned and saw a tiny woman with a crinkled face.

"Yes, ma'am," he answered.

She grinned and her face crinkled even more.

"Oh, a polite one. I like that. Where you from, boy?"

Kel paused awkwardly. The old woman nodded.

"One of those," she said knowingly. "Hope whatever you were running from, or for, was worth it."

Kelly thought of Joy and the way she used to burrow into his side while she slept. She wasn't as hard, then. She was simply herself, Joy with her Kel, and that was the only moment when either of them was truly happy.

"It's worth it, ma'am," he answered.

The woman peered inside the glass store. "Ever go inside?"

Kelly cleared his throat. "They've asked me to leave. Twice. Pretty sure they think I'm going to steal something or knock it over."

She looked at him innocently. "Would you?"

He shook his head vigorously. "Never, ma'am. I just would like to look, that's all."

She was quiet for a while. Then she said, "You seem like a nice boy. Does your family know where you are?"

He shook his head, suddenly unable to speak.

"They cruel to you?"

He shook his head again.

"Think they're worried sick?"

Kelly nodded and dashed at his eyes with his filthy sleeve. The woman patted his arm.

"You're a good boy, and I like to trust good boys. Here's what I'm going to do. Take my phone and make a phone call home. Go on, take it. I'll be browsing in this store for a few minutes while you do. When you're done, you can return the phone. Sounds to me like that would work right well for everyone."

She reached into her purse and handed him the phone. He

couldn't meet her eyes.

"Good boy," she said again, and patted his hands. She wandered into the store.

Kelly stared at the phone as if it couldn't possibly be real. It was more likely that he had caught a fairy in his hands, or a magical talisman. His finger shook as he punched in the numbers and held the phone to his ear.

One ring. Two.

Maybe this wasn't such a good idea.

Three rings. Four.

Nobody was home to answer.

Five.

What would he leave on the answering machine? Should he say anything at all? Hang up? He didn't know what to do, he didn't know what to do, he didn't know...

"Hello?"

Her voice was weary. His mother had grown tired while he was away. Kelly's breath caught.

"Mama?"

He hadn't called her "mama" in years, not since he was a little boy terrified of the monsters in his closet. Joy had real monsters in her house, but Kelly's could be chased away with his parent's love and a little bit of Monster Spray.

"Kelly? Kelly, is that you?"

"M-mama?"

His mama screamed, then made a sound so happy and loud and forceful that Kelly didn't know whether to laugh or cry, so he did both.

"Kelly, I've been so worried, you have no idea! Are you okay? Are you safe? Is that girl with you? Are you coming home?"

Kel wept into the sleeve of his hoodie and assured his mother that yes, he was all right, and yes, they were alive, and yes, he still said his prayers and tried to be a good man and he loved his mama, yes, he did, and he always would, and tell his dad he loved him, too, because he did, it was true, he loved them so much that his soul hurt.

"Kelly," his mother said, and her voice had that Very Serious Tone that made his body chill. "I have to tell you something about your daddy. His heart hasn't been so good and he's been real sick. I think you need to come home, son. Come home and...tell your daddy goodbye."

"It's…that bad?"

Her voice was somber. "It's that bad. But God told you to call today, so you could come home before it's too late. Will she come, too?"

"I don't know, Ma. I don't think so. She never wants to come back."

"I don't blame her. Her daddy is right awful. I think he'll kill her if he sees her. You keep her safe, as much as you can, but you get on back here, even if it's just for a little while. Okay?"

"I love you, Ma."

He hung up the phone and stared at the cold cement under his feet.

The old woman came outside and took her phone.

"Well?" she asked. Her face was a light. It was aglow. Kel wanted to sweep her into his arms and thank her a million times, but his head was full of marbles and thoughts and fears.

He simply looked at her.

"Everything's changed," he said.

#

Joy didn't want to hear it at first.

"You're just trying to get me to go back, you son of a–" She took a swing and missed. She staggered and glared at Kelly as though he had pushed her.

"My dad is dying, Joy," Kelly said. His hands hung limply at his sides. He couldn't have defended himself if he wanted to. He stared at something behind Joy's shoulder, some spot in the distance that had nothing to offer except a place to rest his eyes.

"You'll say anything, won't you?" she spat. "I'm tired of this dance. I'm not going home and nothing you can say will make me." She looked like she was going to say more, but Kelly's strong skeleton betrayed him and he slid down to the ground, seemingly boneless. He wrapped his arms around his skinny legs, his embarrassed face held low, and sobbed.

Joy watched him for just a second, and something seemed to move inside of her heart. Street Joy disappeared and Real Joy came creeping back.

"Kel," she whispered, and squatted down next to him. She pressed her forehead to his and kissed his salty face. "Kelly, I'm so sorry. You're telling the truth. I know you are. I'm sorry I've been so awful. I know how you feel about your daddy."

The tears felt so good, so strong and cleansing, and they had brought Joy back to him. There might be worth in human tears, Kelly thought vaguely. Maybe one day we'll collect them and trade them like diamonds. Tears will be our new currency. Wouldn't that make us appreciate everything we had, if we had to earn each and every item with our tears?

"I'm losing my mind," he said aloud, and Joy was right by his side.

"You're not. You're a good, strong man and a good, strong son. We need to get you home."

He looked at her, puzzled, not sure if he heard her correctly.

"Home?" he asked. The word tasted…sweet.

"We'll need to get you cleaned up first," she said, looking him up and down. "It's been a while and your hair is awful long. Your mom might pass out when she sees it."

He turned his head and watched her flit around, making plans. He had to say it again, say the words slowly and make sure they were absolutely real and that he wasn't stuck in this strange half-shadows/half-light dream world that might be the undoing of him.

"We're going home?"

He hated the hopeful note in his voice. He was disgusted with his weakness. He saw Joy's shoulders slump. She turned to him, brown eyes full of pain.

"No," he said, and shook his head. She took both of his hands in hers.

"Baby," she said, and kissed his fingertips. He shut his eyes, like a child. If he didn't open them, perhaps he'd be safe from the monsters that swarmed underneath his bed and in the dark streets. Maybe he'd be safe from the horrific disappointment he knew was coming.

"Baby. I know you need to go home, but I can't. Do you understand? I can't go with you."

"We won't see your father," Kelly insisted. "You'll stay at my house. I won't let him touch you, I swear. I'll—"

"It's more than that," she said, and she spoke so solemnly and low that he could barely hear her. "There's nothing to go back to. I have nothing left. I can't go like this," she gestured at the bruises and tracks in her arms, "and I don't want to. But you, my love. You need to go home. You know you do."

They huddled together that night, her thin fingers tucked into the hole in the knee of his jeans. A couple of Joy's friends approached them, but she shook her head and mouthed "No." Kelly fell asleep and Joy ran her fingers through his hair. She rubbed her cheek against the filthy sleeve of his hoodie.

He stirred.

"Joy?"

"Shhh," she soothed, and kissed his shoulder. "Go to sleep, love. I'm the last one awake. I'll watch over you."

He faded back into oblivion and Joy pressed her back into the stone wall, staring at the smoggy sky far into the night. There were no stars there. Sometime before daylight, she slipped away. She returned with a torn shirt, cauliflower ear, and a single, solitary bus ticket.

They cleaned up the best they could at the bus station. Kelly washed his face and tried to comb his hair back with his hands. He smiled awkwardly at Joy.

"Is this a face only a mother could love?" he asked, and waggled his brows.

Joy laughed, and it almost sounded normal. "A mother, and me. I love that face more than life."

Kelly's smile faded.

"I love you more than life."

Joy handed him his backpack, staring at the ground. Kel reached out and tipped her chin up so she'd meet his gaze.

"I'll stay if you need me to. You know that, Joy. I'll do anything for you."

Her brown eyes washed over with so many emotions that Kelly was nearly dazzled.

"I know. You've proven it over and over and over again." She took her necklace off, the one with the shiny glass star, and tied it around his neck. "It suits you," she said. She hugged him and it was the old days. He was just a young man worried about school and a job and making sure the lawn was mowed in the right pattern so it looked nice and neat for his mother. He closed his eyes and rested his chin on her hair.

"I'll come right back," he promised. "I'll bring money and more stuff for us. Clean up good and get a job this time. I'll make someone hire me, anyone, doing anything. Things will be different." He pulled back and looked into her eyes again. "Promise me you'll be here. Promise I'll be able to find you."

She reddened at his intensity. "I'll be here, Kel, waiting for you. I can't wait to get into some clean clothes. Will you bring a band for my hair? If I don't tie it back soon, I'll go crazy and chop the whole thing clean off."

"So many bands," he swore. "A hairband for every day of the month." He pulled his hoodie over his head and handed it to her.

She looked confused.

"It's your favorite one. You'll need this."

He shook his head. "No, you're my favorite one. It will keep you warm until I get back. Just…don't forget me while I'm gone, okay?"

"In a week?" she teased. She leaned her forehead against his chest. "I could never forget you, Kel. Never ever, not even if you never come back."

"But I will," he promised. His eyes were fierce, fiercer than he had ever felt them. "Don't you doubt, Joy. Just be where I can find you."

He kissed her again and climbed onto the bus. He slouched down in his seat and squeezed his eyes shut as it began to move. He hoped his hoodie would somehow turn into a magical shield, covering Joy from the top of her head down to her knees, keeping her soul inside instead of letting it seep out through the pinpricks in her arms.

He slept. There was no one awake.

#

His mother met him two days later at the station. He wrapped his long arms around her and she cried into his shirt. "You're filthy," she sobbed. "You're so skinny. I've missed you so much. I've never seen a boy who needs a shower more than you."

"I love you, too, Ma," he said, and slung his arm over her

shoulder as they walked to the car. She couldn't stop touching him the entire drive, picking at lint on his arm or poking at his hand with a shaking finger. Finally, he took her hand and held it.

"I'm here, Ma. You aren't imagining it. I'm real."

She drove the rest of the way home with his hand clenched tightly in hers, occasionally pulling it up close to her heart.

It was late when they got in.

"Take a shower while I put something together for dinner," his mother said.

The hot water was a sin, hitting his face and back as brutally as Joy's father had ever hit her. He scrubbed the city out of his hair and the grime from his body. The horrors of the past months sluiced down the drain along with the dirty water. He climbed out and wrapped a towel around his hips. He studied his face in the mirror, all eyes and too-long hair and still no beard. He wasn't sure he would ever grow one.

*What would Joy do for a shower?*

The thought turned his stomach, because he knew Joy would do just about anything for anyone. But not after he came back. He'd take her and they'd run to another city, a better one where she didn't have regular johns and her sickness and her strung-out friends. They'd start fresh and she'd have sunshine on her hair every day.

He ate dinner with guilty gusto.

He climbed into his bed. It was plenty warm and soft, topped with a quilt his mother had made. After two hours of sleeplessness, he folded the quilt and set it aside as something to bring back for Joy. A blanket for both of them, just like old times. He huddled on his side all night, thinking of Joy shivering in the cold without him.

*You aren't alone,* he mentally told her. *It's safe to fall asleep. I'm awake and watching.*

He held the star pendant in his hand and counted the seconds until the sun rose.

The morning was full of breakfast, a haircut, and a visit to his father in the hospital.

"Kelly," his father said, and his meaty hands, sans meat, clasped around Kelly's fingers. "You're home."

"I didn't mean to worry you, Dad," Kelly answered. He knew the words sounded weak, but they bloomed with truth.

"I know, son. And I feel so much better now that you're

home to take care of your mother."

"Don't talk like that, Dad. You're going to be fine. We can take care of her together."

His dad clapped Kelly's hands again, and met his eyes.

"I wish you could be a child again, Kel, and not have to worry like a man worries. But you are a man, now, and we have to face up to things. I'm not getting out of here. This is where I end. It's up to you to care for your mom now that I can't."

"But Dad…"

His father smiled at him and it was rife with sadness. It was the type of smile a boy should never have to see.

"Make me proud, son."

Kelly tried. Every day he woke up and his first thought was "Joy." Then he thought, "My parents," and he set to work. He painted the house and fixed all of the things his father had meant to get to. He let his mother make him his favorite meals. He sat by his father's bedside and cooled his fevered face with a cool cloth. Days passed. Soon it was weeks. Then the season changed and his father was gone.

Nobody was ready.

Kelly wore a new suit with enough fabric to cover his daddy-long legs, and he carried his father's casket on his shoulder. The physical weight was also born by other men, but Kelly carried the emotional weight alone. His mother had long stopped sobbing and simply stood there at the gravesite, her eyes sightless as she stared at the love of her life being lowered into a hole in the dirt. Kelly stood beside her, scowling at the brazen sun that dared to show its face on this day. Shouldn't it be raining at funerals? Shouldn't the atmosphere itself drip with sorrow like the rest of them? He thought of his father. He thought of Joy.

"I don't know what to do," Kelly's mother murmured. Her fingers picked at her new funeral hat. "What am I supposed to do?"

Kel took her hand to stop the birdlike tremor. "We go home. We serve food and nod our heads. And then we go to sleep. Tomorrow is a new day."

"How do I live without your father? Who do I make breakfast for? How do I sleep in that big bed without him? It's so very big. I…I can't do this alone."

Kelly hugged his mother close.

"You're not alone, Ma. I'm here."

Kelly left his father in the cold, hard ground. The ride home was long and silent. Neither he nor his mother said a word. The car seemed far too empty with just the two of them. No, it wasn't just the two of them. Joy and Kelly's father rode along with them.

The car was full of ghosts.

When they returned, Kelly sat for a second before getting out and opening his mother's car door. He took her elbow and guided her into the house. They walked into a room of hushed conversation and ambrosia salads. Grief is overwhelming, but a casserole seems to help. Neighbors pressed pies into their hands. Baskets of warm rolls. Fragrant breads wrapped in tinfoil.

Kelly's mother stood there, robotically holding the food until a kind woman guided her to the kitchen and helped her find a place to set it down.

The door blew open and the air changed. It became hard, jagged. It pulsed like something with far too many tentacles and a spiny beak.

Joy's father, Buck, stood in the doorway, emanating an energy that made Kelly look up from his untouched plate. The man saw him and strode over.

"Where is my daughter?" he demanded. His eyes were brown like Joy's, but that's all they had in common. "Why didn't she come home with you?"

"Buck, this isn't the place," an older man said, and touched Buck's arm. Buck shook him off.

"Where is she? She needs to be home where she belongs."

Kelly set his plate of food down and drew himself upright. He was taller than Joy's dad, now. When had that happened? How could such a small man do so much damage?

"She needs to be wherever you aren't," he said. "Home is anywhere far away from you."

The nervous chatter stopped. The house of mourning was silent. Kelly looked Joy's father squarely in the face but his mind was far away. Joy cradling her wounded arm. Joy with both eyes swelled shut. Joy damaged in the most private and secret of ways that she couldn't tell even Kelly about. Kelly's brain was full of electric wires. His attention sharpened.

"You little..." Buck's words were lost in the deep roar that was ripped from him while he swung. The sound startled Kelly. It was barbaric, something primal and not altogether human. The beefy fist caught him in the face and his nose spouted blood. His teeth clacked together and he felt a tooth chip. Buck knew just where to hit. He had plenty of practice.

Something in Kelly burst, then. He roared back and started windmilling his arms, connecting with flesh more often than not.

"Kelly!" His mother's voice.

Joy crying over him in the fields when he had his asthma attack. Joy sifting through garbage cans, looking for something to eat, the bone of her spine pressing too hard against her skin.

"Kelly!"

Hands pulled at him, but he was all rage and wiry young muscle.

Joy counting out change so carefully. Disappearing into the night with a man while Kelly squeezed his eyes shut and pretended to be asleep, because it was easier for both of them that way. Returning with dead eyes and a heroin habit and scabbing needle marks and that cheap star pendant that she found so beautiful.

"You did this," he screamed. The only sound in the room was his voice, and it encompassed all. "You did this to her! You broke her, you ruined her, you destroyed your little girl and how could you? That isn't what a father does!"

Worn out, he finally stopped, panting, held back by hands dressed in mourning black. Blood ran from his face onto his new, tattered suit. Buck crouched on the floor, shielding his face with his hands. Kelly's eyes roamed the room until they found his mother. Her face was white. Her hands shook.

"Ma," he said, and had to clear his throat. He spit blood onto the carpet. "Ma, I'm sorry. I don't know what came over—"

"Find her, Kelly," his mother said. She dug into her purse, came over, and pressed her wallet and car keys into his hand. "Don't leave that little girl out there for one more second. You bring her home to us, do you understand?"

Kelly nodded and pulled her into a quick hug. He ran upstairs, his long legs eating the steps, and grabbed the bundle of things he had squirreled away for Joy.

"We won't let him touch her," his mother shouted after him. Kelly slammed the car into reverse and screamed out of the dirt driveway.

He flew. He flew. He drove through the night, as fast as he dared, stopping only to gas up the car.

"Ahem." An attendant cleared his throat politely and nodded toward Kelly's aching face. "Do you want some ice?"

"Oh. No, thanks." Kelly headed toward the bathroom and cleaned up the dried blood. He dabbed at his suit with paper towels and then washed his hands carefully. He ran his wet hands through his hair, trying to look presentable for his Joy.

His nose was swollen and his face scuffed and cut from Buck's rings, but his eyes burned with something dark and deep and full of resolve. This wasn't the lost Kelly who usually looked back at him from gas station bathroom mirrors. His face had changed, the bones somehow shifting beneath his skin until he looked wolfish and whole. His thin shoulders had straightened themselves under the suit he had bought to honor his dead father. This Kelly didn't need his Joy to watch over him while he slept. He would do the watching for both of them.

"I'm coming," he said aloud, and his chipped teeth looked sharp. He felt that he could dip his head down and pierce somebody's jugular if it came to it.

He almost hoped it came to it.

He bought drinks and snacks with his mother's credit card. He bought so many things that the clerk gave him four bags. He was going to shower Joy with treats, cheap gas station chocolates and caramel popcorn and all of the soda she could possibly handle. They were going to be ten years old again, stealing away in the dark to hide in the trees and eat Sweet Tarts and penny candies because they could buy a whole ten with a dime. They were going to stuff themselves with chips until they were sick, until Joy's shriveled stomach nearly burst from the goodness, and she would curl up in the passenger side of the car under his mother's quilt and sleep while he drove. He would drive and drive, under the sun and the stars, while she was safe and warm and protected and every bad memory would leak out the syringe holes in her arms. He would keep watch. He'd be the last one awake.

"Think this will be enough for you?" the cashier asked wryly, eyeing the bags of snacks.

Kelly's face broke into a smile, and it felt deep. Genuine and natural. It spread and warmed his body from the face down.

"Enough for a bit. I'll be back soon. My girl and I will buy out the entire store."

He winked as he left. He held the door open for a striking brunette who was speaking to an Asian man with white sneakers. The man was gassing up an 18-wheeler.

"Sure thing, Lu," the woman called over her shoulder. She smiled her thanks at Kelly and the world was full of stars. It was going to be a day of magic. He could just feel it. He nodded at her companion by the gas pumps, and the man nodded back.

See? Magic.

He jumped into the driver's seat and started on again. He sang with the radio. He sang his beating heart out.

The city was as gray as it had ever been, but this time his heart leapt a little in his chest. Somewhere huddled on that cracked concrete was his Joy. He was so much later coming for her than he intended to be. He hoped she forgave him. He hoped she jumped into his arms and showered his face with kisses like she did when she was happy. He knew she would be happy.

"I beat your dad up," he would say, standing there in his scruffy, ruined-suit glory. "I beat him up in front of everybody after my father's funeral. He'll never touch you again. We won't let him. Mom says to bring you home to live with us, now. We can help take care of her. She needs us, Joy. And we need you."

"Oh, Kel!" she'd exclaim, and her brown eyes would be the warmest things he had ever seen. "We're all rescuing each other. We're all keeping watch. It's perfect. It couldn't be better."

This is what love is. Spark and ashes and light. Ignition and desecration.

He threw his backpack over his shoulder and hurried to their usual squatting spot, but she wasn't there. No matter. He'd look elsewhere.

She wasn't behind the Chinese place, or the gas station, or window shopping at any of the fine stores. His Adam's apple seemed bigger than usual and it was hard for him to swallow.

He'd keep looking. He'd never stop looking.

She wasn't buried in the leaves or strung out in the park. He searched all of her favorite places and a few areas she swore she'd never go again. She wasn't anywhere to be seen.

The sun yawned and cooed about it being a busy day. It slid cozily behind the horizon.

No, no, no. It was so much harder to search in the dark. Kelly walked until he was snowed under by sheer despair. His footsteps were slow and heavy as he made his way to their usual spot.

He huddled against the wall, waiting. The cement seemed harder than it had before, the night more chilled. Without Joy's body warmth, he shivered and shook. Had she been this cold without him, without her Kel-Bear to keep her warm? He felt even more guilty, and he wasn't sure that was even possible.

Morning came, but no Joy. It was an utterly Joyless day.

He didn't find her the next day, either.

Kelly's heart didn't fit in his chest quite right. It wasn't made of muscle after all, but uncomfortable gears and springs. His lungs were too small, tucked incorrectly into his rib cage somewhere. He couldn't breathe, couldn't focus, couldn't think of anything except that he couldn't find his Joy, couldn't find his love. Had she left the city? Started staying in a different spot? Why didn't she wait for him?

Because he hadn't come for her, that was why. Because life and death and everything in between stopped him. No, because he *let* it stop him. It was his watch and he blew it.

He saw some shapes through the steam from the man holes. Heard voices. Voices he didn't particularly like, but voices he recognized.

He stood and approached them.

"Hey," he said. His voice sounded weedy, so he tried again. "Hey. It's Kelly. Have you guys seen Joy?"

Moon faces swung in his direction. Vacant eyes didn't blink.

"Joy," he said impatiently. "Tiny. Blonde. She shoots up that junk with you sometimes."

One of the figures spoke. "Kelly, man. Where have you been? Thought you got out of the city."

"My dad died. I'm back for Joy. Where is she?"

His eyes roamed over them until he saw a girl in back. She was filthy, her hair matted and her skin covered in sores. She was wearing his favorite hoodie. It fell down halfway to her shins.

His arms snaked to her, grabbing her by the collar.

"Where did you get this?" he demanded. "It isn't yours!"

"Screw off," she shouted, and clawed at his face. Kelly winced and grabbed at his smarting skin.

"That…that's Joy's. I gave it to her before I left," he said, trying to keep his voice calm. "How did you get it?"

They didn't speak. Behind them, the city raged and churned and vomited out sirens and whistles and cell phone chatter. But here in this alley, the human silence was so great that it was crushing. It spoke without words. It relayed agony to his great, big, broken, mechanical heart.

"No," Kelly said, and leaned heavily against the wall. "Don't say it."

"Hate to tell you," a boy said, "but she met up with a guy with kinks. Not anyone we'd seen around."

Kelly thought he was going to throw up. He doubled over, staring at the cement, his breathing coming faster and faster.

"What happened?" he asked.

"I don't think—"

"Tell me," Kelly screamed.

The boy was silent as he debated. Finally, he spoke.

"He stabbed her, man. He left her out back. The city cleaned her up."

Cleaned her up. Disposed of his Joy. Just another nameless runaway who didn't matter to anybody. Another junkie out prostituting herself on the street.

"Maybe she was high and didn't feel much," the boy offered. Kelly squeezed his eyes closed. The thought of Joy bleeding out while her soul was so very far away…this almost made it hurt worse.

Didn't they know who she was? How special? Didn't they know how her eyes shone with secrets and how her hair glittered in the sun? That her mother had been inspired by heaven itself when she decided to name her "Joy?"

"When?" The word was a gut punch, a breath forced from his body.

The girl in his hoodie shrugged, already disinterested and drifting away. "Two weeks ago? Maybe. Got anything to eat?"

Kelly shook his head automatically and watched them as they wandered through the mist. They disappeared.

He dropped his backpack to the ground and slumped beside it.

He stared at the sky.

There were no stars.

## Epilogue

Kelly's hair was carefully combed, but still refused to lie flat. It stuck up in wonder, curious, wanting to see everything around it. While Kelly bent over textbooks, his hair waved like plants in the sea. It was an antenna when he mopped the university buildings at night. It peered over his shoulder as he presented in class, and chicken-feathered behind him when he threw his clothes into the car and drove home to visit his mother every few months.

"How's it going, Ma?" he said, dropping his bag on the ground so he could hug his mother. "I've missed you."

"Oh, Kelly, it's so good to have you home," she exclaimed. "Look at you, all grown up and so handsome. You look more and more like your father every day."

He blushed. "You say that every time you see me."

"Because it's true, sweetie. Do you have any clothes for me to wash?"

"I'll do it, Ma. Tell me what's been going on since I was here last."

She would talk, and he would listen. He'd measure detergent and start the washer while she told him about the small parade they had, or the pumpkins growing in the patch, or how the library had just purchased two new stuffed chairs in a beautiful blue. He hung shelves and replaced lightbulbs while he told her about college and how his roommate called him "Hayseed" and only came up to his chest, but they were still inseparable.

"Bring him home next time," his mother said, and Kelly agreed. He knew his roommate would bloom under the love his mother would lavish on them. It would be a house of healing and goodness.

Later, after his mother was sleeping, Kelly sat on his bed for a long time. He listened to the house settle and creak. He could name every sound. The pipes knocked softly and the air conditioner hummed. He realized he was listening for his father's footsteps as he walked around, putting the house to sleep. Closing windows and locking doors. Flipping off lights and unplugging electronics. Kelly had done these things earlier in the evening, but it just wasn't the same. He hadn't realized his mother had heard his quiet footsteps and wept.

He stood up and went downstairs. He slipped outside and closed the door carefully behind him.

It was a warm Southern night, so different from his school back East. He'd grown to love the history and the biting cold, but knew that, deep down, he was a simple thing who wanted bare feet and magnolias.

His footfalls were soft on the grass. He was careful not to disturb anything that ran or slithered. He was simply a shadow ghosting toward the trees.

He'd driven by Joy's house on the way home. Buck was in jail for some petty crime or another, and had a bit more time until release. The house had taken on that forlorn, waiting look of recently abandoned homes. Kelly's chest had squeezed tight, but he drove on. That place had never really belonged to Joy anyway; she had simply slept there sometimes. It was nothing but a building held together with secrets and old nails.

The woodshed looked the same as it always had. It was a place of safety in the dark, beautiful in its familiarity. He thought of two small children curled up in the fragrant grass behind it, their heads close together as they shared crackers and terrors and nightmares.

If Joy was anywhere, she was here. A girl that good inside had to get to heaven somehow, deserved that rest, but he knew she wouldn't go without her Kelly. She would be the last one awake and stand watch over him until his old bones were tucked safely away in to the dirt.

He stood for a long time, the sounds of the night piercing him through with their melancholy remembrances. He remembered Joy's quiet tears threading through the frog song. His young, helpless anger at some school injustice evaporating as she held his hand. The night sounds were the soundtrack to his entire life. The honking horns and heavy bass of the city wasn't music at all; It was simply noise.

"Joy," he said, and fireflies floated lazily away from him, riding his breath to the stars.

He didn't know what to say next. He couldn't put anything

that he felt into words.

He wanted to tell her how he thought of her every day. That there was an enormous hole inside of him that he didn't know how to fill. He wanted to tell her that he studied with an intensity that was almost frightening, driven by a demon he couldn't name. He was doing college for both of them. He was going to make something of himself.

He wanted to tell her that he'd stare every time he'd see a woman with blond hair, and even after all this time, his stomach would be a sinkhole when she would turn around.

It was never Joy.

He removed the necklace that he wore beneath his shirt. The clear points on the star had rubbed smooth with years of use, but it still shone. He held it in his hand for a long time.

"I'll make you proud of me," he said, and hung the necklace on the thin branches of a tree. It rotated slowly, glimmering in the moonlight. The fireflies surrounded it, fading softly in and out.

She was one more thing of beauty in his life. One more star. The universe was awash with them.

## ABOUT THE AUTHOR

Mercedes M. Yardley is a whimsical dark fantasist who wears poisonous flowers in her hair. She is the author of many diverse works, including Beautiful Sorrows, Pretty Little Dead Girls: A Novel of Murder and Whimsy, and the Stabby Award-winning Apocalyptic Montessa and Nuclear Lulu. She won the prestigious Bram Stoker Award for her realistic horror story Little Dead Red and was a Bram Stoker finalist for her story "Loving You Darkly." Mercedes lives and creates in Las Vegas with her family and menagerie of battle-scarred, rescued animal familiars. She is represented by Italia Gandolfo of Gandolfo Helin and Fountain Literary Management.

## Acknowledgements

I want to thank those who were so instrumental in my recovery from own addiction, many who will never read this. Huge thanks to my wife and daughters for living with my obsessions. Sometimes I really do write like I need it to survive. Thanks to my brother Kevin, passed well before his time, who introduced me to horror. We shared a common burden. Thanks to Uncle John FD Taff, who really inspired me to reach big and bold with both this collection and Garden of Fiends. Thanks to Andi Rawson for such solid council, to Julie Hutchings for support and editing and her wings of a Harpy, and to Dean Samed for his magnificent cover. Thanks to the editorial and proof reading support of Jason Parent, and Michael Fowler. Thanks to the authors on the table of contents and also a shout-out to the writers in the initial collection, the late Jack Ketchum, Jessica McHugh, Glen Krisch, Johan Thorson, Max Booth. Without Garden of Fiends there would be no Lullaby. Thanks to the defacto street team of dark fiction bloggers for their incredible support. Mostly, thanks to you, dear reader. You are appreciated.

## Also from Wicked Run Press

### Garden of Fiends: Tales of Addiction Horror
"What fertile ground for horror. Every story comes from a dark, personal place"
—*JOSH MALERMAN, New York Times Best Selling author of Bird Box*

### On the Lips of Children
"A sprint down a path of high adrenaline terror. A must read."
—*BRACKEN MACLEOD, Shirley Jackson Award nominated author of Stranded.*

### Milk-Blood
"An urban legend in the making. You will not be disappointed."
—**Bookie-Monster.com**

### All Smoke Rises
"Intense, imaginative, and empathic. Matthews is a damn good writer, and make no mistake, he *will* hurt you."
—*JACK KETCHUM, Bram Stoker Award winning author of The Girl Next Door.*

CPSIA information can be obtained
at www.ICGtesting.com
Printed in the USA
LVHW032156160220
647076LV00003B/30